PENGUIN

Zero Hour

Clive Cussler is the author or co-author of a great number of international best-sellers, including the famous Dirk Pitt® Adventures, such as *Arctic Drift*; the NUMA® Files, most recently *Medusa*; the *Oregon* Files, such as *The Jungle*; the Isaac Bell Adventures, which began with *The Chase*; and the highly successful most recent series – the Fargo Adventures. He lives in Arizona.

Graham Brown is the author of *Black Rain* and *Black Sun*, and the co-author with Cussler of *Devil's Gate*. A pilot and an attorney, he lives in Arizona.

Find out more about the world of Clive Cussler by visiting www.clivecussler.co.uk.

DIRK PITT® ADVENTURES BY CLIVE CUSSLER

Poseidon's Arrow
(with Dirk Cussler)
Crescent Dawn
(with Dirk Cussler)
Arctic Drift
(with Dirk Cussler)
Treasure of Khan
(with Dirk Cussler)
Black Wind
(with Dirk Cussler)
Trojan Odyssey
Valhalla Rising
Atlantis Found
Flood Tide
Shock Wave
Inca Gold
Sahara
Dragon
Treasure
Cyclops
Deep Six
Pacific Vortex!
Night Probe!
Vixen 03
Raise the *Titanic*!
Iceberg
Mayday!

FARGO ADVENTURES BY CLIVE CUSSLER

WITH THOMAS PERRY
The Mayan Secrets
The Tombs
WITH GRANT BLACKWOOD
The Kingdom
Lost Empire
Spartan Gold

ISAAC BELL NOVELS BY CLIVE CUSSLER

The Striker (with Justin Scott)
The Thief (with Justin Scott)
The Race (with Justin Scott)
The Spy (with Justin Scott)
The Wrecker (with Justin Scott)
The Chase

KURT AUSTIN ADVENTURES BY CLIVE CUSSLER

WITH GRAHAM BROWN
Zero Hour
The Storm
Devil's Gate
WITH PAUL KEMPRECOS
Medusa
White Death
The Navigator
Fire Ice
Polar Shift
Blue Gold
Lost City
Serpent

OREGON FILES ADVENTURES BY CLIVE CUSSLER

WITH JACK DU BRUL
The Jungle
The Silent Sea
Corsair
Plague Ship
Skeleton Coast
Dark Watch
Mirage
WITH CRAIG DIRGO
Golden Buddha
Sacred Stone

NON-FICTION BY CLIVE CUSSLER

Built for Adventure
The Sea Hunters
The Sea Hunters II
Clive Cussler and Dirk Pitt Revealed

Zero Hour

CLIVE CUSSLER
and GRAHAM BROWN

PENGUIN BOOKS

PENGUIN BOOKS

Published by the Penguin Group
Penguin Books Ltd, 80 Strand, London WC2R 0RL, England
Penguin Group (USA) Inc., 375 Hudson Street, New York, New York 10014, USA
Penguin Group (Canada), 90 Eglinton Avenue East, Suite 700, Toronto, Ontario, Canada M4P 2Y3 (a division of Pearson Penguin Canada Inc.)
Penguin Ireland, 25 St Stephen's Green, Dublin 2, Ireland (a division of Penguin Books Ltd)
Penguin Group (Australia), 707 Collins Street, Melbourne, Victoria 3008, Australia (a division of Pearson Australia Group Pty Ltd)
Penguin Books India Pvt Ltd, 11 Community Centre, Panchsheel Park, New Delhi – 110 017, India
Penguin Group (NZ), 67 Apollo Drive, Rosedale, Auckland 0632, New Zealand (a division of Pearson New Zealand Ltd)
Penguin Books (South Africa) (Pty) Ltd, Block D, Rosebank Office Park, 181 Jan Smuts Avenue, Parktown North, Gauteng 2193, South Africa

Penguin Books Ltd, Registered Offices: 80 Strand, London WC2R 0RL, England

www.penguin.com

First published in the United States of America by G. P. Putnam's Sons 2013
First published in Great Britain by Michael Joseph 2013
Published in Penguin Books 2014

001

Set in 12.5/14.75 Garamond MT Std
Typeset by Jouve (UK), Milton Keynes
Printed in Great Britain by Clays Ltd, St Ives plc

PAPERBACK ISBN: 978–1–405–90986–0
OPEN MARKET PAPERBACK ISBN: 978–1–405–91535–9

www.greenpenguin.co.uk

Penguin Books is committed to a sustainable future for our business, our readers and our planet. This book is made from Forest Stewardship Council™ certified paper.

Prologue

April 18, 1906
Sonoma County, Northern California

Thunder shook the unlit cavern as an immense, blue-white spark jumped between a pair of towering, metal columns. Instead of fading, the shimmering charge split in two and the twin streams of plasma began to circle their respective pillars. They moved like flames chasing the wind, racing around the columns and snaking their way upward toward the underside of a curved, metallic dome. There, they swirled together like the arms of a spiral galaxy, joining each other once again before vanishing in a final, eye-searing flash.

Darkness followed.

Ozone lingered in the air.

On the floor of the cavern, a group of men and women stood motionless, night-blind from the display. The flash had been impressive, but they'd all seen electricity before. Every one of them expected something more.

'Is that it?' a gruff voice asked.

The words came from Brigadier General Hal Cortland, a burly, squat figure of a man. They were directed at thirty-eight-year-old Daniel Watterson, a slight, blond-haired man wearing spectacles who stood by the controls of the great machine from which the artificial lightning had come.

Watterson studied a bank of dimly lit gauges. 'I'm not actually sure,' he whispered to himself. No one had ever gotten this far, not even Michael Faraday or the great Nikola Tesla. But if Watterson was right – if his calculations and his theory and years of serving as Tesla's apprentice had led him to understand what was about to occur – then the display of light they'd just witnessed should be only the beginning.

He switched off the main power, stepped away from the controls, and pulled the wire-rimmed glasses from his face. Despite the darkness, he could make out a soft blue glow coming from the columns. He raised his eyes to the dome above. An effervescent hue could be seen coursing around its inner surface.

'Well?' Cortland demanded.

Back at the console, one of the needles ticked up. Watterson saw it from the corner of his eye.

'No, General,' he said quietly, 'I don't think it's quite finished.'

As Watterson spoke, a low rumble made its way through the cave. It sounded like heavy stones tumbling in some distant quarry, muffled and distorted, as if the vibration had to traverse miles of solid rock just to reach them. It rose for several seconds, then faded and ceased.

The general began to snicker. He switched on a

flashlight. 'Uncle Sam ain't paying for a show with wet fireworks, son.'

Watterson didn't reply. He was listening, feeling for something, for anything, at this point.

The general seemed to give up. 'Come on, people,' he said, 'the party's over. Let's get out of this mole hole.'

The group began to move. Their shuffling and mumbling made it impossible to hear.

Watterson raised a hand. 'Please!' he called out loudly. 'Everyone, stay where you are!'

The observers stopped in their tracks, and Watterson edged over to where the steel columns penetrated the rock floor. From there, they descended another five hundred feet 'to get a firm grip on the Earth,' as Tesla once put it.

Laying a hand on one of the columns, Watterson felt a cold vibration. It surged through his body as if he'd become a part of the circuit. It wasn't painful like electricity and didn't make his muscles spasm, nor did it find its way to the ground and electrocute him. It was almost soothing, leaving him slightly dizzy, even a bit euphoric.

'It's coming,' he whispered.

'What's coming?' the general asked.

Watterson looked back. 'The return.'

Cortland waited a few seconds before scowling. 'You scientists are like barkers at a carnival: you think if you say something loud enough, and often enough, the rest of us will begin to believe it. But I don't hear any –'

The general swallowed his words as the deep rumble made a second appearance. It surged through the cavern more emphatically this time, and the blue glow around the towers intensified, pulsing and matching the sound waves identically.

This time, when the waves faded, everyone held still. They were waiting for more. Forty seconds later they were rewarded. A third wave came through like a freight train passing by. It shook the cave underfoot and brought the swirl of lightning back to the polished surface of the dome above. The visible spiral of energy began descending the pillars, making it halfway down to the ground before vanishing.

Watterson pulled back, stepping away from the danger zone.

Moments later, a fourth reverberation surged into the cavern. The columns flared as it hit. Flashes of light jumped back and forth between them. The cavern began shaking. Dust and tiny bits of stone rained down from above, sending the witnesses scurrying for cover.

Watterson caught sight of General Cortland bathed in the light and grinning manically. Their roles had reversed. Now it was Cortland looking satisfied as Watterson began to worry. The scientist stepped toward the panel, slid his glasses back on, and studied the display. He couldn't account for the vibration.

Before he could determine anything, a fifth wave hit. The vibration and the artificial lightning grew so intense, even the general seemed to realize something was wrong. 'What's happening?'

Watterson could barely hear him, but he was wondering the same thing. The power gauges – all but dead moments before – were heading toward their redlines.

A brief respite gave way to a sixth harmonic return, and the needles went off the scales. The shuddering was unbearable. Rocks were falling from above. A huge crack began to zigzag its way across the reinforced wall of the cave where the army had poured concrete to shore it up. Watterson had to grip the panel to stop from falling down.

'What's happening?' the general repeated. Watterson wasn't sure, but it couldn't be good.

'Get everybody out of here,' he yelled. 'Get them out – now!'

The general pointed toward the cagelike elevator that would take them four hundred feet to the surface. The group ran for it like a stampeding herd. But the tremors intensified and the far wall gave way before they could climb inside.

A thousand tons of rock and concrete plunged down on them. Those too close were crushed instantly. Others scrambled away just in time as the scaffolding-like frame of the elevator was bent and shoved aside.

Watterson began to panic. His hands flew back and forth across the controls, flicking switches and tapping gauges. The vibration was constant. The sound deafening.

Cortland grabbed him by the shoulder. 'Turn it off!'

Watterson ignored him. He was trying to understand.

'Did you hear me?!' the general shouted. *'Turn the damned thing off!'*

'It is off!' Watterson shouted, pulling free of the general's grasp.

'What?'

'It's been off since after the first spark,' Watterson explained.

The latest wave faded, but on the panel he could see the next wave building. The needles went off the scale and Watterson's face went white. Each wave had been bigger than the last. He feared to imagine what kind of power was on its way.

'Then where's the energy coming from?' Cortland demanded.

'From everywhere,' Watterson said. 'From all around us. That's what the experiment was supposed to prove.'

The cavern began to shake once again. This time the lightning was not contained on the columns; it jumped around the room, flying into the walls, the ceiling and the floor. Shards of stone and clouds of dust blasted out into the open space.

Amid the screams and panic, Watterson stood helpless, his moment of victory fading to utter catastrophe. From above him came the ominous sound of cracking.

With the cave shaking so badly they could barely stand, both Watterson and the general looked up.

A dark fissure snaked across the ceiling. It went from wall to wall and then spidered in different directions.

The ceiling collapsed all at once and a million tons of rock dropped toward them.

Death came instantly, and neither Watterson nor General Cortland would ever know the fury they'd unleashed or the utter devastation that the ensuing earthquake caused in the city of San Francisco.

I

December 2009

In the midst of a growing tempest, Patrick Devlin stood on the aft deck of the *Java Dawn*, an oceangoing tug linked by a single massive cable to the rusting hulk of a cruise ship known as the *Pacific Voyager*.

Huge swells came at the tug sideways, slamming against the hull with the sound of a shotgun blast. The rain fell in diagonal sheets, though it was hard to distinguish from the wind-whipped spray.

Surrounded by towing and loading equipment, including a fifty-foot crane and a powerful winch array, Devlin looked positively small. In truth, he stood nearly six feet tall, with broad shoulders that were hunched against the cold.

With gray stubble on his cheeks and folds of burnished flesh hooding his eyes, Devlin appeared every bit the wizened old sailor he was. Taking stock of the deteriorating weather, the increasing strain on the cable and the condition of the sea, he came to a grave conclusion: they'd made a ruinous choice to leave port, one they'd be lucky to survive.

As Devlin grabbed the ship's phone, another swell

rolled the tug severely. The captain picked up on the other end.

'What's our heading?' Devlin yelled into the receiver.

'Due south,' the captain said.

'It's no good,' Devlin replied. 'We'll never survive this side-on beating. We have to turn into the swells.'

'We can't, Padi,' the captain insisted. 'That'll take us into the teeth of the storm.'

Gripping the bulkhead to keep from falling, Devlin watched a wave crash over the deck. 'This is madness,' he said. 'We should never have left Tarakan.'

Tarakan was the primitive, almost backwater port where they'd picked up the *Voyager*. The old liner had berthed there for repairs some years ago after an accident. She'd ended up marooned when her shipping line went bankrupt several days later.

At some point, the ship was sold to a mystery buyer, but, for reasons unknown, the *Voyager* sat and rusted at Tarakan for three more years. Issues with the bankruptcy and squabbles about who would pay for the repairs, Devlin guessed.

Whatever it was, the ship looked like a derelict when they'd found her; covered in corrosion from stem to stern, barely seaworthy. The hastily repaired damage from where the freighter had holed her looked like a jagged H near the bow.

Now, caught up in a storm that was rapidly getting worse, she was certain to go down.

'How's the line?' the captain asked.

Devlin glanced at the thick cable that stretched from the gigantic winch across the aft end of the tug and out toward the *Voyager*. The cable tensed and strained with the load before going slack again.

'The cable's taut,' Devlin said. 'That rust bucket is starting to pitch with these waves. She's definitely riding lower as well. We need to get the inspection crew back.'

Against Devlin's wishes, the captain had allowed three men to stay aboard the cruise ship to watch for leaks. It was dangerous in these conditions and a waste of time as well. If she was taking on water, there was nothing they could do to stop it. And if she started to go down – like Devlin thought she was – they would need to cut the cable and let her go before she dragged the *Java Dawn* into the depths alongside her. But with three men on the ship, cutting that cable would be the closest thing to murder Devlin had ever done.

The big tug nosed over and dropped into the largest trough yet. As it did, the cable stretched so tight that it actually began to sing. The tension pulled the aft end of the tug backward, the water churning around the hull as the propellers fought against the strain.

By the time the tug rose up on the next swell, the *Voyager* must have been dipping into a trough of her own because the tow cable pulled downward, bending over the reinforced-steel plating at the tug's transom and forcing the aft end of the deck into the water.

Devlin raised binoculars to his eyes. The action of

the waves had a way of obscuring the truth, but only to a point. The *Voyager* was definitely riding lower.

'She's down at the bow, Captain. Listing slightly to port.'

The captain hesitated. Devlin knew why: this tow was worth a small fortune, but not if the ship didn't make it.

'Call them back!' Devlin shouted. 'For God sakes, Captain, at least call the men back.'

Finally, the captain spoke. 'We've been calling them, Padi. They're not answering. Something must have gone wrong.'

The words chilled Devlin's core. 'We have to send a boat out.'

'In this? It's too dangerous.'

As if to emphasize the point, another wave hit them broadside and a thousand gallons of water crashed over the rail, flooding the aft deck.

The sturdy tug quickly shed the water, but moments later another wave swamped it more drastically than the first.

As the *Java Dawn* recovered, Devlin looked toward the *Voyager*.

She was definitely going down. Either a couple of hatches had blown or the shoddy repair job had caved in.

The captain must have seen it too. 'We have to let her go,' he said.

'No, Captain!'

'We have to, Padi. Release the cable. The men have a boat of their own. And we can't help them if we go down.'

Another wave crashed over the deck.

'For God sakes, Captain, have pity.'

'Cut the cable, Padi! That's an order!'

Devlin knew the captain was right. He let go of the phone and took a step toward the emergency release lever.

The deck pitched hard as another swell overran the stern and sloshed toward him. It hit like a wave at the beach, knocking him off his feet and dragging him.

As he got up, Devlin saw that the cable was now disappearing into the water. Through the rain and spray, he could see that half the cruise ship was submerged. She was going down fast, plunging to the abyss and about to drag the tug down with her. The back quarter of the tug's rear deck was already awash.

'Padi!'

The shout came over the dangling phone, but Devlin needed no more urging. He pulled himself up, grabbed the emergency release handle, and wrenched it down with all his might.

A loud crack rang out. The giant cable snapped loose and flung itself across the deck like a speeding python. The tug lurched forward and upward, and Devlin was thrown into the bulkhead, splitting his lip and bruising his eye.

Stunned for a moment, he gathered his wits and

turned. The old liner was sliding beneath the waves at a gentle, almost peaceful angle. Seconds later, it was gone. The men they'd left behind were almost certainly dead. But the *Java Dawn* was free.

Devlin grabbed the phone.

'Take us back around,' he demanded. 'The men may have gone overboard.'

The deck shifted as the rudder and the directional propellers kicked in. The tug began a sharp, dangerous turn. By the time she'd made it around, Devlin was at the bow.

It was almost dark. The sky held a silver hue above the black sea. The whole scene was so devoid of color, it was like living in a black-and-white movie.

Devlin gazed into it. He saw nothing.

As darkness enveloped them, the tug's spotlights swept the area. No doubt every available eye was straining to find the men just as Devlin was. It was all to no avail.

The *Java Dawn* would spend the next eighteen hours searching in vain for her lost crewmen.

They would never be found at sea.

2

Present day

Sebastian Panos made his way through the narrow corridor like an alley cat on a dark street behind restaurant row. The passage was dank and wet, more like a sewer tunnel than a gangway. Condensation dripped so persistently that he often wondered if the poisonous waters from outside the submerged station were leaching through the walls and slowly killing them all.

Still, it wasn't as bad as the island where the main work was done, with the notorious quarry at its heart. Compared to that place, this station was a pleasure. And yet, Panos had become obsessed with thoughts of escape.

A Cypriot engineer of mixed Greek and Turkish background, Panos had been lured to this underwater nightmare by the promise of a big contract and enough money to set his family up for a generation. All it required was three years of his life and utter secrecy. Six months in, he'd begun to feel uneasy. Before the year rolled over, he knew he'd made a terrible mistake.

Requests to leave were denied. All communications were monitored and often interrupted. The slightest hint of protest resulted in veiled threats. *Something might happen to his family if he didn't stay and complete the work.*

As the project neared fruition, Panos and the other engineers were played off against each other. It was impossible to know who to trust and who to fear, so they feared one another, did as they were told, and one year stretched into two.

All that time Panos lived like a sailor press-ganged on to a ship. He had no choice but to do the master's bidding or forfeit his life, though he felt certain that his end would come that way eventually. The project was so secret and dark that his logical mind told him there would be no witnesses left when it was done.

No one gets out alive, a fellow worker had joked. One day later, the man disappeared, so perhaps it was true.

Panos remembered an offer to bring his family along. He wasn't a religious man, but he thanked whatever god or fate or random instinct had caused him to decline. Others had brought their families in. He'd seen them on the island, wretched and miserable, prisoners to an even greater degree than he. He knew not to trust them. They were the easiest to control; they had more to lose than their own lives. Some had even borne children in the depths of that putrid, sulfur-tinged world. They lived like indentured servants, like slaves building a modern-day pyramid.

Panos was at least free to *think* about escape, though he'd never had any real expectation of pulling it off. At least, not until the note appeared in his locker.

It was the first in a set of mysterious contacts from an unseen angel of mercy.

Initially, he assumed it was a trap, a little test to see if he would lunge at the bait. But he'd reached a point where it no longer mattered. Freedom beckoned. Whether it came through escape or the cold sting of death, he welcomed it either way.

He tested the offer and received more notes. They arrived at odd times. Help to escape would be made available, the notes promised, but it would come with strings attached. He was to bring the plans of this terrible weapon to those who might stop the madman constructing it. A drop had been arranged. All Panos had to do was make it to the location alive.

With that goal in mind, he continued down the wet gangway and into the dive room. It was late, well past the hour for anyone to be there. Using a key left in his locker by his unknown contact, Panos opened the door and slipped inside. He shut the door and switched on a desk lamp.

The dive room was a twenty-by-forty rectangle with a sealed airlock protruding at its center. Visible through the airlock's thick observation glass was a circular pool of dark water.

Panos switched on the pool lights. The water lit up perfectly clear, for the poisons filling it made it absolutely sterile. But instead of blue or turquoise or green, the water shimmered in a reddish tint, a color like translucent blood.

He took a deep breath. He would be all right. The dry suit would keep the toxins out. At least he hoped it would.

He glanced over at a whiteboard. Three numbers had been scrawled on it: 3, 10, and 075. His unseen helper had been there before him, just as he'd promised.

Panos memorized the figures and then quickly erased them. He went to the third locker and opened it. A dry suit and an oxygen tank had been prepared for him. A dive watch, hanging with the suit, had its bezel twisted to the ten-minute mark. This was the time it would take him to ascend, moving at thirty feet per minute, a pace calculated to help him avoid the bends. A handheld compass had also been left for him. When he surfaced, he would look to a heading: 075 degrees. In that direction, he would find help.

A dive knife would be his only weapon, if he needed it.

He strapped the watch around his wrist and carried the tanks to the airlock. He slipped the compass into his pocket and then double-checked that the cargo he'd promised to carry – the schematics of the station and a portable hard drive filled with data – were secured in a watertight container.

He shoved them back inside his shirt and grabbed the bulky suit, sitting down to pull it on. Before he could get a leg in, a clicking noise sounded from across the room.

A key in the lock.

The handle turned and the door swung open. Two figures stepped in, chatting between themselves.

For a second, they didn't notice Panos. When they did, they looked more confused and surprised than angry. But Panos knew the suit and tanks would give him away.

He charged the men before they could react, swinging the knife downward at the closest figure, stabbing the man in the shoulder. The man fell back, grabbing at Panos and dragging him to the desk. The second man jumped on him, putting an arm around his neck.

Panos reared up and forced himself backward until the two of them collided with the desk, fell to the ground, and separated.

Spurred on by adrenaline, Panos was up first. He kneed the man in the face, then grabbed the desk lamp and slammed it into the man's forehead. The man hit the ground and didn't move again, but the one who'd been stabbed was running out the door.

'No!' Panos exclaimed.

With no way to barricade the door and precious little time before an alarm sounded, he made a fateful decision. He left the dry suit on the floor and stepped into the airlock. Pressing a switch, he closed the inner door and began to pull on the harness and an oxygen tank.

Panos felt his ears popping as a hissing noise told him the airlock was sealed and being pressurized. Even though the station's pressure was twice the normal atmosphere, it wasn't enough to keep the water from flooding in through the open pool. Thus, the airlock was needed.

He pulled on the dive helmet. The seal wasn't too bad. He made sure the air was flowing, pulled his fins on, and dropped into the glowing red water.

Stillness surrounded him. He swam downward, away from the light, and out into the dark. When he'd passed the edge of the submerged structure, he began to kick his way upward. Or what he thought was up.

Three hundred feet down, there was no light. He quickly became disoriented. Vertigo set in, and it seemed like his body was doing somersaults even though he was completely still.

Flicking on a light did little good. The red water gave nothing away. He began to panic, knowing men from the station would be following him soon.

What had he done?

He exhaled a cloud of bubbles. Quite by accident, he noticed the direction they raced off in. It seemed to Panos that the bubbles were traveling sideways, but his rational mind knew this was not the case. The bubbles could *only* be moving upward. The laws of nature could not be altered or tricked like his sense of balance.

Forcing his mind to override what his inner ear was telling him, he began to follow the bubbles. It felt like he was swimming into the pit, to the bottom of this great red pool of death, instead of upward.

He kept going until his mind began to accept it. His

equilibrium began returning to normal. He exhaled more bubbles and kicked harder, swimming for the surface as fast as he could.

In his haste, Panos forgot about the ten-minute warning. By the time he neared the surface, he was in the grips of pain. His knees, elbows and back all felt as if they were cramping up.

Despite the pain, Panos broke the surface and stared at the evening sky for the first time in months. It was periwinkle blue. He guessed it was almost dusk.

He looked around. High sandy walls rose up on every side. He'd never seen them before. He didn't even know where he was. Arrivals and departures always took place under sedation. They would fall asleep here and wake up on the island, or vice versa.

Despite the pain in his joints, Panos managed to pull the compass from his pocket. He began to swim, heading 075 degrees. The wretched throbbing in his joints got worse and was soon accompanied by blinding flashes of light that seemed to shoot through his brain.

Still, he fought on, eventually crawling out of the water and on to the sandy beach. He made it several yards before coming to a terraced wall of rock. It rose no more than ten feet, but it might as well have been a mountain.

How could he scale it? He couldn't. Not in this condition. He tried to stand and then collapsed in agony.

The sound of feet rushing toward him signaled his end. But when a pair of hands lifted him up, they did so caringly.

He saw a face hidden by a bandanna.

'You surfaced too quickly,' the man behind the bandanna said.

'I . . . had to . . .' Panos managed. 'They . . . found me.'

'Found you?!'

'In the airlock . . .' Panos said.

'That means they'll be coming.'

The unknown helper grabbed Panos and dragged him over the ridge with no concessions to the pain. He carried him to a waiting SUV, tossed him in the back and slammed the tailgate down.

Panos curled up in the fetal position as his savior climbed into the front and turned the key.

The engine roared, and they were soon bouncing over the rough terrain, each jolt spurring new waves of pain. To Panos, it felt as if his body were being crushed and exploding from within all at the same time.

'I'm dying,' he cried out.

'No,' the driver insisted. 'But it's going to get worse before it gets better. Use your regulator. It will help.'

Panos managed to get the regulator back in his mouth. He bit down on it and breathed as deeply as he could. Even with that, a new series of spasms gripped him as the SUV careened across uneven ground.

Panos bent his head closer to his chest. It seemed to ease the agony a bit. He noticed his fingers and arms curling inward.

'Do you have the papers?' the driver asked. 'And the computer?'

Panos nodded. 'Yes . . . Can you tell me where we're going?'

The driver hesitated, perhaps afraid to say too much in case they were captured. Finally, he spoke. 'To someone who can help,' he said. 'To someone who can put a stop to this madness once and for all.'

3

Sydney, Australia, 1900 hours

Kurt Austin sat in a comfortable seat eight rows from the main stage in the Opera Theatre, the smaller of the two sail-and-seashell-inspired buildings of the famous Sydney Opera House. The larger Concert Hall lay next door, vacant at the moment.

For years, Kurt had planned to visit Sydney and attend a performance there. Beethoven or Wagner would have been nice, and he'd almost made the trip when U2 played the venue, but the timing hadn't worked out. Unfortunately, now that he'd finally made it, the only sound coming from the stage was a dry, academic speech that was quickly putting him to sleep.

He was there for the Muldoon Conference on Underwater Mining, put on by Archibald and Liselette Muldoon, a wealthy Australian couple who'd made their fortune together through four decades of risky mining ventures.

Kurt had been officially invited because of his expertise in underwater salvage and his position as Director of Special Projects for the National Underwater and Marine Agency. But it seemed the Muldoons also wanted him there because of the modicum of fame he'd earned within the salvage industry – if there even was such a thing.

Over the past decade, he'd been involved in a series of high-profile events. Some of those exploits were classified, with nothing more than rumors to suggest anything had ever occurred. Other events were public and well known, including a recent battle to clear a swarm of self-replicating micromachines from the Indian Ocean before they changed the weather patterns over India and Asia, potentially starving billions.

In addition to whatever notoriety he'd earned, Kurt was easily recognizable. He had a rugged look about him, tan-faced, with prematurely silver-gray hair and sharp eyes that were an intense shade of blue. All of which meant his absence from any particular event was easily noticed, something the constant attention of one or both Muldoons had so far prevented.

They'd certainly been gracious, but after three days of seminars and presentations, Kurt was plotting his escape.

As the lights dimmed and the speaker began a photo presentation, Kurt sensed the chance he'd been waiting for. He pulled out his phone and thumbed the switch that made it buzz audibly as if it were ringing.

A few glances came his way.

He shrugged a sheepish apology and put the phone to his ear.

'This is Austin,' he whispered to no one. 'Right,' he

added in his most serious tone. 'Right. Okay. That does sound bad. Of course. I'll look into it right away.'

He pretended to hang up and slipped the phone back into his pocket.

'Is something wrong?' Mrs Muldoon asked from one seat over.

'Call from the head office,' he said. 'Have to check something out.'

'You have to go now?'

Kurt nodded. 'A situation that's been building for several days has reached breaking point. If I don't go now, it could be disastrous.'

She reached out and grabbed his hand. She looked crestfallen. 'But you're missing the best part of the presentation.'

Kurt made a grim face. 'It's the price I have to pay.'

Bidding the Muldoons good-bye, Kurt stood and strolled down the aisle to the waiting doors. He pushed through them and jogged up the steps into the foyer. Fearing he might get trapped in a conversation if he ran into other attendees, he took a left, sneaking down a curving hallway toward an unmarked side door.

He pushed it open and stepped out into the humid air of the Australian evening. To his surprise, he wasn't alone.

A young woman sat on the step in front of him, fiddling with the heel of a strappy shoe. She wore a white cocktail dress with a matching white flower in her strawberry blond hair. Kurt thought it might be an orchid.

She looked up, startled by his sudden appearance.

'Didn't mean to scare you,' he said.

For a second, she looked apoplectic, like he'd caught her stealing the Crown Jewels or something. Then she glanced around and went back to work on her shoe, wiggling the offending heel back and forth until the delicate little spike snapped off in her hand.

'That's probably not going to help,' Kurt guessed.

'My favorite shoes,' she said in a melodic Australian accent. 'Always seem to be the ones you break.'

Dejected but exhibiting admirable common sense, she slipped off the other shoe and broke off its heel, then compared the two.

'At least they match,' he said, offering a hand. 'Kurt Austin.'

'Hayley Anderson,' she replied. 'Proud owner of the most expensive flats in all of Oz.'

Kurt had to laugh.

'I suppose you're escaping the keynote,' she said.

'Guilty as charged,' he admitted. 'Can you really blame me?'

'Not in the least,' she replied. 'If I didn't need to be here, I'd be off to the beach myself.'

She stood up and stepped toward the door from which Kurt had emerged. It seemed a shame to have the encounter end so soon.

'Flat shoes work well on the sand,' Kurt offered. 'Almost as well as bare feet.'

'Sorry,' she said, 'can't miss this or someone will have my guts for garters. You could come back in with me; I promise to keep you entertained.'

'Tempting,' Kurt said. 'But my hard-won freedom is worth too much at this point. If you get bored in there, you'll find me on Bondi Beach. I'll be the one who's slightly overdressed.'

She laughed lightly and grabbed quickly for the door. She seemed to be rushing, but as she pulled the door open, she stopped, her gaze drifting past Kurt. She was looking across Sydney Harbour.

Kurt turned. In the fading light, he spotted the curving wake of a powerboat. It cut across the harbor, coming dangerously close to the front of a ferry. A scolding blast from the ship's horn followed, but the boat never slowed.

An instant later, Kurt saw why. A dark-colored helicopter raced over the top of the ferry, flashing across the crowded vessel in the blink of an eye and dropping back toward the water in hot pursuit.

The speeding boat turned left and then right, carving an S in the water and intentionally skirting the edges of a slow-moving sailboat. It was a madman's path across the harbor.

'He must be insane,' Hayley said, gawking at the boat.

Kurt took a good look at the helicopter, a dark blue

Eurocopter EC145. A stubby, bulbous cabin that jutted forward gave its nose an odd, compact look, something like the snout of a great white shark. A four-bladed rotor whirled overhead, leaving a white blur, while its short, boomlike tail ended in three small vertical stabilizers something like a trident.

Kurt saw no markings or navigation lights, but he noticed flashes coming from the open cargo door: muzzle flashes.

He grabbed his phone and dialed 911. Nothing happened.

Hayley took a step forward. 'They're shooting. They're trying to kill those people.'

'What's the emergency number here?'

'Zero zero zero,' she said.

Kurt typed it in and hit CALL. By the time he was connected, the speedboat had turned head-on toward the Opera House. It raced toward them at full throttle, aiming for the rounded promenade that stuck out into Sydney Harbour like a great pier.

Most of the promenade was a wall of solid concrete, but a single flight of stairs on the left-hand side led down to the water. The speeding boat was drawing a line right to them. The helicopter was following, trying to set up a kill shot for the sniper.

More flashes lit out from the door.

The boat jerked to the left as the popping sound of gunfire reached the shore. It swerved a bit, then came back on course and hit the stairwell at high speed. It flew up into the air at an angle, like a stunt car launching off a jump ramp in catty-corner fashion. It traveled fifty feet and rolled halfway over before it slammed down on its side.

From there, the boat skidded across the concrete deck, hit a lamp post, and came apart. Shattered fiberglass fluttered in all directions as the post bent over and its bulbs exploded with a flash.

'Emergency Service,' a voice said over the phone.

Kurt was too mesmerized by the accident to respond.

'Hello? This is Emergency Service.'

As the shattered boat settled, the Eurocopter thundered overhead, barely missing the pointed top of the Opera House.

Kurt handed the phone to Hayley. 'Get help,' he shouted, taking off down the stairs. 'Police, ambulance, national guard. Anything they've got.'

Kurt had no idea what was going on, but even from up on the platform he could see two people trapped in the boat's wreckage, and he could smell leaking fuel.

He reached the bottom of the stairs, ran a short distance, and hopped over a wall on to the promenade. As he raced up to the mangled craft, the still-spinning prop touched the concrete walkway. A shower of sparks lit out from it. They flew into the gasoline vapors, and a flashover roared outward.

In the wake of this small explosion, a sea of flames rose from where the ruptured fuel had spilled.

Despite the conflagration, Kurt rushed forward.

*

Four hundred feet above and a mile away, the Eurocopter made a steep turn above the outskirts of Sydney.

Even though he was strapped in, the sniper put a hand out and held on.

'Take it easy,' he shouted.

He was already wrestling with the long-barreled Heckler & Koch sniper rifle, trying to attach a high-capacity fifty-round drum. The last thing he needed was to be dumped out the side.

'We have to make another pass,' the pilot called back. 'We have to make sure they're dead.'

The sniper doubted anyone could have survived the crash, but it wasn't his call. As the helicopter leveled out, he gave up trying to attach the drum and jammed a standard ten-round magazine in the weapon.

'Keep it steady this time,' he demanded. 'I need a stable platform to shoot from.'

'Will do,' the pilot replied.

The sniper eased toward the open door, folding one leg underneath him and stretching the other leg down to brace himself on the step that was just above the copter's skid.

They'd come around now and were approaching the sails of the Opera House more slowly. He racked the slide and readied himself to fire.

By the time Kurt reached the shattered boat, fire had engulfed its stern. A hunched-over figure in the passenger seat was trying to get free. Kurt pulled him loose and dragged him over the side, ignoring the cries of pain.

Fifty feet from the boat, Kurt laid the injured man down, noticing the strange way his hands and fingers curled up. It was an odd enough sight to stick in Kurt's mind even as he raced back to help the driver.

Fighting through the acrid smoke, Kurt clambered on to the boat. By now, flames were licking at the driver's back.

Kurt tried to pull the man upward, but he was held in place by the crushed-in section of the control panel.

'Leave me,' the man shouted. 'Help Panos.'

'If that's your passenger, he's already safe,' Kurt shouted. 'Now, help me get you free.'

The man pushed and Kurt pulled, but the crushed panel held him tight. Kurt knew they needed leverage. He grabbed a harpoonlike boat hook that lay in what remained of the bow and wedged it in between the trapped driver and the mangled wreckage.

Leaning on it with all his weight, Kurt forced some space between the driver and the panel. 'Now!' he shouted.

The man shook his head. 'I can't,' he said. 'I can't feel my –'

In a sudden recoil, the driver's head snapped back, and blood spattered across the dashboard. The smoke swirled with new abandon and the rising flames danced in odd directions as gusting wind from the helicopter's downwash swept over them.

Realizing the driver was dead and that he was probably next, Kurt dived over the side of the boat and tumbled out.

Shells hit left and right as he scrambled for cover.

Hidden in the smoke, Kurt looked up. The Eurocopter hovered sixty feet above. He could see the sniper searching for a target, moving the long barrel of his rifle back and forth. Then the helicopter drifted to the left and turned away.

The sniper must have seen the injured passenger limping down the promenade. He opened fire with abandon.

Ricochets hit all around the man until a shell found its mark and dropped the poor soul to his knees. Before the shooter could finish him off, another bystander rushed in. It was Hayley. She dragged the limp figure behind a large concrete planter and ducked down.

The sniper opened fire once again, the shells digging chips out of the concrete and throwing up chunks of dirt. But the planter might as well have been a giant sandbag. It was too thick for the bullets to penetrate.

The helicopter began to drift sideways. Kurt had only seconds before the sniper found a clear line of fire.

He grabbed the wooden boat hook once again, the business end of which was now in flames. He gripped it near the center, ran forward, and hurled it like a javelin.

The helicopter was broadside to him now, and the

fiery lance tracked toward the open cargo door like a heat-seeking missile.

It hit the target dead center, missing the sniper by inches but lodging in the cabin and spreading a wave of fire in the process. In a moment, smoke was pouring from the helicopter's side door. Kurt saw the sniper's body erupt in flames, and he could only guess that he'd hit a fuel or oxygen line.

The orange firelight surged through the helicopter as it began to turn. For a second, it looked as if the pilot would regain control and speed off across the harbor, but the angle of his turn tightened, and the helicopter began to corkscrew back toward the Concert Hall. By now, the interior of the cabin was an inferno, smoke billowing from it in all directions.

Burning and falling and accelerating at the same time, the Eurocopter flew right into the famous glass wall of the Concert Hall, shattering the fifty-foot panes of clear glass. Shards from the impact burst inward, while other sections dropped in huge sheets and exploded into thousands of fragments when they hit the ground.

The helicopter dropped straight down along with them, its rotors gone and its hub turning like a weedwacker that had run out of string. It landed with a great crunch. In moments, it was a barely recognizable hulk at the center of a small inferno.

By now, emergency units were arriving. A squad of patrolmen raced up on foot. Fire trucks were pulling in.

Workers from the Opera House came running out with extinguishers. Another group opened a fire hose from a stanchion in a wall.

Kurt was pretty sure it wouldn't help the occupants of the helicopter, neither of whom had managed to get free of the blaze.

He made his way over to Hayley and the lone survivor from the boat. The man was lying in Hayley's arms. His blood had soaked her white dress. She was trying desperately to keep him from bleeding out where two bullets had hit him.

It was a losing battle. The shells had gone right through him, entering his back and coming out through his chest.

Kurt crouched down and helped her keep pressure on the wounds. 'Are you Panos?' he asked.

The man's eyes drifted for a moment.

'Are you Panos?!'

He nodded weakly.

'Who were those people shooting at you?'

No answer this time. Nothing but a blank look.

Kurt lifted his head. 'We need help over here!' he shouted, looking for a paramedic.

A pair of men were running toward them, but they weren't first responders. They reminded Kurt of plain-clothes policemen. They stopped in their tracks as he looked their way.

'I brought . . . what was promised,' the injured man said in an accent Kurt thought might be Greek.

'What are you talking about?' Kurt asked.

The man grunted something and then extended a shaking hand in which he clutched several bloodstained sheets of paper.

'Tartarus,' the man said, his voice weak and wavering. 'The heart . . . of Tartarus.'

Kurt took the papers. They were covered with odd symbols, swirling lines, and what appeared to be calculations.

'What is this?' Kurt said.

The man opened his mouth to explain but no sound came out.

'Stay with us,' Hayley shouted.

He didn't respond, and she began to perform CPR. 'We can't let him die.'

Kurt felt for a pulse. He didn't feel one. 'It's too late.'

'No, it can't be,' she said, compressing the man's chest rapidly and trying to force life back into him.

Kurt stopped her. 'It's no use, he's lost too much blood.'

She looked up at him, her face smeared with soot and tears, her white dress stained red.

'I'm sorry,' he said. 'You tried.'

She sat back and turned away, looking exhausted. Her hair fell around her face as she looked to the ground. Her body shook as she sobbed.

Kurt put a hand on her shoulder and gazed at the damage surrounding them.

The wreck of the boat still burned on the promenade, while the blazing hulk of the Eurocopter lay where the shattered façade of the Concert Hall should have been. Volunteers were hosing it down, desperately trying to keep it from setting fire to the building, while onlookers poured from the keynote address on underwater mining, half of them gawking as the rest moved quickly in the other direction.

It all happened so fast. Chaos sprung on them from nowhere. And the only man who might have known why lay dead at their feet.

'What did he say?' Hayley asked, wiping the tears from her face. 'What did he say to you?'

'Tartarus,' Kurt replied.

She stared. 'What does that mean?'

Kurt wasn't convinced that he'd heard the man correctly. Even if he had, it made little sense.

'It's a word from Greek mythology,' he said. 'The deepest prison of the underworld. According to the *Iliad*, as far below Hades as Heaven is above the Earth.'

'What do you think he was trying to tell us?'

'No idea,' Kurt said, shrugging and handing her the papers. 'Maybe that's where he thinks he's going. Or,' he added, considering the grime, dust and stench that covered the poor man, 'maybe that's where he's been.'

4

Red and blue lights flashed across the famous sails of the Opera House in a series of intersecting patterns, while blinding white spotlights illuminated the wreckage of the powerboat and the charred shell of the dark blue helicopter. They remained where they'd crashed, smoking and smoldering, as fire trucks poured waves of foam on to both vehicles to prevent any chance of re-ignition.

The spectacle drew a crowd from both the land and the water. Police tape and barricades kept the shore-based onlookers at bay, but the number of small boats crowding the harbor had grown to more than a hundred. Cameras and flashes snapped in the dark like fireflies.

From the shadows of a doorway, Cecil Bradshaw of the Australian Security Intelligence Organisation studied the man responsible for all the damage.

An aide handed him a dossier.

'This is awful thick,' Bradshaw said. 'I need only the highlights, not every bloody clipping on the man.'

Bradshaw was a stocky man in his mid-fifties. He had pile-driver arms, a thick neck and a short buzz cut.

In a way, he resembled a giant human bulldog. He liked to think of himself in similar terms. *Get on my side or get out of my way,* he often said.

The aide didn't stammer in his response. 'Those are the highlights, sir. If you'd like, I have another fifty pages I could print out for you.'

Bradshaw offered a grunt in response and opened the file. He leafed through the pages quickly, studying what the ASIO knew about Mr Kurt Austin of the American organization NUMA. His activities read like a series of high-stakes adventure novels. Before that, he'd apparently had a successful career in the CIA.

Bradshaw couldn't imagine what strange permutations of fate had brought Austin to this very spot at this precise moment, but it just might have been a break the ASIO desperately needed.

Austin might do, Bradshaw thought to himself. *He might do very nicely.*

'Keep an eye on him,' he ordered. 'If he's as smart as the file shows, he'll be trying to get information out of Ms Anderson in no time. He does that, you bring them both to me.'

'Why would we want to do that?'

Bradshaw glared. 'Did you get a promotion I'm not aware of?'

'Um . . . No, sir.'

'And you're never going to if you keep asking stupid questions.'

With that, Bradshaw slapped the file back into the agent's hands and moved off down the hall.

Across the plaza, Kurt sat beside Hayley as a paramedic treated her for a number of scrapes and abrasions and then checked them both for shock.

In the midst of this treatment, a ranking detective from the Sydney Police Department grilled them about the event. *What did they see? What did they hear? Why on earth did they do what they did?*

'Look at the damage,' the captain said, pointing to the ruined façade of the Concert Hall. 'You're lucky the building was empty.'

Indeed, Kurt felt very lucky on that score. But he also felt he'd had little choice but to act. 'Would you rather I'd just let them keep shooting?'

'I would rather . . .' the detective began, '. . . that both of you had stayed inside until proper tactical units arrived.'

Kurt understood that. Police were no different than any other group of trained individuals. *Leave it to the professionals.* Something Kurt would have been glad to do except there hadn't really been any time. Besides, he was getting the feeling there had been other professionals on-site anyway.

'Next time,' he said, 'I promise.'

'Next time?' the detective muttered. He shook his head, closed his book and moved off to check with another witness.

Left alone for a moment, Kurt studied Hayley. 'You're a brave woman.'

She shook her head softly. 'Not really. I just . . . Never mind.'

'You ran right through a hail of bullets to rescue a guy you've never seen before,' Kurt said. 'That's pretty much the definition of brave.'

'So did you,' she pointed out.

'True,' Kurt said. 'But I thought the helicopter was out of the picture. You dragged that guy behind that planter while they were actually firing at him.'

She looked away. She'd been able to clean her face with a water-soaked cloth, but her dress remained tattered and covered in blood. The victim's blood.

'A lot of good it did,' she said.

There was definite sadness there. More regret than one usually felt for an unknown man.

'How long were you waiting for him?' Kurt asked.

'What are you talking about?' she replied.

'You were sitting out here all by yourself,' he reminded her. 'As soon as I showed up, you tried to get me back inside. I'm guessing you didn't want me in the way because you were waiting to make contact with our friends in the boat. More than likely, they chose a public place where they figured they'd be safe. You chose a white dress so you'd be easy to spot when everyone else was wearing black or gray for the gala ball tonight. You sat out here on the wall so you could watch anyone approach.'

She tried to smile, but it looked forced.

'Either you hit your head very hard or you have an active imagination,' she said. 'I'm here for the conference. The Muldoons are old family friends. I chose white because I like to stand out, and because it's summer here, and because someone recently told me white is the new black.'

He shrugged and turned away. 'Maybe you're right,' he said. 'Maybe it is just an overactive imagination. Tell me, though, whatever happened to the papers?'

'What papers?'

'The bloodstained pages our dead friend was grasping when he spoke his last. I notice the police haven't asked us about them. Me and my overactive imagination think someone might have misplaced them before the police arrived. Maybe even handed them to the two guys in suits who came running toward us but stopped when they realized it was too late.'

The false smile vanished, replaced by a look of surprise and then almost tears. Kurt sensed her reaching out to him. 'I didn't –'

Before she could say anything more, a young man in a dark suit appeared on the steps beside them. Kurt could see the bulge of a shoulder holster under his jacket and the earbud in his right ear.

'Could your timing be any worse?' Kurt muttered.

The man ignored him. 'Ms Anderson, Mr Austin, come with me.'

Hayley looked as miserable at this suggestion as she

had about the possibility of answering Kurt's question, but she stood dutifully, and Kurt did the same.

Two minutes later, they were inside one of the undamaged structures. One of the agents, who'd run their way and then stopped during the incident, let them into a conference room.

Kurt followed Hayley inside. There, two other men and a woman stood around the table, examining the bloodstained pages. They used tweezers and wore gloves. One of them seemed to be taking photos of the contents under a UV light. In the far corner, a second woman tapped away on a laptop.

'Nothing on that,' she said, answering some question that had been asked before Kurt and Hayley entered. 'Next line, please.'

The group froze at Kurt and Hayley's arrival.

A stocky man with rolled-up sleeves and a buzz cut stood at the head of the table. 'Clear the room,' he grunted.

This was the boss, Kurt guessed. He looked none too happy.

The others began to move, putting down whatever they were working on and filing out one by one. The last one to leave pulled the door shut.

'Are you okay?' the burly man asked Hayley.

'No, I'm not okay,' she said. 'People are getting killed right in front of me now. You said nothing like this would happen.'

'I thought this would be the last time,' the man said.

Kurt had guessed right. Some kind of rendezvous was in the works, but the way Hayley was acting, she didn't sound like an operative.

'Don't mean to be rude,' Kurt said, 'but would someone clue the dumb foreigner in as to just what's going on here?'

The boss man turned toward Kurt. 'You've walked yourself into a dangerous situation, Mr Austin.'

'You'd be surprised how often that happens.'

'Actually,' the man said, 'in your case, I wouldn't be. I've read your file. Trouble seems to find you. And when it doesn't, you go looking for it.'

'My file?' Kurt asked. 'Why would you have a file on me?'

'Because I'm Cecil Bradshaw, deputy chief of counterterrorism for the ASIO, the Australian Security Intelligence Organisation. And *you* are a wayward member of the National Underwater and Marine Agency as well as a former specialist with the CIA.'

'I agree with everything but the wayward part,' Kurt said. 'I'm here on vacation.'

Bradshaw looked like he didn't believe that. 'Really? And your *vacation* just happened to land you in the middle of the most sensitive operation we've conducted in years.'

Kurt could imagine how it looked, especially considering his background. 'Bad timing,' he insisted. 'I'm not a spy or anything. I'm a nautical engineer and head of NUMA's Special Projects Branch, which generally involves research and development, though we do get into our share of scrapes. As for the CIA, I did salvage work mostly. Refloating sunken ships. Retrieving important parts from inside them, or blowing them up to keep others from doing the same. And even that was a long time ago.'

'So it says in your file,' Bradshaw replied.

'Look,' Kurt said, 'I'm just here for the conference. And, once it's over, I plan on surfing, diving, and knocking back a few Fosters. But I don't stand around and watch people burn to death or let them get shot, if I can help it. That's how I got involved.'

Bradshaw seemed to be weighing this up, perhaps acknowledging Kurt's actions in his mind. His tone softened a bit, but his face remained gruff.

'Okay, Austin, I'm going to cut you a little slack,' he said. 'I'm also going to assume you're not dumb enough to open your mouth about what you've seen here. But if you're not sure you can stay quiet, I can find a nice ovenlike jail out beyond the Black Stump where you can sit and think about it to your heart's content.'

Kurt wasn't sure where exactly the Black Stump was, but it sounded far away. Like a trip to Siberia only hotter.

'I remember the drill,' he said. 'You want me to sign something? See a hypnotist to forget this ever happened? That's fine too. Just show me the way out, and I can head to the beach like I intended. But you might want to check your own ranks for a leak because someone knew this little meeting of yours was going down.'

Hayley and Bradshaw exchanged a glance. Something unspoken passed between them.

Bradshaw turned back to Kurt. 'Not likely,' he said with a smug look on his face, then changed subjects. 'But since you're here, maybe you'd care to offer your professional opinion.'

'On what?'

'Start with the dead man's last word: *Tartarus*. Does that mean anything to you?'

Kurt looked at the setup once again. They were prepared to digest a lot of information. At least three analysts were on-site, plus Bradshaw. Whatever they were hoping for, it came in short. Way short.

'Only what I told Hayley,' he said.

'We're dealing with a threat to Australian national security,' Bradshaw insisted. 'Maybe even to other countries. We have four dead contacts, two before this event. One of them led us to a shipload of exotic mining equipment. You said Tartarus was underground.'

'That's right,' Kurt said. *'In Greek mythology.'*

He glanced at the desk where the laptop was. 'As you've no doubt discovered, it's a mythological prison for the gods. But unless you know something I don't, it's not real. Whatever that guy was trying to tell you, I doubt he meant it literally. Tartarus is probably a code word or a cipher for something. Maybe related to the papers he gave you.'

Bradshaw took a second to digest this and then waved Kurt over to the conference table. 'You claim to be an engineer. These look like schematics to me. You see anything here that might ring a bell?'

Kurt studied the cryptic papers. There was so much blood on them, the writing was obscured and smeared in places. What he could see looked like gibberish. He saw complex equations populated by symbols he didn't recognize. The second page was definitely part of a schematic, but it seemed to describe a circular-shaped dome.

'Afraid not,' Kurt said. Despite his earlier guess, he couldn't imagine a single word unlocking the clutter he was looking at.

'What about the boat?' Bradshaw asked. 'Did you see anything in it before it burned? A backpack? A suitcase? A computer?'

'Is that what they were bringing you?'

'Just answer the question.'

'No,' Kurt said, 'I didn't see anything like that.'

'What about the driver?'

Kurt's mind drifted back to the scene on the promenade. 'He asked me to leave him and help this guy. He called him Panos.'

'That's it?'

'We didn't exactly have a long conversation.'

Hayley looked away sadly, and Bradshaw sighed with disappointment. 'Well, you've been a tremendous help,' he said sarcastically.

'He did save my life,' Hayley pointed out.

'That he did,' Bradshaw agreed, speaking with a note

of humility in his voice for the first time. He stepped toward the door. 'Sorry to be so nasty, Mr Austin, but it's been a damned awful day. Enjoy your vacation.'

'Hold on a second,' Kurt said.

His mind was drifting back to the incident. He couldn't recall any luggage in the boat or anything else out of the ordinary except that he remembered Panos wincing in pain when he was dragged from the boat. He recalled the odd way the man's fingers had curled up and how he struggled to walk. There was something strange about his hunched-over appearance as he lumbered away from the boat. Something familiar too. Kurt had seen that gait before.

'That guy was your informant?'

Hayley went to speak, and Bradshaw stopped her.

'Come on,' Kurt snapped, 'either you want my help or you don't.'

'The dead men were couriers,' Bradshaw said reluctantly. 'Bringing us something.'

'Do you know where they came from?'

Bradshaw shook his head. 'If we knew that, there would be no need for this lovely conversation.'

'I suggest you start looking underwater,' Kurt said, 'because that man was suffering from DCS.'

'DCS?'

'Decompression sickness,' Kurt said. 'Bubbles of nitrogen in the joints. It causes horrendous pain and a hunched-over appearance – if the patient can even walk, that is. You get it from deep, prolonged diving, then surfacing too quickly. Normal treatment is one hundred per cent oxygen and time in a hyperbaric chamber to force the gas back into suspension. But wherever this guy came from, I'm guessing he didn't have the time to go back down. Kind of hard to do when you're running for your life.'

Bradshaw all but snickered. 'He'd just been in a crash, playing stuntman without a seat belt or a helmet. More likely, he was injured in the wreck.'

'He wasn't limping,' Kurt noted, 'he wasn't favoring one side. He was bent over like the Hunchback of Notre-Dame and unable to straighten up. Those are the most typical effects of a disease commonly called the bends.'

Bradshaw seemed to be considering Kurt's guess. He sucked at his teeth and then shook his head. 'Not a bad thought,' he said, 'but here's why you're wrong.'

He pointed to a brownish red smear on the blood-stained papers. It was oddly iridescent under the light.

'He was covered in this,' Bradshaw said, 'every pore, every fiber of his clothes. So was the last courier we found dead.'

'What is it?'

'It's a type of soil, called a palaeosol,' Bradshaw explained. 'Common in the outback. Not found under-water. If it tracks with the other guy, it'll contain a mix of heavy metals and various toxins, including traces of man-ganese and arsenic. Which tells us these guys are operating in the desert somewhere. Not from a submarine.'

'He could have been in a lake and gotten dirty afterward,' Kurt pointed out.

'Have you ever been to the outback?' Bradshaw asked. 'The lakes out there are mostly transient. Even during the rainy season – which it is not right now, by the way – they're shallow and wide. Like your Great Salt Lake.'

Kurt was stumped. 'Don't know what to tell you,' he said, 'but I'd stake my reputation on it. That man came up from a depth where he was exposed to great pressure.'

'Thanks for your opinion,' Bradshaw replied. 'We'll be sure to check into it.'

He waved a hand toward the exit.

'So this is what it means to be shown the door,' Kurt said.

Hayley looked as if she'd have preferred to leave with him. Kurt felt differently about her now. A damsel in distress. He wondered once again what her deal with Bradshaw might be.

'Good-bye,' she whispered sadly. 'Thank you.'

Kurt hoped it wasn't quite final. He guessed that suggesting as much would annoy Bradshaw. *A win-win situation.*

'Until we meet again,' he said. And then he stepped out through the door and left her and Bradshaw behind.

5

Two hours after the incident, Kurt found himself back in his suite at the Intercontinental Hotel. He'd taken a shower, sent a long e-mail to NUMA headquarters, and finished a tumbler of Scotch before climbing into bed.

Forty minutes later, he was still wide awake, staring at the ceiling and listening to the hum of the air conditioner. The events played on an endless loop in his mind. As they did, the questions chased one another in circles.

What was the ASIO dealing with? Why would a man covered in desert dust also be suffering from decompression sickness? And what part was Hayley Anderson playing in all of it? She seemed to be there by her own choice, but she didn't seem happy about it.

Despite a little voice that told him to leave it alone, Kurt found he couldn't let it go.

He glanced over at the nightstand. He'd covered the bright face of the alarm clock with a towel to keep the light out of his eyes, but his Doxa watch was resting beside it. He scooped it up, checked the luminous hands, and realized it was almost two o'clock in the morning.

He threw the covers off, climbed out of bed, and walked over to the desk. If he couldn't find sleep, maybe he could find some answers.

He opened his laptop and took a drink of water while it booted up. A quick Internet search regarding the ASIO brought up numerous articles. He didn't expect to find a list of secret operations, but he thought there might be something indicating what they were dealing with. Maybe something obscure enough that he could put two and two together.

With no luck there, he thought about Hayley.

'Who are you, Ms Anderson?' he muttered. 'And what are you mixed up in?'

He ran a Google search on her, and a wealth of links appeared.

To Kurt's surprise, Hayley was a scholar: a theoretical physicist tenured at the University of Sydney. She'd authored a number of papers with incomprehensible titles. There was a more easily read article about her turning down an invite to Oxford. He found another where she was trying to explain something about gravity and why Einstein was wrong in his understanding of it.

Kurt poured himself a glass of Scotch. He found himself more baffled than before. *What on earth was a young woman who could prove Einstein wrong doing in the middle of a terrorist investigation?*

Finding no answer to that question, or any public link between her and the ASIO, he turned his attention to the dead informant.

Kurt was certain the man had been suffering from decompression sickness. The question was: how did he get it?

DCS had once been called caisson disease, because it was originally noticed in construction workers who were toiling away in the pressurized caissons used to build the foundations of great bridges. But it was most commonly seen in scuba divers.

The dead man Panos had arrived in a boat, racing across Sydney Harbour. That also suggested he might have been diving. But he wore grimy street clothes, not a wet suit, and he smelled like days of perspiration, not the fresh salt of the sea. That, along with the mining connection and the ASIO's belief that some terrorist group was operating in the outback, weighed against Kurt's theory.

He found a register of lakes in Australia and painstakingly scanned through them. Just as Bradshaw insisted, most of them appeared to be shallow or even transient, drying up completely in the summertime.

'Not the kind of places one gets the bends,' Kurt said.

He put the list down and began scanning a satellite image of Australia. Moving westward from Sydney and out over more arid territory, it was easy to see how quickly the terrain became barren. Occasionally, he came across a swath of green.

Much like the American Southwest and the Egyptian Nile, wherever a stream or river flowed, vegetation grew up around it. Even if it didn't flow year-round, there was often underground water to be had. But that water was locked away in permeable sands and aquifers, not hidden lakes that one could swim in. And even if he could find a lake, that didn't explain the toxins on the man's skin.

About ready to shut down, Kurt used the touch pad to scan a few more sections of the map. He stopped when a strangely colored spot caught his eye. He tapped the ZOOM IN command a couple of times and waited.

The map blurred and refocused, with the iridescent spot taking up a quarter of the screen.

He was staring at a lake. A lake of brilliant rainbow hues, brighter than anything in nature had a right to be.

Right away, Kurt knew what he was looking at. The pieces came together quickly after that. He knew why the lake was so outrageously colorful, and he also knew why the informant had both DCS and metal toxins all over his body.

It seemed he and Bradshaw were both correct.

He reached for the phone, dialed up a number from memory, and waited for an answer.

'Come on, Joe,' he whispered to himself.

A click on the line followed.

'Hello,' a sleepy American voice said.

Joe Zavala was Kurt's best friend, his most loyal and trusted ally. Others would use the term *partner in crime*.

'I hope the women of Cairns haven't worn you out,' Kurt said, 'because I need your help on something.'

A yawn came over the line. 'I have to ask: is it dangerous, illegal, or otherwise likely to result in serious bodily injury?'

'Would you believe me if I said no?'

'Probably not,' Joe said. 'Especially considering what you've been up to down there.'

'You heard?'

'HQ called and left a message. Aside from that, you're all over the news,' Joe explained. 'CNN is reporting that an "unnamed American" brought down the house in Sydney.'

'That's witty of them,' Kurt said. 'Too bad they weren't performing the 1812 Overture; it would have been a showstopper of an ending.'

'And you said the conference was boring.'

'Seems I was wrong,' Kurt said. 'So do you want to join in the fun or not?'

'Well,' Joe said, 'I'm supposed to show off our new diving speeders to a group of reporters and a fifth-grade honors class from Cairns tomorrow as part of the Great Barrier Reef Project, but considering how repetitive their questions are, I think I'd rather throw my lot in with you. What do you need me to do?'

'Have the speeders been tested?'

'We checked them out today.'

'Perfect,' Kurt said. 'Pack them up and bring them to the airport. I'll have a plane chartered for you.'

'You got it. So what are we doing with them?'

'Just following up on a hunch,' Kurt said.

'You know you could phone it in,' Joe suggested. 'Let the Aussies handle it.'

'If I had any brains, I would,' Kurt replied, 'but my last conversation with them didn't go so well. I figure I'll have to show them instead of telling.'

'Sounds about par for the course,' Joe said. 'So where are we going anyway?'

'Not entirely sure yet,' Kurt said. 'But you'll find out when you get to the airport. I'll meet you at our destination.'

'You know you can count on me,' Joe said. *'Hasta mañana, amigo.'*

Before Joe could hang up, Kurt spoke again. 'One more thing,' he said. 'Keep this under your sombrero. It's not exactly an approved NUMA operation.'

6

Janko Minkosovic stood in the center of the octagonal room. The lighting was dim and subdued, the air around him chilled below fifty degrees. Despite that, Janko was sweating. That the room was kept near one hundred per cent humidity didn't help, but fear and anxiety were the real causes.

He tried to control it, but the longer he stood in silence, the more his mind wandered.

All those who'd been called to this room felt great trepidation. Their master resided here. He ruled from here like a dictator, gave pronouncements from here like a judge.

No one knew that better than Janko. He'd brought many here against their will and dragged them out of the room afterward, either sentenced to some awful punishment, or dead.

Two members of the guard stood behind him. Short-barreled versions of the American M16 rifle were clutched in their hands.

In a way, they were Janko's men. After all, he was Captain of the Guard. He chose not to look at them. They were not here to support him; they'd received an order to bring him in.

Across from the group, staring out of a window into utter darkness, their master waited. 'What's your main function, Janko?'

The imposing figure spoke without turning. There was a strange hushed quality to the voice. It came from scorched and damaged vocal cords.

'I am chief of security, as you well know,' Janko replied.

'And how do you judge your performance in light of recent events?'

Maxmillian Thero turned around. Janko saw familiar burn scars that ran up the man's neck and on to his face. Only Thero's mouth was visible, twisted into a scarred cut by what must have been a horrible fire. The nose, eyes, the right ear, and the rest of the face lay beneath a black latex mask. The mask hid features too hideous to show, but it also put a sense of fear into those who looked upon it. It separated him from them. It made him seem less, or perhaps more, than human.

Janko had the impression he was looking upon a demigod of some type, a being that should have been dead several times over – from fire, from gunshots, from radiation – and yet he still lived. Janko did not want to disappoint this demigod, but he could not bring himself to lie. He summoned all his courage.

'We have been endangered,' Janko admitted. 'Our purpose may have been compromised. Despite great effort, I've failed to find the one who puts our goals at risk. The failure is mine. And mine alone.'

'You speak the truth,' Thero said. 'How did it occur?'

'The dive master is in possession of all keys. He cannot explain how Panos was able to gain access to the airlock. Either the dive master is lying or there is a conspiracy. One that goes beyond Panos and the other traitors. But there is no way to account for all the strange things that have occurred. No one single person has access to all areas that have been breached. You know how tightly things are watched.'

Thero nodded, the soft latex of the mask catching the small amount of light that was present. The reflections danced up and down the mask, as if it was sending and receiving signals.

'Panos was driven from here,' Thero said. 'That can mean only one thing: the help comes from the outside. From one of those we have trusted to do our business in the secular world.'

Janko did not agree, but he kept that to himself.

Thero shifted his weight. 'You see the difficulty of my position, don't you, Janko? I no longer know who to trust. Either here or on the island. Particularly because the next diamond shipment is ready to be sent. This one is the largest yet. But I can't count on the other men to carry out the transactions.'

'Postpone it,' Janko suggested.

'The longer those diamonds sit, the bigger men's eyes get,' Thero said. 'I won't delay the cargo any further. You will return to the island and take it personally.'

Janko's eyes lit up. 'Me?'

'First, you will kill the others, all those who have done our business before,' Thero explained. 'Then you will take possession of the shipment and travel to Jakarta, where a buyer awaits us.'

Janko could hardly believe what he was hearing. He'd come to Thero's chambers expecting to be tortured or even killed. Instead, he was being offered a great honor.

He knew to grasp it immediately. Thero's mercurial personality ran hot and cold, munificent at one moment, cruel and murderous the next. All those around him had learned to fear the strange pauses he was prone to, the odd looks he gave, as if searching the mist for something only he could see. Paranoia and power were a dangerous combination.

'I will do as you require,' Janko said firmly.

'Take these guards and go to your task. I will meet you on the island. I expect to see the bodies of the traitors when I get there.'

Janko stood taller and glanced at the men behind him. They snapped to attention. 'The traitors will talk and then die,' he said, doubting the other men were traitors at all but far happier to put them to death than to die himself.

Janko turned and strode out the door with the two guards following close behind.

Thero remained where he was, watching as the rusted steel door slammed shut behind them. In the muted silence, he considered the situation. Janko could be trusted, he thought. He'd been with them for so long.

The sound of footsteps emerged from the darkened room behind him. Thero turned in time to see a young man coming forth from the shadows. He had cropped blond hair, a slight build, and a sad and weary look about his eyes. He wore a lab coat.

'It won't take long for the Australians to find us here,' the young man said. 'Not now. Not after this.'

'True,' Thero said.

The young man was Thero's son, George. He was also the chief designer of the latest version of Thero's system, a weapon that would literally shake the Earth to its core.

'You're quite right, my son,' Thero said. 'What would you have me do?'

'There's no reason to keep this station around,' George said. 'We should leave. Have Janko stay behind and scuttle the station. Then he can join us and complete his other task.'

'But this station will help us inflict the pain we seek,' Thero countered.

'The main system on the island will soon be operational,' George said. 'Once it is, we will be invulnerable. We should move everything of value there.'

'When will it be up and running?'

'Within days.'

'Excellent,' Thero said, beaming with pride. 'You've succeeded where so many others have failed. Soon, we'll show the world how they've lived in ignorance. We'll make the nations that shunned us pay.'

The young man looked downcast.

'You disagree?'

'Proving the system works, proving that we can draw unlimited energy from the void around us, surely that's vindication enough? That and the wealth that will follow.'

'No,' Thero said sharply. 'It's not even close. Look what they've done to us. To me. To you. They've stolen everything. Mocked us and murdered your sister. They sent us away like we carried the plague, abandoned us to certain death. All the nations of the world are complicit in this. All the nations we could have helped.'

Thero's tone softened. George had always been the merciful one. George's sister had been more like her father. 'You're too forgiving,' Thero said. 'I can't afford to be that way. I won't hand them the gift we've created. Not without extracting my pound of flesh first.'

Thero's son looked up at him. He nodded grudgingly.

'The system must be tested,' he reminded his father. 'If we can't fine-tune it, then neither dream will come to fruition.'

'Only the most minor tests,' Thero said. 'The world must remain in the dark until the zero hour arrives.'

7

Joe Zavala stood on the ramp at Cairns airport as the speeders he'd brought with him were secured on a pallet and towed toward a waiting aircraft.

Five foot ten, with the dark smoldering eyes of his mother and the solid build of a middleweight boxer like his father, Joe was an engineer and a connoisseur of living to the fullest.

Life was good, Joe felt, especially his. He traveled the world having adventures, met interesting people, and worked on the most fantastic machines imaginable: high-speed boats, experimental submarines, and the occasional aircraft or car. It was like getting paid to play with one's favorite toys in fantastic, exotic locations.

Unlike most who had their dream jobs, Joe knew it. It kept a smile on his face and a spring in his step that usually rubbed off on those around him. So far, it was doing nothing for the burly loadmaster of the small aircraft Kurt had chartered.

'This just can't be correct,' the man said, repeating himself for the third time and flipping through a detailed bill of lading.

Joe was wearing a dark suit with a white shirt and a pink tie, a disguise of sorts he'd decided to don after

Kurt told him this mission was not to have any official NUMA involvement.

'What can I tell you?' Joe said, taking on the air of a harried middle manager. 'It's got to go on board. Those are my instructions. *Accompany the item to the delivery point.*'

The loadmaster's face scrunched up, and he squinted in the sunlight. 'But you're shipping diving gear and a pair of one-man submarines?'

'Apparently.'

'To the middle of the desert?'

'Really?' Joe said, feigning ignorance.

The big Aussie nodded. 'Alice Springs is out in the red center, mate. You might as well fly these things to the Sahara.'

Joe hemmed and hawed. 'Well, I wouldn't be surprised if we did that next. This company of mine. We get a little crazy.'

The guy sighed and handed the paperwork back to Joe. 'Well, they're too heavy with the rest of the cargo anyway,' he said. 'And I'm not off-loading half my shipment to put a mistake on board.'

He turned away to halt the offending pallet's approach, but before he could say a word Joe put his arm around the big man's shoulders, leaning in close, all friendly-like.

'Now, listen,' Joe said. 'I know this is a mistake. And *you* know it's a mistake. But if I don't take these tubs out there in person, there's going to be hell to pay.'

Joe stuffed a wad of Australian cash into the man's hand, five hundred dollars in total. 'For the inconvenience,' he said, patting his newfound friend on the shoulder.

The loadmaster thumbed through the money, keeping it low and out of sight like a man hiding his cards at the poker table. A smile crept over his face. It was a big payday.

'This is really a waste of time,' he muttered, far more subdued than he'd been before. 'But, then again, who are we to question why?'

'My thoughts exactly,' Joe said.

The loadmaster turned and whistled to his crew. 'Pull the other pallets off and load her up with this one. And make it quick,' he grumbled. 'We're not getting paid by the hour.'

As the ground crew went to work, a young woman from inside the charter company's office brought Joe an ice-cold bottle of water. She smiled at him, all dimples and sparkling eyes.

'Thank you,' he said.

'My pleasure, sir.'

She winked and turned with a swish, and Joe had to fight hard to keep himself from following.

He stood and considered the situation. He was accustomed to being covered in grease and neck-deep in the hands-on work. He'd certainly never considered himself the supervisor type. But as he sipped the cool drink and watched from the shade while the heavy cargo pallets were pulled off and rearranged in the strong morning sun, he began to consider it an option.

He straightened his tie and glanced once more at the smiling customer service rep.

'A guy could get used to this.'

A few hours later and a thousand miles away, Kurt Austin waited in the cab of a boxy-looking flatbed. He watched as the CASA-212 landed on the centerline of the tiny Alice Springs Regional Airport and taxied toward him.

As the aircraft eased to a stop, Kurt put the truck in gear and drove up. While the ground crew went to work on the plane, Kurt climbed out of the cab and on to the flatbed. He activated the truck's hydraulics and tilted the flatbed down until its far edge touched the ground like a ramp. By the time he locked it in place, the ground crew had begun wheeling the pallet with the speeders on it toward him.

Kurt attached a cable to the front of the pallet and used the flatbed's winch to haul it up on board. After locking it in place, he leveled the flatbed once again and jumped down.

Joe Zavala sauntered out of the aircraft cabin a moment later, wearing a tailored suit and sunglasses.

'Looking sharper than I remember,' Kurt said.

'I'm in management now,' Joe said. 'We have to dress for success.'

Kurt chuckled. He and Joe had been friends for

years. They'd met at NUMA, finding themselves to be kindred spirits who'd rather be doing *anything* than sitting around bored. They'd been called troublemakers, undesirables, and been thrown out of at least twenty bars in their lifetimes, though none in the past year or so. But in the often tense and dangerous world that NUMA worked in, there were none better at keeping their cool and getting the job done.

'By the way,' Joe said, 'you owe me five hundred dollars.'

Kurt paused at the door. 'For what?'

'I had to grease the skids to get these things here.'

Kurt pulled the door open and climbed in. 'You're in management now. Put it on your expense account.'

Joe got in on the other side. 'You are my expense account,' he said. 'Now, how about telling me what we're doing out here in the driest of the dry with a truckload of diving equipment.'

'I'll explain on the road,' Kurt said, starting the engine. 'We're burning daylight.'

They drove off the airport grounds and were soon rumbling west, out of Alice Springs and into the desert.

As they drove, Joe changed his clothes, and Kurt explained the situation, starting with the events in Sydney and his odd meeting with Hayley Anderson and Cecil Bradshaw of the ASIO.

'The courier had red dust on him. It was packed into the mesh of his clothing. Bradshaw called it a palaeosol. It's very old and infertile and commonly found here in the outback. Half the reason this place is so barren. The dead guy also had a mix of toxic metals on his skin. The kind usually found in mining operations.'

'Again pointing in this direction,' Joe said.

'Exactly,' Kurt said. 'The problem was the decompression sickness. I'm certain the guy had the bends, but most of the lakes out here are transient. Even the year-round ones are shallow.'

He motioned to the surroundings. There was nothing but desert and dust in every direction, right out to the horizon.

'And yet, you've found a place out here where the water is both deep and poisonous.'

Kurt nodded. 'Ever hear of the Berkeley Pit?'

Joe shook his head.

'It's an open-pit copper mine in Montana. It flooded when the miners went too deep and water began seeping in from aquifers in the surrounding rock. Took years to fill up, but at last check the water was nine hundred feet deep and rising. The minerals give the water an odd color, reddish orange. It's so toxic that a flock of geese landed there a few years ago and never took off again, promptly dying from exposure to the poisons.'

'Interesting,' Joe said. 'But we're not in Montana anymore, Toto.'

'No, we're not, Dorothy. But as it turns out, here in Oz the Aussies have a few open-pit mines of their own. The outback is full of them. And some of them appear to be filled with water.'

Joe nodded, he seemed impressed. 'I'll buy that,' he said. 'Are they deep enough to cause the bends?'

'Some are deeper than the Berkeley Pit.'

'Maybe you're on to something,' Joe said. 'But even if you are, why on earth would someone be diving in a poisoned lake?'

'Not sure,' Kurt said. 'But Bradshaw told me these guys were a threat to Australian national security. And a flooded, toxic mine like this has two attributes that might make it interesting to such conspirators.'

'And those are?'

'For one thing,' Kurt said, 'people stay away from toxic lakes that may or may not leak poisonous gas. And for another, they're hard to see through.'

'You think they're hiding something in the lake,' Joe said.

'Hiding it very effectively from a world filled with satellites.'

Joe nodded. 'Technically, it's a world surrounded by satellites. But I get your drift.'

Kurt almost laughed. 'Thanks for that dose of editorial genius. I'm sure it'll come in handy when the bullets start flying.'

After two hours on an empty highway, they were a hundred miles from Alice Springs and cruising a secondary dirt road. They hadn't seen another soul for the last ninety minutes.

Kurt glanced in the mirror. A thick cloud of dust trailed out behind them, enough that they might have been followed from space. But if someone was tailing them, their engine would have choked out long ago.

He slowed the truck. They'd come to a gap in the barbed wire fence that ran along the side of the road. An even more primitive trail led through it and off toward a low rise.

'This should be it.'

Turning the wheel to its stops, Kurt maneuvered the big truck through the opening.

'Just so I'm clear,' Joe said, 'we have no idea what's going on. No idea what we're getting ourselves into. But we're doing all this because some snotty bureaucrat didn't like your theory.'

Kurt nodded. 'Yep.'

'You have issues, amigo. Starting with a pathological need to prove yourself right.'

'The least of my flaws,' Kurt insisted as they neared the top of the ridge, 'but it's not that they didn't believe me. They didn't even take me seriously.'

The big flatbed crested the ridgeline. Ahead of them was a massive depression filled with crimson water. It had once been known as the Tasman Mine, but a thousand feet down the miners had cracked into a pressurized section of the water table. Just like the Berkeley Pit in Montana, the Tasman Mine had slowly filled with poisoned water. By now, it had risen to within a hundred feet of the rim.

Kurt eased the truck on to a sloping ramp that snaked its way around the walls of the pit and down toward the water's edge. To his surprise, a group of vehicles were already parked there. Four dust-covered SUVs and a pair of Jeep Wranglers. They appeared to be new builds. The tinted windows and the matching colors just screamed government motor pool.

'Looks like they took you more seriously than you thought,' Joe said.

Kurt put his foot on the brake, slowing the truck until it lurched to a stop. There was something odd about the scene. It took a moment to notice.

'Where are they?' Kurt asked.

Joe shook his head.

There were six vehicles parked at strange angles, two of them with open doors, a third had its tailgate up. There were piles of equipment strewn about on the poisoned beach as if some type of activity were in the works. But there was not a single human being anywhere in sight.

8

Kurt scanned the perimeter of the lake and studied the water. He saw no one.

'Maybe they were abducted by aliens,' Joe said, glancing up at the sky.

Kurt cut his eyes at Joe.

'I'm not kidding,' Joe said. 'I've been reading up on UFOs. Australia is a hotbed of sightings. And this is *exactly* the kind of place they love to frequent.'

'And me without my tinfoil hat,' Kurt said.

He glanced down at the arrangement of parked cars, thinking about the dead geese found near the Berkeley Pit. He wondered if some kind of poison gas had overcome the occupants.

He opened a cargo bin that sat between the two seats. A pair of compact oxygen tanks, each the size of a large thermos, sat upright in it. Two masks and an air sampler, designed to check for toxic levels of one hundred and seventy different airborne poisons, sat beside them.

'The Australian EPA lists this place as a danger,' Kurt said, 'but only to the water table. The air is supposed to be clean. I figured we'd err on the side of caution.'

Kurt pulled out the sampler and switched it on as Joe checked the tanks for pressure.

Kurt cracked the window just enough to poke the nozzle through. After thirty seconds a green light flashed. 'Air quality is okay. Better than Los Angeles in the summertime.'

'It wouldn't hurt to keep checking,' Joe suggested.

Kurt nodded and took his foot off the brake.

The big truck began to coast down the long ramp, rolling slowly. When it reached the flat section by the parked cars, Kurt pulled in beside them and stopped.

A second green report from the air sampler gave Kurt some confidence.

He opened the door. It was deathly silent. There was no wind. No birds. No insects. Not a blade of grass or even a sprout of the hardiest weed grew on the poisoned shore.

'Desolate,' Joe whispered.

'I feel like we're on the moon,' Kurt said, clipping the air sensor to his belt and grabbing one of the small oxygen tanks before stepping out of the truck.

As Joe climbed out the passenger door, Kurt eased over to the closest SUV. The tailgate was up. Several carbines stood untouched in a rifle rack while a pile of windbreakers that read ASIO in big block letters lay folded neatly in a box.

'Looks like they were planning a raid,' he whispered.

'A batch of test tubes over here,' Joe said, calling from beside one of the Jeeps. 'Some of them are full of water. I'd say they were taking samples. The rest of this is sonar equipment. Maybe they went into the lake?'

Kurt looked forward. The poisoned lake sat undisturbed, reflecting the sky like a pane of dark glass. Kurt wondered if the bodies of the ASIO team were in there somewhere.

'They wouldn't all go in,' he said. 'Not by choice anyway.'

A fly buzzed past Kurt's ear. The first sign of life he'd encountered since entering the pit. It zipped by him in one direction and then flew off into the distance again. A trickle of sweat ran down Kurt's temple.

He glanced up toward the rim. Nothing there, nothing moving, no sign of struggle in front of them. Something was very wrong.

He pulled a rifle from the rack and slid a clip into place, racking the slide as quietly as he could.

Joe arrived beside Kurt. 'You think someone bounced them?'

'If they did, it was the neatest ambush of all time,' Kurt said. 'You see any bullet holes? Any blood?'

'Nope,' Joe said.

'Maybe you're on to something with this UFO business. Grab a rifle just in case.'

As Joe pulled a weapon from the rack, the sound of rocks sliding turned Kurt. He spun just in time to see a trickle of pebbles coming down the side of a dune made of red Australian soil. He crouched and drew a bead with the rifle, but no one came at them.

Joe crouched beside him. 'What do you think?'

Kurt's eyes were on the dune. 'Cover me.'

Joe nodded, and Kurt eased to a new spot and then dashed toward the small dune. He scrambled up the side and popped up over the top, ready to blaze away at whatever might be there.

The tension in his body vanished. Replaced by remorse.

Down below lay a pile of bodies. Men and women thrown in a heap. They were dressed ruggedly, but they were clean-cut. Their gear and clothing looked almost identical.

Kurt slid down toward them, tracking a series of marks in the sand made by someone who'd tried, and failed, to climb out. He arrived beside a burly man with a buzz cut who looked all too familiar.

'Bradshaw,' Kurt shouted, crouching beside him and rolling him faceup.

As Kurt checked for a pulse, a slight groan of pain escaped Bradshaw's lips.

'Joe, get over here!'

Joe came over the top of the dune.

'Check the others.'

As Joe slid down, Kurt ripped a piece of fabric from Bradshaw's shirt and tied a tourniquet around his leg where the worst wound seemed to be. He spotted two other wounds, but they looked superficial.

With the tourniquet cinched up, Kurt pulled out his canteen and splashed some water on the ASIO chief's face.

'Bradshaw, can you hear me? What happened?'

Bradshaw moved his lips, mumbling something incoherently.

Kurt took his small oxygen bottle and placed the mask over Bradshaw's face. As the O_2 began to flow, Bradshaw became more animated. He pawed at the mask. Kurt held it in place until Bradshaw's eyes began to focus.

'What happened?' Kurt asked, pulling the mask away.

'They went down,' Bradshaw replied.

'Who went down?' Kurt asked.

No response.

'Bradshaw, can you hear me?'

Joe returned. 'The rest of them are dead. Gunshots. Close range. I'd say they were thrown on the ground and machine-gunned.'

'Damn,' Kurt said.

Joe's eyes were searching the sloping walls that rose up like cliffs around them. 'I don't like this, amigo. We're sitting ducks in a shooting gallery.'

'We'd be long dead if someone was watching,' Kurt replied. He kept the oxygen mask on Bradshaw's face and turned the valve to full. Bradshaw's eyes opened a fraction more. Finally, he seemed to become more coherent.

Kurt pulled the mask away once more.

'Austin?' Bradshaw muttered in disbelief. 'What are you . . . What are you doing here?'

'Playing a hunch,' Kurt said. 'What happened?'

'I . . . don't . . . know,' Bradshaw said. 'Somebody

waylaid us. Next thing I knew, I was on the ground, listening to gunfire.'

Bradshaw coughed like a man choking on dust, and Kurt put the mask back against his face. Bradshaw pushed it away. 'Must have been a setup,' he said. 'You were right. There has to be a leak.'

'Did you see who it was?' Kurt asked. 'Where they came from?'

'No,' Bradshaw managed. He seemed about to fade out.

'We have to get you out of here,' Kurt said, trying to lift the big man. 'Joe, help me.'

Joe ducked under one of Bradshaw's arms while Kurt ducked under the other.

'Hayley . . .' Bradshaw mumbled.

Kurt looked around. He didn't see her among the dead. 'Was she with you?'

Bradshaw nodded. 'She went down.' He pointed toward the lake. 'She went down with the other diver.'

'What's down there?'

'A structure of some kind. We thought it might be the device. But it's huge. More like . . . some kind of lab. She went down to look because only she would know. But they hit us, and then . . .'

'And then what?'

The chief wavered but recovered, his face displaying great pain.

'And then they went down after her,' he said. 'They're down there now. All of them.'

9

Kurt and Joe dragged Bradshaw to a spot by one of the SUVs. He had three bullet wounds. He'd lost a lot of blood. Kurt doubted he would survive for long.

He grabbed a first-aid kit and tossed it to Joe.

'Do what you can for him,' he said. 'And find a way to call for help. If you can't reach anyone, get him out of here.'

'What are you going to do?'

Kurt was climbing on to the back of the flatbed, yanking the tarp off the one-man submersibles. 'I'm going in.'

'But you don't know what's down there.'

'A laboratory and a device,' Kurt said, repeating Bradshaw's cryptic explanation as he dropped from the side of the flatbed and landed back down on the beach. 'And a young woman who's in way over her head.'

'So what are you going to do?' Joe asked. 'Just swim around looking for this device?'

Kurt jumped back into the cab of the boxy truck and turned the key. 'No,' he said. 'I'm going to drive.'

The big diesel rumbled to life. Kurt jammed the truck into gear and began to roll forward. He turned slightly to the left, toward the deadly lake, and pressed down harder on the throttle.

Had anyone but Joe Zavala been watching him, Kurt might have explained in greater detail what was about to happen, but Joe knew vehicles like no one else. He'd eyed the truck strangely at the airport and most likely put two and two together shortly thereafter. If he hadn't figured it out already, he'd understand any moment now.

The rig accelerated across the slope, its heavy tires carving deep tracks in the soft red sand as Kurt drove it straight into the water. It quickly came up off the wheels and began coasting forward.

As soon as he was afloat, Kurt grabbed a stainless steel lever on the dashboard and forced it upward and over into a notch, where it locked. The truck's big wheels rose up, pulling free of the water, while a propeller attached to the drive shaft extended from the rear.

Kurt glanced at a monitoring board. All the lights were green. That was good news. It meant the prop was connected to the power train and there were no detectable leaks.

Kurt stepped on the gas. The prop churned the red water behind him, and the amphibious craft began to plow forward, completing its conversion from slow-moving truck to an even slower-moving boat. It drove like a nose-heavy barge, but fortunately Kurt didn't have far to go.

Flipping another set of switches, Kurt activated a sonar system he'd brought along. A weighted spring kicked the small towed array off the back of the truck. It began to sink, spooling out a cable behind it and bouncing mid-frequency sound waves off the bottom of the lake. A pattern soon appeared on the display screen.

As Kurt moved away from the sloping edge of the pit, the bottom dropped away sharply. The pit was a mile across at the very top but shaped like a giant elongated V, with a wide, flat bottom.

'Six-forty and dropping,' he said to himself as the numbers continued to change. 'Let's see how deep you are.'

The top of the rim was over a thousand feet from the original bottom, but the water level was at least a hundred feet below the rim, and most likely years of erosion had begun to fill in the pit. He noticed a leveling at eight hundred and fifty. It was hard to fathom being in the middle of the desert and floating on a lake so deep that a World War Two submarine would be crushed if it went more than halfway down, but there he was.

At roughly the center of the lake, the sonar picked up a dome-shaped object. It appeared something like a sleek water tower, rising above the cornfields of the Midwest, bulbous at the top, with a group of pipes descending from the bottom in a tight bunch. As far as Kurt could tell, they went right down into the center of the lake bed.

He wondered what he was looking at. What was its purpose?

Bradshaw had used the term *device*, which conjured up images of a nuclear warhead of some kind. Unfortunately, in today's day and age, one didn't need to build a giant tower with a sixty-foot dome on top to unleash atomic fury.

The dome passed out of sight and a new target came into view. This one didn't have the curving, artistic lines of the dome. It looked more like a pile of cylindrical pods and shipping containers stacked on top of one another. From top to bottom, it was the height of a seven-story building. It appeared to be anchored to the steeper wall of the lake and connected to the dome by gantries and thick cables. An intermittent response on the sonar suggested guide wires anchoring it to the wall.

The roof of this structure sat near a depth of two hundred and fifty feet, the bottom checked in below three hundred and twenty. The dome loomed above it and off to one side.

Kurt was grudgingly impressed. Building a structure like this at a depth of three hundred feet was quite a task to begin with. To do it in a toxic lake, in secret . . . He was more than grudgingly impressed.

He took his hand off the throttle, and the amphibious rig coasted to a halt near the center of the lake. Kurt got out of his seat and climbed on to the flatbed behind him.

He was directly over the main structure. Now all he had to do was get down there.

Joe spent a few minutes tending to Bradshaw and trying to patch him up with the meager offerings of the first-aid kit. Despite the effort, Bradshaw looked bad, ghostly pale, with skin that was cool to the touch. He needed *real* attention and he needed it soon.

Joe left Bradshaw and began to rummage around in the SUV beside them. He grabbed a handheld radio and turned it on. The LED, which should have lit up nice and green, remained dark. Joe fiddled with the power switch a few times and then keyed the mike. He got nothing: no squelch, no static. The battery was dead.

Looking for a charger, Joe noticed that the keys were still in the SUV's ignition. He also noticed that both doors were open and yet the dome lights were dark, and the dash wasn't emitting any kind of annoying ping.

He reached over and turned the key. He twisted it to OFF and then back to the ACC position. Nothing changed. No warning lights, no voice telling him the door was ajar, nothing.

'That's odd.'

He climbed out of the SUV and grabbed his rifle. Moving quickly from one vehicle to the next, he checked them all. Each one of them was as dead as the last.

Six new vehicles. Not one with an ounce of juice. A

rack of radios and two cell phones in the same condition. A flashlight in the glove box of the last vehicle had just enough power to make the old-style filament glow for a second or two, but then it too went dark.

Joe felt the hair on the back of his neck stand up. He glanced at the sky. This was exactly the kind of thing that happened right before the mother ship arrived.

He moved back to Bradshaw. 'Why are all the batteries dead?'

'Dead?'

'The cars, the radios, they're all dead,' Joe explained. 'You need to be medevacked, but I can't find a way to call for help.'

Bradshaw's eyes went glassy. He had no answers. Joe wasn't even sure he was hearing the questions anymore.

Joe stood up and glanced out over the water. Bradshaw needed to be moved ASAP, but the only vehicle with any power was the amphibious rig now sitting a half mile from him in the center of the poisoned lake.

10

Kurt donned a wetsuit and approached the small one-man submarines that rested near the back end of the flatbed. The bright yellow machines were affectionately called speeders. They resembled Jet Skis, with a set of small dive planes forward and a clear canopy that the driver pulled down and locked into place once he or she was seated on the vehicle.

The machines were rated to five hundred feet, powered by a lithium-ion battery pack similar to those in modern electric cars and equipped with a pair of grappling claws, headlights and an internal air/water bladder.

The canopy and much of the body were made from hyperstrong polymers designed to resist the pressure at great depths. Though they'd yet to be tested on a deep dive, Kurt had great faith in them. Joe was the main designer, and Kurt had found all of Joe's designs to be even stronger than the specs indicated.

After a quick series of checks, he was ready to go. He released the strap holding the speeder in place and then set the flatbed gradient lever at thirty degrees. The hydraulics kicked into gear, and the flatbed began to tilt like the back of a dump truck.

Kurt climbed on to one of the speeders and pressed

the switch that closed the hatch. The canopy quickly locked into place, covering Kurt snugly. Straddling the seat with his arms stretched forward and his legs out behind him, Kurt felt like he was on a nautical motorcycle.

The tail end of the flatbed reached the lake, and water came up around the sides of the speeder. Through the canopy Kurt noticed the hue of the water. Pink at the very top but darker red as the light was absorbed.

He wondered for a second just how toxic the mess was. Then he twisted the throttle and drove off the ramp, wondering about the sanity of anyone who would dive into a soup like this.

At first, the speeder cruised a few feet beneath the surface. Then Kurt adjusted the dive lever, and the ballast tank filled with water. Pushing the handlebars forward caused the dive planes to tilt downward, and the speeder began to descend.

Kurt continued forward for twenty seconds or so and then leaned to the left, bringing the unit around in a wide turn. By the time he was eighty feet deep, the water around him looked like red wine. Fifty feet deeper, it was the color of dried blood. Whatever compounds were suspended in it, they filtered out the light very efficiently. But as he dropped lower, Kurt was able to make out the top of the dome.

It was smooth but mottled in appearance, as if some kind of mineral had precipitated out on the curved surface. Perhaps it was calcium or copper or manganese, but, whatever it was, it reflected more light than the surrounding water.

As he finished his pass across the dome, Kurt feathered the throttle and ejected the last of the ballast air. The speeder began to sink again.

Kurt stared into the blackness. The roof of the laboratory structure rested about seventy-five feet below the top of the dome. He hoped its surface would be covered with the same minerals and that he'd spot the roof before he banged into it and let everyone inside know he was there.

'Two hundred and ten,' he said, reading the depth gauge out loud. 'Two hundred and twenty.'

He scanned the void around him. Nothing but darkness. It was like he was sinking into a black hole.

'Two hundred and thirty,' he said quietly.

If the gauge was reading correctly, he would hit the lab's roof in twenty feet or so. Still, he saw nothing.

He pumped a smidgen of air into the bladder like a motorist trying to top off his tyres to the perfect pressure. One quick hiss, then another one. The descent slowed.

The depth gauge soon read two hundred and forty feet, and Kurt still saw nothing outside. At two hundred and forty-five, he put a slight bit of pressure on the air switch again. And by two hundred and forty-seven, his nerves gave out.

He jabbed the switch until the speeder reached

neutral buoyancy. The descent stopped, and the speeder hung motionless in the dark.

Kurt slid his thumb upward and tapped the light switch. He hit it just hard enough to send some juice through the circuit, but not enough to fully switch it on. The lights flashed dimly and went dark again. In a brief flash, they revealed a world of neon red and the corroded top of the laboratory a mere three feet below him.

'At least I'm in the right place,' he muttered.

If this ungainly construction was indeed a laboratory, there had to be a way in. Toxic water or regular, the safest, most efficient way to build an airlock in a marine environment was to put it underneath the structure.

Kurt risked another flash, got a bearing on the edge of the structure, and went over the side. Dropping downward once again, he began to make out a soft glow around the bottom of the lab: illumination spilling from the airlock.

'Nice of someone to leave a light on for me,' Kurt muttered.

At just that moment, the speeder tilted violently to the right, and a strange metallic twang reverberated through the water.

Kurt knew instantly what had happened. Drifting down, he'd hit one of the guide wires that held the dome and its shaft of pipes in place. The impact had wrenched him to the side and spun him around. Far worse, it sent a vibration through the water like the striking of a gigantic guitar string. The noise reverberated off the walls of the pit and came back at him in a shadowy echo.

Kurt righted the ship and looked around for leaks. The cockpit appeared to be secure. He breathed a sigh of relief and continued on downward, hoping to avoid any more trouble.

'What was that noise?'

The question was posed to Janko by one of his men, who was nervously placing a block of plastic explosives beneath a set of computer servers.

'I'm not sure,' Janko admitted. He'd listened to all kinds of creaks and groans during his time on the station, especially when the techs were testing the dome or drawing power from it, but nothing like the strange reverberation they'd just heard.

'Water has a way of distorting sound,' one of the techs mentioned.

That was true, but Janko was not alone in wondering if the structure was safe. One didn't need to be a scientist to imagine acids slowly etching their way through the metal walls.

'Who knows what the chemicals in this lake have been doing to our hull all these years,' he said. 'Finish setting the explosives. I want to get out of here and blow this thing before it dissolves around us.'

The men seemed to agree. They doubled their labors, and moments later the demolitions expert slid out from under the computer bank. 'All set.'

'Good,' Janko said. The explosives would tear apart the circuit boards and memory banks. The fire that followed would melt the remnants to sludge before the water poured in. Even assuming they had the ability and fortitude to recover the remnants from beneath nearly a thousand feet of poisoned water, the high-tech labs of the world's intelligence agencies would get nothing from what they found.

That meant only one job remained.

He turned around and pointed his rifle at a pair of gagged figures sitting on the floor. One man, one woman. Both with their hands tied behind their backs.

The man was either law enforcement or military. Strong willed, he stared at Janko, almost daring him to shoot them. The woman was softer, pretty, with strawberry blond hair, and fear in her eyes. Janko figured he would shoot her first. Put her out of her misery. He raised the weapon.

'Are you insane?!' the tech shouted.

Janko glared at him.

'We've turned the oxygen to full,' the tech explained. 'We also opened the acetylene tanks. This whole station is filling with flammable gas. If you pull that trigger, the whole place might go up in flames. You want to kill them, use a knife.'

Janko lowered the rifle and looked back at the

captives. Had they realized this? Had they been goading him into destroying himself? It didn't matter. They would face the painful fate of an explosion and fire on their own in a few minutes.

'Set the timer,' he said. 'We're getting out of here.'

Janko watched as the demolitions man set the timer to 10:00 and pressed INITIATE. The clock ticked over to 09:59 and began winding down. Without glancing back, Janko turned and made his way toward the main ladder. Their submarine awaited.

Joe stood on the beach, considering his options. As much as he believed Kurt would make it back one way or another, waiting around for him to return wasn't going to work for Bradshaw. Nor was Joe interested in a half-mile swim through a toxic lake to retrieve the amphibious truck.

His mind turned to the dead vehicles. They had chargers in them. Assuming he could get one of them started, he could power up the radios and call for help. It would come in the form of a helicopter or three – one to whisk the gravely injured chief of the ASIO to a hospital and two or three more filled with military commandos or SWAT teams to surround and secure the lake.

It was a two-hour drive to Alice Springs but only thirty minutes by air. For Bradshaw, that might be the difference between life and death.

'If only these things came with hand cranks,' Joe muttered, thinking of vintage cars.

He considered push-starting one of them. The two Jeeps had manual transmissions, and the beach sloped down to the water. That would help, but he wasn't sure he could get up enough speed.

He reached into one of the Jeeps, put the transmission in neutral, and put his shoulder into the doorframe. Pushing with all his might, Joe got the rig moving. But the sand was soft, and he couldn't get the speed up beyond the pace of a slow walk. He stepped aside as the vehicle reached the water's edge.

He expected to see the front wheels roll into the water and stop, but the nose of the vehicle went over, and the cabin filled with water from the open door. Seconds later, it plunged downward and disappeared beneath the surface. The last thing he saw was the trailer hitch that stuck out from the rear bumper like the battle flag on the aft end of a sinking ship.

He glanced over at Bradshaw, who appeared to be out cold. 'You didn't need to see that anyway.'

Joe stood perplexed for a second, wondering about what had just happened. Then it made sense. Like most open-pit mines, the entire excavation was done in terraces. A steep slope, then a flat section, and then another steep cut. The beach was nothing more than a wide terrace. A sixty-foot wall lay behind them at an almost vertical angle. A similar drop must lie just beyond the water's edge.

Joe looked around at the remaining vehicles, and a new plan formed in his mind. It would cost the ASIO at least one more vehicle, but if Joe was right, it would get the other Jeep started.

Kurt looked upward into a pool of cherry-colored light. He'd brought the speeder in beneath the station and found the airlock.

Carefully, he maneuvered into the bay and surfaced. The pool and the surrounding deck space appeared empty.

Kurt nudged the throttle and bumped it up on to a shelf of some type. He popped the canopy back and stepped out on to the deck. A moment later, he was through the primary airlock and into an equipment room.

A pair of tanks and two full-face helmets sat nearby. The same type of equipment the ASIO had in one of their trucks.

The dive team had made it this far, he thought. *But where were they now?*

Kurt had managed to bring the short-barreled M4 carbine, but the odd, almost nervous energy that he'd quickly begun to feel told him he was breathing a high-oxygen mix. That was surprising.

He would have expected a tri-mix of gasses, or even an oxygen-helium mixture, that worked better at sustained depths. To be sure he wasn't imagining it, Kurt spoke briefly. 'Four score and seven years ago . . .'

He should have sounded like Mickey Mouse or Donald Duck, but he sounded exactly like himself. There was no helium in the air, or very little of it anyway. He put the rifle aside. There would be no gunfight at the bottom of the Tasman Lake. One shot would destroy the entire place.

He pulled a large diving knife from a sheath on his leg, wondering if this turn of events made his odds better or worse.

Twenty feet down a hall, he found water at the base of a ladder. He went up it and explored the next floor, finding two rooms filled with stacks of batteries. A wall panel displayed power states, most in the green and a few odd ones in yellow or red. Kurt wondered where they were getting the power to charge the huge stack or what they were using it for.

He went up another level and found what looked like the crew's living quarters. Empty lockers and unmade beds gave him the impression the place had been abandoned.

He moved back to the central ladder, ascended to a third level, and found the next hatch resting on its stops. He was about to open it when he heard the sound of footsteps pounding down the ladder toward him.

He held completely still.

Voices echoed. 'Come on,' someone shouted. 'Move.'

Kurt was about to slide back down a level and hide, when the footsteps abruptly moved to the left, pounding on the deck above, and headed away from him. It sounded like several people in a hurry.

He opened the hatch just a sliver and looked through. No one there.

Quietly, he pulled himself up and peeked around the corner. Three men stood in front of another airlock. This one reminded Kurt of the revolving doors in a center-city office building. As it opened, two of them went in and the third waited.

The sound of more footsteps descending the ladder came next. Kurt looked up just as another man dropped in beside him.

'What the . . .'

Kurt clapped a hand over the man's mouth and plunged the carbon steel blade into the man's chest, slamming him against the wall in the process. A second man dropped in, landing on Kurt's arm and knocking the knife to the floor.

Kurt spun around and threw an elbow into the second attacker's temple. It sent the man sprawling to the deck near the airlock.

By now, a third man had come down the ladder, his hands and feet sliding on the rails instead of using the rungs. He landed and grabbed Kurt from behind, wrapping an arm around Kurt's throat and trying to choke the life out of him.

Kurt pushed backward, ramming the man into the bulkhead wall. The grip loosened only a bit. Kurt pushed back again, this time trying to snap his head back in a reverse head butt of sorts.

The second impact shook the man loose, just as the airlock pinged like an elevator in a hotel lobby. Kurt was pushed to the ground as this third assailant rushed past.

By the time he got up, the airlock door was closing. The four remaining men were crammed into it, looking back at him. One of them shook his head, smiling sadistically.

Four against one, and they'd run off. Kurt could only think of a single reason for that: they were about to scuttle the station.

A quick glance at the dead man in the ladder well confirmed it. He carried wire strippers in his breast pocket, a roll of electrical tape on his belt, and a length of red-and-blue flat cable. In all likelihood, the station was set to explode.

Kurt grabbed the wire cutters and continued up the ladder. Based on the escaping group's show of haste, he doubted there was much time.

11

Joe's plan was in full bloom now. He'd set up a pulley system, running the cable from the front of the last Jeep, around the tubular steel brush guard on one of the SUVs, and attached it to the tail end of another SUV.

His plan was simple: push the hooked vehicle into the water and over the edge. As it dropped, the cable would drag the Jeep forward rapidly enough for Joe to pop the clutch and get the engine going.

Ready to go, he checked on Bradshaw once more, crossed his fingers, and moved to the SUV he was using as a deadweight. He couldn't open the windows without power, so he smashed them in. He opened all the doors and the tailgate and even popped the hood. Anything to let air out and water in to help the SUV sink faster.

He put the transmission in neutral, released the brake, and then hopped out. Digging his feet hard into the sand, Joe began pushing. Little by little, the SUV began to move, its pace quickening as it reached the firmer soil at the water's edge. With a last great shove, Joe pushed it off and stepped back, almost losing his balance and tumbling into the toxic soup.

The SUV rolled out and began to fill with water. It

nosed over just like the first vehicle had, then stopped as the wire cable pulled taut.

Joe ran back to the Jeep and hopped in. He made sure the key was turned and released the brakes. It began to move forward, slowly at first, but then picking up speed as the sinking SUV pulled on the cable.

Joe waited as long as he could and then popped the clutch.

The engine surged, stuttered, and then fired up. He pressed in the clutch and held it as he hit the brakes. The Jeep stopped a few feet shy of ramming the pulley vehicle.

Foot still on the clutch, he gave the Jeep some gas, revving the engine. After a few seconds, it began to hum nicely, and when he finally let off the gas, it went into a steady idle. With the parking brake firmly set, Joe got out and moved to the winch at the front of the Jeep.

He put a hand on the release lever and yanked it downward. The jaws of the drum parted, releasing the metal cord. It flung forward under great tension and whiplashed across the pulley car, shattering the windshield, before sliding across the sand and following the sinking SUV down into the lake.

Joe gave a salute to the departing vehicle and climbed back into the Jeep. He put the radio on the charger and watched as the red light lit up.

He glanced at his own reflection in the mirror. 'You're good, Zavala,' he said to himself. 'You're very good.'

Guessing it would take several minutes for the radio

to store up enough power to be useful, Joe decided to check on his patient.

He jumped out of the idling Jeep and moved quickly to where Bradshaw lay. The man was unconscious, but he was still breathing.

'Hang in there,' Joe whispered.

Out on the lake, the water began to stir. A slight bulge was forming near the center, halfway between the shore and the floating truck. Something was moving beneath the surface, like a killer whale charging the beach.

For a second, Joe hoped it might be Kurt in the speeder. But the object broke through and revealed itself as a twenty-foot-long submersible with a wide, rubber-skirted bottom. The reason for that design became clear seconds later as the sub rose up out of the water and began racing across the surface, leaving a wide swath of foam beneath and behind it.

'A submersible-hovercraft,' Joe marveled. 'That's even better than a truck that swims.'

For twenty seconds, the hovercraft traveled northward along the surface, then it turned slightly to the east, raced out of the water on the far side of the pit and up on to the ramp.

Joe realized he was witnessing the group who'd ambushed the ASIO making their escape.

'I don't think so,' he said. He rushed to the idling Jeep and climbed in. He paused for a second, considering Bradshaw. There was nothing he could do for him. But as soon as the radio was charged, he'd call for help.

He jammed the transmission into gear and stomped on the gas pedal. The tires spun in the gravel as he tore off after the fleeing hovercraft.

Down in the empty station, Kurt continued to look for Hayley. He climbed and checked two additional levels as quickly as he could before finally pushing through the uppermost hatch and coming out in some kind of control room.

In the far corner, two figures sat bound and gagged on the floor. Kurt ran over to them and pulled the gag off Hayley's mouth.

'Explosives,' she blurted out, not even uttering a hello. 'Under the panel.'

Kurt cut her loose and left her with the knife as he rushed to the panel and slid beneath it. He found the blocks of plastic explosives and the timer. It read 01:07 and was counting down by the second.

He took out the wire cutters as Hayley freed the guy beside her. He was about to snip one of the wires when they rushed up behind him, crowding him more than he would have liked.

'Either of you know anything about explosives?' he asked.

They shook their heads.

'We should get out of here,' Hayley said, gulping.

The clock hit 00:59. They had less than a minute. Kurt shook his head. 'We'll never make it.'

The guy from the ASIO reached for the timer. Kurt

slapped his hand. 'Press the wrong button and you'll blow us to bits.'

He pointed. A tiny lock symbol was illuminated at the top of the screen. If Kurt was right, they would need to enter a code to stop the countdown.

'Wc can't just sit hcrc,' thc guy said.

'Forty seconds,' Hayley mentioned.

Kurt studied the detonator. It was a standard industrial design, not a bombmaker's toy. He'd used similar devices scuttling a few ships. If he was right, it should fail-safe instead of fail-deadly. It was connected to two wires, red and blue.

'Thirty seconds.'

The ASIO guy bumped Kurt, trying to get a better look.

'What's your name?' Kurt asked.

'Wiggins.'

'Back up, Wiggins,' Kurt said.

'Twenty seconds,' Hayley said stressfully.

'What good will that do?' Wiggins asked.

'It will get you out of my space.'

They eased off of him a bit, and Kurt opened the wire strippers as wide as possible.

'Ten seconds,' Hayley said. 'Nine . . . eight . . .'

Kurt didn't wait for her to hit seven. He reached out and snipped both wires as emphatically as he could.

Nothing happened. No fire, no explosion, nothing. The timer stopped at 00:00.

'Oh, thank goodness,' Hayley said.

Appearing ready to collapse, she put her arms on Kurt's shoulders and lay her forehead against his back.

'Great job,' Wiggins said. 'Did Bradshaw send you?'

'Not exactly,' Kurt replied. Before he could explain, a rumble shook the structure, followed by several concussions in rapid succession. It sounded like distant thunder. The floor tilted slightly and then came back to level. The whole station swayed and creaked like an old tree in the wind.

'The dome,' Hayley said. 'They were going to blow that too.'

Another round of explosions went off, and this time the shock wave hit like a sledgehammer. The sound of snapping cables followed. Moments later, the crunching impact of a collision knocked all of them to the floor.

Kurt remembered that the dome was above them and anchored to them, and he could only imagine what its destruction would do to the dilapidated laboratory. The sound of metal sliding on metal and the appearance of pinpoint jets of water blasting across the room gave him his answer.

12

Joe was racing across the desert in a V-8 Jeep Wrangler. With its big knobby tires, powerful engine and high centerline clearance, the Jeep's off-road capabilities were among the best in the world. But they didn't compare to the ability of a hovercraft to cross rugged terrain.

Joe had to work hard to keep the Jeep upright as it scrambled through ravines, across uneven ground, and around patches of scrub too thick to drive through. The hovercraft simply flew over them and continued in a straight line.

He was losing ground fast until he came to a smooth section that reminded him of the Utah Salt Flats. Out on the level terrain, Joe began to catch up. As he closed the gap, the light on the handheld radio finally turned green.

Joe snatched it off the charger and pressed the talk switch.

'ASIO, do you read?' he said, assuming that's who was listening. 'Anyone out there?'

A scratchy reply came back. 'Bradshaw, is that you?'

'Negative,' Joe said. 'Bradshaw has been injured. You have several agents down.'

'Who is this?' the voice on the other end of the line asked.

Joe explained the best he could, and also explained that he was chasing the suspected shooters westbound through the desert.

'What road are you on?'

'I'm not on any road,' Joe said. 'We're heading cross-country, due west from the flooded mine. Right into the sun.'

A garbled reply came back, and then the radio cut out once again. Joe slammed it back on to the charger. Ahead of him, the hovercraft was turning, skidding sideways. It ended up rotated 180 degrees and pointing right at him.

Joe began to swerve, but it was a little too late. Something flashed, as much in his mind as in his eyes, and Joe's world went instantly dark.

'We have to get out of here,' Kurt shouted, ushering everyone to the ladder.

Hayley went first, Wiggins in the middle, and Kurt bringing up the rear.

Another impact jarred the structure, and Kurt almost lost his grip. He grabbed the hatch above and pulled it down, but it wouldn't seal. Like a door that couldn't be closed because the frame had swollen, the hatch would not pull flush.

'The impact must have warped the deck plates,' Wiggins suggested.

Kurt gave it one more try, putting all his weight on it, but the tiny gap remained. Water began to run down the inside of the ladder well, water that Kurt had no interest in touching.

'Go,' he said to Wiggins.

The two of them slid to the bottom level and soon made it to the airlock. Hayley was already there, pulling on her helmet. They were wearing dry suits. With gloves and full helmets, they theoretically wouldn't be exposed to the toxins of the lake.

Water was now pouring down, accompanied by the creaking and groaning of metal stressed to the limits. The station would implode in moments.

'We can't go straight up,' Kurt said. 'You've both been down here for too long. You'll end up with the bends like the courier did.'

'We have to get away,' she said.

'Grab on to the handholds,' Kurt said. 'I'll tow you as far away as we can go.'

She nodded and sealed her helmet.

Kurt climbed on to the speeder and then closed and locked the canopy. The lights went out as Hayley and Wiggins were pulling on their tanks. Kurt switched on the headlight of the speeder so they could see.

With their air supplies attached, Wiggins gave Hayley the thumbs-up. She returned the gesture.

'Here we go,' Kurt said to himself.

They pushed the speeder back into the immersion pool and dropped in after it. As soon as they'd grabbed on, Kurt expelled all the air from the flotation tank, and they began to sink.

They cleared the bottom of the portal in three seconds.

'Hold on!' Kurt yelled, hoping they could somehow hear him.

He twisted the throttle slowly, and the water jet that powered the speeder began to thrust. He accelerated gently, but to only about half speed. Any faster and his passengers would be pulled off.

With the headlights blazing, Kurt stared through the rose-tinted water. He dove a few feet to avoid one of the guide wires and continued forward. Compressional explosions came from behind as compartments of the station gave way.

A group of flashes traveled up and down the vertical collection of pipes that hung from the center of the damaged dome. More explosives being triggered.

Each flash backlit the structure the way lightning might silhouette an abandoned building. What was left of the dome had already collided with the station and slid off to the side. It scraped downward and lodged against a seam, an act which proved to be the last nail in the coffin for the lab.

The hull plating buckled, and the water crushed it inward, mashing it like a giant foot stepping on a tin can. A surge of light and air blasted outward, sending a shock wave across the flooded pit. Hayley and Wiggins were actually sucked backward toward the station for a second before being thrown violently forward as clouds of sediment exploded out of the dark.

As the concussion wave hit, the speeder was tossed around like a child's toy. Kurt banged his head against the canopy as it tumbled. He spun around and caught sight of Hayley and Wiggins just as the churning waves of silt swallowed them whole.

13

The noise reached Joe through the fog of sleep. At first, it sounded like a sprinkler irrigating a field, repetitive and sharp, only slower: *chih-chih-chih-chih-chih* . . .

Joe's mind wandered to the stretches of farmland he'd grown up around in New Mexico and the high-pressure irrigation that was used to bring the desert to life. Somehow, even half asleep, he knew he wasn't in New Mexico.

When he opened his eyes, the world was a blur. He tasted something salty and put a hand to his mouth; it came away red with blood. Blood that was trickling from a gash in his forehead, running down his nose and on to his lips.

His vision began to clear, and he realized he was in the driver's seat of a motor vehicle. The windshield in front of him was smashed in a starburst pattern that lined up with his head. The nose of the vehicle was pointed down at a sharp angle, like he'd driven into a ditch.

Even as his other symptoms cleared, the strange noise continued. It even became more distinct, sounding for all the world like a giant fan turning at moderate speed.

Shouts from outside the Jeep reached his ears.

'Over here,' someone said.

'Get a crowbar.'

The door beside him moved. Fingers appeared around the edge and wrenched it several inches. A face appeared in the gap.

'Are you okay, mate?' a man in army fatigues asked.

Joe put a hand to the gash on his forehead. 'I've been better.'

'Sit tight. We're gonna get you out.'

The soldier went to work on the bent and twisted door, helped by another soldier who'd brought a crowbar. Together, they forced the door wider an inch at a time.

As they worked, Joe's memory returned. He was in Australia. He'd been chasing after another vehicle. He tried to peer around the starburst in the windshield for any sign of the hovercraft, thinking for a moment that they might have hit head-on. He saw only the dirt wall of the gully he'd gone into.

The door beside him finally broke loose, and the soldiers reached in to help him. With care, they pulled him free of the mangled wreck. As one of them searched the Jeep, the other led Joe out of the ditch and toward a tan-colored NH90 helicopter with Australian military markings.

Now Joe realized where the odd sound had been coming from. The rotors above the big transport were still turning.

A stern-looking man in a black suit met him a few feet from the helicopter's door.

'Are you the one who called us in?' the man asked. 'On Bradshaw's radio?'

Joe nodded. 'What happened?'

'What do you mean?'

'The guys I was chasing,' Joe explained, 'did you catch them? They were in a hovercraft.'

The man raised an eyebrow. 'Hovercraft?'

'I know it sounds crazy,' Joe said, 'but that's what they were driving. Afraid I can't give you a make and model.'

The man shook his head glumly. 'Whatever they were in, we didn't find them.' He motioned toward the open door of the helicopter. 'We have to debrief you. This bird will take you back to Alice Springs.'

'What about Bradshaw?' Joe asked.

'He was medevacked out thirty minutes ago.'

'Thirty minutes ago?' Confusion swept over Joe. He felt like he'd made the call no less than thirty seconds ago. Even given his few minutes of unconsciousness, they couldn't have gotten to Bradshaw that quickly.

Only then did he realize it was nearly dark. The sun had been dropping toward the horizon during his chase, but it was long gone now. Only a faded orange glow lingered in the darkening sky.

The helicopter blades began to accelerate above them as the pilot spooled up for liftoff. 'It took us a while to find you,' the man explained.

‘What about Kurt?’

‘Who?’

‘Kurt Austin.’

‘I don’t know that name,’ the man said. He took Joe’s arm and ushered him toward the door. ‘Please, we have to go.’

Joe shook loose from the man’s grasp. ‘I’m not going anywhere until you tell me what happened to my friend. He went down into the mine to rescue your divers.’

The official made a strange face. ‘There was an explosion,’ he said. ‘If your friend survived, he’s been flown out. But no one’s left at the lake now except the dead.’

With a sick feeling in his heart, Joe climbed aboard the helicopter and strapped himself in. As he flew, night tightened its grip on the land. By the time he arrived at the Australian military base outside Alice Springs, the sky was like black cloth punctured by some of the brightest stars Joe had ever seen.

He was taken to the infirmary first. A young doctor looked him over and tested for signs of chemical or metal poisoning. After informing Joe that he’d live, the doctor left and an even younger nurse came in. She stitched up the gash in his head where he’d smashed it into the windshield.

Shortly after finishing, she jabbed him in the arm with a shot.

‘Oww!’

‘Tetanus and antibiotics,’ she said.

'Sure,' Joe said, rubbing his bicep. 'But aren't you supposed to warn me or tell me that it's not going to hurt first?'

'Why lie?' she asked. 'Besides, I thought you Yanks were tough.'

'It's been a rough day,' he admitted. 'Speaking of Yanks, have you treated any other Americans tonight? Maybe a guy six feet tall with silver hair.'

'Sorry,' she said, packing up her things, 'you're the first.'

After the nurse left, Joe was taken to a different section of the base. It seemed like basic housing or perhaps quarters for the NCOs.

His escort/guard opened the door to reveal a room with two bunks, a utilitarian desk placed between them, and cinder-block walls. It reminded Joe of a dorm room, right down to the roommate already lying on one of the beds with his feet up.

Joe stepped inside, the door was locked behind him, and Kurt Austin sat up.

'Damn, I'm glad to see you,' Joe said. 'They had me thinking you'd become part of the junk pile at the bottom of that mine.'

Kurt stood and gave Joe a bear hug. 'I had a similar fear about you. Didn't expect to surface and find Bradshaw, sunning himself on the beach unattended. I was afraid those thugs got the drop on you.'

'I figured he wasn't up to four-wheeling through the desert,' Joe replied.

Kurt looked at him oddly. 'I'm guessing by the stitches that your chase ended with some extracurricular activities?'

'No,' Joe said, 'I didn't catch them. I ended up in a ditch somehow. But considering how well I was doing up until that point, I'm thinking about entering the Baja 1000 next year.'

'You don't win the Baja by crashing, Joe. You know that, right?'

'I didn't crash, amigo, I was . . .' Joe paused. 'Okay, I guess I did crash, but I'm pretty sure it wasn't my fault.'

The vagueness of his own recollection was puzzling to Joe. He tried hard to remember. 'One second, I was going head-on with them . . . there was a flash, like the glare of sunlight off a pane of glass, and then . . . I must have swerved, though I honestly can't remember.'

'You sound like Bradshaw,' Kurt noted.

'How is he, by the way?'

'Alive, thanks to you. They had him in surgery.'

Joe was glad to hear that. 'Did you find your scientist down there?'

'Her and another diver from the ASIO. They were basically strapped to a bomb. We escaped, but the station imploded.'

'Are they all right?'

'As far as I know,' Kurt said. 'I lost track of them for a moment when the station blew. When I found them, both were unconscious. But thanks to the gripper claws you put on the front of the speeder, I was able to grab them and bring them slowly to the surface.'

Joe smiled with pride. 'So the speeder performed like a champ. I knew it would.'

'You may have a future in this submarine business,' Kurt said. 'That is, if you can give up your dreams of middle management and off-road racing.'

Joe laughed and took a seat at the desk between the two bunks. He rapped his knuckles against the cinder-block wall. 'So are we in prison or protective custody?'

'No idea,' Kurt replied. 'Nor do I have any idea what I've gotten us into. But if they ever let me talk to someone, I'm damned well determined to find out.'

'Or,' Joe said, 'just go with me on this – we could pretend it was all a big misunderstanding and be about our business.'

The furrow in Kurt's brow showed his feelings on that idea. 'What fun would that be?'

Joe knew Kurt so well, he could have predicted that answer. Once his friend sunk his teeth into a mystery, there was no turning back, not until he found what he was looking for.

Unfortunately, no answers would come for the next few hours. In fact, no one bothered them until well past midnight, when the door was unlatched and a pair of Australian military personnel came in. MPs, or the Aussie equivalent, dressed in fatigues. One male, one female.

'Mr Austin?' the male soldier said. 'Please come with me.'

Kurt stood wearily. Joe did the same.

'Not you, Mr Zavala,' the female guard said. 'You stay here.'

Joe feigned great indignation. 'What? Nobody wants to interrogate me? I might know a thing or two.'

Kurt moved to the door. 'I'm sure they'll bring you in when I'm done. Don't wait up.'

The male guard allowed Kurt to pass by and then escorted him down the hall.

Joe lost sight of him and leaned stoically against the wall. To his surprise, the female guard remained behind even as the door was shut.

Joe studied her. She was pretty, despite the lack of makeup and the baggy uniform. It occurred to Joe that she might be there to conduct a surreptitious interrogation. He figured he'd make it easy on her and attempt to find out what she might know in the process.

'Here to keep an eye on me?' he asked.

No reply.

'You know,' he said more smoothly, 'there's something I love about a woman in uniform.'

Still nothing. If she was supposed to charm him, the statue routine was not going over with high marks.

'Not a people person, are you?' Joe said. 'So how do you feel about . . . UFOs?'

She still didn't speak, but this time the corners of her mouth curled into a slight but apparently irrepressible smile. Joe smiled back. Now he was getting somewhere.

*

While Joe attempted to charm his guard, Kurt was led on a hike across what seemed like half the military base. They passed the infirmary and continued on until they reached a long hallway. Additional guards or MPs stood at the far end.

'Third door on your right,' Kurt's escort said.

The corridor was gloomy. The paint on the walls peeling. Equipment covered by dusty tarps lay stacked against the wall, as the fluorescent lights flickered. It looked like the kind of place where they might keep the electroshock therapy equipment.

'Aren't you going with me?' Kurt asked.

The guard stood with his hands behind his back. He said nothing.

'Guess not.'

Kurt took a deep breath and moved slowly down the hall until he reached the third door. He twisted the handle and stepped into a moderately lit room with all the equipment of an ICU. Lying in a bed on the right – with an oxygen line attached to his nose and an IV drip hooked up to his arm – was Cecil Bradshaw. He did not look well.

Kurt closed the door.

Bradshaw turned his head. His eyes were dark, sunken and half closed.

'Glad to see you,' Kurt said. 'Thought I was about to get hooked up to the power grid for a moment.'

Bradshaw's eyes crinkled a bit, the closest he could come to a smile. He stretched for the switch that controlled the hospital bed, but he couldn't reach it.

‘Prop me up, will ya?’

Kurt found the button that raised the back of the bed and pressed it, holding it down until Bradshaw was almost in a sitting position.

An alarm began to flash on the monitor for a second, indicating Bradshaw’s pulse had dropped into the fifties and that his pressure was a little low.

‘That’s what happens when you lose half your blood,’ Bradshaw said. ‘They’ve been pumping it back in all night.’

‘Surprised you had *any* left to begin with,’ Kurt said.

‘I’m a heartless bastard,’ Bradshaw insisted. ‘We don’t require much.’

‘Lucky for you.’

‘I made them take me off the painkillers,’ the ASIO chief went on to explain, ‘so I could talk to you clearly. First, I want to thank you for being the type of idiot who doesn’t know when to quit. I reckon that Hayley, Wiggins and I all owe you our lives.’

Kurt appreciated the sentiment. ‘There’s a rugby match I’ve been wanting to see. Get me good seats, and we’ll call it even.’

Bradshaw laughed a little, but it made him cough. ‘The other night, after you intervened at the Opera House, I almost asked you to help out. I had a feeling about you. But once you mentioned the decompression sickness, I was able to put the puzzle together, so I let it go. Good thing I did or you’d have been right alongside us when we got hit. And then we’d *all* be dead.’

‘A bit of luck,’ Kurt noted.

'Seems so,' Bradshaw agreed. 'I hope there's more where that came from. I don't have enough wind to beat around the bush, so I'll just say it straight. I want you to take over the investigation.'

Kurt's eyes narrowed.

'You guessed right,' Bradshaw explained, 'I have a leak in my department. I don't know how it's possible, but it's the only logical explanation. Despite my efforts, someone seems to know what we're doing almost before we do. They're batting a perfect record at beating us to the punch.'

'Is that why we're here on the air base instead of in a civilian hospital?'

'That's exactly the reason,' Bradshaw said. 'My men are being told I'm still in surgery, and then they'll hear that I haven't regained consciousness. Aside from Wiggins and Hayley – who are temporarily being held in solitary like you and Zavala – no one is being informed of your presence or interference.'

'These things have a way of leaking out,' Kurt noted, 'especially if we start poking around asking questions. Which, considering that we're Americans, might be a little tricky down here on Australian soil.'

'It would be tricky,' Bradshaw agreed, 'if you were *staying* on Australian soil.'

Kurt leaned against a desk. 'What are you saying?'

'We're dealing with terrorists here,' Bradshaw replied. 'We believe the next phase of their plan will be launched from somewhere offshore.'

'Based on what?'

'Our informant,' Bradshaw said. 'We've been told the project in the outback has been superseded by a larger, more dangerous plan. Evidence bears that out. Considering the effort it must have taken to build and hide that lab – or whatever you might call it – it's completely irrational to blow it up unless you have something else to fall back on.'

Kurt nodded. It made sense to him.

'In addition to that,' Bradshaw added, 'the shipment of mining equipment we intercepted was some of the latest self-contained, ocean-going gear available. It's designed for use in the most hazardous environments and the worst weather. We plucked it off a freighter that left Perth and was officially bound for Cape Town, but the ship's track was southbound, toward Antarctic waters, not west to South Africa.'

'There's no accounting for bad navigation these days,' Kurt joked. 'Where do you think they were headed?'

'We think Thero is hiding on the Antarctic shelf.'

'Thero?'

'The leader of this mess.'

Kurt pulled up a chair, swung it around, and sat down with his arms resting on the back, leaning toward Bradshaw. He considered what the man was asking. His own curiosity spurred him on, but there were bigger issues.

'NUMA is not exactly a law enforcement agency. Maybe you want to contact Interpol.'

'And wait six months for the paperwork to clear?' Bradshaw shook his head in answer to his own question. 'Besides,' he added, 'this is a science problem as much as it is a terrorist threat. From what I've heard, you NUMA guys seem to specialize in that combination. And if they're using the ocean as cover . . . well, that's right up your alley, isn't it?'

Kurt nodded. 'It is.'

'Then let me pass the baton.'

'It's not my call,' Kurt explained. 'All this . . . our involvement . . . It was just me being an idiot, like you said. But if we're going to involve NUMA officially, I have to run it up the flagpole. I can't promise you anything. But from what you've told me, I think our Director will see it your way.'

'Pitt?' Bradshaw said. 'Yeah, I've heard of him. Sounds like a good man.'

'The best,' Kurt said. 'But before I go to him, I have to know exactly what we're dealing with. What are these people up to? Who is this guy Thero and what does he want?'

Bradshaw didn't hesitate. He'd brought Kurt here to talk and he was ready. 'Have you ever heard of zero-point energy?'

Truth was, Kurt hadn't. At least not until he'd done the Internet search on Hayley Anderson.

'I saw the term on a scientific paper,' he admitted. 'Can't say I read more than a paragraph or two, but it sounded like some type of power source.'

'I won't pretend to understand the physics,' Bradshaw said, 'but the concept involves drawing energy from background fields that are supposedly all around us. As the theory goes, tapping into these fields would provide an unlimited and inexhaustible source of energy for the whole world, one that would cost almost nothing to use and distribute.'

'Sounds like a pipe dream,' Kurt said.

'Maybe it is,' Bradshaw said. 'Who knows? But this group we're dealing with believes in it. They claim they've unlocked its secret.'

Bully for them, Kurt thought. 'How does that turn into what we saw today? If free energy is all about peace, love and kilowatts, why are people getting shot and blown up?'

Bradshaw coughed and winced in pain. 'I'll give you a file with everything we *think* we know, but here's the short version. As I told you, it starts with a guy named Thero, Maxmillian Thero. He's an American, actually. A nuclear engineer by trade and a self-taught physicist. He spent eight years in your navy, working on submarines and aircraft carriers. He was discharged in 1978 and began work at Three Mile Island a few months before the meltdown in 1979.'

'Great timing,' Kurt noted.

'It was for him, apparently. Feeling like the world had narrowly avoided an epic disaster, he began to rethink his career choice. He bounced around a lot and eventually launched a crusade to find an alternate system of generating power. At some point, he hit on the idea of zero-point energy. As near as we can tell, he spent years trying to get funding and prove the concept was workable. Unfortunately, he was never taken seriously.

'After a while, he came to believe there was a sinister reason for this, that his efforts were being thwarted by big shots in the nuclear industry, the oil companies, and other power brokers in your Energy Department. He claimed in an interview that your government had tapped his phone lines and bugged his home and his laboratory. An IRS investigation into his funding only added fuel to the fire.'

'Sounds like a persecution complex.'

'A CIA profile your government shared with us concluded exactly that. He's a paranoid bugger. That seems to be what drives him. Shortly after Y2K, he fled the US and came to Australia.'

'Why Australia?' Kurt asked. 'From what I recall, you guys don't even use nuclear power.'

'We don't,' Bradshaw said. 'And that's exactly why he came here. He figured that would level the playing field. That, along with the fact that Australia and New Zealand were pushing back against visits by American nuclear warships. From what I understand, he seemed to think my government would embrace him.'

'Did they?'

'At first,' Bradshaw said. 'He received the first real grant he'd ever seen and found work as a professor at the University of Sydney, while trying to perfect his theory. By 2005 he claimed he was only a year away from a workable system. But before he could run his big test, my government got involved and shut him down.'

'Why?'

'I have no answer to that,' Bradshaw said, 'but there were people who thought his experiments were dangerous.'

That really wasn't a surprise. Paranoid nuclear scientists doing unregulated trials in the dark tended to make people nervous.

'How does Hayley fit into all this?'

'She's a physicist. She was a grad student when Thero arrived. She worked with him the entire time he was here. Hayley, along with Thero's son, George, and his daughter, Tessa, all of whom were physicists, formed a tight little triangle looking up to Thero.'

'All part of the crusade,' Kurt guessed.

'True believers.'

'So you guys shut him down eight years ago,' Kurt noted. 'Somehow, I'm guessing that's not the end of his story.'

'It's not. Thero and his family were ordered to leave the country or be deported. They might have gone back to the US, but a Japanese venture capitalist named Tokada gave him a lifeline. As near as we can tell, Tokada promised that Japan, unlike your country or mine, would support his work.'

'Makes sense,' Kurt said. 'Japan has always been dependent on imported energy.'

'Massively dependent,' Bradshaw said. 'They import ninety-eight per cent of their oil and ninety per cent of their coal. Their nuclear industry is pretty large, but because of Hiroshima and Nagasaki, nuclear power has always been a sore spot, even before the tsunami wiped out those reactors on the coast.'

Kurt could see the dominoes lining up. 'So if Thero could tap into this zero-point energy, Japan could do away with all of that, and the whole country would hail him as a hero and probably make him a billionaire overnight.'

Bradshaw nodded again. 'Thero moved there in 2006, setting up shop in a secret laboratory on a small island in the north known as Yagishiri. His son and daughter went with him. Hayley stayed behind.'

'Why?'

Bradshaw tried to make himself more comfortable, pulling at a pillow. 'Well, for one thing, she'd begun to think they were headed down a dangerous path. Beyond that, she suffers from a debilitating fear of travel. She doesn't fly, doesn't even own a car. She mostly walks or takes the train. Until yesterday, she hadn't been out of Sydney for nine years.'

That surprised Kurt, considering the bravery he'd seen in her.

'How'd you get her out here?'

'Sedatives.'

Kurt laughed.

Bradshaw coughed again and cleared his throat.

'Two years after Thero went to Japan, there was an incident, a massive explosion on Yagishiri. His lab was completely obliterated.'

'What happened?'

'No one knows for sure. Some say his experiments literally blew up in his face. Satellite photos showed nothing left but a smoking hole in the ground. It seemed impossible that anyone could have survived. Funerals were held for everyone believed to be present, including Thero and his children.'

'Case closed,' Kurt said. 'A little too easy.'

'Yeah,' Bradshaw agreed. 'Fast-forward to last year, and my government received a letter, claiming to be from Thero. It insists he's come for revenge and that he intends to tear Australia apart, the way his family was torn apart.'

Kurt sat back. 'Tear Australia apart? As in create chaos, social upheaval, or something like that?'

Bradshaw shook his head. 'As in rip the continent in two.'

Kurt studied Bradshaw's face. There was nothing to suggest he was joking or delusional. 'Come again?'

'That's where the worm turns,' Bradshaw said. 'Like any form of energy, there are beneficial uses and harmful uses for this one. Thero claims he's finally succeeded in his quest and unlocked the secret to limitless energy. He insists that he would have used it for the benefit of the world, but because the world rejected him and brutalized his children, he'll now use this newfound power for revenge, beginning by ripping this island in half.'

'Even with some type of energy source I've never heard of, that sounds a little absurd,' Kurt said. 'A thousand nuclear bombs couldn't split Australia in half.'

'No,' Bradshaw agreed, 'but plate tectonics can.'

'Why don't you cut to the chase here? What are you telling me?'

'I'll let Hayley explain the details, but Thero claims he can use this zero-point energy to unleash earthquakes and affect the movement of continental plates.'

Kurt had seen a study some years back, suggesting such a thing might be possible on a minor scale. High pressure, deep-well injections of certain chemicals were known to lubricate fault lines and cause minor tremors in places. But for the most part, these were quakes felt only on the readouts of seismic monitors, not in the streets of cities and towns high above.

Then again, this zero-point energy was like nothing Kurt had ever heard of before.

'Thero's already proven it to us,' Bradshaw said. 'In the letter detailing his threat, he promised to unleash an earthquake exactly two months from the date of his signature. He insisted it would occur somewhere between Adelaide on the southern coast and Alice Springs, where we are now.'

'There was an earthquake last month,' Kurt said, recalling the news. 'A big one.'

'Six-point-nine,' Bradshaw said. 'One hundred and

twenty miles north-northwest of Adelaide. It hit on the exact date Thero promised. Largest quake we've had in years.'

'But there are no fault lines here,' Kurt said, remembering his geology. 'Australia sits in the middle of a plate, not on the boundary like California or Japan.'

'So I've been told,' Bradshaw said. 'Thero insists he can change all that. That when he's done, Australia will be cleaved down the middle and there will be, in effect, two smaller plates where there is currently one.'

Kurt's mind reeled. *Was it really possible?*

'Is there any way it could be coincidence?' he asked. 'A lucky guess that just happened to come true? Even an educated prediction based on some new sensing device he created?'

Bradshaw shrugged. 'Even Hayley isn't sure. But we can't exactly wait around to find out.'

No, Kurt thought, there was no way they could do that. Not when they were dealing with a madman looking for poetic justice who'd already lost everything of importance.

'Why is Hayley still involved?' he asked. 'She's no agent. She sounded like a woman on the verge of a nervous breakdown the other night. Why do you have her meeting with these couriers?'

Bradshaw sighed. 'I told you, we have an informant, an unknown person inside Thero's organization who's been feeding us data. He or she contacted Hayley out of the blue shortly after the threat first came to light.

Whoever this person inside Thero's organization is, he or she is willing to deal with us only if Hayley acts as the go-between.'

Kurt could see Bradshaw's dilemma. 'She's a brave woman,' he said, 'too brave for her own good. You should put her in protective custody somewhere.'

'There is no protective custody from what Thero is about to unleash. Not down here anyway. And since she won't travel, that kind of limits the options. Besides, she wants to keep helping. And if you take this on, you're going to need her. She's the only one who understands what we're really dealing with.'

Kurt could see that Bradshaw was right, but he didn't like the idea. Bad things happened to civilians who got tangled up in a mess like this.

Bradshaw pointed to a sealed manila envelope on the desk. It looked to contain a thick file. 'That's everything we know. Read it, talk to your people, and let me know your decision as soon as you can. You'll get your rugby tickets either way.'

Kurt smiled. Bradshaw was a good soul, tough as nails and gutting out the pain so he could pass the torch and yet still able to crack a joke. Kurt figured he deserved some more happy juice so he could fade off to dreamland for a while. The thought reminded him of another mystery.

'What happened out there?' he asked. 'How'd those guys get the drop on you?'

Bradshaw shook his head. 'One minute, I was getting

ready to make a radio call. The next thing I know, I was on the ground, and someone was shooting.'

'Did you see a flash?'

Bradshaw paused.

'Like sunlight reflecting off glass?'

'Yeah,' Bradshaw said slowly. 'Yeah, I think I did.'

Kurt nodded. He was no closer to an answer. But he was pretty sure that whatever happened to Bradshaw had also happened to Joe. Maybe Thero had more than one weapon at his disposal.

He grabbed the file and stood. 'I'll send the nurse in.'

'I'll rest better when I know you're on the case,' the ASIO chief grunted.

'Then I'll let you know as soon as I can.'

14

Washington, DC, 2200 hours

Under the soft light of antique chandeliers, a crowd of ambassadors, congressmen and other dignitaries mingled in the East Room of the White House. They spoke quietly, accompanied by the subdued tones of the gilded Steinway piano that graced the room.

At the conclusion of a state dinner for the Prime Minister of India, the attendees were given the chance to talk, network, and discuss ideas unencumbered by the constraints of long-held official positions. It had been said that more business was done after business hours than during all the official meetings, negotiation sessions and carefully orchestrated mediations of the world's governments combined.

Dirk Pitt didn't doubt it.

As he moved through the room, he overheard deals being closed, wiggle room in treaties being discussed, and myriad other activities. As Director of NUMA, he'd used such occasions himself, putting a bug in the right ear or two. Tonight, however, he was on hand mainly as a favor to an old friend.

Tall and rugged, with the weathered good looks of

an outdoorsman, Pitt was a man of action and a decisive leader who exhibited the greatest sense of calm amid the worst types of chaos. Were an explosion to go off down the hall and others begin racing for the exits, Dirk Pitt might assess the situation, finish his drink, and then calmly find the closest fire extinguisher.

With that mind-set, he moved slowly around the room, looking for the only potential flash point he expected to find that evening: his good friend James Sandecker, NUMA's former director and the current Vice President of the United States.

Pitt found him, standing proudly on the far edge of the reception. Sandecker's red hair was now partially gray, but his bantamweight frame still taut and fit. He stood with his hands clasped behind his back, presumably to discourage anyone from attempting to shake them. That stance and the scowl on his face seemed enough to warn most of the spurious human traffic to steer well clear.

Most but not all.

'How many senators does it take to screw in a lightbulb?' a stocky, red-faced congressman asked him between swigs of a Scotch on the rocks.

Dirk Pitt watched the exchange with amusement. He pegged the odds of a profanity-laced reply somewhere around fifty-fifty. They would have been higher, but they were in the White House, after all.

'How many?' the Vice President said curtly.

The congressman began laughing at himself. 'No

one knows, but if you like we can form a blue-ribbon committee, study the issue, and get back to you in a year or two.'

Sandecker offered a fleeting smile, but the scowl returned almost instantaneously. 'Interesting,' he said, offering nothing more.

The congressman's laugh faded and then stopped cold. He seemed confused by Sandecker's response and unnerved by it at the same time. He took another sip of his drink, gave a polite wave and walked off, glancing back once or twice with a bewildered look on his face.

'I do believe you're mellowing,' Pitt said, easing up beside the Vice President. 'It's a testament to your self-control that you didn't slug that guy.'

At that moment, the shrill beeping of an alert tone sounded in one of their pockets.

'You or me?' Sandecker asked.

Pitt was already reaching for his phone. 'I believe it's me.'

He pulled the phone from his jacket pocket and typed in a code. The screen lit up with the words PRIORITY 1 MESSAGE.

Sandecker offered a serious look. 'I remember the days before cell phones and pagers,' he began, 'when some poor soul had to actually come running like the dickens to tell you bad news.'

'Times have changed,' Pitt said, waiting for the message to download.

'Not for the better,' Sandecker suggested. 'Shooting the messenger isn't half the fun when it's nothing but a damned machine. What's the word?'

'Kurt's gotten himself involved in something down under.'

A grin lit upon Sandecker's face. 'I heard he smashed up the Opera House pretty good,' he said, barely suppressing a laugh.

'What's so funny about that?' Pitt asked.

'They're like grandchildren,' Sandecker explained. 'Paying you back for the havoc you and Al used to cause me. When I think of all the things I had to smooth over or sweep under the rug . . .'

Sandecker laughed again and shook his head. 'You know the IRS still wants to tax you on that Messerschmitt you brought back from Germany.'

Pitt cut his eyes at Sandecker. 'Considering all the money I've put into it, that thing's more of a liability than an asset anyway.'

The answer rolled off Pitt's lips almost subconsciously; he wasn't really focused on the conversation anymore. He was scanning the text as it was decrypted by the security software on the phone. In other company, he might have kept his emotions hidden. But around one of his oldest friends, it didn't matter.

'Something's wrong,' Sandecker guessed.

'Nine members of the ASIO killed in an ambush. It looks like Kurt and Joe stumbled on to the scene and managed to save two others and a scientist of some kind. Kurt wants to talk on scrambled satellite feed. Says he's at the air force base in Alice Springs.'

'Alice Springs,' Sandecker said. 'Interesting.'

Pitt looked up. 'Interesting like the senator's joke? Or interesting for real?'

'Interesting for real,' Sandecker said, though he didn't elaborate.

Dirk slid the phone back into his pocket. 'I assume you have somewhere in this building I can talk to Kurt?'

'The Situation Room is available,' Sandecker said, pulling out his phone and firing off a text. 'I'll have the communications team set it up. The lights will be on and the coffee piping hot by the time we get there.'

'*We?*'

'I can't let you walk around the White House unattended,' Sandecker explained, as if Pitt were part of a tour group or something. 'Besides, I need an excuse to get out of here before I pummel someone and sully the reputation of my office.'

Twenty minutes later, Pitt and Sandecker were in a secondary area of the Situation Room, a smaller section no larger than an average household den. A single large monitor and three smaller ones were set into a wall. Two rows of comfortable chairs completed the kit. All in all, it felt like an upscale home theater.

True to Sandecker's word, some of the best coffee Pitt could remember was ready and waiting. He sipped it as a technician from the communications crew finished the setup and stepped out.

Pitt sat front and center, Sandecker took a seat beside him.

Seconds later, an incoming signal was locked, and the stubble-covered face of Kurt Austin appeared on the screen.

'Two-way link established,' the tech's voice said over the intercom. 'You can see and hear them, they can see and hear you.'

'Thanks, Oliver,' the Vice President said.

On-screen, Austin straightened. 'Mr Vice President?' he said. 'Didn't expect to see you on this call.'

'Would you have shaved if you'd known?'

'If they'd loan me something sharper than a butter knife, absolutely.'

Sandecker flashed a smile. 'Not to worry. By the way, the good people of Pickett's Island send you their best. We recently swore them in as United States citizens. They've chosen to keep the island as it is, for the most part, with one notable exception. They've renamed the cove where they found you. It's now called Austin's Bay.'

'Sounds terrific,' Kurt said. 'Hope I live to see it again.'

Pitt spoke next. 'You've been on vacation for less than a week, Kurt. So far, you've managed to destroy a world-famous landmark, get yourself and Joe Zavala tangled up in a matter of Australian national security, and, apparently, land yourselves in the hospital. I'm starting to worry about your definition of recreation.'

'I shouldn't have involved Joe,' Kurt admitted.

'Probably shouldn't have involved yourself,' Pitt corrected. 'On the other hand, you've saved lives. That has a tendency to even things up.'

Kurt nodded. 'In case it hasn't totally balanced out, the head of the ASIO's counterterrorism unit has asked for some additional assistance.'

Kurt went on to explain the events of the past two days, the existing situation and the perceived threat. He finished up by describing what he knew about zero-point energy and laying out Bradshaw's request.

As Pitt listened, he found the story almost too incredible to believe, but he'd learned long ago that ignoring what seemed impossible usually meant dealing with it face-to-face at some later date. He noticed Sandecker, sitting tight-lipped and appearing less surprised by what Kurt was saying.

'The immediate danger affects Australia,' Kurt finished. 'But according to Bradshaw, Thero's letter indicates that Australia will suffer first and that other countries will feel his wrath in the future.'

'So you want to search for him,' Pitt said. 'Any idea where to look?'

'Based on the contraband mining equipment and some other facts, the ASIO believes the next phase of Thero's work would be conducted offshore, either at a submerged facility or on the Antarctic shelf.'

Pitt nodded thoughtfully. 'That's an awful lot of space. You're talking hundreds of thousands of square miles. We have to find some way to narrow down the search area.'

'According to Bradshaw, Ms Anderson's been working on some type of detector,' Kurt said. 'She believes the initial earthquake was caused by the prototype device in the flooded mine, but that the larger device Thero is building will require several calibration tests before he can use it at full strength. Those tests could bring some danger, and cause some havoc, but, if she's right, they'll give us a way to hone in on the weapon site.'

A grunt came from Sandecker's direction. Pitt glanced at his old friend. 'Does that mean something to you, Mr Vice President?'

Sandecker sat back in his seat and began stroking the neatly trimmed Vandyke beard on his chin. After a moment, he sat straight up and leaned forward. His face was fixed, his eyes unblinking. He was the very picture of a commander who made instant and authoritative decisions.

'What I'm about to tell you men is confidential,' he said. 'Top secret, in fact. The NSA has developed a special kind of remote sensing array. It's designed to locate nuclear explosions through the neutrino bursts and gamma rays they produce. The new detectors are far more sensitive than our satellite-based systems when it comes to studying underground nuclear tests and blasts. There are twenty-four of them located at various military bases around the world. For reasons unknown, several of them received an anomalous signal at 0735 GMT a month ago, immediately prior to the earthquake in Australia.'

'Which stations?' Pitt asked.

'Cape Town, Alice Springs and Diego Garcia, with the strongest signal coming in at Alice Springs.'

'Can we get access to that data?' Pitt asked.

'I'll make sure of it,' Sandecker replied.

'It sounds like it could be connected,' Kurt said. 'Might help us narrow down the search zone.'

Pitt agreed. 'What do you need to take your next step, Kurt?'

'I'll need a few ships,' Kurt said, 'as many as you can spare. We'd like to set up a picket line and listen for anything louder than a peep. And I'll need some technical help. Paul and Gamay Trout should fit the bill, if you can pull them in. Also, I'm forwarding a list of high-tech equipment that Ms Anderson has requested. If you can ship it to Perth, that would be great. We'll arrive there in a couple of days.'

'A couple of days?' Pitt repeated. 'Perth is no more than three hours from Alice Springs by air.'

'I know,' Kurt said, 'but we're not traveling by air. Joe and I have to escort Ms Anderson. And she's deathly afraid of flying. So, apparently, we'll be traveling by train.'

Pitt would have preferred to send a jet for them, but it would take several days to get the ships and equipment in place anyway. 'Understood,' he said. 'Plan on shoving off the minute you arrive at the dock.'

'We'll be ready,' Kurt said.

He signed off, and Dirk Pitt considered the task ahead of them. Pinpointing an experiment in the vast expanse of the Great Southern Ocean would not be an easy task even for a small fleet of high-tech vessels.

He turned back to Sandecker. 'Do these neutrino detectors of yours have a directional-sensing component?'

'To some extent,' Sandecker admitted, 'but not in a pinpoint-accurate kind of way, if that's what you're getting at.'

Pitt's gears were turning. 'Any chance we could have them tuned to look for these waves? In case our friends do exactly what Kurt is suggesting but that this sensor Kurt's scientist friend is building doesn't pick them up?'

'What are you thinking?'

'Even if it's a vague directional vector, three stations receiving a signal means we should be able to cross-reference and triangulate. That'll help us narrow down the target zone.'

Sandecker grinned. 'I'll see what I can do.'

15

NUMA vessel Gemini
Indian Ocean, 140 miles due west of Christmas Island

The NUMA vessel *Gemini* was a rakishly designed, hundred-and-fifty-foot vessel. In profile, she looked like a bulked-up yacht, thicker and heavier, designed to carry instruments and ROVs and a crew of scientists packed into tiny cabins.

At the moment, *Gemini* was moving due west, as the crew tested a new type of sonar designed to penetrate the seafloor.

With a walkie-talkie in his hand, Paul Trout moved to the very front of the forward deck. He leaned over the railing and gazed downward. Just aft of where the ship's bow met the water, an eleven-foot triangular flange stuck out from the side of the hull. This protrusion, along with an identical one on the port side, gave the ship's bow an odd shape, like the head of a stingray, and the crew had nicknamed it the Skate.

Perhaps it was appropriate. Like her namesake, the Skate was designed to scan the seafloor far below, searching for things hidden beneath eons of piled-up sediment.

It was expected to be a huge leap forward in the hunt for and development of underwater resources. But first, it had to work, which, so far, had proven hit or miss.

Paul pressed the talk switch on the radio. 'Flange folded down and locked in place. The hookup bars are secured, the alignment indicators are matched up. The Skate is visually in the correct location.'

'Okay, Paul,' a female voice said over the radio. *'We're still getting an odd signal on the processor.'*

The female voice belonged to Gamay Trout, Paul's wife. She was in *Gemini*'s information center, monitoring the data stream from the Skate's bell-like housing.

Paul preferred to be out on the deck, partly because the information center was cramped and tight and he was six feet eight inches tall, but also because the idea of signing up for a mission at sea and spending most of it in a darkened room surrounded by computers struck him as the height of absurdity.

'Do you see any dolphins?' Gamay asked.

'Dolphins?'

'During a test run, there were dolphins bow-riding with us; they seemed very interested in the Skate. They kept blasting it with their sonar. It was a similar kind of staccato display.'

Paul hadn't heard that one before. He checked both sides of the ship. 'No dolphins, no pilot whales.'

A long pause followed. Paul figured Gamay was running through a diagnostic protocol or something. He took the time to stretch out and marvel at the blue sky, the fresh breeze and the warm sun.

After more silence, he decided to risk prodding her. 'Everything okay?'

There was no answer, and Paul imagined the computers crashing and all manner of swearing going on in the control room. For the moment, he was doubly glad not to be down there.

He turned as a figure appeared outside the *Gemini*'s bridge and descended the stairs toward the main deck.

Paul smiled at Gamay as she approached. At five foot ten, she was relatively tall for a woman, but her proportions were such that she looked neither thin nor reedy the way many tall women do. Glamorous when she needed to be, for now she was dressed like the rest of the crew, in khaki pants and a NUMA polo shirt. Her dark red hair was pulled sleekly back in a ponytail and tucked beneath a NUMA cap that read GEMINI in gold letters. She flashed a smile at him, and her blue eyes sparkled with a mischievous quality.

'Decide to join me for a stroll?' he said, a New Hampshire accent detectable in his voice.

'Actually,' she said, 'I came to tell you the bad news. We have to pull up stakes and head south.'

'South? Why? I'm sure you can get the Skate back online.'

'It's not the Skate,' she said. 'We have new orders.'

Paul sensed the ship beginning a turn to port. 'Not wasting any time.'

'Dirk wants us to go help Kurt and Joe with what he called a critical project.'

'Last I heard, Kurt and Joe were on vacation,' Paul reminded her. 'Does this project involve bail money or sneaking them out of the country somehow?'

'You know Dirk,' she said, looping an arm around Paul's waist. 'He's a man of few words. Said we'd be given more details when we arrived on-station.'

Now Paul became deeply suspicious. In addition to Gamay's words, he could feel the *Gemini* picking up speed.

'Where exactly are we going?'

Gamay shook her head. 'All I know is, Dirk told me we'd better break out the cold-weather gear.'

'So that's why you're out here,' Paul said.

'Figured I'd better enjoy the sun while I can.'

Paul and Gamay often worked closely with Kurt and Joe. And, in most of those cases, once the ride picked up speed, they got more than they'd bargained for. If the pattern held, the next day or two would probably be their last chance to relax for quite a while.

'How about that stroll?' Paul asked.

'Don't mind if I do,' Gamay replied.

16

Eastern Siberia, 1700 hours

Mist fell on the grassy steppes of the Kamchatka Plain. The mottled gray sky obscured the mountain peaks and threatened rain.

'Pull!'

With that shout, the gates of several cages were opened. The flutter of wings burst forth.

Three shots rang out. Three birds, fleeing in different directions, fell in rapid succession, feathers exploding outward like dust.

Standing in the middle of the carnage, Anton Gregorovich pumped another shell into the shotgun's breach. Three shots, three hits.

Grinning at his own prowess, he placed the weapon down and glanced at his two assistants, teenage boys who crouched by a circle of cages. 'How many left?'

'Four,' one of the boys said.

'All of them, this time,' Gregorovich demanded.

The boys nodded and rigged the cages. Gray-winged birds jumped nervously in the traps.

Gregorovich stood calmly. He lowered his head and closed his eyes, listening for the sound of flight.

Six foot two, two hundred and forty-five pounds, Gregorovich wore fatigue pants in an Arctic-camouflage pattern and no shirt at all, despite temperatures barely out of the thirties. His muscular body was no more than one per cent fat. He subsisted on a diet of almost pure protein, engineered supplements and nutrient cocktails developed by the Russian Olympic Team. Standing motionless, he looked like a statue, like some sculptor's version of the ideal man carved from a block of stone.

In many ways, he was more fit than any athlete since his regimen included steroids and human growth hormones and other factors banned by the athletic associations of the world.

It was only fair. In his world, the consequences of failure were not represented by second-place medals or dismissal from an event. If Gregorovich faltered, he died.

'Whenever you're ready,' he said quietly.

Silence for a moment. He could sense the boys creeping into position, moving the cages quietly, unwilling to give anything away. He appreciated that they wanted to test him. He kept his eyes closed, his heart rate steady and his mind clear. Seconds ticked by, followed by the sudden bang of the cage doors opening.

Gregorovich snapped his head up and opened his eyes. In an instant, he'd fixed on the birds, once again flying in different directions. He yanked a pair of Makarov pistols from holsters on his hips like those of a gunslinger from the Old American West.

He spun to the right with a gun in each hand and pulled both triggers. The two pigeons on that side went down simultaneously.

He twisted to the left, spotted the third target, flying low. He took aim with his right hand and fired twice. The pigeon dropped into the long grass. The fourth was fifty yards off by now.

Gregorovich fired both guns at it, clipping a wing. The bird fell in a spiral, like a World War Two aircraft that had been shot down. It hit the ground before he could fire again and finish it for certain.

'Damn it!'

The boys glanced at him nervously, still crouched as low as they could get. He could see fear in their eyes. Before he could reassure them, a new sound reached out across the tundra: a helicopter coming toward them.

Gregorovich turned and saw one of the monstrous Mi-24 models, lumbering beneath the overcast sky. A phalanx of missile pods and multibarreled cannon were displayed on pods beneath its stubby wings. Its six-bladed rotor churned overhead in a great and constant whirl.

The helicopter dropped lower and lower, slowing as it approached and then hovering. Finally, it touched down on the grass fifty yards away. Before the engines even reached idle, a side door had been thrown open and a man in a heavy overcoat had climbed out and begun hiking toward Gregorovich.

Even from this distance, Gregorovich recognized him: Dmitry Yevchenko, one of Russia's oil billionaires.

With the fall of the Soviet Union, Yevchenko had joined the scramble for wealth, transforming a dying Siberian oil field into a Eurasian empire of sorts. Like many of the new billionaires, Yevchenko had been ruthless on his way to the top. But, unlike most, he'd seen the need to change when the writing appeared on the wall.

His corporation now filled the coffers of Communist Party stalwarts. He hired their friends and family members. He ignored the graft and theft he had to deal with, considering these things another form of taxation and calculating them into his business plan as a separate line item.

But the past was hard to hide, it did not vanish just because Yevchenko wanted it to. A few months back, a reporter had begun probing for the truth, getting fairly close to some answers, before dying suddenly in a plane crash. An overzealous politician who'd asked for too much met a different fate: drowning in the Black Sea.

It wasn't by chance that Yevchenko was called the Siberian Butcher; the bodies of his enemies lay everywhere. But the name itself was a misnomer. Yevchenko had never killed anyone. Gregorovich had always done it for him.

'Take the horses,' Gregorovich said to the boys. 'I'll meet you back in the village.'

The boys did as they were ordered, disappearing as Yevchenko approached.

'Playing with children these days, Gregorovich?'

Yevchenko had always been portly, now he looked rotund, even beneath the heavy coat. Apparently, he'd been eating well in Moscow.

'Boys from the village,' Gregorovich replied. 'Their mother is appealing to me, and they have nothing better to do.'

'I see,' Yevchenko said. 'And do you?'

Gregorovich pulled a gray shirt over his head. 'What are you bothering me for?'

'I've been at an emergency meeting with members of the party,' Yevchenko explained.

'Are they trying to take control?'

'No, nothing like that. They have learned that what's good for us is good for Russia.'

'Then why do you look as if you've seen a ghost?'

'Because I have.'

Yevchenko's hands were stuffed deep into his pockets, the collar of his coat was pulled up high. It was mid-March, and he was freezing. The Siberian Butcher had gone soft. 'Why don't you come to it, my friend?' Gregorovich said to him.

'What do we fear?' Yevchenko asked rhetorically. 'Either the failure to get what we desire or the loss of that which we have. Our business, our economy, our nation's very existence, is linked primarily to one thing and one thing only: energy. Coal, oil, natural gas. We're now the world's largest producer of crude, outstripping the Saudis for the past two years. For a decade, we've been the largest producer of natural gas, and we possess the most extensive reserves of coal on the planet. These are the resources that will sustain us. We will sell them to power-hungry China, India, Europe for ever-increasing prices. It is nothing less than our life's blood. But now we face a threat that could take it away in the blink of an eye.'

Gregorovich picked up the shotgun and began walking, more interested in finding the wounded bird than continuing this conversation. Unfortunately, Yevchenko followed him.

'Five years ago, I sent you on a mission,' Yevchenko explained. 'The Japanese were developing a way to extract energy from the air around us. They were planning a fleet of purely electric cars, a national grid that did not require power plants of oil, coal or natural gas. And they were greedily looking forward to exporting the technology to the rest of the world, gaining more wealth for themselves and slamming the door of poverty in our faces yet again.'

'The Yagishiri experiments.'

'So you remember.'

'Of course I remember,' Gregorovich snapped. 'I destroyed the laboratory and killed the scientists.'

Yevchenko raised an eyebrow. 'Are you sure?'

Gregorovich was looking in the grass for the pigeon. He found feathers and a trail of blood. 'What are you suggesting?'

'Much like this wounded pigeon,' Yevchenko said, 'it seems you did not obliterate the threat as completely as you claimed.'

Gregorovich stopped his search and turned toward Yevchenko. 'The lab was annihilated. We used enough explosives to bring down a city block. The thermite burned everything to cinders. All record of what they were attempting was destroyed. And, before that, I shot every one of those poor bastards myself.'

'Someone survived.'

'Impossible.'

'The experiments have begun again,' Yevchenko explained, 'in secret.'

Gregorovich looked away, taking a deep breath of the pure Siberian air. He figured there was a less sinister explanation.

'You knew we were merely delaying the inevitable,' he said. 'If this scientific theory is valid, eventually someone else will stumble on to it and complete the work. Even if this theory proves false, change will come from another avenue. One day, there will be a solar panel that is one hundred per cent efficient or a way to economically harvest energy from the tides or the waves or the wind. When that happens, there will be no more need for the Gazproms, Aramcos or Exxons of this world.'

'Yes, of course!' Yevchenko shouted. 'But let it happen a hundred years from now. We've spent a hundred billion dollars over the last three years, buying up new reserves of oil and natural gas. Huge portions of the government budget have gone into infrastructure for our industry. We cannot have those investments wasted. Not now, not at this juncture.'

Gregorovich went back to his search, pressing down the long grass with his boots, following the trail of blood. 'Even if the Japanese develop this system, it will take decades to build out the infrastructure,' he said. 'Decades more to change the world.'

'No,' Yevchenko said. 'When the change comes, it comes suddenly. Ten years ago, cell phones were the gadgets of the rich. Now they blanket the Earth. The trillion dollars spent on landlines for the world's phone companies are fast approaching worthlessness.'

Gregorovich still hadn't found the pigeon. He paused to focus on his old mentor once more. 'Not like you to show fear, my friend. Perhaps you've lived in the comfort of Moscow's bosom for too long.'

'No need for jealousy, you could have joined me.'

'And live in fear like you?' Gregorovich shook his head. 'You're screaming bloody murder over a pipe dream and a long-shot possibility. That doesn't add up to me. What is it that really scares you?'

Yevchenko seemed to shiver a little more. He hesitated and then finally spoke. 'I've received a threat. It claims we will suffer for what we did. It comes from Thero himself. It includes details only someone who was there would know. It promises that the martyrs of

Yagishiri will be avenged, that their blood will be repaid a millionfold. What once was designed for peace will now be used for war.'

Gregorovich considered this. He couldn't imagine anyone surviving the explosions and fire he'd caused. The lab had been turned into a smoking crater two hundred feet wide. The fire had burned so hot that Gregorovich and another commando had been singed from a long distance away. 'Someone is using his name to scare you.'

'Perhaps,' Yevchenko agreed. 'But, either way, they must be stopped. And the technology destroyed once and for all.'

Gregorovich paused, wondering who might be perpetrating this hoax. 'As I recall, there was a woman, an Australian. She was a colleague of Thero's, a friend of his son and daughter. She denounced the work as a waste of time, and remained in Australia when Thero and his team went to Japan.'

Yevchenko nodded. 'We put tabs on her already, she's not the cause. But she's a danger to us nonetheless, especially now that she's working with the Americans.'

'How did they get involved in your little mess?'

'There was an incident in Australia,' Yevchenko said. 'The woman you spoke of was rescued by an American from their National Underwater and Marine Agency. We believe they're also looking for Thero. Two of their ships have just been diverted toward Perth, a third toward Sydney.'

Gregorovich had heard of NUMA. Though their work was civilian in nature and their staff mostly scientists and environmental do-gooders, some in Russia were convinced that it was an offshoot of the NSA. Gregorovich doubted this. But even he had to admit they ended up in more scrapes than the Central Intelligence Agency.

'Why NUMA?'

Yevchenko shrugged. 'No one knows. But, most likely, they intend to steal whatever they discover and develop it for America. As I'm sure you can understand, such an outcome is completely and categorically unacceptable.'

Perhaps this was what Yevchenko and the party leaders feared the most. 'You should have listened to me the first time,' Gregorovich said. 'I would have brought Thero and the other scientists to you. This would have been your prize to exploit.'

'All we want is the status quo,' Yevchenko explained. 'It was your job to ensure that. As far as the party is concerned, *it still is*.'

Yevchenko's gaze was harsh, his voice firm and bitter. Apparently, there was a little fire left in his soul after all, at least on this subject.

'What are you saying?'

'You must find Thero or this imposter and destroy him. You must erase from existence all record of their research, all evidence of their efforts. And you must not leave any loose strings to haunt us this time.'

He understood the context. This was not a request. 'I did not fail.'

'Something slipped through your grasp.'

Gregorovich fumed at the insinuation. There had to be another explanation. It seemed he would have to find that explanation himself. 'If you want to stop Thero, you'll have to locate him first. The woman is the key. That's undoubtedly why the Americans and Australians are using her.'

'What do you suggest?'

'You have men watching her?'

Yevchenko nodded.

'Have them capture her and bring her to whatever command post you're setting up for me,' Gregorovich suggested.

'We have a ship awaiting your arrival. A team of commandos were flown to it yesterday. They have no knowledge of the situation but will follow your orders.'

'I'd rather hire my own,' Gregorovich said.

'No,' Yevchenko said.

Gregorovich turned away, noticing movement in the long grass ahead of him. The pigeon he'd wounded was there, trying desperately to drag its damaged body through the pasture. For a moment, he thought of blasting it with the shotgun. But it no longer mattered to him. He had a new quarry to hunt now.

Yevchenko saw it as well, stepping forward.

'Leave it,' Gregorovich said. 'Let it suffer.'

Yevchenko stepped away. He seemed half pleased and half apprehensive. 'You're a very cold man, Anton Gregorovich. This is why we choose you. Do not fail us again or the suffering will be yours.'

17

Jakarta, Indonesia, 0540 hours

The sun rose over Tanjung Priok Harbor shrouded in a blanket of haze. It lit up a thicket of cranes and booms sprouting from an endless line of ships and the lengthy concrete piers. Only seven degrees south of the equator, and a recipient of constant humidity from the Java Sea, the harbor was a sweatbox even at this hour of the morning.

At least that's how it felt to sixty-five-year-old Patrick Devlin, as he meandered along in the early morning sun.

After forty years at sea, Devlin was approaching retirement. That looming thought, and a long night of drinking, had left him in a reflective mood. What exactly was he retiring to? He had no family, no real friends aside from those he crewed or drank with.

'Can't believe this is the last time I'll see this stinking place,' he said, speaking to an equally exhausted drinking companion, another Irishman named Keane.

'If it was your last night here,' Keane said, 'then you did it up right, Padi. In true Irish fashion . . . you drank everyone under the table. And left them with the tab.'

Despite Indonesia's Muslim status, there were plenty of places to drink in the city of Jakarta. A good thing too, because the harbor had become so busy that ships often anchored for days waiting their turn to load and unload. Traffic in the port had doubled threefold in the past decade. Despite frantic levels of construction, the harbor could not keep up.

'Think about it,' Keane added. 'Back home, you'll never wake with dust caking your throat and sweat dripping from your face.' Keane almost tripped but regained his balance. 'And none of these damned blaring speakers, waking the dead in the morning like air-raid sirens.'

The call of the muezzins from the mosques in Jakarta was known to be exceedingly loud and to ring out at an exceedingly early hour. Only recently had the time for their song been moved from 3 a.m. to the somewhat more reasonable hour of four thirty.

Still too damned early, Devlin thought. But, in some ways, he'd miss even that, such was the lure of exotic lands.

'Always thought I'd make captain,' he said.

'And give up all this?' Keane asked, slurring every word.

Devlin laughed. He'd longed to be a captain and ship's master for most of his life, but an event several years back had made him wonder if he wanted the responsibility. It had also set his drinking on a dangerous course. Captains didn't tie one on with their crews, they drank alone in their cabins. And they were often forced to make harsh decisions, the kind that haunted Devlin as it was.

'Not on your life,' Devlin said with false bravado. He threw an arm around Keane's neck in a move that was half headlock and half hug.

The two men were laughing as they reached the motor launch they'd brought from their ship: a freighter loaded with rolls of copper, anchored offshore in the never-ending queue.

As they climbed into the small runabout, Devlin stepped to the controls. Keane, on the other hand, found himself a comfortable spot to lie down, stretching out across a trio of seats and pulling an orange life vest under his head for use as a pillow. Before Devlin had even cleared the bowlines, Keane was passed out and snoring loudly.

'That's right,' Devlin mumbled, 'you sleep. I'll do all the work as usual.'

He cast off the bowlines and then fired up the small boat's engine. A moment later, he was picking his way across the crowded harbor.

Small boats moved here and there. A pair of tugs worked to drag a monstrous bulk carrier out into the channel, while crewmen, painting and scraping and fighting the endless battle against rust and corrosion, scampered over other vessels like crabs on the rocks.

Devlin guided the launch past all this and out into the anchorage. He kept a fair course, moving slowly past the waiting ships, until a particular vessel caught his eye.

Slowing the launch just a bit, Devlin stared at a black-hulled vessel with a dark gray superstructure. It looked vaguely familiar, like a small cruise liner, though the dark paint was neither festive nor striking. The more he studied the ship, the odder her appearance was to him. She didn't seem to carry any lifeboats, radar masts, or even antennas. In fact, she carried none of the normal appendages that sprout from modern ships.

In his inebriated state, Devlin struggled to make sense of it. He saw no one on deck and no sign of activity. The ship itself reminded him of a derelict, stripped for parts. Her black-gray color was like that of charred steal, but the coating wasn't soot, she'd been deliberately tinted that way.

Subconsciously, Devlin angled the launch toward her, moving closer and then coming around the bow. There he spotted something new, something unmistakable.

'It can't be,' he said out loud.

In front of him lay the overlapped plating of a hasty repair job. Plates of different thickness and consistency had been welded and riveted into place to cover a breach in the hull. The heavy black paint covered it all, but the jagged, H-like shape of the repair was unmistakable.

He shouted to Keane. 'Wake up,' he said, 'you have to see this.'

Keane grunted something and rolled over.

'Keane?!'

No response. Devlin gave up on him and turned back to the ship. He was wide awake now.

'You're a bloody ghost,' he whispered, edging closer to the black hulk. 'A bloody ghost or a bloody trick.'

He was still muttering various curses of disbelief when the launch bumped up against the ship. He reached out and touched her. There was an odd, almost rubbery feel to the paint. But the ship itself was real enough.

A sense of uncontrollable anger began to well up inside Devlin, a dark Irish rage. Years of guilt and self-hatred fueled it. Someone was tricking him, or had tricked him years ago.

He passed around the bow and headed for the stern. A gangway sat in the lowered position, resting diagonally across the aft end of the ship. Its bottom step was eight feet above the harbor's oily waters. Devlin pulled up next to it.

He cut the throttle and lazily tied a line to the sloping stairs. He didn't bother with Keane and instead climbed on to the launch's roof. From there, he clambered awkwardly up on to the gangway.

It shook with his weight and banged against the hull, but it held. Despite the racket, no one appeared to welcome him aboard or shoo him away.

Devlin began to climb. He moved slowly at first on shaky legs, and then faster as he became more certain of the truth. 'I saw you go down!' he shouted at the ship. 'I saw you bloody well go down!'

He stumbled as he neared the top and sprawled out on the last few steps, breathless and almost weeping. He could see raised letters on the stern. They were hidden beneath the rubbery black paint, but they hadn't been scraped off before the new paint was slapped over the top.

He ran his hand across the letters he could reach. They were real, just like the ship itself.

Pacific Voyager.

Like a man caught in the surf, Devlin was bowled over by waves of emotion. Confusion, sadness and elation hit him almost simultaneously, one after another. *How could the ship be here? Had someone salvaged her? Last he knew, the wreck hadn't even been located.*

He sat there, sobbing like a child and hoping he wasn't in the middle of a dream, until the sound of footsteps came from above. The squeak of a gate followed as a section of the rail was pulled back where the gangway met the main deck.

Devlin looked up as a man appeared. The face was bearded now but familiar to him. An odd moment passed as two sets of eyes tried to connect what they saw to distant, faded memories.

The bearded man won the race. A sad smile crept over him. 'Hello, Padi,' he said in a kind and melancholy way.

'Janko?' Devlin said. 'You're alive? But you went down with this ship.'

The bearded man offered a hand and helped Devlin

to his feet, bringing him aboard and steadying the inebriated old sailor as he stood on the main deck.

'I wish you hadn't found us,' Janko said.

'Us?'

'I'm sorry, Padi.'

With that, Janko shoved a handheld device into Devlin's ribs. The blow stunned the old sailor, but the massive shock that followed did more damage. Devlin convulsed as he fell backward. He was unconscious by the time he hit the deck.

A watertight hatchway opened behind Janko, and two other men came running out.

'Is everything all right?' one of them asked.

Janko nodded and slipped the device back into his pocket. 'Check the launch.'

One of the men raced down the stairs. The other glanced at Devlin, lying still on the deck. 'How the hell did he know who you were?'

'He was the chief on the tug I signed on to,' Janko explained. 'The one who cut us loose in the storm. From the look of it, he's been beating himself up ever since.'

'What should we do with him?'

'Take him below,' Janko said. 'Bodies bring attention. Disappearance is more easily explained. Especially that of a drunk.'

A shout came up to them from the launch below. 'There's another man in the boat. He's passed out cold.'

'He must have been unconscious when they got

here,' Janko thought aloud. 'Doubt he'll remember a thing. Untie the launch and let it drift. By the time he wakes up, he'll think this one went overboard. Another sad accident at sea.'

The man below untied the launch and shoved it off before coming back up the stairs.

'We need to get under way,' Janko said as the two men picked Devlin up and carried him toward the hatch.

'And then what?' the first crewman asked. 'What do we do with him when he wakes up?'

'We show him what became of the ship he lost,' Janko explained. 'And then we toss him in the pit, along with the crew from those Korean freighters. He can dig for Thero's diamonds like all the rest.'

18

Australian outback, just south of Alice Springs

The *Ghan* raced through the desert like a great metal snake: twenty shimmering passenger cars pulled by a pair of matching diesels in a brick-red paint scheme.

Named in reverence to Afghan explorers who helped map Australia's desolate interior and adorned with a camel logo, the *Afghan Express* traveled a route that stretched vertically across the continent, from Darwin in the north down to Adelaide on the island's southern coast, pulling into Alice Springs every few days near the halfway point of its journey in each direction.

A four-hour whistle-stop allowed passengers to explore the small town, but, as dusk approached, the train began to fill up once again. Kurt and Hayley boarded shortly before departure.

'Where exactly are we going?' Hayley asked.

Kurt said nothing. He just kept moving forward until he reached the Platinum Car, in which the train's most luxurious accoutrements resided. A steward opened the door to their compartment, revealing a compact lounge, complete with a private bathroom and shower, a small table, and a pair of large plush chairs that folded out into beds at night. The space was tight, like a ship's stateroom, but the modern design and décor made it seem more spacious.

'Pick a side, any side,' Kurt said, 'and then relax and await the gourmet dining to follow.'

Hayley pointed, and Kurt placed her small carry-on beside the chair.

'Are you trying to impress me?' she asked.

'Possibly,' Kurt admitted. 'But mostly I figured you could use a little taking care of after all you've been through. It's not every day someone steps out of their regular life and takes on something like this.'

A soft smile appeared on Hayley's face. She seemed surprised and reassured all at the same time. 'It feels like forever since someone gave a bit of thought to what I might need. Thank you.'

'You're more than welcome,' Kurt said, putting his own pack away as the train eased off the stops and began to move.

An hour later, night was falling. The view through the picture windows of the cabin was that of an indigo sky blending slowly with the matte black of the MacDonnell mountain range. With this for a backdrop, dinner arrived, brought in by a private steward on a rolling cart.

Kurt paid the steward, included a generous tip, and then acted as a combination sommelier and maître d', laying a cloth napkin across Hayley's lap and presenting the wine.

'A 2008 Penngrove Cabernet Sauvignon.'

‘I love a good cabernet,’ Hayley said, her eyes sparkling like a child awaiting a present.

‘I haven’t had this one,’ Kurt said. ‘I’m told it’s very smooth, with a hint of licorice and vanilla.’

He uncorked the bottle and took her glass, pouring it from about ten inches above. ‘A good fall helps the wine to aerate,’ he said. ‘It speeds up the breathing process. But we should still give it a few minutes.’

‘Why not?’ Hayley replied. ‘The poor crushed grapes have been in there for years. Be a shame not to give them a few minutes to soak up the fresh air.’

Kurt poured a glass of his own and set the bottle down.

Next, he lifted the insulating covers from the plates set up before them. An avocado-green-colored soup with dashes of red was first. ‘Pea-and-ham soup, with a hint of garlic.’

‘Looks delicious.’

Pulling the cover off the second scrumptious-looking dish, Kurt continued, ‘Braised short ribs with silver-beet gratin. And the pièce de résistance . . .’ He removed the final lid. ‘Bread-and-butter pudding, soaked in sweetened custard and brandy.’

‘I might just start with that,’ Hayley said. ‘How on earth did you conjure up such fantastic foods on a train out here in the never-never?’

‘Platinum service,’ Kurt said. ‘And, besides, the chef is a personal friend of mine. At least he has been for the last few hours.’

She took a deep breath. 'If this is traveling, perhaps I could get used to it.'

Kurt sat down as Hayley sampled the soup.

'Must say I've never met someone so brave and intelligent who's afraid to travel,' Kurt said.

'I know it's strange,' she said. 'I know all the statistics, how the most dangerous part of any trip is the drive to the airport. I understand aerodynamics, and I spend half my life dreaming about far-off places, but something grips me when I leave home.'

'You seem okay now,' Kurt pointed out.

She smiled. 'Maybe it's the company.'

'Consider me your personal guide and protector wherever we go.'

'Truth is, I'd love to see the world,' she said. 'And the universe. I used to dream about being an astronaut. Seems a little silly, when getting out of Sydney makes me feel like I'm going to be ill.'

'The universe is a big step,' Kurt said. 'Let's start by getting to Perth.'

The *Ghan* would take them south to Port Augusta, where they'd board another of Australia's great trains for the journey west.

For the next twenty minutes, they ate and chatted lightly, enjoying the atmosphere and the gentle motion of the train. Only after they'd had their second helpings of bread pudding did Kurt ask the question that was most on his mind.

'So tell me about zero-point energy,' he said.

She finished the last sip of her cabernet and slid her glass toward him. Kurt filled it halfway and then topped off his own glass.

'Zero-point energy is a relatively simple concept,' she said. 'It's the energy remaining in a system when all that can be drawn from it has been taken out.'

She pointed to the bottle of wine. 'Imagine this bottle is a system or an energy field, and you or I decide to drink from it with a straw.'

'Which we would never do,' Kurt pointed out.

'Not unless we were outrageously desperate,' she replied with a conspiratorial smile. 'But assuming we'd lost all sense of decorum and decided to give it a try, we'd be able to siphon off the energy from it right down to the bottom of the straw. But any wine below the reaches of the straw would remain behind untapped. That wine that can't be reached is the zero-point energy.'

'Unless we found a longer straw,' Kurt said.

'Exactly,' she said, 'except that physics tells us that, at some point, there's no such thing as a longer straw.'

'Can you give me a real example?'

'The classic case is helium,' she said. 'As it's cooled, the molecular activity within the sample begins to slow, and the helium turns from a gas to a liquid. At absolute zero, it should freeze into a solid, and all molecular activity inside it should stop. But no matter how far one lowers the temperature, right down to absolute zero, helium will *never* turn into a solid under normal atmospheric pressure.'

'Meaning?'

'Some energy remains in the system. Some energy that can't be removed.'

'And that's zero-point energy?'

'Exactly,' she said once again.

'So if it can't be removed,' Kurt said, 'what hope is there in accessing it?'

'Well,' she hedged, 'all things are impossible until they're proven otherwise. Theoretically, there are fields of energy all around us sitting at their zero point. The same theory that postulates the existence of such fields suggests it may be possible to *dislodge* this hidden energy the way someone dislodges electrons in a power grid and reaps the benefits of electricity. Only, no one has been able to do it yet.'

It sounded a little like the mythical ether of the old days to Kurt, a substance that was once believed to fill the emptiness between planets and galaxies when scientists of the day couldn't believe there was such a thing as a vacuum.

'Has anyone tried?' Kurt asked. 'Before you and Thero, I mean.'

'A few brave souls,' she said. 'I assume you've heard of Nikola Tesla?'

Kurt nodded.

'Tesla was one of the first,' she said. 'In the 1890s he began developing what he called his Dynamic Theory of Gravity. He tinkered away on it for years until 1937, when he claimed it was finally complete and promised boldly that it would displace Einstein's Theory of Relativity, at least in explaining how gravity works.'

'Don't we know how gravity works?'

'We know *what* gravity does,' she corrected, 'but we don't know *how* it causes what it causes. Tesla believed it was connected to a kind of energy field that existed everywhere, but in some places this field had greater concentrations than others. He also believed that that field could be tapped and the result would be an unlimited energy source, one that would bring peace and prosperity instead of thermo-nuclear explosions and genocide.'

'So you're telling me that zero-point energy and gravity are connected?'

She nodded. 'If Tesla's right – and Einstein and the others are wrong – then, yes, the two are connected in very complex ways.'

Kurt considered this. 'Complex enough to cause what Thero is threatening?'

She seemed to need a second to think about it. 'Tesla spent four decades working on his theory,' she said, 'more than half his life. He made his great announcement, insisting to the world that he'd finally completed the Dynamic Theory of Gravity, that all the details were worked out, and then he never published it. After all that work, he locked it away and never spoke of it again. Despite years of ridicule and the crushing poverty he'd fallen into thanks to the treachery of

Westinghouse and Edison, Tesla took the Dynamic Theory of Gravity to his grave.'

Kurt had never heard this story. 'Has any record of it ever surfaced?'

Hayley shook her head. 'When Tesla died, your government seized all his belongings and papers – despite having no legal reason to do so. They were held for a year or so and then finally released to his family. His work on zero-point energy and the Dynamic Theory of Gravity were not among them.'

Kurt considered what she'd told him. He knew Tesla's reputation as a genius and as a mad scientist of sorts. He also knew Tesla was primarily considered a pacifist. It was fully conceivable that Tesla had destroyed all records of his theory. It was also possible that somewhere in the vast archives of the federal government there lay a file with Tesla's name on it with the missing papers inside. He made a mental note to relay this information to Dirk the next time he checked in.

'The fact is,' Hayley continued, 'we're dealing with a primal force of nature. Many would tell you it's something best left alone.'

'But Thero isn't leaving it alone,' Kurt pointed out. 'So what happens if he makes a breakthrough?'

'If he's successful, a vast output of energy and a side effect of short-lived, extremely powerful gravitational fluctuations.'

'Can you try that in English?' Kurt said.

'The Earth isn't going to be vaporized or anything,'

Hayley said. 'We're not going to start floating out of our chairs like astronauts in zero g.'

'What will we see?'

'The first and most *dramatic* manifestations will be noticed in the seas,' she said.

'The tides,' Kurt said.

'Exactly,' she replied. 'The oceans of the Earth are drawn by the gravitational pull of the moon. The land is pulled on as well, but, unlike the liquid of the ocean it's locked in place except at the fault lines.'

'How much power are we talking about here?'

'If the papers sent to us are valid,' she began, 'potentially more energy than all of humankind has produced and expended since the beginning of the industrial revolution.'

Kurt paused before responding. For the second time in as many days, he found it hard to believe what he was being told.

'How is such a thing possible?'

'The same way it's possible to run a nuclear submarine on a small chunk of uranium for years. Or to obliterate a large city with only twenty pounds of plutonium. There are vast amounts of energy hidden in places the normal human eye can't see.'

'But splitting a continent in half?' Kurt asked. 'I've seen big earthquakes in California. They knock down highways and buildings, but, contrary to popular belief, half the state doesn't float off into the Pacific.'

'No,' she agreed. 'No one is suggesting you're going

to see a divided continent with the ocean in the middle. But Thero is no fool. His first earthquake was a test, probably triggered from the station in the Tasman Mine. We have every reason to believe that that was just a small prototype. He'll hit us harder next time, much harder, and he'll hit us where Mother Nature has already done half the work.'

'What are you talking about?'

'Australia has the beginnings of a rift valley,' she explained. 'Like the Great Rift Valley in Africa. Ours runs from Adelaide northeast toward the Great Barrier Reef. It began to form a hundred and fifty million years ago and then stopped for reasons unknown. The crust is thin and fractured in this section, and the pressure built up by a hundred million years without movement is waiting to be released.

'If Thero can direct his weapon toward this point and create a gravitational distortion that wedges the plate apart even fractions of an inch, the pressure that's been built up over the millennia might be released all at once. We're talking about a series of earthquakes, hundreds even, all in quick succession along the rift. What normally takes ten thousand years might happen in a day, or a week, or even hours. The devastation from that kind of tremor will not be measurable on the Richter scale, or any other scale ever devised. Every city, every town, every village in Australia will be reduced to rubble. Not a single building will remain standing.'

Kurt considered her point quietly. It was a grim scenario.

'I know,' she said, taking his silence for disbelief. 'I'm a silly academic pointing out the worst-case scenario. *The sky is falling – once again.* The thing is, when these scenarios *actually* happen, there's always someone running around, wondering why no one told them it could be this bad. I'm telling you, right here and now, it's going to be horrific.'

Kurt's face was dark. A new thought occurred to him. 'I have to ask why you?'

'I'm not sure what you mean,' she said.

'The informant sent the papers to you,' Kurt clarified. 'Why not send them straight to the authorities?'

Hayley shrugged. 'I can only guess it's because of my background. The claims and calculations would seem like gibberish to someone else. Had the package been sent directly to the ASIO, I can only assume it would have ended up in the wastebin.'

'Okay,' Kurt said, 'but why not some other scientist?'

'It's a very obscure field,' she explained. 'We're a tiny group.'

'Tiny but not infinitesimal,' Kurt said.

'No,' she agreed, 'not infinitesimal.'

'So I have to ask you one more time: if there were other options, why do you think they picked you?'

She paused for a long moment. 'I don't know,' she said finally. The sadness had returned to her voice.

There was a tinge of weariness to it, and a stronger hint of guilt. 'I don't know.'

She looked away, averting her eyes and staring out into the night. And, in that instant, Kurt knew that she was lying.

He considered pressing her for the truth but held back as he felt a subtle change in the train's motion, like the engineer had taken his hand off the throttle.

Hayley looked up. 'Something wrong?'

'Not sure,' Kurt said. He stood just as the brakes went on at full pressure.

The car lurched. Kurt braced himself and caught Hayley's arm, keeping her from falling as the dinner plates and wineglasses flew off the table. The screech of the steel wheels sliding on the rails overrode all other noise as the quarter-mile-long train began skidding to a halt.

Still holding Hayley, Kurt glanced out the window. The train itself was in a turn, on a slight uphill grade. Looking forward, Kurt saw two other passenger cars and the twin diesel engines. Sparks were flying from the wheels as they dug into the track. But something else caught his eye: tiny points of crimson burning in the night, flares along the track bed and, a little farther on, the outline of a tractor trailer stalled across the rail line at a crossing. Two men stood in front of it, waving their arms frantically.

The breaking continued until the *Ghan* lurched awkwardly to a stop a few hundred feet from the crossing.

At this point, Hayley could see the truck as well. 'Lucky we were able to stop,' she said.

Kurt glanced around. 'Somehow, I don't think luck's got anything to do with it.'

Before Hayley could reply, he spotted just what he expected to see: men in ski masks, coming out of the night and headed straight for the motionless train.

19

The masked men came aboard the train at several different points, climbing on to the couplers between cars and forcing the doors.

'What's happening?' Hayley asked in a panicked voice.

'I'll give you one guess.'

Hayley's mind quickly grasped the truth. 'They're after us.'

'Either that or this is a Butch Cassidy reenactment no one told me about.'

Hayley grabbed her cell phone and dialed out in an attempt to call for help. 'I have a signal, but I can't seem to get through.'

'Waste of time,' Kurt said. 'They're probably jamming the tower.'

He glanced outside. Two car lengths down, another man stood out away from the train, scanning back and forth.

'They've got a guy outside,' Kurt said. 'Probably watching for anyone who might make a break for open ground.'

A voice came over the public-address system. It had a bit of an accent, one that Kurt couldn't place immediately. It certainly wasn't the conductor.

'Please remain calm,' it said. *'We have hijacked the train, but we're not interested in harming anyone. We're looking for two people. A man with silver-gray hair, about six feet tall, and a woman about six inches shorter than him, with blond hair. Her name is Anderson. Cooperate with us, and no one will get hurt. Interfere or argue, and you will be beaten or killed.'*

As the announcement ended, Kurt cracked the cabin door a fraction and glanced down the narrow corridor.

He saw two men down the hall, pushing their way into one of the compartments. They were wide-bodied brutes, with thick arms and legs and faces hidden by ski masks. They moved without a hint of elegance or remorse. Kurt pegged them as street thugs hired for money.

A third man trailed behind them. He was thinner and taller. Even with the man's ski mask, Kurt could tell he had a narrow face and sunken eyes. Though not as imposing physically, there was a more menacing air about him. Kurt guessed he was the headman.

A wave of shouting erupted. The sound of a scuffle and someone being thrown around reverberated throughout the railcar. A moment later, a man about Kurt's height was dragged out of the room. Beside him was a young woman. They looked like newlyweds.

The leader examined them. 'No,' he said without emotion, 'not them.' Then he hauled off and punched the defenseless man. 'That's for resisting.'

The man sagged, held up only by the two bandits. Their leader wasn't done. He wound up and kicked the man in the chest, sending him tumbling back into his compartment.

Every instinct in Kurt's body told him to intervene, but the headman was clearly armed, and his two henchmen might have been. Besides, he had one job right now: keep Hayley Anderson safe.

He went to the window again, preparing to smash it. Charging out into the dark and battling one opponent seemed like a better play than a close-quarters fight against three.

He grabbed a chair and raised it over his head. Before he could use it, the door flew open.

'Drop it!' a voice shouted.

Kurt let the chair go, and it clattered to the ground.

He turned around slowly as the intruders measured him up and gave Hayley the once-over.

'I assume you guys are here for the dishes,' Kurt said, pointing to the pile of flatware, cups and glasses on the floor.

The two men looked down, their eyes instinctively drawn in the direction Kurt had pointed. It was an amateur response, but they *were* amateurs, local muscle hired to do someone else's dirty work. In the fraction of a second before they corrected their mistake, Kurt moved. He pivoted on his left foot and fired his right leg toward the closest man's gut.

The heel of his boot hit like a pile driver and knocked the man backward. He crumpled like a folding chair, sucking wind and grabbing his stomach as he hit the ground. The second thug lunged at Kurt, his huge paw-like hands going for Kurt's neck.

Kurt blocked the effort, grabbing the man's wrist and twisting it. Using the attacker's considerable momentum against him, Kurt spun him off balance and body-slammed him to the ground. The man hit the floor with a thud, and Kurt dropped down and hammered him with a forearm smash to the face.

He would have slugged the guy again, but he knew the boss would be coming. He spun to his feet and turned.

It was too late.

The gaunt leader of the crew was already there with a black pistol in hand, holding it sideways, gangster style. He studied Hayley, nodded approvingly, and then turned back to Kurt.

'I don't need you,' he said.

Kurt dove to the right as the man fired mercilessly. The first shell missed, the second grazed Kurt's arm. The third bullet shattered the window behind him. Before the would-be killer could trigger a fourth shot, a different sound rang out. It was a sickly thud, like the sound of a broken-bat single being hit in a baseball game.

The gunman's head snapped forward, and the pistol flew from his hand. He fell into the cabin, hitting the table and splaying on the ground like a marionette whose strings had been cut.

Behind him, Joe Zavala stood in the doorway with a piece of cabinetry in his hands.

Kurt snatched up the black pistol. 'Way to make an entrance.'

Joe grinned. 'What I do, I like to do in style.'

The leader was out cold, the other two assailants were moving but not interested in any more combat. They hadn't expected to take a beating, and now that they were outnumbered and outgunned, they seemed more interested in surrender.

Kurt pulled the mask off the leader. 'Anyone recognize this face?'

Joe shook his head, Hayley did likewise. 'Never seen him before,' she said.

'I figure they're not our friends from the flooded mine,' Kurt replied.

'What makes you say that?'

'The fact that we're still conscious,' he said.

A radio began to squawk in the downed leader's pocket. *'What's the delay? We heard shooting. Do you need assistance?'*

This time, Kurt thought he recognized the accent. 'Russians?'

'That's what it sounded like to me,' Joe said.

'What are they doing mixed up in this?'

'No idea,' Joe said. 'But I saw another group of them heading to the back, where the caboose would be if this train had one.'

'And at least two more outside,' Kurt said.

Kurt aimed the pistol at the man with the busted face. 'How many friends did you bring to this party?'

The man answered slowly. 'Eight or nine in the truck. I didn't count 'em.'

Kurt pointed to the Russian. 'How many like him, the guys who did the hiring?'

'There were four of them.'

Kurt looked up. 'That means at least three more with guns.'

'And plenty of muscle to do the heavy lifting,' Joe added.

'We have to get out of here,' Hayley said.

Joe nodded. 'The lady *is* a rocket scientist. We should probably listen to her.'

Kurt couldn't have agreed more, but how and to where? Going on foot into the outback wasn't going to get them very far.

The radio squawked again. *'Victor, respond. What's happening?'*

Kurt grabbed the radio and pressed the talk switch. 'Victor's not available right now, mostly because he's taking an unintended nap. But please stand by, your call is important to us.'

'What are you doing?' Hayley asked, her eyes all but bugging out of her head. 'Now they know we're here.'

'They already know we're here,' Kurt said. 'Thanks to Joe, we took the first round. Time to go on the offensive, at least enough to throw a little doubt into their minds.'

The radio crackled. *'Screw with us, and you're going to regret it,'* the voice growled.

'We'll see about that,' Kurt replied. 'Just so you know,

I have your friend Victor's gun, and, unlike him, I don't miss what I shoot at.'

Kurt figured that would give them something to worry about. He stepped outside and checked the corridor. Seeing it was clear, he motioned for Joe and Hayley to follow.

He figured the group that went to the back of the train was now headed forward at double speed. He had a plan to slow them down. Making a few threats was the first step, finding the breaker panel at the front of the car was the second. He flipped it open just as the radio came to life again.

'Leave the woman, and you get to live.'

Kurt put his hand to the car's master switch and spoke into the radio once more. 'You want her,' he said, 'then come and get her.'

With that, he flipped the switch, cutting power and plunging the fifty-foot car into darkness. A wave of muffled shouts came from the passengers.

Kurt ignored them and continued to the forward door, not hesitating for even a second. He pulled the door open and stepped through. Joe and Hayley followed. And all three stood in the gap between the cars out on the coupler.

'I hope you have a plan,' Joe said.

'Don't I always?'

'I'm not sure you want me to answer that right now.'

Kurt studied the metal plating that covered the knuckle-shaped coupler below them. Next, he looked up, glancing through the dusty window into the railcar ahead of them.

It was an observation car. Warmly lit, half full. The passengers inside were hunkered down in various places, hands on their heads, too scared to move. At the far end, he saw two more of the hijackers.

'Check the sides.'

Joe and Hayley peaked around the edges of the car, looking backward.

'Our friend is still out there,' Hayley said. 'He's got a partner now. They seem to be ambling this way.'

'There's a guy on this side too,' Joe said, 'also coming forward. Probably moving in lockstep with the men inside.'

'Which means my plan is mostly working.'

Joe's eyebrows went up. '*Mostly* working? We're almost surrounded.'

'Exactly,' Kurt said.

Joe looked confused. 'I'm not sure I want to know what total success looks like.'

'Complete encirclement,' Kurt explained. He glanced forward into the lighted Pullman car once again. 'Finally,' he whispered, 'a couple of heavies, coming this way.'

The approaching thugs moved slowly, checking each row of seats to make sure Kurt and Hayley weren't among the passengers in the car.

'Congratulations,' Joe whispered. 'You've now graduated from the General Custer School of Tactical Brilliance.'

Kurt smiled, reached over, and gently opened a trapdoor in the floor plating. The gravel and railroad ties of the railbed could be seen through the opening. 'If Custer knew what I did, he'd have tunneled under Sitting Bull and popped up behind him. Crawl forward, quick and quiet.'

'And then what?'

'And then we hijack the train. Or *rehijack* it, I should say.'

'Hijack the hijackers?' Joe said. 'Now you're talking my language.'

Joe went down first, Hayley followed. Kurt squeezed his way through behind them, gently lowering the metal plate once he'd climbed down. He'd only crawled a foot or two when the door opened above him.

He held still as heavy footfalls scuffed and clunked on the decking.

The thugs were hesitating, either waiting for directions or a signal to make a coordinated attack.

'We're in position,' a voice said.

Kurt's hand went to the radio to cover it, but no sound came forth. The hijackers had switched channels to keep him from hearing their plans.

'Move in,' a tinny voice replied. *'And make it fast. We're running out of time.'*

Through a narrow gap in the plating Kurt saw the door to the darkened railcar open and watched as the men entered. As soon as they did, Kurt began to move, scrambling forward on his forearms and knees, moving like a lizard on its belly. There were twenty-four inches of clearance between the axles of the cars and the track bed. It wasn't much headroom, but enough to make the escape work.

Enveloped by the smell of oil, dust and creosote, as the sharp edges of the gravel stones dug into his knees and elbows, Kurt moved with all possible haste.

He worried mostly that the men on the ground would spot him, but he needn't have been concerned. The light spilling from the other railcars was bright enough to affect their night vision. From their vantage point, looking into the dark space beneath the train was like gazing into a black hole.

Kurt made it past the two bogies on which the Pullman-type car's wheels rested, continued forward under the next car, and caught up to Joe and Hayley. She was struggling.

'Not exactly enjoying this part of the trip,' she said.

'At least you fit under here,' Kurt said. 'This is a little tight for me. And considering the size of Joe's head, I'm not sure how he's avoided knocking himself out yet.'

Joe chuckled. They kept going and quickly reached the aft of the two diesel engines.

'Afraid we've run into a roadblock,' Joe said.

Kurt looked past them. There was much less clearance under the engine than under the passenger cars.

'These modern engines have the electric motors down on the wheels,' Joe explained, pointing. 'The gearing too. Not to mention the fuel tank in the middle, and probably a cowcatcher up front.'

'You sure we can't squeeze by?'

'Not a chance.'

Kurt frowned. If they couldn't go under, they would have to go over or around. 'If you were a hijacker in a locomotive, what would you be watching?'

'The engineer,' Joe said.

Kurt's eyebrows went up. 'My thoughts exactly.'

'What are you going to do?' Hayley asked.

Kurt glanced out behind them. The guards on foot still had their attention on the passenger car, but not for long. Due to the way the train had stopped on the curve, there was more space on one side than the other.

'We're going to break in and surprise whoever's in the lead engine. Hopefully, without having to do any shooting.'

Kurt eyed the foot patrol once more. As they turned toward the tail end of the train, he climbed out from under the passenger car and sprinted forward in the dark. He reached the lead engine and went up the ladder on to the catwalk, or sill, that ran the length of the engine like a running board on an old car.

Joe came up behind him, and Hayley followed quickly as well.

They eased their way toward the cab of the diesel. The throbbing of twin sixteen-cylinder diesels masked their approach.

Kurt reached the door, managed a quick peek inside,

and saw exactly what he'd hoped to see: a single gunman with his back to the door and his pistol leveled at a burly man in the driver's seat.

He put his hand on the door, testing the resistance in the handle. He felt pretty certain it wasn't locked. He opened it with a start and stepped inside.

The hijacker didn't react quickly. He turned as if expecting to see one of his kind. His eyes widened only when he saw the gun pointed at his head.

'G'day, mate,' Kurt said.

The hijacker hesitated and then handed the pistol over.

20

Victor Kirov woke to darkness and a pounding, migraine-like pain in his head. It took a moment, but he soon remembered where he was and what his mission required. The lights came on in the passenger car, and, seconds later, a group of his men dashed into the compartment.

'Where are they?' one asked.

'How should I know?' Kirov replied. 'I was unconscious when they left.'

One of the locals who'd taken a beating pointed forward. 'They went to the front.'

'We just came from there,' another guy said. 'We never saw them.'

Kirov stood, angry and wobbly. He steadied himself. 'They're hiding. Check everywhere. Check the roof. Check the baggage compartments. Double-check every space.'

The men fanned out, looking nervous.

Kirov's partner sidled up to him. 'We've been on this train too long as it is.'

Kirov looked at his watch, having trouble focusing. He wasn't sure how long it had been, but it didn't matter. 'I'm not going back without the woman.'

'This isn't some third world country,' his partner reminded him. 'The authorities will be coming here soon.'

Kirov considered this. It wouldn't do to get caught out in the open with the lights on. It might require cyanide, a thought he wanted nothing to do with.

Suddenly, the train lurched forward. The sound and vibration of the diesels straining to pull the load could be felt.

'They're in the engine,' Kirov said, heading forward.

'We'll never get to them in time,' his partner pointed out.

'You forget: the truck is still across the road. This train isn't going very far.'

In the cab of the forward diesel, Kurt was watching the door with one eye and the hijacker they'd surprised and subdued with the other. He could sense Hayley and Joe staring at the big truck in their path about five hundred feet away.

At first, the train was only inching toward it, but it slowly began to pick up speed, the thundering roar of eight thousand horsepower in the two locomotives beginning to win the battle over inertia. When they were four hundred feet out, the truck driver began flicking his lights on and off and blowing his horn. As if everyone didn't know he was there.

'He'll move,' Kurt said confidently.

'What if he doesn't?' Joe asked.

'Would you stay there?'

'But trains derail,' Hayley cried. 'Two hundred and fifty-three worldwide in the last six months alone. And not all of them hit trucks!'

Kurt looked at her sideways. 'How would you even know such a thing?'

'I keep abreast of all travel-related accidents,' she said, 'to remind myself why I stay at home.'

At three hundred feet, the train's blazing headlights began to light up the broadside of the big truck. The driver could be seen blocking the light from his eyes.

Kurt flipped the radio back on, switching channels until he heard someone speaking.

'. . . do not allow the train to pass,' another Russian-sounding voice was saying.

Kurt broke in as soon as the frequency cleared. 'Whoever you are in the truck, I'd move if I were you.'

Kirov's voice came next. *'Driver, if you move that truck, I will personally cut your heart out.'*

Two hundred feet from impact, with the train beginning to gain momentum, the truck driver made a decision that split the difference. He threw open the door, jumped from the rig, and ran for the hills.

'Didn't see that coming,' Joe muttered.

'Oh no,' Hayley gasped.

'You have to stop now,' Kirov threatened.

'Don't stop,' Kurt told the burly Australian engineer.

'No worries,' the big man said.

'I really don't want to be in a train wreck,' Hayley cried.

The engineer looked at Hayley. 'Don't worry, love,' he said. 'At this speed, we're not really a train anyway.'

The truck was only a hundred feet ahead.

'What are we, then?' Hayley asked.

The engineer grinned manically and held the shuddering engine's throttle wide open. 'The world's largest, most powerful bulldozer!'

There was something both inspiring and borderline crazy about the engineer. Either way, he wasn't slowing down. And Kurt was glad for that.

'Brace yourselves!' the engineer shouted.

The last hundred feet vanished in ten seconds. The rumbling train thundered into the broadside of the truck, shoving it forward. The diesels alone weighed six hundred thousand pounds. The sheer power they were generating, and the weight of the entire train, made quick work of the truck, lifting it and then discarding it to the right as if it were made of tin.

The impact was incredibly loud, a thundering boom followed by the wrenching sound of shredding aluminum. The feeling was like that of a ship breaking a large wave. The train shouldered through the blow with great power. The headlights blew out, and the windshield cracked, but the safety glass stayed in place. And when the last bits of the truck were finally tossed aside and sent tumbling down the embankment, the train itself was still on the tracks.

*

Four cars back, the impact had felt like a sudden application of the brakes. Kirov and his partner had to grab the handholds to keep from being thrown to the ground. They saw the remnants of the truck thrown off to the side and felt the train continuing on, accelerating smoothly once again.

'How are we going to get into that locomotive now?' his partner asked. 'They'll be waiting to pick us off the second we open the door. If we can even get there, that is. There's no door between the two engines. They're separate units.'

'Maybe we could go on the roof,' Kirov said.

Even as he suggested it, Kirov considered the insanity of the attempt. He'd seen it many times in the movies, but he doubted it was really possible. To walk on a swaying train roof in a fifty-mile-per-hour slipstream was not really feasible. Crawling might work, especially if they got up there before the train picked up too much speed.

Before he came to any conclusions, the sound of an announcement came over the public-address speakers.

'This is Kurt Austin,' the voice said. *'We've taken the train back from the hijackers and are resuming our regularly scheduled journey. To the passengers of the* Ghan*: we apologize for any inconvenience tonight's festivities may have caused. A satellite link has been established with dispatch. They've been apprised of our situation and assure us that help is on the way.*

'To the hijackers who came on board during our unscheduled stop: if you want to end up surrounded by Australian SWAT

teams and military units, then, please, sit back, relax, and make yourselves comfortable. Otherwise . . . get off this train!'

To Kirov's surprise, a cheer went up from the passengers. It rang out through the compartment and echoed around him on all sides.

He looked at his partner. 'The tables have turned.'

Both of them started for the door together. Ten seconds later, they were standing in the open space between the two cars, staring at the ground as it began to roll by at an ever-faster clip.

One car behind, a man jumped and tumbled across the gravel. It looked to Kirov like an agonizing landing. Two more followed, doing little better with their dismounts.

'We have to jump,' Kirov's partner said.

Kirov didn't want to jump, but the alternative was worse. Capture followed by embarrassment, suicide, or imprisonment as a spy and a terrorist. He looked ahead for an open spot. 'You first!'

Without delay, Kirov's partner launched himself. He seemed to land and tumble more than slide.

The train's horn howled through the night, and Kirov knew time was running out. Any faster and he'd be facing certain death. He took a deep breath and stepped into the breach.

For a long second, he flew, waving his arms for balance. Then he landed sideways and tried to tuck and roll. His face slammed into the gravel. His neck and shoulders were wrenched in the process. He flipped several times, covered at least fifty feet, and ended up facedown in an unconscious heap the second time in less than an hour.

In the forward engine, Kurt, Joe and the engineer were celebrating as the *Ghan* continued to pick up speed and leave the original hijackers behind. Hayley was in a seat, shaking and looking like she might be sick.

'Are you going to be okay?' Kurt asked, moving a wastepaper basket into range just in case she wasn't.

'I think so,' she said. 'At least that's over.'

'Good,' he replied. 'Because as soon as we make the next stop, we're hopping on a helicopter and flying the rest of the way.'

She looked up at him, her eyes bulging out. 'Helicopter accident rates are five times higher than that of passenger trains . . .'

The words trailed off. It was too much, too fast. She turned toward the bucket and promptly threw up.

21

NUMA Headquarters, Washington, DC

Dirk Pitt stepped from the elevator and on to the tenth floor as soon as the doors opened. Unlike the other floors of the NUMA building, the tenth had no receptionist to check people in or workers busy with different tasks. In fact, the only real noise in the open space came from the hum of exhaust fans and the climate-control unit that kept the computer servers and other processers cooled to the correct temperature.

Walking at a brisk pace, Dirk passed through the symmetrical stacks of computing power. Somewhere in the center, he found the goal of his search: a man with a long ponytail, wearing blue jeans and a corduroy shirt.

The lanky figure stood in the middle of three rectangular glass screens that were the size and shape of full-length mirrors. In fact, the arrangement was somewhat like that of a department store fitting room, which allows the customer to view his or her potential clothing purchase from all angles.

In this case, the angled glass screens did not reflect much, except perhaps the obsessive nature of their designer and chief user: one Hiram Yaeger.

Yaeger was a certified genius. He'd been designing and building computers since he was twelve years old. At NUMA, he'd been given almost unlimited resources to build his own systems, collect his own data, and apply it how he saw fit. The tenth floor of the NUMA building had long been given over to Yaeger's machines. In recent years, he'd expanded, taking over portions of the eleventh, much to the chagrin of the meteorology group, who were moved to the basement.

In a constant search for the most efficient human/machine interface, Yaeger had redesigned his system countless times over the years. He used multiple keyboards, voice activation, even virtual reality and talking holograms. This setup was his latest.

Oddly enough, even as the systems continued to evolve, Yaeger remained the same, as if he were the only constant in an ever-changing equation.

As Pitt approached, Yaeger's eyes darted around the glass screens upon which data was flashing here and there. He gestured and touched and moved things from one screen to another. A strange headset covered one ear and placed an additional tiny screen a finger's length in front of his right eye, which seemed to flicker. Even from ten feet away, Pitt could see information flashing up on it.

'One day, I'm going to come in here and find you hardwired to the system,' Pitt said.

In his zeal, Yaeger hadn't sensed Pitt coming. He turned abruptly, startled by Pitt's voice. 'You might have knocked.'

'All this technology, and you don't have a doorbell?' Pitt said. 'Or one of those things in the mall that ping when someone enters the store. Maybe I should get you a dog.'

Yaeger's face scrunched up at that thought. 'I already have a dog. I leave him at home because he pees on things and chews up the wires.'

'Sensible choice.'

'What brings you down here?' Yaeger asked.

Pitt placed a thick manila packet down on the table. 'From the Aussies. Their file and technical data. I figured you and the computers could analyse it.'

'They sent it on paper?'

'Some people still use the mail, Hiram.'

'Might as well write with a quill pen,' Yaeger grunted.

Pitt climbed up on to the platform. 'So what is all this?'

'New interface.'

'What's that thing over your eye?' Pitt asked. 'You look like a cross between Colonel Klink from *Hogan's Heroes* and one of the Borg from *Star Trek*.'

'Unfortunately, I feel more like Sergeant Shultz,' Yaeger said. 'Because *I know nothing* at this point.'

'That doesn't sound right.'

'The NSA doesn't want to share,' Yaeger explained. 'Despite their promises. I've got nothing from them.'

'Didn't they send a batch of data over this morning?'

'It's all seismic data,' Yaeger said, 'which we do need, I admit. But you asked me to look into this Dynamic

Theory of Gravity that Tesla supposedly came up with. I've requested a boatload of documents on that end and received nothing. They're stonewalling me.'

Pitt figured they would have to do something about that.

'Let me show you something,' Yaeger said, waving Dirk to the platform area between the three screens.

Pitt stepped forward. 'I feel like you're going to measure me for a suit.'

'The system could do that if you wanted it to,' Yaeger insisted. 'But it's a waste of processing power.'

'Depends on how the suit fits,' Pitt replied.

Hiram ignored him and pointed to the left-hand screen, where the photo of a one-story brick building appeared. It had ten evenly spaced windows, five on each side of a central door. It looked like a schoolhouse.

A half-finished structure stood behind the building. It was made of latticework, somewhat like the Eiffel Tower but with little of the French construction's graceful lines. In fact, it looked very utilitarian. At the top of the tower was a dome. Altogether, the setup resembled a giant metal mushroom.

'Wardenclyffe,' Yaeger said. 'Tesla's million-dollar folly, they called it. Construction began in 1901. Tesla insisted it was the first of many to be placed around the world. Towers that would allow instant transmission of data and, more important perhaps, the wireless diffusion of electrical energy.'

'Amazing,' Pitt said.

'It really is,' Yaeger said. 'Tesla worked on this tower in conjunction with his Dynamic Theory of Gravity. He exhausted himself on it, financially, physically and mentally. He just about broke himself trying to see it through. In 1905, he ran out of money. The building remained in his possession for years but was eventually foreclosed upon. Finally, in 1917, a demolitions crew blew up the rusting tower. In many ways, it was the biggest setback of Tesla's life. And yet, we have this letter.'

As Yaeger spoke, the photocopy of a handwritten letter flashed up on the central screen. It was signed by Tesla and addressed to a man named Watterson. It was dated March 1905.

'Who's Watterson?' Pitt asked.

'Daniel Watterson,' Yaeger replied, 'Tesla's prodigy at the time. Computer, please read the letter.'

The computer began speaking aloud, using a convincing foreign accent. 'Is that Tesla's voice?' asked Pitt.

'No,' Yaeger said. 'But it's an authentic re-creation of Tesla's English. The way he probably sounded.'

'You taught it to do that?'

'No, it made the choice itself based on a thousand different dialects.'

Pitt shook his head, feeling a sense of disbelief and wonder as he listened to the voice over the speakers.

'Young Daniel, we have both been afraid this day would come. Ever since the patents on my motors of alternating current expired, the incoming funds have been drastically reduced. Neither

Mr Astor nor Mr Morgan seem willing to put up more funding . . .'

Yaeger leaned over to Pitt. 'That would be J. P. Morgan and John Jacob Astor IV, the one who went down on the *Titanic*.'

Pitt nodded. 'Our paths have crossed before.'

'So I recall.'

'. . . *they have intimated that perhaps they would be willing to grant us more if we're able to demonstrate the transmission of power, but considering our inability to neutralize the anomalies we've encountered, I feel it is too dangerous to try at this point.*

'Remember, poverty can be overcome with hard work. Death cannot be. And I will not be the instrument of harm to so many who know nothing of our struggle. For this reason, I must decline the other offer you arranged as well.

'Please inform General Cortland that I appreciate his efforts but cannot move forward until I have been able to render the danger moot.

'With all hope, Nikola.'

The computer had finished.

'Who's this Cortland fellow?'

'Harold Cortland,' Yaeger said, 'a brigadier general in charge of special procurements at the time.'

'So Tesla decided not to seek more money from Jacob Astor because he thought it was too dangerous, and then he turned down money from the US Army as well?'

Yaeger nodded. 'According to the letter. But aside from this reference, I've found no proof that the army ever spoke to Tesla, let alone offered him something.'

Pitt turned back to the photo of Wardenclyffe. 'It looks a lot like what Kurt and Joe found in that flooded mine.'

'The ratios of the dome to the piping are almost identical,' Yaeger said. 'And just like that mine, Tesla's Wardenclyffe tower had electromagnetic conduction pipes that ran hundreds of feet down into the ground. According to Tesla, this was to *"get a firm grip on the Earth,"* which he insisted would not only conduct the power but *provide* it.'

'Million-dollar folly,' Pitt mused, 'except it sounds like Tesla was glad to let it go. Almost relieved. Why? What was he afraid of?'

Yaeger tilted his head as if the answer were obvious. 'Probably the exact effect Thero is striving to achieve: tipping over the applecart of this zero-point field and wreaking havoc as all the apples tumble out.'

Pitt nodded. He was beginning to sense a pattern.

'From what you've said,' he began, 'and what this Australian scientist has said, the zero-point field is connected and intertwined with gravitation. Tesla began work on his gravity theory and these towers at about the same time, around the turn of the century. He seemed to give up on both until . . . when?'

'Nineteen thirty-seven,' the computer replied.

Pitt looked around. 'Thank you,' he said, feeling odd about responding to the machine. 'Why then?'

'Insufficient data,' the computer said.

'Can it guess?' Pitt asked Yaeger. 'And, if not, can you?'

'Tesla was older by then,' Yaeger said. 'And broke. Maybe he needed money.'

'From what I've read, he always needed money. Why should 1937 be any different?'

'What are you suggesting?'

Pitt shrugged as if it were obvious. 'He buried this Wardenclyffe project when he could have saved it or at least kept it afloat. Then, thirty years later, he insists he's ready to spring the theory on the world. What are the chances he would do that unless he thought he'd found a solution?'

Again it was the computer that answered. *'Considering Tesla's adherence to his principles, the chances are less than ten per cent.'*

'I was asking Hiram,' Pitt said. 'But thank you anyway.'

'You're welcome.'

Pitt made a strange face.

'This is how we work,' Yaeger said. 'I talk. It talks back. This is how I've always worked.'

'I liked it better when there was a hologram involved,' Pitt said.

'Only because she flirted with you.'

'You might be right about that. Can we get back to Tesla?'

Yaeger nodded. 'You're suggesting Tesla found a way to eliminate the danger, these anomalies he talks about in the letter.'

'It fits,' Pitt said.

'Maybe,' Yaeger said, 'except he still never published his theory. And when he died, it vanished.'

'I wonder where,' Pitt said sardonically.

'You think the NSA has it?'

'They have something.'

'That I don't doubt,' Yaeger said.

Pitt considered calling Sandecker and asking him to lean on the NSA, but the VP was in London at a G-20 meeting, and that kind of fire took a while to stoke.

'What would happen if we nudged their database?' Pitt asked.

'Nudged it?'

'You know,' Pitt said, 'like a vending machine that you put your money in but then it doesn't give you what you paid for. You shake it a little until something falls out. What would happen if we did that to the NSA's computers?'

'Aside from prison and hard labor?'

'Yeah, aside from that.'

Hiram sighed. 'Maybe we can find another way.'

'You can always blame it on the . . .' Pitt nodded his head toward the computer display, wondering if the machine could pick up on the inference he was making.

'I don't think we'll need to do that,' Yaeger said.

'Maybe not,' Pitt said. 'What about this Watterson character? You find anything on him?'

Yaeger sighed. 'He didn't really do much after working with Tesla. As I recall, he died young.' He cocked his head. 'Computer, are there any events in Daniel Watterson's life of material relevance to our current project?'

The computer calculated for a second, scouring billions upon billions of records, cross-referencing them and looking for any link, connection, or bit of data they might have missed. Finally, it spoke:

'No meaningful influence on this project can be derived from Daniel Watterson's post-1905 actions,' it said. *'One statistical improbability detected.'*

Yaeger turned toward the main screen. 'What would that be?'

'According to obituary records, Daniel Watterson and General Harold Cortland both died on the same day. Their deaths occurred in separate states and from different causes. However, both obituaries were exactly fifty-one words in length and contained identical phrasing, except for the name of the deceased, cause of death, and location. Statistical probability of that occurring, considering the difference in their ages, occupations and domiciles, computes to less than .01 per cent.'

Pitt and Yaeger exchanged glances. 'Sounds like I'll be nudging the NSA's database,' Yaeger said.

'Sometimes, it's easier to apologize than get permission,' Pitt noted.

Yaeger nodded. 'Remind me of that when we're breaking rocks at Leavenworth.'

22

Pacific Voyager
2,400 miles southwest of Perth

Patrick 'Padi' Devlin stood on the black-painted deck of the sailing abomination that had once been the *Pacific Voyager*. The wind was bitterly cold as it whipped around the front of the ship. Sleet had begun spitting from the steel gray sky, and mist in the air had reduced visibility to less than a mile for the past few hours.

Devlin pulled his coat tight, shoved his hands deep into his pockets, and wished mightily for a scarf. Still, he didn't want to go back inside.

'Thank you for letting me out on deck,' he said to a figure, hovering behind him: Janko Minkosovic, his old crewmate and current jailer.

'I can't see any harm in it. Not like you're going to swim back to Jakarta.'

'I noticed you didn't extend the same courtesy to the others in the hold.'

'There are twenty-six of them,' Janko said. 'They come from a pair of vessels we hit. Together, they could be a danger.'

Devlin considered that. *Did it mean Janko had only a small crew on board?*

The wind gusted and the sleet intensified. From the temperature and the cobalt blue of the sea, Devlin guessed they'd been traveling south. He couldn't see the sun, but he guessed they were well into the Roaring Forties now, maybe even farther south. It looked like a storm was brewing.

'Remind you of anything?' Janko asked.

'The day this hulk went down,' Devlin replied.

'The day you cut us loose.'

'You know that was the captain's choice,' Devlin shot back. 'I begged him to hold on.'

'Stop blaming him,' Janko said. 'For that matter, stop blaming yourself, Padi. Look at you. You're a worse wreck than this ship. And you thought you'd make captain someday.'

Devlin cut his eyes at Janko.

'There was nothing any of you could have done,' Janko said. 'We set it up that way. If you hadn't released the cable, we'd have cut through it ourselves.'

'Who?' Devlin asked sharply. 'Who's we? And why? To fake the ship's destruction? She was already a derelict. She wasn't even insured.'

'The man I work for bought her,' Janko explained, 'years before. All that time in dry dock at Tarakan, he had people working on her. Making changes. When the moment came, he needed her to disappear. So he ordered us to tow her into the storm.'

Devlin stared at Janko. 'But you were part of the crew. Our crew!'

'For six months, along with the other two. He arranged that with your employer.'

'Fine,' Devlin said. 'So he got you on with us and had you put aboard the *Java Dawn*. But the ship – *this ship* – it went down. I saw it. That was no illusion.'

Janko exhaled like a parent tiring of questions from a curious child. 'No, Padi, it wasn't.'

'How the hell did you do it, then?'

'Follow me,' Janko said. 'You're about to find out.'

Janko led Devlin in through the main hatch and then through a second, inner hatch. For the first time, Devlin noticed that the outer section of the ship was left pretty much as it had been when he'd seen it years back. It looked neglected, disused. But once they passed the inner hatch, things were different.

Soon, Devlin found himself in a modern control room. Chart tables, propulsion gauges, radarscopes and graphic displays surrounded him. Large screens on the front wall were set up like the forward view from the bridge; in fact, they showed the gray sky and the cold sea ahead of the ship, piped in from the highest vantage point of a group of video cameras.

'When did all this get done?'

'I told you,' Janko insisted, 'the changes were made before the ship was towed off the beach.'

'But we inspected it for leaks.'

'The outer hull only,' Janko reminded him. 'Besides, I was with you to make sure you didn't stray into any sensitive areas.'

Devlin remembered now. They'd checked the repair job and the lower decks, the engine room and the bilge. No one had bothered with the inner spaces of the ship.

Janko turned his attention to one of the crewmen. 'Switch to infrared.'

The crewman flicked a switch, and the right-hand screen cycled. The color changed from gray to an orange hue. Suddenly, the clouds, mist and spitting rain were gone. The visibility that had been less than a mile was no longer a problem. Like magic, the shape of a large, cone-shaped island suddenly took up the center of the monitor. The central peak soared thousands of feet into the sky. It seemed impossible to have been a mile or so out and yet have the mist hiding the island so thoroughly.

Even as his eyes were growing wide, Devlin's ears began to pop. 'What's happening?'

'Inner hull pressurized,' one of the crewmen said, 'outer hull flooding.'

On the left screen, Devlin saw the bow of the ship settling toward the sea. A few moments later, the water rushed in from all sides as air surged out of hidden vents in the decking. In seconds, the foredeck was submerged. The water level moved rapidly higher, traveling up the superstructure and engulfing the camera.

Suddenly, all Devlin saw was darkness and the swirl of water in front of the lens. It took a minute for the view to clear, but even then there was nothing in the frame but the ship's bow.

'A submarine?' Devlin said. 'You turned this ship into a bloody submarine?'

'The central section of this ship is a pressure hull,' Janko explained. 'The rest is just camouflage.'

Despite his anger, Devlin found himself impressed. 'How deep can it go?'

'No more than eighty feet.'

'You'll be spotted from the air.'

'The black paint reflects almost no light, and it also absorbs radar.'

That explains why the paint is so thick and rubbery, Devlin thought.

'And all the radar masts and antennas?'

'We had to do away with them,' Janko said. 'They tend to cause problems when we submerge.'

'You'll still be picked up on sonar.'

Janko seemed exasperated. 'We don't travel around like this, Padi. We travel on the surface, like we have been. We merely do this to hide. And . . . to park.'

'Park?'

'Activate the approach lights,' Janko said to a crewman.

In the far distance, a line of yellow-green lights came on. They ran along the seafloor. To some extent, they resembled the dashed centerline on a dark highway.

'Five degrees to port,' Janko said. 'Reduce speed to three knots.'

As Devlin watched, the crewman to his left tapped away on a keyboard. 'Auto guidance locked. Auto-docking sequence initiated.'

The ship continued toward the dim lights.

'In position,' the crewman said.

'Open outer doors.'

A few more taps on the keyboard, and a thin crack of light appeared in what looked like a wall of rock. Before Devlin's eyes, the crack widened as huge doors slid open, revealing a narrow portal in the sloped side of the island's submerged foundation.

Using bow and stern thrusters, the *Voyager* countered the current and moved slowly into what proved to be a gigantic, naturally formed cave.

'All stop,' the helmsman said.

'Cave doors closing,' the other crewman reported.

'Surface the *Voyager*,' Janko ordered.

The sound of high-pressure air forcing water from the ship's tanks became audible. It reached a crescendo just as the four-hundred-foot vessel broke the surface.

Devlin watched in awe as the water drained away from the cameras and then shed itself from the decks. More artificial lighting came on, illuminating the cave around them, a space just slightly larger than the *Pacific Voyager* itself.

A slight bump was felt.

'Docking ramp is in position,' the crewman said.

Janko nodded. 'Bring the prisoners,' he said. 'I'll show Padi his new home personally.'

'New home?'

'That's right,' Janko said. 'Welcome to Tartarus. Prison of the Gods.'

23

NUMA vessel Orion, *1530 hours*
1,700 miles southwest of Perth

After thwarting the hijacking of the *Ghan*, Kurt, Joe and Hayley had switched modes of transport, taking a chartered jet to Perth and then boarding a Sea Lynx helicopter that flew them to the NUMA vessel *Orion* when she was still three hundred miles from the coast.

From there, the *Orion* had turned southwest, heading back out to sea. Three other ships in the NUMA fleet were joining them and heading in different directions. They were moving south, attempting to set up a picket line using the sensing devices Hayley had designed. The plan was simple. If Thero tested his device, they should be able to locate him.

As Hayley began the long task of calibrating the sensors, Kurt made his way up to the bridge. He arrived just as the third watch began.

Through the large plate-glass windows, he could see that the sky had darkened and lowered, and the sea had turned a dark iron gray. The western swell continued at four to five feet, surprisingly calm for this section of the world. Still, Kurt didn't like the look of things.

He grabbed two mugs with the name ORION on them and a small representation of the constellation's stars embossed on the side. He filled them with coffee and wandered over to Joe, who was standing with the *Orion*'s captain, studying the charts and the weather report.

'Captain?' Kurt said, offering one of the mugs.

'No thanks,' Captain Winslow replied.

'I'll take one,' Joe said.

Kurt handed one mug to Joe and kept the other for himself. He took a sip and then nodded toward the weather report. 'What's the word?'

'No storm yet,' Joe said, 'but the pressure's dropping. We're looking at a disturbance coming in from the west.'

It was March, which meant it was early fall in the southern hemisphere. The worst of the weather would not hit for another month or so, but south of 40 degrees latitude they'd entered an area known as the Roaring Forties. At this latitude, the Great Southern Ocean encircled the Earth uninterrupted by land. It could brew up a monster storm whenever it chose.

'So far, we've been lucky,' Winslow said. 'But my old bones tell me this weather isn't going to hold.'

'Quiet before the storm?' Joe asked.

'Something like that,' the captain said.

'We have to keep going,' Kurt said, 'even if the weather hits hard.'

Winslow seemed determined as well, but only to a degree.

'We won't let you down,' he assured Kurt. 'But if there's a point at which the danger to the ship and crew becomes too great, I'll have to make that call. The *Orion*'s a strong ship, but she wasn't built for a full-on gale.'

Kurt nodded. The captain was master of the ship, and though Kurt was in charge of the mission, the captain's word would hold sway. 'What about the others?'

Joe pointed to the chart. 'Paul and Gamay are aboard the *Gemini*.'

On the map, she was a long way out of formation.

'Why is she so far behind us?'

'She had to come all the way from Singapore.'

'Frustrating,' Kurt said. 'But it's worth the wait to get Paul and Gamay on the team. What about the others?'

'*Dorado*'s here,' Joe said, pointing to a different section of the map well to the east, almost directly under the center of Australia.

'And the *Hudson* is way over here, south of New Zealand. They just got the equipment delivered. Two days, at least, before they come online.'

Kurt studied the chart. Four tiny ships, just dots on the map in the vast sea. They were the only real hope of finding Thero before he acted.

'You think this is going to work?' Joe asked.

'It all depends on Hayley's sensors.'

'You don't seem as certain as before,' Joe noted.

'She's hiding something,' Kurt said.

'And yet, you like her,' Joe noted.

'All the more reason to be careful,' Kurt said.

At this, Joe nodded. 'It's always the punch you're not looking for that hits the hardest.'

Kurt took a sip of the coffee and glanced out the bridge windows into the deepening gloom. He couldn't help but wonder which direction that punch might come from.

Eighty-six miles behind the *Orion*, a different kind of vessel loomed out in the darkness. From all appearances, the MV *Rama* was a containership. A check of her logs and cargo would prove that she spent most of her time transporting goods from Vietnam to Australia and back. In fact, she'd been fully loaded with electronics and only hours from Perth when Dmitry Yevchenko had bought her, lock, stock and barrel, and diverted her to the south, turning her into a floating command ship for Anton Gregorovich and the commandos the Russian government had put at his disposal.

The *Rama* was smaller than most containerships of the day, only five hundred and sixty feet at a time when seven-hundred- and eight-hundred-footers were rapidly being dwarfed by thousand-foot behemoths. But what she did not have in size, she made up for in speed, with a top rate of twenty-eight knots.

As Gregorovich gazed at a satellite feed downloaded to them from a Russian satellite, he was thankful for that choice. The Americans had been racing south at nearly thirty knots since the moment Gregorovich had found them.

'Why are we following them?' a man with a heavily bandaged face asked.

'Because you failed to capture the woman,' Gregorovich said.

'We have helicopters and jamming equipment,' Victor Kirov replied. 'And twenty trained commandos on board. We could take her now with ease.'

Gregorovich didn't like having official Russian agents on his team, or even the Red Army commandos they'd sent him, but at least he could trust the soldiers. With an ambitious GRU man like Kirov, that was not possible.

'You're lucky I allowed you to come aboard, Victor. You've lost face with me in more ways than one.'

Kirov bristled at the comment but didn't respond.

'Don't you see?' Gregorovich asked. 'The Americans know something. They wouldn't be driving through the waves at flank speed if they didn't. They are the hounds chasing the fox. We are the hunters on horseback. At this point, it's best to shadow them from a distance, using the satellite granted us by the Kremlin to keep an eye on them from over the horizon. When they settle on a final location, we'll act.'

Kirov snorted and shook his head. 'If Thero proves to have a workable weapon, the Americans will swarm here like a horde of angry bees. Our little force will be no match for them. We must find him and destroy or take what he is building before he tests it in a way that alerts the world.'

'Take it?' Gregorovich said. 'So we have alternate plans now?'

'If some of the technology can be recovered, we are to do so,' Kirov noted.

'Those were not my orders,' Gregorovich said.

'They're mine,' Kirov replied.

This was odd, Gregorovich thought, but not totally unexpected. He shrugged it off, more concerned with the fact that he hadn't been told than the actual task.

'And what are we to do with the little toy you brought along?' He nodded toward a case secured to the far bulkhead. A nuclear warhead lay inside. A suitcase bomb. The mother of all suitcase bombs, really.

The Russian designation was RA-117H. While most tactical warheads yield a few kilotons at best – enough to vaporize several city blocks and perhaps devastate a square mile or so – the RA-117H yielded far more. Nearly three times the power of the Hiroshima bomb.

'Once we have samples of the technology, we are to activate the weapon and obliterate the site. There are to be no remnants of Thero or his experiments this time.'

24

Maxmillian Thero walked past a line of his engineers and technicians, a group of misfits he'd molded into a production team. Among them was a North Korean who'd escaped Kim Jong-il, an Iranian couple who'd fallen under suspicion of the radical Ahmadinejad government when their efforts in building his bomb were sabotaged by an American or Israeli computer virus, a Pakistani scientist wanted by Interpol for selling nuclear secrets, a middle-aged German woman whose radical thoughts made her persona non grata in her homeland, and a youth from Chechnya who was brilliant beyond his years but who'd been forced into hiding under the threat of a death sentence for killing Russian soldiers.

In a way, they were his children, Thero mused. But only in a way.

A mixture of fear, promises, and lack of other options kept them at his side, working like devout believers.

'You are the lost sheep whom I've gathered beneath my wings,' Thero said, the arrogance in his baritone voice echoing in the semi-darkened control room. 'Together, we shall witness the fruits of our labor. The brilliance of my genius.'

He moved to a control panel and flipped a series of switches. Lights came on around them, and a suite of computer monitors lit up. Beyond the panels lay a large Plexiglas window. On the other side, a great cavern was illuminated. Perfectly spherical, it stretched nearly five hundred feet from the polished stone floor to the curved, domelike roof. Much of it was natural, but Thero's believers and his slaves had worked it into the shape of a perfect sphere.

Inside the sphere sat a mechanical orb, made of metal pipes and scaffolding. It resembled a monstrous gyroscope, and, in a sense, it could act as one, pivoting in any and all directions.

This was Thero's weapon, the ultimate expression of his genius. With it, he could direct vast amounts of energy toward any point on Earth. But, unlike most weapons, Thero's would not rain destruction down from above. It would send it surging up from below.

By disturbing the zero-point energy contained within the Earth, Thero could channel this energy through the heart of the globe if he chose to.

One by one, a bank of indicator lights went green.

'All systems go,' announced the Chechen.

'Set for minimal power draw,' Thero said.

The engineers busied themselves with Thero's protocol. They went through checklists and procedures and soon came to the point of no return.

'Switching from geothermal input,' the German

woman said. The lights dimmed for a second and then returned to full brightness.

'Initiating the priming sequence,' the Iranian man said.

Several seconds later, a flashing icon on the panel in front of Thero indicated the priming was complete. The moment of truth beckoned. Thero pressed the ignition switch.

The lights dimmed again, much lower this time. Several went dark. The immense power draw of the ignition sequence was straining the electrical grid.

On a screen placed above the viewport a flat line was displayed. For a moment, nothing happened. Then, the line began to oscillate as a shallow wave pattern ran across the screen over and over.

Out in the cavern, a dim specter of ethereal light spiraled along the tubing and around the interior of the globe-shaped room. It flashed and faded. A second pulse of energy followed. But, unlike the first, this one remained, moving back and forth like a ghost trapped in some kind of man-made purgatory.

'Magnetic containment field holding,' the Iranian woman said.

Slowly, the lights around them came back up.

'We are now running on zero-point energy,' the German woman said proudly.

As the sounds of subdued celebration spread throughout the room, Thero watched the monitor ahead of him. The peaks and troughs of the wave continued to build until a yellow indicator began to flash.

'Something's wrong,' the young Chechen said. He returned to his desk. 'The pattern is unstable.'

'It can't be,' someone else insisted.

'Look for yourself.'

Thero stepped over to the panel and studied the three-dimensional pattern. It should have been a perfect sphere like the cave, but it was distorted in one section near the top. The lines pulled to the side, snapped back, and pulled again, like the picture on an old television getting bad reception.

'Counteract it,' Thero said.

Even as he spoke, a second alarm went off.

'Modulate the field.'

The Pakistani began tapping the keys on his computer. Out in the cave, the monstrous, gyroscope-like construction began to pivot in the huge rig. It turned slowly like a giant telescope, trying to align itself with a specific section of the sky. As it moved, the second alarm shut itself off. Only a flashing yellow marker on the oscilloscope-like screen continued.

The giant array of pipes locked itself into place. Ghosts of electromagnetic energy chased one another around the interior and across the polished walls of the sphere. The whole setup continued to glow as if it were covered in St Elmo's fire.

'The counterbalancing pulse is in effect,' the Iranian

man said. 'It should be tuned perfectly, but there is still a slight distortion.'

Thero was furious. He was ready to exterminate whoever had failed him. A slight distortion at low power would be fatal at higher energy levels. It would render his threat impotent.

'Explain the failure!' he demanded.

The engineers and technicians pored over their individual screens, checking and rechecking for any sign they'd missed. They chattered among themselves trying to understand what they were looking at.

'Well?!'

'It's not us,' the German woman said finally. 'Our energy output is balanced perfectly.'

'Then what is occurring?'

The Chechen youth spoke hesitantly, as if he were unsure. 'Something out there is reading our signal, absorbing part of it. It's creating an interference pattern, upsetting the balance.'

'Reading our signal?' Thero's mind whirled.

'Yes,' the youth replied. 'I think I can counteract it and restore . . .'

Understanding came to Thero suddenly, hitting him like a hammer. 'No,' he said. 'Shut it down. Shut everything down!'

'What?' someone asked. 'Why?'

'They're probing us. Waiting for us to power up and homing in on our signal. Shut the system down!'

Thero went to switch the system off himself, when an arm barred him. He turned to see his son, George.

'How dare you stay my hand!' Thero shouted.

'It's too late,' his son told him. 'Like radar, we've already been painted. There's no point in shutting it down now.'

'That may not be true,' Thero charged.

'You know it is,' George said.

'Then we must stop them,' Thero blurted out.

He looked over to the engineers. 'If they can detect us, then we can find them. Pinpoint the origin of this distortion. Quickly.'

The Korean and the two Iranians sprang into action, glancing up at Thero nervously, gawking at him as he conversed with his son.

'Do not raise your eyes to us!'

They looked back down at their work, made a series of calculations, and came up with a solution.

'Typing the location in now,' the Iranian woman said.

A map appeared on the monitor above the Plexiglas viewport. It displayed Thero's location, his island of Tartarus. It also displayed the waters of the Southern Ocean and the southwestern tip of Australia. A flashing dot indicated the location where the offending distortion was located. Almost due east, only nine hundred miles from the island.

'How could they be so close?' he gasped. 'Traitor. There must still be a traitor among us!'

'It must be a ship,' the Korean said.

'Of course it's a ship!' Thero bellowed.

'Perhaps we should shut down,' Thero's son suggested.

'Now?!' Thero barked. 'I think not! Like you said, it's too late. Prepare to destroy them.'

'It's not wise to risk full power without testing.'

The crew continued to gawk at the argument between father and son. The embarrassment enraged Thero even further. 'No more questions!'

'The system isn't ready!' his son pleaded.

'Silence!'

With that, Thero's son retreated, and Thero gazed out at his crew.

'Set the machine for a short impulse,' he ordered. 'Align the dislocation to occur directly in their path. The distortion alone should swallow them whole.'

25

Kurt and Joe were still on the bridge, waiting for a printer to churn out the latest weather map, when it jammed midpage and wouldn't restart.

'What'd you do?' Joe asked.

'I didn't touch it,' Kurt said.

Joe stepped to the computer to restart the printing process. 'That's weird.'

'What?'

'No signal.'

'Telemetry's down,' Captain Winslow told them. 'It's been in and out all day. Something to do with solar flares messing up our satellites.'

Kurt remembered hearing how that would be a problem this year as the sun was entering the most active phase of its eleven-year cycle. Sunspots and flares were stirring up powerful electromagnetic storms in the upper atmosphere, creating incredible displays of light over both the northern and southern poles.

Kurt glanced out the windows. If they weren't socked in under a thick blanket of clouds, the aurora australis, or southern lights, might have been a treat to see.

'I'm going to get some air,' Kurt said. 'Let me know when the link is reestablished.'

He opened the bulkhead door and stepped outside. A chilly blast hit him, chasing away the cobwebs that had been creeping over him. The wind from the ship's motion whistled past, biting his exposed skin. He pulled his coat tight and shoved his hands into its pockets.

He stepped to the rail and stood there, enjoying the solitude, until a bulkhead door opened behind him.

He glanced back to see Hayley coming out on to the deck. 'Kurt,' she shouted, 'I think we've found them. I think we've found Thero.'

She moved toward him, eyeing the rail cautiously. A couple sheets of paper fluttered in her grip as the wind tried to pull them loose.

Kurt took them from Hayley, and she grabbed on to the ship's rail with both hands.

He looked down at the printouts. On top was a map with arcs and lines drawn on it. They angled off to the west. It looked like nothing but open ocean. On the edge of the page was a numerical bearing to the target.

'They're on that line somewhere,' she said. 'Without a second sensor operating, I can't get a precise fix, but they're on that line somewhere.'

'Are you sure?'

'I did the calculations three times,' she said. 'I checked everything. There were no errors. Something in this exact direction is disturbing the zero-point field.'

She looked up at Kurt, positively beaming. Then she stretched up and gave him a quick kiss.

'Just trying out the spontaneity thing,' she said.

Kurt smiled. 'I like it.' He reached toward her, slid a hand behind her head, and pulled her toward him for a proper kiss.

'Okay, I like yours better,' she said. 'Can we try that again?'

'Let's talk to the captain first.'

'Do we really need his permission?' Hayley asked. 'I know it's his ship, but . . .'

'About the map,' Kurt said. 'And our new heading.'

'Oh . . . all right,' she said.

He took her by the hand and stepped toward the hatch, stopping as a flash on the horizon caught his eye.

He turned and gazed directly into the night but saw nothing but darkness.

'Did you see that?' he asked.

'See what?'

'That flash.'

'No,' she replied. 'I didn't see anything.'

As they stood and gazed into the darkness, like two people waiting to see fireworks go off, a strange feeling began to creep over Kurt. He could sense the hair on the back of his neck standing up.

Finally, another flicker of light appeared. This time, Kurt saw it plainly, but it wasn't a flash on the horizon like a strobe light or even a definable bolt of electricity, it was more like heat lightning in the summer, covering the whole horizon, flickering dimly. Only, it wasn't coming from the sky. The sea itself was flashing, as if the whole of the ocean were bio-luminescencing.

'Could this be an effect of the aurora?' he asked.

Hayley pulled back trembling. 'It's not the aurora,' she said. There was a chill in her voice. The sound of fear.

'What is it?'

'Electromagnetic discharge,' she said. 'It's a side effect of disturbing the zero-point field.'

'Because of your sensor?'

'No,' she said, shaking. 'It's not us. It's Thero.'

The sea flickered again, much brighter this time, and the ship lurched downward. It happened so suddenly that Kurt and Hayley were flung to the deck. The bow dug into the water, and a towering wall of spray blasted up into the air and then fell in sheets around them.

Kurt pulled himself up and looked aft. A line of foam stretched out into the dark, straight as a ruler and perpendicular to their path, but he saw no retreating wave.

'Kurt,' Hayley cried.

He swung his eyes forward. The ocean was flickering again, a pale blue-green, just enough to show its contours in the dark. Fifty yards ahead, another line was forming on the sea. It peeled back like skin being cleaved open and formed a deep trough right in front of them. It stretched across the ocean in a straight line, but it wasn't a wave. There was no raised vertical component to it. It was more like a gap in the water, like a drainage ditch cut across a road.

The *Orion* hit this gap at a slight angle. The ship rolled awkwardly as she plunged into it.

Kurt wrapped one arm around Hayley, crushing her to him with all his strength and lacing his other arm through the rail.

The ship's bow knifed into the bottom of the trough, all but submarining. It was already rising as it reached the far side, coming up in a corkscrew motion, and flinging Kurt and Hayley into the air like riders who'd been tossed off a prize bull.

They landed on the deck just as a second curtain of icy water cascaded down upon them, soaking them to the bone.

Kurt tasted the salt of the water. It stung his eyes and the abrasions he'd taken from the first impact. Without waiting for her to stand, he grabbed Hayley, pulled her up and began running toward the safety of the bulkhead door.

A foot of water had covered the foredeck. It sloshed out through the drainage holes, taking Hayley's printed papers along for the ride.

A klaxon blared above them, and Kurt realized it was the ship's alarm sounding for a collision. The ship was turning hard.

'Brace for impact!' the captain's voice called over the loudspeakers. 'All hands, brace for impact!'

Kurt glanced forward, looking past the bow. The ship's lights had come on, illuminating a new trough directly in front of them, perhaps a hundred yards off. This one was deeper and wider than the other one, wide enough to swallow the ship. From Kurt's angle, it looked like the edge of a great cliff in the center of the sea, an edge they were about to go over.

The *Orion* leaned hard over as the rudder hit the stops. Kurt felt the vessel shudder as the props went into reverse.

One look told Kurt it wasn't going to be enough.

He pulled the hatch open and shoved Hayley through, scrambling inside right behind her and slamming the steel door shut. He wrenched the handle down, locking it just as the deck began to fall out from beneath him.

A moment of weightlessness followed, like they were on some gigantic amusement ride. Then Kurt was slammed into the deck. A tremendous boom reverberated throughout the ship, like a dozen cannons being fired off together. It was the sound a wall of water made when it struck the hull flush.

A muted silence followed, and Kurt knew the ship had gone under. If she was buttoned up tight, she would come to the surface again. But, for the moment, Kurt couldn't feel her rising.

Several seconds went by before the momentum of the ship changed and she began to rise, several more before the sea released her.

She heaved up, bursting free of the water, and then crashing back down like a breaching whale. Kurt pulled Hayley to her feet and helped her forward.

They reached the bridge to find water sloshing about. One of the windows had been shattered and smashed in completely. The captain was hanging on the wheel, a bloody gash across his jaw. The XO was down on the floor and out cold, having been flung against the far bulkhead.

Joe was slamming a metal plate into the slot where the shattered window had been. He wrenched a lever tight, locking it into place just as the main lights went out.

'Power's gone!' the captain said.

The sea flashed again, a beautiful and deadly blue that raced outward in all directions. Another trough began opening in front of them, the waters parting like the Red Sea.

The ship was still moving as the lip of the disturbance raced underneath them. She dropped once again.

In the darkness it was terrifying, a free fall that lasted for seconds but seemed endless. As the ship hit the bottom of the trough, the jarring impact was accompanied by the sound of wrenching metal. Rivets popped as high up as the bridge and, somewhere deep, the keel broke. As if to finish them off, the towering walls of seawater slammed together around the *Orion* like giant hands clapping.

This last act of the angry sea might have killed everyone on board, except that the two great hands spent most of their energy smashing each other. As they rebounded off each other, the current they created dragged the stricken vessel to the surface.

She came up for only a minute and was soon awash and sinking.

The bridge was flooded from the impact, with the

remaining windows smashed out. The water was frigid, cutting into their skin like knives.

Kurt still had his arm around Hayley. In the glimmer of the emergency light, he saw Joe opening a life-raft container, and Captain Winslow desperately trying to order the crew to abandon ship.

Kurt grabbed a life jacket, pulled it over Hayley's head and cinched it tight.

'Stay with Joe!' he shouted.

She nodded as Kurt waded to where the XO had fallen. Heaving him up, he passed the unconscious man to the captain and then glanced at the stairwell to the lower deck.

He saw a crewman staggering upward as the water flooded down upon him. The man was injured. He could hardly fight the current. Kurt pulled him up and passed him to Hayley, who helped him into a life jacket of his own. Holding the rail, Kurt began to climb down.

'There's no use,' the crewman said, 'they're all gone. Those that weren't pulled out when she broke are drowned. It's all water below this deck.'

Kurt ignored him, splashing down into the stairwell and diving into the icy black liquid. He inched forward, one hand on the wall, the other outstretched and numbly feeling around for any sign of a crewman. He found no one and turned back.

When he came up, water was pouring in through the shattered windows again. The top of the bridge was all that remained above water.

Joe grabbed him under the arm and yanked him free of the stairwell. 'I'm not going to let you kill yourself,' he shouted, dragging Kurt to the hatch and toward the inflated orange raft.

Joe flung Kurt on to the raft and jumped on behind him. His momentum carried them away as the *Orion* sank beneath the waves. It vanished to the sound of random, muffled explosions as the last air pockets in the ship were purged one by one.

Kurt glanced around. Aside from the single crewman who'd struggled up from belowdecks, only those on the bridge had escaped.

The hexagonal life raft rolled up on one of the low swells, and Kurt stared into the dark, his eyes straining for any sign of another raft or anyone in the water. He saw nothing. But neither did he see another flash like those that had preceded the strange ruts appearing in the sea. 'Do we have any flares?'

Joe dug into the raft's survival kit. 'Six,' he said. 'Three white, three red.'

'Fire a white one,' Kurt said. 'We have to see if anyone else is out there.'

Joe pointed the flare gun skyward and fired. With a whoosh, the blazing little sphere rocketed upward, casting a harsh glow across the rolling waves. Kurt stared and stared, his eyes darting about, as the moving carpet of the swells stretched out before him.

Plenty of wreckage and debris had come to the surface. Insulation, packaged stores and unworn life jackets, anything with buoyancy. He saw no sign of another raft but spotted two people bobbing among the wreckage.

'There,' he said, pointing and grabbing an oar.

The flare only lasted another ten seconds, but Joe had also found a flashlight. He kept it trained on the floating crewmen as Kurt and Captain Winslow rowed the life raft in their direction.

Kurt hauled the first crewman on to the raft. She was a young woman he recognized from the radio room. The second survivor was the boatswain's mate Kurt had seen on the previous night's watch. Neither one appeared to be responsive. Two others were found, who Kurt didn't know by sight.

'Are . . . they . . . alive?' Hayley asked through chattering teeth.

'Barely,' the captain said. 'They're all but frozen. Hypothermia doesn't take long in thirty-eight-degree water. We've got to get them warmed up.'

'With what?' Hayley asked.

'Body heat,' Kurt said. 'Everybody needs to huddle together. We're all wet. We're all going to lose our heat fast if we don't conserve it.'

The group began to move to the middle of the raft, leaning against one another and pulling a microfiber survival blanket over themselves. All except Kurt and Joe, who were aiming the flashlight around and looking for other survivors.

They pulled in a few empty life jackets and several

pieces of cloth and plastic, things that might prove useful at some point, but they found no other survivors. Eventually, they knew there was no more point in looking.

'Better save the battery,' Kurt said.

Joe waited until he and Kurt were safely in the huddle with the others before he shut it off.

'Thirty-nine men and women,' the captain said. 'What happened to the sea? What was that? I've never seen waves like that. They looked like craters appearing in our path.'

Kurt glanced at Hayley.

'Thero's weapon did this,' she said grimly. 'It distorts gravity.'

'And that gravity affects liquids far more easily than solids,' Kurt added, repeating her earlier statement in a somber tone.

'It's like a bubble,' she managed. 'Highly localized but very powerful. It forces the water to the side, and then, when it passes, the crater, as you called it, collapses on itself.'

'And the water comes crashing back in,' the captain added, showing that he understood.

She nodded. 'I'm so sorry.'

'It's not your fault,' the captain said.

'But it is,' she replied. 'I helped construct the theory. And the sensor I used must have given away our position somehow. That's the only explanation. The only way they could find us.'

Kurt tried to comfort her, but he didn't have the words. Nor, in his most optimistic dreams, did he have any idea how they were going to survive, let alone prevent Thero from fulfilling his venomous threat.

26

NUMA Headquarters, Washington, DC

A twelve-hour time difference separated Washington, DC, and the small fleet of vessels approaching Antarctica. At eight o'clock, the morning shift took over from the night owls in the NUMA communications room, a large, modern workspace that looked something like an air traffic control center.

From there, NUMA teams and vessels were monitored and tracked twenty-four hours a day, seven days a week, all around the globe. Data and communications were sent and received a variety of different ways, the preferred method becoming encrypted satellite communications. It was the most efficient means, the most secure, and the most reliable. Except when it wasn't working.

Within five minutes of arriving, Bernadette Conry could tell that this was going to be one of those days when all the technology was more trouble than it was worth.

A ten-year NUMA veteran with short dark hair, light green eyes, and a strong sense of duty, Bernadette Conry wore fashionable glasses, little in the way of jewelry, and was known to be a detail-oriented manager.

Her first order of duty on any shift was to run through the list of ongoing operations with the communications specialists, with an eye toward fixing or avoiding any problems. All week long, an uptick in solar flare activity had made that a difficult task.

After going through a lengthy list of ships and operations teams that had experienced trouble during the night, she wondered how naval commanders had even functioned in the days without satellite tracking and communications.

Thankfully, she noticed that almost all the problems from the previous twelve hours had been cleared up. All except one.

She eased over to a console upon which the designation REGION 15 had been marked. Region 15 included most of the Southern Ocean beneath Australia and what NUMA termed Antarctic Zone 1.

'What's the story with *Orion*?' she asked the specialist.

'No data for the last hour,' he replied. 'But it's been up and down like that for the past two days.'

'Are you getting data from *Dorado* and *Gemini*?'

The technician tapped away at the keys and received a positive answer. 'We lost them for a while too,' he said. 'But we have clean links to both ships now.'

That raised the supervisor's sense of doubt. She reached over and tapped the F5 key on the technician's computer. It brought up a map, which included the *Orion*'s last-known position.

'She is a lot farther south than the other ships, but

the solar activity has backed off considerably. We should be getting a signal. Have you received any radio calls?'

'They're on a "run silent" protocol,' the specialist reminded her.

'Who's on board?'

'Austin and Zavala.'

Ms Conry sighed. 'Those two are bad enough about reporting in to begin with. Who put the run silent order on?'

'Came from Dirk Pitt himself.'

The vast majority of NUMA's work went off without any type of conflict, at least nothing greater than the usual bureaucratic rigmarole found throughout the world. But right from the beginning, the organization had been willing to tangle with those who were up to no good in one way or another. If a 'no contact,' 'run silent,' or 'monitor and track only' order was in place, it usually meant that a delicate or outright-secret assignment was in the works. That ship or team was not to be disturbed or contacted in any way that might risk alerting other parties to its presence.

Satellite communications gave them a way around that. The bursts could be coded and then sent and received without giving a ship's position away like radio broadcasts could if they were intercepted. But if the satellites were being interfered with by a solar storm, it left the distant ships, and the supervisors who were supposed to keep track of them, in the dark.

'Anything unusual in their last transmission?'

The specialist shook his head. 'All data was normal when the link was broken. There was no sign of trouble. Nor has *Orion*'s emergency beacon been activated.'

The emergency beacons were automatic, designed to go off when a ship sank even if there was no one around to activate them. But Bernadette Conry recalled at least one instance of a ship going down so fast that the beacon never had a chance to send out a message.

'What's the weather report?'

'Nothing to write home about,' he said. 'Westerly swell, five to six feet. Moderate-sized storm forming about five hundred miles from their last-known position.'

Not bad weather at all, she thought. And it *was* Austin and Zavala. 'Keep an eye out for any change,' she said. 'I'm going to let the Director know we've lost their telemetry.'

Dirk Pitt nodded at the report. He had a sense that something was wrong. That feeling was reinforced by the next call, which came in from Hiram Yaeger.

'The NSA just sent me a new batch of data,' Yaeger explained. 'They picked up a large neutrino burst just over an hour ago. It was detected in the *Orion*'s general vicinity.'

'That's not good,' Pitt said.

'Why?'

'She's gone dark,' Pitt replied. 'We lost contact with her an hour ago, just as they were about to activate the zero-point detector. Either she's suffered a massive failure, or worse. Either way, our only hope of finding Thero is if the other ships can get their detectors online in a hurry.'

Yaeger was silent for a moment. 'I don't know if that's such a good idea,' he said finally.

'Why?'

'None of us really understand how the sensor works,' Yaeger said. 'And this zero-point energy is like a genie in a bottle, a moody genie at that. The simulations I've run do not yield consistent results. Considering that fact, it's slightly possible, however unlikely, that the sensor itself interacted with the zero-point field and either shut all systems on the *Orion* down or caused a more catastrophic event.'

Pitt considered the possibility before responding. 'That's not what you're really concerned with, is it?'

'No,' Yaeger replied. 'More likely, the sensor gave away their position somehow. And if Thero knew he was being monitored . . .'

'He would respond,' Pitt said.

'Precisely,' Yaeger said. 'And if he has the power to split a continent in half, attacking a small ship would be like swatting a fly.'

Pitt thought of the *Orion*'s crew; there were thirty-nine men and women aboard that ship, including some of his closest friends. 'Why wouldn't she warn us?' he wondered aloud. 'If there was a possibility of this, why wouldn't Ms Anderson make us aware of it?'

'No idea,' Yaeger said. 'But I'd say we have to leave those sensors off.'

'It's not that simple,' Pitt said. 'We have a job to do and we're running out of time.'

'I wasn't aware we were on any particular clock.'

'A new letter has arrived,' Pitt explained. 'Bradshaw from the ASIO sent it over, even used e-mail. I'll forward it to you. Thero claims he's waited long enough. He promises to strike Australia as the sun rises over Sydney two days from now. He's calling the moment zero hour.'

Yaeger remained silent.

'I need answers and I need them fast, Hiram. Right now, those detectors are the only way of finding Thero. I need to know if they're safe. And if they aren't, I need you to find me another way to locate him before this zero hour hits. Or, better yet, a way to stop it from hitting even if he makes his move.'

'I'll do everything I can,' Yaeger said. 'So far, we've identified a strange sequence to these energy bursts. According to Ms Anderson's research, they create a type of three-dimensional wave, somewhat like a bubble. Perhaps we can figure out some way to stop that bubble from forming. Or a way to collapse it once it does.'

'Let me know as soon as you have more.'

Yaeger acknowledged him, and Pitt hung up. He hesitated for only a second before deciding to dial the communications room.

He spoke quickly. 'Ms Conry, please attempt to contact *Orion* by any means at your disposal. If you hear nothing from them, alert *Dorado* and *Gemini*. Transmit the *Orion*'s last-known position to them and order them to begin search-and-rescue operations.'

'Anything else?'

Pitt gave one more order. 'Advise the other ships not to activate the new sensors they've been working on. Not under any circumstances, unless further ordered by me.'

As he hung up the phone, his second line buzzed. It was Vice President Sandecker. His voice was distorted by a shrill electronic hum. It sounded like he was airborne.

'There's going to be a marine Black Hawk on your roof in four minutes,' Sandecker said. 'I need you to be on it.'

'I'm a little busy right now,' Pitt replied.

'I know,' Sandecker said. 'Hiram's been busting the NSA's chops to release more data on Tesla. When they didn't give in, he hacked their computer system to liberate a few extra files. Knowing Hiram, he wouldn't do that without your orders.'

Pitt figured they'd get caught, just not this quickly. 'I may have given him the impression I'd look the other way,' he said, 'but they shouldn't be holding back on us. Not at a time like this.'

'You're lucky, old friend, because I've finally gotten them to agree with you. They're going to give you everything they have on Tesla. But they want you to see something first. You now have three minutes. See you on the roof.'

Pitt really had no choice. He exhaled. 'Where are we going?'

'The chopper will take us to Andrews,' Sandecker explained, referring to the air force base ten miles to the southeast of Washington.

'And from there?'

'You'll find that out when our wheels leave the ground.'

27

NUMA vessel Gemini, *approximately*
750 miles northeast of Orion's
last-known position

In the *Gemini*'s darkened communications room, Gamay Trout stared at the computer screen. A new set of operational orders were coming in from NUMA HQ.

Paul sat beside her, reading it out loud.

'Orion *is not responding to any method of communication. Proceed to* Orion*'s last-known position with all possible speed. Be prepared to launch search-and-rescue operations or search-and-recovery if no survivors are found. A satellite pass detected no infrared signature within fifty miles of* Orion*'s position. Due to heavy cloud cover, visual confirmation is not possible at this time.*'

The report seemed so cold. As if the ship weren't filled with their friends and colleagues.

'It can't be,' Gamay said. 'No emergency signal? No distress call? There's no way one of our ships could go down that fast.'

Paul continued. '*Further orders refer to the sensing array provided by Ms Anderson. Under no circumstance is the array to be activated. If already completed, the unit is to be rendered inop-*

erable by hard-wire disconnection from Gemini*'s systems. A direct time-based correlation has been made between the activation of* Orion*'s sensor array and a high-energy neutrino burst detected by the NSA ground stations and* Orion*'s last communication. It remains unknown if the array was at fault, but at this time it cannot be ruled out.'*

They were only hours away from activating their own array.

'Could they really have blown themselves up?'

'The explosion at Yagishiri that obliterated Thero's lab was never adequately explained,' Paul said, 'but Yaeger thinks it more likely that the sensor might have given away their location and allowed Thero to strike.'

The *Gemini* was already turning. The thrum of her engines and propellers could be felt strengthening. Gamay looked at the map.

'Seven hundred and fifty miles,' she muttered. 'Thirty hours. That's too long. They'll never survive.'

Paul looked glum as well. 'If they're in the water, they're already gone,' he said. 'Three hours or thirty, it won't make a difference. Let's just hope they made it to the boats.'

Gamay appreciated what he was trying to do, but she knew the score. 'If the ship went down too fast for the emergency beacon to send out a signal, what are the chances anyone got off in a lifeboat?'

Her mind was imagining what the crew of the *Orion* might be experiencing. The water temps had to be in the thirties, with the ambient air temperature dropping into the teens at night.

Paul reached over and wrapped his arms around her. 'We can't give up hope. And we won't.'

'This is why I love you, Paul,' she said. 'No matter how crazy you make me at times, you really know what I need.'

'I also know that Kurt and Joe are survivors,' he said. 'And that every man and woman on that ship has been well trained. Let's not write them off yet. Instead, let's be ready to lend assistance when we get there.'

She wrapped her arms around Paul's waist and nodded. 'Okay, but don't stop hugging me just yet. I need a few more moments of this before I get back to the real world.'

Seven hundred and fifty miles from the *Gemini*, the *Orion*'s survivors huddled in the small orange life raft as it wallowed in the persistent western swell.

For the better part of four hours, they rose and fell in a circular motion, surrounded by utter darkness. Neither the moon nor the stars were visible through the heavy layer of clouds. Aside from the dim glow of his watch, Kurt saw no light in any direction.

Worse than the darkness was the silence. But, worst of all, was the cold.

The frigid air was painfully debilitating to the men and women in their wet clothing. Even huddled together under a thermal blanket, their core temperatures were slowly dropping. A process that would only accelerate as their bodies digested the last meal they'd eaten.

Kurt was already hungry, though he did his best not to think about food and instead tried to imagine himself on a beach in the Mediterranean with the sun beaming down on him and a drink in his hand. Somehow, the image wouldn't last.

A sort of trancelike state had come over them. It was akin to depression. Kurt figured they'd better break it somehow.

'Any chance those alien friends of yours might come pick us up?' Kurt muttered to Joe. 'I'd take a warm spaceship with little green men over this freezing life raft.'

Joe shrugged. 'They don't seem to like cold weather either. Roswell. Ayers Rock. Chichen Itza. If we were shipwrecked a little closer to one of those locations, we'd have a shot.'

Kurt didn't bother to point out that there was little water near any of those places.

'*Dorado* and *Gemini* are not too far away,' Kurt said. 'If our beacon went off, they'll be on their way.'

'Do they have a hot chocolate dispenser on board?' Joe asked.

'I hope so.'

'What about a sauna?' someone else asked.

'Something tells me NUMA didn't spring for that.'

'Too bad,' Joe added.

'I'll settle for dry clothes and a warm rack,' Kurt replied. 'In the meantime, I'm trying to imagine a dry sauna, with smooth wood paneling and the smell of eucalyptus oil. But it doesn't seem to be working. Apparently, this mind-over-matter stuff is harder than you think.'

'I don't know,' Joe said. 'I've convinced myself I hear a ship approaching.'

Kurt tilted his head. He heard nothing.

'What kind of ship?' he asked. The words came out funny. Their lips were nearly frozen.

'A nice big yacht,' Joe said. 'With a few playmates, some Hawaiian Tropic girls, and a fully stocked bar. I think I even hear a jazz band playing some Louis Armstrong.'

'You're losing it,' Kurt said. 'But if you must fantasize . . .'

He stopped midsentence. Strange as it was, he thought he could hear the thrum of engines in the distance as well. Had there been any wind at all, he might not have heard it. But the still air was awfully quiet.

He threw the edge of the thermal blanket back, much to the consternation of the others. 'Hey,' someone grumbled. 'What are you doing?'

'Quiet.'

'What?'

'Joe heard a ship, and so did I.'

Kurt was staring out into the night. If there was a ship out there, its running lights should have been visible in the darkness. He saw nothing.

'I hear it,' Hayley said. 'I hear it too.'

With an abundance of caution, Kurt considered the

possibility of mass hysteria. It happened often enough among shipwreck survivors, but usually after days of exposure and dehydration.

'Give me a flare,' Kurt said.

Joe handed the flare gun to Kurt. By now, the thrum of heavy diesel engines could be heard clearly. There was a ship out there, running dark for whatever reason and moving closer.

Kurt aimed the gun skyward and pulled the trigger. The flare rocketed straight up, casting a white light down on the sea around them. A half mile off, Kurt spotted the prow of a freighter. It was heading roughly in their direction, though it would miss them to the east.

'It's not one of ours,' Captain Winslow said.

'Nor is it a yacht with a band and a bar,' Joe replied. 'But I'll take it.'

The flare had a forty-second life, and the darkness returned once it dropped into the sea.

They waited.

'There's no way they didn't spot that,' Joe insisted.

Kurt loaded another flare into the firing chamber. 'Let's hope they're not sleeping or watching TV.'

He was about to fire the second flare when the sound of the big engines and the reduction gearing changed.

'She's cut her throttles,' Winslow said gleefully.

Kurt held off on firing the precious flare. Waiting. Hoping.

A spotlight came on near the aft of the big ship. It played across the water until it locked on to the orange raft. It went dark for a second and then began to flash a message.

'Use the flashlight,' Kurt said.

Joe moved to the edge, snapped on the light, and began to signal an SOS in Morse code.

More flashes followed from the ship.

'They're coming around,' the captain replied, reading the message before Kurt could speak. 'They're going to pick us up.'

A cheer went through the boat.

With the spotlight blazing down on them, the survivors watched as the freighter heaved to. It slowed appreciably and then came around, settling a hundred yards to the west of the lifeboat, blocking the swells to some extent.

Kurt and Joe rowed with great enthusiasm to close the gap. Their efforts were rewarded when the orange inflatable bumped into the side of the blue-painted hull.

Thirty feet above, a wide cargo hatch opened in the side of the ship and a few faces appeared. A basket was lowered to haul up the injured crewmen. After they'd been secured, a cargo net was draped against the hull like a ladder for the rest of the survivors to climb.

One by one, they went up until only Kurt and the captain remained.

'After you,' Kurt said.

The captain shook his head. 'My ship went down without me,' Winslow insisted. 'The least I can do is be the last man off the lifeboat.'

Kurt nodded, secured the flare gun to his belt, and climbed on to the cargo net.

He glanced down to see Winslow latching on to the net and the orange lifeboat drifting away. Truth was, they'd been lucky. Lucky to have survived the sinking, lucky to have avoided hypothermia, lucky to have been picked up.

In fact, they'd been extremely lucky. Their rescuers weren't from NUMA or any navy or coast guard. The ship was a merchant vessel. Forty feet above him, Kurt could just make out the boxy outline of shipping containers stacked three high.

A thought began to form in his mind, a spark of insight that struggled to flare brightly in his weary, half-frozen brain. They were a thousand miles from the nearest trade route, he told himself. So what on earth was a containership doing there?

He got part of the answer as he was pulled into the hatchway. It came in the form of a black pistol pressed up against the side of his head.

He looked around. The other survivors were down on their knees. Stern-looking men wielding AK-47s stood around them.

Captain Winslow climbed in and received the same treatment.

Kurt received the rest of the answer a moment later as one of the gun-toting men got on the ship's phone.

'Da,' he said, holding the phone to his ear and turning back toward the captives. 'We have been most fortunate. The woman is among them.'

'Russians,' Kurt muttered.

The man hung up the phone as the sound of the ship's propellers reengaging shuddered throughout the vessel. He came toward Kurt. He was tall, but a little on the thin side. Half of his face was covered with scabs. Despite that, Kurt recognized him.

'So we meet again,' Kirov said, slamming the barrel of his AK-47 across the back of Kurt's legs.

Kurt dropped to his knees. For a moment, he was thankful that his legs were almost numb.

He resisted the urge to fight back or fire off a snarky comment. And since Kirov refrained from shooting him, it seemed Kurt had made a wise choice. Or so he thought until Kirov stepped toward the open hatch, through which a bitter air was beginning to flow as the ship picked up speed.

'You made me jump from a moving train,' Kirov said, peering down at the cold sea below. 'It seems Karma wishes me to return the favor.'

Kirov nodded to his men. 'Throw him out.'

Two men grabbed Kurt and tried to drag him to the door. Kurt pulled free of one and slugged the other, but a third man jumped into the melee.

With all eyes on Kurt, Joe spun and batted away the AK-47 aimed in his direction. From his knees, he threw an uppercut into the guard's groin, and the man fell, dropping the weapon and releasing a grunt of agonizing pain.

Captain Winslow joined the fray, lunging at one of the guards and tackling him before he could fire.

This second commotion distracted Kirov. As it did, Kurt managed to kick free of the remaining guard. He lunged at Kirov, grasping him in a headlock before the others could regroup.

'Enough!'

Kurt's voice boomed off the metal walls of the small compartment. Everyone looked his way. He was all but choking the life out of Kirov with one arm. He was also holding the flare gun to Kirov's cheek with his other.

An uneasy stalemate settled over the room. Joe went for a rifle that was lying on the ground, but the guard closest to him raised his weapon.

'Tell your men to lower their guns,' Kurt growled, 'or I'm gonna give you a chemical peel you won't ever recover from.'

Kirov gulped hard, his Adam's apple moving up and down against the crushing force of Kurt's forearm.

'Lower your guns,' Kirov said, 'but do not discard them.'

Half a win, Kurt thought. It was better than nothing.

He was pondering what to do next when the sound of the bulkhead door being unlatched caught his ear.

Kurt turned as the door swung wide and an oak tree of a man stepped through the hatch. Despite his size, he moved fluidly. He wore dark khaki pants and a black sweater. His cheekbones were high on his face and angular, almost like the mirrors on a sports car.

The Russian commandos immediately stood a little taller in his presence. Kurt guessed this was Kirov's superior. He seemed it in every way. He was armed with two black pistols, though for now they sat in shoulder holsters, one on each side of his chest.

'What have we here?' he asked.

'A small disagreement,' Kurt said. 'Your slug here wanted to toss me into the ocean. I didn't feel like being part of any catch-and-release program.'

'So it would appear,' the man said.

'Who are you?' Kurt asked. 'You weren't on the train.'

'My name is Gregorovich,' the man said. 'And you're right, I avoided that pitiful episode.'

Gregorovich glanced around. 'You seem to have made the best of your situation,' he said to Kurt. 'However, you're outnumbered and outgunned. The woman is the only one of you with any value. And Kirov is not much of a bargaining chip to me.'

He turned to one of the commandos. 'Shoot them both.'

As the commando raised his rifle and took aim, Kurt prepared to fling Kirov forward as a human shield and fire the flare into Gregorovich's face.

'Wait!' a voice cried.

Of all people, it was Hayley.

'He's the only one who knows,' she exclaimed.

Once again, all activity stopped just short of a bloodbath.

'The only one who knows what?' Gregorovich asked.

'I know about the threat,' Hayley said. 'First, my country will be punished, then Russia, then the United States. You guys are Russian. You must be after Thero just like we are. That's why you're here. That's why you tried to pull me off the train. You must think I can help you find him, but you're wrong. Kurt's the only one who knows where Thero is.'

Kurt felt a glimmer of hope. It was quick thinking.

'You really expect me to believe that?' the muscle-bound Russian said. 'You're the scientist. They brought you along for a reason. The same reason we tried to kidnap you. Because you are the only one who understands what Thero is doing. Therefore, it stands to reason that *you*, not him, have discerned Thero's whereabouts.'

'The computer determined Thero's location,' Hayley said desperately. 'It gave me a printout. I ran to Kurt to show him. It had numbers and lines on it, but I don't know anything about azimuths and ranges and coordinates. For God sakes, I don't even like being away from Sydney. I showed it to Kurt, he saw it. He read it. He told me we were going in the wrong direction. And then the wave hit, and it broke our ship and sank us in thirty seconds.'

The commandos exchanged glances.

'We were wondering what happened,' Gregorovich

said. 'We came across a lot of debris and some of your crewmen. I'm afraid they were all dead.'

'Thero's weapon is operational,' Hayley said. 'He found us because we sent out a pulse. Which means even if I build you a detector, you're just signing your own death warrant by turning it on. He'll destroy you like he did us.'

Gregorovich turned to Kurt. 'She makes a good case, but it only changes things momentarily. You will give me what I want or I will kill your friends one by one.'

Kurt was pretty sure that would happen anyway. 'No,' he said, 'that isn't how this is going to go.'

The Russian's eyebrow went up. 'It will go how I say it goes,' Gregorovich insisted.

'You don't seem like a fool,' Kurt began, 'so don't treat me like one. If I give you what you want, then you don't need us anymore. And we all end up dead. I'm not dumb enough to think I'm saving any lives by handing you our only bargaining chip.'

'Then I'll torture it out of you,' Gregorovich insisted. 'I will make you talk.'

Kurt stared the Russian killer in the eye. 'Go ahead and try. Maybe I'll talk. Maybe I'll give you a location. Maybe I'll give you a dozen different locations, and you'll spend forever bouncing around Antarctica looking for your prize. Or maybe I'll put you right in front of him so he can tee you up and crush this ship the way he crushed ours. You want to chance that? Then go ahead, try to force it out of me. You never know what you'll get.'

Gregorovich seemed impressed with Kurt's challenge. He actually began to chuckle. 'An inspired response,' he said. 'And, what's more, I believe you. Not because I must, but because I would do exactly that in your position. However, I have my orders and I will fulfill them . . . *to perfection*.'

'Then let me help you,' Kurt said.

Gregorovich narrowed his gaze.

'We're after the same thing,' Kurt explained. 'To stop Thero. You may not care about the timing, but in our case we'd like to do it before he lays waste to Australia.'

'We have the power to stop him,' Gregorovich insisted. 'Tell me where to find him and I'll destroy his lair. I give you my word, you and your crew will be released when we're finished.'

'I have a better idea,' Kurt said. 'I'll lead you to him and we can destroy him together.'

Gregorovich inhaled deeply. He seemed angered by having to negotiate or consider any form of compromise. If he didn't like the first offer, Kurt thought, he really wasn't going to like the fine print.

'And,' Kurt said, 'you'll be giving us guns. Rifles and spare clips for myself, Joe, the captain, and any other member of our crew who wants one.'

'Count me in,' Hayley said.

'And one for me,' the XO added.

Gregorovich raised an eyebrow. 'You expect me to arm you? Here on this ship?'

'I do,' Kurt said. 'And I'm not giving you a thing until you do.'

Gregorovich was fuming. His eyes narrowed, and he ground his teeth with a clenched jaw. He was trapped and he knew it. But he didn't reject the offer outright. That meant he was at least considering it.

'A countryman of mine used the term *peace through strength*,' Kurt said, quoting Ronald Reagan. 'Your nation and ours held nuclear weapons to each other's head for half a century. It made for a stable – if somewhat tense – relationship. But no one ever pulled the trigger, so it obviously worked. I figure we can make it through a few days with a similar setup and a common goal.'

'This is madness,' Kirov said.

Kurt choked his words off and kept his eyes on Gregorovich.

'Do we have a deal?'

Gregorovich leaned against the bulkhead. He stroked his chin thoughtfully. Kurt could almost hear the gears turning in his mind.

'I will give you one pistol,' he said finally. 'And to a friend of your choosing, I will give exactly one rifle. You will get nothing more from me except death.'

'Until we achieve our common goal,' Kurt added.

Gregorovich did not comment on that statement. He only looked to Joe. 'You. Arm yourself.'

Joe was allowed to pick up a rifle. He checked it

quickly and pointed it at Gregorovich. Two of the commandos pointed their own weapons at him in response.

'See?' Kurt said. 'Nice and stable.'

He released Kirov. He then handed the flare gun to Captain Winslow and grabbed one of the Makarov pistols from the deck. He pulled the slide back an inch to make sure there was a bullet in the chamber and then eased the hammer back down.

'You have your weapons,' Gregorovich said. 'Now you will accompany me to the bridge and tell the navigator which direction to go.'

Kurt glanced at the others and received a smattering of *I hope you know what you're doing* looks. He nodded confidently. 'Lead on.'

The Russian stepped through the hatch. Kurt followed, with Kirov and all the others trailing behind.

It would take no more than a minute or so to reach the bridge, a time frame Kurt could expand by dragging his feet. But that was it, all the time he had in which to come up with a plan. A plan that would somehow point the freighter in the right direction and satisfy the Russians without simultaneously making himself and the rest of the NUMA survivors expendable once again.

Two minutes at most, Kurt thought. And the clock was ticking.

28

Bridge of the MV Rama, *2340 hours, five miles southeast of where the* Orion *went down*

'We're waiting, Mr Austin.'

The words came from Gregorovich, but they might as well have been spoken by any of the commandos, or the Vietnamese crewmen who ran the freighter, or even from the NUMA survivors, all of whom were standing around looking at Kurt expectantly.

Twenty people, half of them with guns, crowded into a room more fit for eight or ten. *If ever there was a recipe for disaster . . .*

'Give us a heading,' Gregorovich added, raising a pistol of his own and setting the hammer.

Kurt kept his eyes forward. He stood over a surprisingly modern chart table. In reality, it was a giant touchscreen monitor laid flat. The screen was white with black demarcation lines. The display was almost identical to how the old charts used to look when lit up from below. The difference was, this screen could pan or zoom. It could indicate currents and wind and tides. It could bring up information in dozens of different ways.

None of which helped Kurt at the moment.

Right now, it was centered on the MV *Rama*'s location, with nothing but deep sea around it right out to the chart's edge.

'Zoom out,' Kurt said.

The Vietnamese navigator glanced at Gregorovich, who nodded his approval.

The navigator touched the screen, tapping a magnifying glass icon with a little minus sign inside it. The screen adjusted its resolution and settled at the new level of magnification, displaying four hundred miles from corner to corner.

'Zoom out,' Kurt said.

This went on for several more rounds until the chart covered most of the southern hemisphere.

'If it's not on the map now, we're going to need more fuel,' Gregorovich said.

His men laughed, but it was a nervous laugh.

'Zoom in twice,' Kurt said.

This time, the map refocused with Perth and the southwestern edge of Australia in the top right corner. Along the bottom of the screen, the jagged edge of the Antarctic coast could be seen. At the far left, the tip of Madagascar poked into the picture.

Kurt stared at the very center of the map, locking his eyes on the dot that marked the MV *Rama*. He tried to *see* with his peripheral vision, not willing to even glance in the slightest in any direction lest he give away what he was looking for. His mind was racing. There had to be a way.

He knew where the ship needed to go, but how could he get the *Rama* pointed toward the target without letting the Russians know the location?

Gregorovich stepped closer, he pressed the cold muzzle of the gun to the back of Kurt's head. 'I won't ask you again,' he said.

The answer came to Kurt in a flash, a memory derived from years of studying warfare at sea. They would zigzag, changing course almost randomly every few hours like the allied convoys dodging the U-boats during World War Two.

Such a tack had two benefits. First, it would keep the Russians guessing and therefore keep Kurt and the NUMA crew alive. And, second, if anyone happened to be watching, they might notice the containership lost at the bottom of the world and question the crazy path she was taking.

'Helmsman,' Kurt said, still keeping his eyes locked on the center of the map, 'would you please set the ship on a heading of 195 degrees true.'

Gregorovich lowered his pistol and stepped back. All eyes looked at the map. The helmsman plugged in the coordinates. A line appeared on the chart. It led almost due south, with a slight westerly lean. It ran aground at the tip of a jagged little peninsula jutting out from Antarctica.

'So Thero's station is there?' Kirov asked, bluntly. 'In Antarctica?'

Kurt said nothing. He kept his eyes still, calculating the ship's speed.

The *Rama* began to turn, the first of Kurt's zigs. He checked his watch. Four hours, he told himself. In four hours, he would give them a new heading.

'Answer me,' Kirov demanded, grabbing Kurt.

'Wait,' Gregorovich shouted. 'We are on our way. I'm assuming if we get off course somehow, our polestar, Mr Austin, will reroute us.'

Clearly, he saw what Kurt was doing. For some reason, he seemed okay with it. That thought gained strength when Gregorovich handed another weapon to Captain Winslow.

'Détente,' he said, explaining. Then he snapped his fingers at one of the Vietnamese crewmen. 'Show them to their quarters. Mr Austin and I are going to share a drink.'

The situation had worked out better than Kurt might have hoped. They'd bought some time, and they now had two rifles plus his pistol. They just might survive until morning.

Dirk Pitt found himself standing in the mist on a low rise surrounded by tall pines and cedars. He and Vice President Sandecker had hitched a ride on a B-1 bomber making a transcontinental trip. Traveling at Mach 2, they'd arrived at Travis Air Force Base in Northern California nearly a full hour before they'd taken off, at least according to the local clock anyway.

It had been a great ride, and one that Pitt enjoyed as a pilot. He might have enjoyed it more had he known the purpose of the trip.

From Travis, a CH-53 Sea Stallion had brought them northwest. It thundered across the landscape, finally setting them down on a rocky outcropping high atop an inaccessible ridge overlooking Sonoma Lake.

There, Pitt and Sandecker met with Jim Culver, head of the NSA. He was fuming mad, and he and Pitt might have come to blows had Sandecker not been there to intervene.

'Who do you people think you are? Hacking an NSA secure database?'

'I'd say it wasn't all that secure if we could do it in a day,' Pitt replied, though he realized there were few people out there with skills like Yaeger's.

'Beyond that,' Pitt added, 'I wouldn't have needed to if you'd have been forthcoming with some answers about Tesla and a theory he either burned or hid seventy years ago.'

'So you admit it?'

'Sure do,' Pitt said. 'There's a terrorist out there threatening to turn an entire country into a parking lot. And I'm not going to leave a single stone unturned in my effort to stop him. If that ruffles your feathers, then I don't happen to care. One of my ships is already missing. It may have gone down with all hands. Compared to those lives, whatever secret you're trying to protect doesn't mean a thing to me.'

Culver shrank back. Years on Wall Street and in the boardroom, followed by a successful political career, had not prepared him for the kind of life-and-death intensity that Pitt unleashed. The anger in Pitt's opaline green eyes caused Culver to forget that he was an inch taller than Pitt and thirty pounds heavier.

He turned to Sandecker. 'I know he's a friend of yours, Mr Vice President. And I'm sure you're going to defend him. But this is inexcusable.'

'Not only is he a friend of mine,' Sandecker said proudly, 'but he's a patriot who's done more for this country than you and your whole army of schemers and bureaucrats ever will. So whatever your problem is, you need to get over it. The President has ordered that there be cooperation on this matter. That's why we're here.'

'Do you two have any idea what's at stake?' Culver said.

'Do you?' Pitt replied.

Culver fumed. Whatever stand he thought he was going to make had crumbled. 'Fine. But understand this. What I'm about to show you has been known only to the presidents of the United States and a select few others. Not even ranking members of Congress. It's considered a national secret of the highest order. To speak of it, or otherwise disclose what you see here, is punishable. And I'm quite sure this even applies to you, Mr Pitt.'

Pitt looked around. 'Not sure how this qualifies as

some big secret. As far as I can tell, we're standing in a national park or something.'

'No,' Culver said, 'you're standing on top of a catastrophe. This is the true epicenter of the 1906 San Francisco earthquake, a natural disaster in the eyes of the world. But, in actuality, the largest self-inflicted wound in US history.'

'April 18, 1906,' Pitt said. 'The day Daniel Watterson and General Hal Cortland died.'

'That's right,' Culver said. 'Only they didn't die in Topeka, Kansas, and San Diego, California, like it says on their papers. They died right here, twenty stories beneath our feet, along with eighty-one others. Casualties not counted in the official death toll of the earthquake.'

'The obituaries,' Pitt said, understanding what happened. 'They were all the same, just a few words changed: name, cause of death and location. They were all written by one person as part of the cover-up. No one bothered to distinguish them. Whoever it was, they didn't count on modern computer analysis to pick up the similar patterns.'

'It was 1906,' Culver said sarcastically. 'I'm guessing they didn't think that far ahead. Come with me.'

Together, the three of them walked back into the forest. They passed through a length of electrified fence and came to a sealed hatch that was as sturdy as any Pitt had ever seen on a ship. In fact, it reminded him of the doors to NORAD's mountain bunker, only a lot smaller.

Culver entered a code on the outside and then used a key card. A seal cracked and the hatch opened like an oyster, revealing steps.

The three of them went inside, and Culver flipped a bank of switches. Old 1940s-style fixtures came to life, illuminated by modern halogen bulbs. A short walk brought them to another sealed door. Once through this door, they entered an elevator. It took them down into a lighted cave.

The cave was mammoth in size, but it appeared to be man-made, or perhaps shored up by man. Concrete lined the walls in places. Steel I beams spanned the cave in dizzying directions, welded and cross-braced in places. To Pitt, it looked like some giant had gone crazy with an Erector set.

They came to an open section. Pitt stared down into a chasm. It dropped hundreds of feet. Water filled the bottom.

'This is where the experiment happened,' Culver said. 'Using Tesla's theory, Watterson claimed he could create and transmit limitless energy. They built a machine much like what your friend found in the mine.'

Pitt guessed at the series of events. 'After Tesla shut down Wardenclyffe, Watterson took the idea back to the army, making his own deal with General Cortland.'

Culver nodded. 'According to Watterson, he'd developed an improved version.'

'Depends on your definition of the word *improved*,' Sandecker added.

'That it does,' Culver said, pointing to some sparkling residue on the cave wall. 'See this? It's shocked quartz. You're only supposed to get it when a meteor hits the Earth or an A-bomb goes off. The whole cave is filled with it, right down into the chasm.'

'From the experiment,' Pitt surmised.

Culver nodded. 'Watterson activated his machine and began to get feedback. A data line running from down here up to a small receiving station on the surface recorded what happened. Multiple waves of energy, all from an initial impulse of minor proportions. Each wave of energy was many times more powerful than the one before it.'

'So Watterson's experiment was a success,' Pitt noted.

'It went too well, in fact,' Culver said. 'He couldn't shut it off. Couldn't control the energy he'd released. The waves grew, flowing in and out of this cave, shaking it to pieces. The observers and military personnel were crushed and buried down here. But the devastation didn't end until they triggered a long-overdue movement in the San Andreas Fault.'

'This experiment caused the 1906 San Francisco quake?' Pitt asked, just to be sure.

Culver nodded. 'By extension, that means the US government did it and never owned up to it. Three thousand people died, countless more were badly burned or wounded. Eighty-five per cent of the city was destroyed. So now you can see why it must remain a secret. People would never trust the government if they knew.'

Dirk Pitt could hardly believe what he was hearing. 'I've got news for you, Culver: no one really trusts the government anyway. Keeping secrets like this is reason number one.'

'What you've been told does not leave this cave,' Culver grunted.

'Fine,' Pitt said. 'What happened a hundred years ago doesn't really concern me. What I'm trying to do is stop it from happening again. Only a thousand times worse. To that end, I need Tesla's theory. I know you guys have it. The Office of Alien Property took his papers when he died. They were folded into the OSS, and somehow that all leads up to you.'

'We do have it,' Culver admitted, 'but not because it was stolen. The OSS brought Tesla here in 1937 when he was finally threatening to publish the theory. We showed him this place. Gave him the data and told him what happened. He handed the theory over that same day. The Office of Alien Property was just making sure no other copies existed.'

'You'd better give us yours, then,' Pitt said.

'I'll turn it over,' Culver said. 'But let me be clear: the theory and the technology must be kept under wraps. Ever since this accident, we've watched people approach what Tesla discovered. Ninety-nine per cent of them touch on it and then go the other way, even the serious ones. Those that don't turn back have fallen on hard times.'

'So you guys were watching Thero,' Pitt said wryly. 'Probably helping make sure he failed.'

'It wasn't hard,' Culver said. 'He's a nut. Delusional, and possibly schizophrenic. We just helped people see that more clearly.'

Pitt glanced at Sandecker. 'Just because you're paranoid, doesn't mean they're not out to get you.'

'Indeed,' Sandecker said.

Pitt turned back to Culver. 'You probably could have saved the world a lot of pain if you'd brought him into the fold.'

'We should have put a bullet in him,' Culver said bitterly. 'We don't want him, or anyone like him, in the fold. We don't want anyone messing around with this. Ever.'

Pitt narrowed his gaze. 'Why? We pursue every other technology. Nuclear bombs, biological and chemical weapons. Why not this?'

Culver didn't blink. But he took the long way around in explaining. 'My wife and I have a farm, Mr Pitt. We have a few cows, a few goats, a few ATVs, and a whole lot of dogs. Some big dogs, some little dogs, even a few mean dogs. But there's one scrawny mutt that just never was right. He never behaves the same way twice. Friendly one second, trying to tear your arm off the next. That dog scares me more than the mean ones. He scares the other dogs too. They give him a wide birth. Even the big alphas.

'Zero-point energy is like that. It's unpredictable. Erratic. The NSA has had people studying it for decades. We're too damned scared to do anything like this experiment because each time we run the numbers, we come up with a range of possible outcomes instead of just one. Could you imagine firing a gun if you had a fifty-fifty chance of hitting the target or having the gun blow up in your face?'

'No,' Pitt admitted.

'Nor can I,' Culver said. 'But that's how it is. With a gun, you pull the trigger and the bullet fires. With a bomb, you hit the detonator and the explosives blow. Even a hydrogen bomb has an established yield. But with this stuff . . . With this stuff, the results seem to be random, like it has a mind of its own. And that means once you press the switch, all bets are off. At that point, anything can happen.'

Pitt recalled Yaeger's comment describing it as a moody genie, best kept in a bottle. It seemed the NSA agreed with him. He had a feeling Culver was making the point for a reason. 'What are you really trying to say?'

Culver still wouldn't shoot straight, perhaps enjoying the little bit of power he was still holding.

'Have your man run the numbers,' Culver said. 'If he disagrees with our people, then we can argue about it. But this device must be prevented from operating under any circumstances. I assure you that's how the President sees it. We have two nuclear attack submarines moving into the area. As soon as we have a location, they're going to destroy the site with nuclear-tipped cruise missiles.'

Pitt glanced at Sandecker, who nodded gravely. He'd already been told.

'It has to be done,' Sandecker said.

To his surprise, Pitt found himself agreeing.

29

MV Rama, *0330 hours local time*

After a stop in the mess hall, and a change of clothes, Kurt sat in a dingy cabin with gray-brown walls lit by a single incandescent light.

A chessboard sat in front of him on a small table. The game was in mid-progress, the pieces already in motion. A quarter of them stood on the side, fallen soldiers already taken by the other player.

To the left was an almost empty bottle of Stolichnaya vodka and two shot glasses, which Anton Gregorovich had just finished topping off for the seventh time. To the right – easily within both men's reach – sat the Makarov pistol that Gregorovich had given Kurt.

Kurt had been in there for most of the night. This was their third game. Occasionally, Gregorovich asked him questions, which Kurt did his best to deflect. More often than not, he sat silently brooding.

Kurt figured it was some kind of test to see if he could hold his liquor or his tongue.

Eyeing the board stoically, Gregorovich finally moved, sliding a bishop into Kurt's section. The move created options, forcing Kurt to choose between saving a pawn or a rook or making an offensive move and letting both pieces go.

Done with his move, Gregorovich pushed one of the overflowing shot glasses toward Kurt and lifted the other to his mouth.

He knocked it down and then turned to the bottle for a refill. As he did, Kurt dumped the contents of his shot glass in a planter with a dying fern in it and quickly brought the glass back to his mouth.

He finished the last sip as Gregorovich turned back to him. 'I wouldn't do that,' Kurt suggested, putting the glass down firmly.

'What?' Gregorovich asked. 'The bishop or the vodka?'

'You leave yourself open to check,' Kurt said.

'Only if you give up one of your pieces,' Gregorovich said and then downed the shot.

Kurt studied the board carefully. He moved the rook to a spot next to the pawn, protecting them both, instead of threatening Gregorovich with check, which the Russian could have easily escaped.

'You don't understand this game, I think,' Gregorovich said. 'You play defensively, protecting your pawns. This game, like life, is all about attacking.'

Gregorovich took another of Kurt's pieces, moving his queen recklessly into danger.

'What would you know about life?' Kurt said. 'Except how to end it.'

This time, Kurt reached for the bottle and poured the shots. He allowed his hand to shake and appear unsteady.

Gregorovich snickered. 'I know that life is about finding your place in all of this madness,' he said. 'Some of us find it easily, maybe you did. My path was more complicated. When I was a boy, my mother left us. My father's temper and the back of his hand were too much for her. So, naturally, he took it out on me. When he drank, everything was my fault. When he didn't drink, everything was my fault.'

Gregorovich shook his head. 'Somehow, I always failed him. And when I did, he would beat me. His favorite game was to force me outside and make me stand in the ice water of the bog. It came up to my thighs and it numbed my legs, and then he would whip me with a belt until the water turned red or until my knees buckled and I fell in it. I couldn't feel my lower half, but I could feel every inch of that belt on my back with heightened awareness.'

Kurt looked up from the board.

'One day,' Gregorovich said, 'I decided I would stay up. Stay up until he killed me, and then I'd be free. I stood as he thrashed me and I kept myself from falling. It infuriated him more until eventually he charged into the water and tried to force me under. This triggered something in me. Something I had never felt. I had forced him to change. And so instead of letting him drown me, I fought him. For the first time ever, I raised my fist to him. And when I'd beaten him to a bloody mess, I took that belt and strangled the life from the miserable bastard.'

Kurt remained silent.

'The look in his eyes,' Gregorovich continued. 'The look in his eyes as he died. It wasn't shock. It wasn't fear. It was pride. For the first time in my life, and the last time in his, I had impressed him.'

Kurt tipped back another shot of vodka. 'Why are you telling me this touching family story?'

'Because from that day on, I knew who I was,' Gregorovich said coldly. 'From that day on, I understood life. It revealed what I was meant to be. An assassin. A killer. It is my gift. I have *never* failed at an assignment. Never failed to destroy the selected target. It is perfection. I am perfection.'

'Except for Thero,' Kurt guessed.

Gregorovich seemed to brood at the mention of the name.

'Come on,' Kurt said, 'it's not that hard to figure. Thero's facility was blown to bits. Somehow, he survives, and now Russia ends up on his hit list. It was you guys who blew him up. Seems you got everything except the head of the snake. I'd say you failed pretty badly on that one.'

Gregorovich lunged across the table, his hand blasting the chess pieces all over the room as it plowed through them on the way to the Makarov. He reached the pistol before Kurt could react.

Kurt had made a different choice. His left hand went for the vodka bottle, grabbed it, and smashed it against the bulkhead wall and brought the shattered stub up to Gregorovich's neck like a blade. It met the Russian's neck at the very instant the barrel of the Makarov lodged against Kurt's gut.

The safety was off, Kurt's liver unprotected. But so was his opponent's jugular. Either man could have ended the other's life in a blink, but it was a standoff. If Gregorovich fired, Kurt's body would convulse, and the jagged glass of the bottle would slice his artery. If Kurt flipped the edge of the glass, he would mortally wound the Russian, but death would not come quick enough to stop the 9mm bullet from blasting through his liver and tearing apart his internal organs.

They stared into each other's eyes. Two men on the brink.

'In chess they call this blood,' Gregorovich said. 'A piece for a piece, an even trade. But our trade wouldn't be even, would it? End my life and I end yours, but Kirov will have your crew shot before dawn. The pawns you fight desperately to protect will die along with their king. And I sense you have no stomach for that kind of outcome.'

'That may be true,' Kurt said. 'But if you kill me, you lose your only chance to find Thero, your only chance to erase your one big failure. And your pride won't let you give that up. No matter how badly I've angered you.'

The Russian began to laugh. 'At least we understand each other.'

Gregorovich released the pistol and dropped it into Kurt's lap. He then pulled slowly away from the glass.

Kurt grabbed the pistol and tossed the broken bottle away.

'I will find and destroy Thero,' Gregorovich said matter-of-factly. 'Whether it happens before or after he obliterates Australia, Russia, or the rest of the world matters little to me. I will hunt him down and kill him because it is personal to me. And I will do so if I have to drive every man and woman on this ship to their deaths in the process.'

Kurt nodded. He recognized a modern-day Ahab when he saw one.

'Why would you need to drive your men so hard,' Kurt asked. 'Don't they have the same orders as you?'

'Orders, yes. But they lack my zeal. They're uneasy and have been since we determined what happened to your ship. Like the men with Columbus, they're afraid we're sailing off the edge of the map.'

'So that's why you gave us the guns,' Kurt said.

'You and your men are quite an effective counterbalance against them,' Gregorovich said. 'Now they have something else to worry about beyond getting rid of me.'

'How Machiavellian of you,' Kurt said.

'It's worked so far,' Gregorovich boasted. 'But for how long, I don't know. Kirov prods them and plots against me. They may find the heart to challenge me yet. If they do, you and your men will certainly die.'

'Or fight for you,' Kurt guessed.

'Odd as that sounds, yes.'

'I guess we'd have no choice,' Kurt said. 'The question is: how much time do you think we have until that occurs?'

Gregorovich shook his head. 'No,' he said, 'that's not the question. The question is: how far will you go to stop Thero?'

So that was it. Gregorovich was looking for a partner, a blood brother, in his quest for the prey that escaped him. Kurt was up for that, as long as they got there in time.

'To stop Thero from killing millions,' Kurt said. 'To the ends of the Earth, if necessary.'

Gregorovich nodded. It was the answer he wanted to hear. It also happened to be true.

'This far south,' the Russian said, 'it would seem we're almost there.'

'Not quite,' Kurt replied. He stood and checked his watch. It was time for a new heading. 'Tell your helmsman to change course. Our new heading should be 245 degrees.'

'So we don't journey to Antarctica after all?'

'Not yet anyway,' Kurt said, keeping the truth to himself. 'I'm going to my quarters so I can sleep this off. Assuming Kirov doesn't kill me during the night, I'll have more course changes for you in the morning.'

Gregorovich nodded, and Kurt stepped out into the hall. One of the commandos waited there.

'You must be the bellhop,' Kurt muttered. 'Take me to my cabin.'

He was escorted aft until he reached a pair of the Russian commandos standing outside the cabin in which the NUMA crew had been placed. He stepped past them and went inside, only to find an argument in full bloom.

Captain Winslow and his XO were on one side, Joe and Hayley on the other.

'. . . he's got us this far,' Hayley insisted.

'He's playing a game with our lives,' the XO replied.

'We'd be dead if he told them what they wanted to hear,' Joe added.

Apparently, more than one mutiny was brewing on the ship.

'Told who what they wanted to hear?' Kurt asked.

The group turned in unison.

'The Russians,' Captain Winslow said. 'While you were out drinking with their leader, they came and took our injured crewmen to the sick bay. Only now they tell us no one will be receiving medical treatment until we give them more information.'

Kurt didn't like the sound of that. But there was no turning back.

'I don't know if this is the right course of action,' Winslow added.

'It's the only course left,' Kurt said.

'We have to give them something,' Winslow said. 'At least a hint.'

'No. If they guess right, we're all dead,' Kurt explained. 'They'll tie weights to our feet and drop us over the side to save the cost of a bullet.'

'My crewmen are in shock,' Winslow said. 'They're dying. For God sakes, Kurt, be reasonable.'

'There's no room for reason,' Kurt snapped. 'Can't you see that?!'

The others stared back at him, taken off guard at an uncommon burst of fury.

'We're caught in between a madman and a lunatic,' he explained. 'Gregorovich is insane. This isn't a *job* for him. It's some kind of vendetta. Maybe even a suicide mission. His failure to kill Thero years ago is eating him alive. If he has to, he'll murder every one of us just to get another shot at it. And Thero is worse. He was a schizophrenic, a sociopath, years ago. Can you imagine what time and pain have done to him since? He's called his lair Tartarus, the Prison of the Gods. What do you think that says about him? He considers himself a god. A persecuted one at that. You think he's going to let up on his threat?'

They gazed at Kurt oddly. No doubt he looked half deranged himself at this point.

'It can't be that bad,' the XO said.

'It can be and it is,' Kurt said. 'If anyone's making plans to survive this, I suggest you stop wasting your time because most likely we won't. The only thing we can hope for is to prevent Thero from acting. And to do that, we need the Russians as much as they need us.'

Joe stood with Kurt, the loyal friend that he was. Hayley seemed to understand the truth and had resigned herself to it. Even the XO seemed to soften his posture. But Winslow shook his head.

'They're my crew,' he said. 'My responsibility.'

Kurt understood that. He figured lack of sleep and guilt were weighing on the captain's mind too.

'Most of your crewmen already gave their lives to fight this,' Kurt said. 'So did nine members of the ASIO, and at least four civilians who've tried to escape Thero's grasp. The only way to give those deaths meaning is to stop Thero from winning. We have a chance to do that if we side with Gregorovich. It's a long shot. But it's the only shot we have.'

Winslow seemed unsure.

Kurt put his hand on the captain's shoulder and looked him in the eye. 'I know what you're going through. None of us would even be in this situation if I'd kept my nose out of it. Those crewmen's lives are on me, not you. But we can't bring them back. We can only do our best to make sure their deaths are not in vain.'

Winslow looked back at Kurt. He seemed to understand. 'So what do we do now?'

'We have to reduce the number of commandos at their disposal,' Kurt said. 'Even the odds a little.'

'How? They have us under guard.'

Kurt had been thinking about this while losing in chess to Gregorovich. 'They eat buffet style around here,' he said, having noted the setup on his single pass through the mess hall. 'This ship is filthy. It has to be crawling with bacteria. Scrape up any kind of grunge you can find. I don't care where you get it from, and, frankly, I don't want to know. Collect it up and find a way to drop it in the food right around chow time – after we've gotten our fill of course.'

'Germ warfare,' Joe noted.

'If the commandos are too sick to fight, Gregorovich will have no choice but to take us along.'

'I like it,' Joe said. 'What if he leaves us behind anyway?'

'Then we take over the ship and radio NUMA if we can.'

Joe nodded, and Hayley offered a sad smile. Even the XO cracked a grin at the thought of going on the offensive for a change. Winslow agreed. 'Okay,' he said. 'I'm with you.'

30

Tartarus

Deep beneath the surface of the ice-covered island, Patrick Devlin found his ears ringing. The bone-shaking sound of a huge rock drill grinding away had all but deafened him over the past hour. When it suddenly stopped, the silence was almost painful.

'That's deep enough,' a burly foreman shouted.

Devlin backed away from the wall. The heavy drill was mounted on an ore cart of sorts. Padi's job was to keep pressure on it and drill a series of boreholes in the wall. Covered in dust and grime, he stepped back as another man placed a series of charges in the holes and began attaching wires to the caps.

A sharp whistle sounded. 'Everyone to the tunnel,' a foreman demanded.

Spread about the large cavern, a dozen other workers busy crushing rocks and scooping the rubble on to a conveyor belt stopped what they were doing and began trudging toward a small tunnel entrance on one side of the room.

They fitted themselves inside, taking shelter under

the steel-reinforced arch, weary souls glad to put down their tools for a moment. Devlin noticed their faces were drawn but their bodies fit.

With the armed foreman and his assistant checking the explosives, he took a chance. 'What's your name?' he asked a black man who stood beside him.

'My name is Masinga,' the man replied in a distinct South African accent.

Devlin nodded. 'I'm Patrick,' he said. 'Sometimes, people call me Padi. What is this place?'

'Don't you know?'

Devlin shook his head.

'Diamond mine,' Masinga said.

Devlin studied the crumbled rock sitting on the motionless conveyor belt. 'I don't see any diamonds.'

'They're in the rock,' Masinga explained. 'Not much of a miner if you don't know that.'

'I'm not a miner,' Devlin said.

'Then what are you doing here?'

'I was bloody well shanghaied,' Devlin swore under his breath. 'Weren't you?'

'No,' Masinga said. 'I signed a contract. We all did. Paid us twice the rate De Beers was offering. Only when it came time to leave, we were kept on against our will.'

'Have you tried to escape?'

The man laughed. 'Do we look like fish? We're on an island in the middle of the ocean. Where would we escape to?'

'But your families,' Padi said. 'Surely, they can protest.'

'They've been told we died in an accident,' another man said. He sounded like he might be from South America. 'And they never knew where we were in the first place. None of us did until we got here.'

It sounded like madness to Devlin, but then little had made sense since he'd spotted the *Voyager* in the harbor off the coast of Jakarta.

'What about you?' Masinga asked. 'Maybe someone will come looking.'

'Not likely,' Padi said, remembering that Keane was unconscious when he found the *Voyager*. 'If I had to guess, the whole world probably thinks I'm dead too.'

'You are, then,' Masinga said. 'We all are.'

'Tartarus,' Devlin mumbled, prison of the underworld. Now it made sense to him.

'Fire in the hole!' the foreman called out.

The burly man pressed a switch. A dozen small charges went off in rapid succession. The wall bulged out, holding its shape for an instant and then crumbling in a great clamor and cloud of dust.

Fans designed to draw the dust and heat out of the room kicked on, and the cloud was evacuated up a large vertical shaft that led to the surface. It swirled past them, sticking to their sweat-covered bodies. By the time it cleared, Padi's face was as dark as Masinga's. In fact, all of them were the same gray color no matter the shade of their skin.

The foreman looked over, the shotgun resting on his shoulder. 'Break's over,' he shouted. 'Back to work.'

Masinga and the others rose up and wearily began moving into position. Against his will, Devlin followed.

31

MV Rama, *1745 hours*
Location 61° 37′ S, 87° 22′ E

Fifteen hours after abruptly ending his chess game, Gregorovich stood over the lighted chart table as another new course line was drawn. This one led off to the northwest.

Kirov stood across from him with one of the commandos at his side. 'That's the ninth course change he's ordered.'

The MV *Rama* could be felt turning to starboard.

'Approaching new heading,' the navigator called out nervously. 'Three hundred twenty-three degrees.'

'He's toying with us,' Kirov said dangerously. 'And you're indulging him.'

Gregorovich stared. The presence of the second commando was Kirov's idea. A show of force. No doubt the mutiny he felt brewing was close to being launched.

The men were getting nervous. It was palpable. They were land-based commandos far from home in a dangerous situation with deteriorating conditions. The ship was rolling appreciably in the growing swells, and the sky had turned gray-white. It looked like snow would be falling soon. At Austin's direction, they'd come so far south they'd begun dodging small icebergs, an effort not helped by the reduced visibility.

Worst of all, they'd heard in detail how the *Orion* was crushed and dragged to the depths as if by a monster from the deep. So far, order remained, but Gregorovich sensed it would not last.

'At least we're heading north,' he said, turning to the navigator. 'What's in this direction?'

The navigator tapped the screen, and the map zoomed out slowly until finally Gregorovich spotted a yellow dot directly in their path.

'Heard Island,' the navigator said.

By tapping the screen at the island's location, Kirov was able to bring up a block of information about it.

'Australian territory,' he said, reading from the screen. 'Volcanic. Last appreciable eruption 2005. Covered in glaciers and completely uninhabited.'

Kirov looked up, a grin plastered from ear to scabbed-over ear. 'That's it,' he said. 'Heard Island is the target. That's where Thero's hiding. Austin finally showed his hand. We can kill him now along with his crew and finish the job without worrying about them.'

Gregorovich didn't like the idea of losing his counterweight. Nor did he think, after proving so crafty for so long, that Austin would have been dumb enough to blunder into revealing his secret with such ease.

'Zoom out,' he ordered.

The Vietnamese navigator did as he was told, and

the map expanded again. Another set of dots appeared. These were roughly two hundred and seventy miles beyond Heard Island, directly on the same course line, 323 degrees.

Austin had maneuvered the *Rama* to a point where they were approaching both islands simultaneously.

'French Southern and Antarctic lands,' the navigator said.

'What kind of a name is that?' Kirov blurted.

'One you won't forget, I trust,' Gregorovich said. 'The same course line takes us to both of them. Thero could be hiding on either one. Or Austin could take us a little closer and then turn us in a new direction. We can't kill him until we know for sure.'

'And once we know for sure?'

'Can you not think more than one move ahead?' Gregorovich asked. 'Suppose Thero's lab is on Heard Island. Our orders are to destroy it with a nuclear weapon. It's Australian territory. Do you not see the advantage of leaving a few charred and radiated American bodies at the outer limit of such a blast?'

Kirov nodded.

'Launch the long-range drones,' he said. 'If anything's moving on Heard Island, I want to know about it.'

The noisy hum of piston engines caught Joe Zavala's attention as he neared the ship's mess with Hayley Anderson at his side.

'What's that?' Hayley asked.

Joe cocked his head to listen. The sound reminded him of unmanned military aircraft he'd worked with a few months back. 'The Russians are launching something up on deck,' he said. 'A small plane, or maybe a drone.'

'Why would they be doing that?'

Joe considered several possibilities but put the thought aside when he saw a gaggle of the Russian commandos coming down the passageway. 'No idea,' he said. 'But let's get in that chow line before those guys do.'

Turning quickly, he ducked into the mess hall. Hayley lingered just behind him, keeping an eye on the hallway.

Stepping to the buffet, Joe inhaled deeply. He loved Vietnamese food, the spices and all the vegetables. The ship's cook had whipped up a pretty good spread. It almost seemed a shame to ruin it.

'They're coming,' Hayley whispered.

Joe nodded, smiled at the chef, and began to load up his plate with heaping piles of everything on the menu. It was enough food for him and two others.

As the cook stared at him in wonder, Joe rubbed his stomach. 'Nothing works up an appetite like being shipwrecked in frigid waters and then being kidnapped by your would-be rescuers.'

The cook's face remained blank. Joe guessed English was not one of his languages. He put his hands together and bowed slightly. *'Kam ung,'* he said, "thank you" being one of the few phrases he knew in Vietnamese.

The cook smiled, his smooth face genuine and true. In a way, the *Rama*'s crew were as much prisoners of the situation as the *Orion*'s survivors.

Hayley sidled up to him, and began filling her own plate. 'It's now or never,' she said.

Joe pointed behind the cook to a wok that was smoking and starting to catch fire. As the cook turned around and went to put it out, Joe slipped a pouch from his sleeve as neatly as any magician. With a quick swish of his arm, he sprinkled the contents across everything in the buffet line. When the pouch was empty, he drew his hand back and stuffed it in his pocket.

As the Russians came in, they eyed Joe and Hayley for a moment and then moved to the head of the line. However odd they found the situation, they seemed more interested in feeding themselves than starting a confrontation they would catch hell for later.

Joe and Hayley sat down in the corner, trying not to watch as the commandos all but inhaled generous helpings of the tainted food.

Eight hours later, Kurt found himself on the bridge, staring at photos of Heard Island and wondering if the jig was up.

About fifteen miles long and ten miles wide, the island was roughly almond shaped and tilted at a forty-five-degree angle. A thin tail of land called

Elephant Spit jutted out to the east like a breakwater, and a small blob called Laurens Peninsula clung to its northwest corner connected by a narrow isthmus.

In profile, Heard Island was obviously volcanic. The central peak, named Big Ben, towered nine thousand feet above the sea in a classic conical shape. It was actually one of the highest peaks in Australian territory, higher than anything on the continent itself.

A satellite view showed glaciers spreading out from Big Ben like the spokes of a wheel. They followed the steep grades down to the ocean in every direction, calving icebergs where they met the water. White chunks of ice, many larger than the MV *Rama*, encircled the island like pilot fish around the head of a great shark.

As Kurt studied the photos, Kirov and Gregorovich stood quietly, looking smug and very pleased with themselves. They were more than happy to show Kurt everything they'd discovered.

'Do you have any infrared shots?' Kurt asked.

Gregorovich slid a new series of photos across the table toward him.

These shots, taken by the Russian drones, showed seals and penguins and colonies of nesting birds. The next photo depicted a series of distinct heat sources grouped on the southeast coast of the island. A spot called Winston Lagoon.

'The first group of targets are thermal vents of some kind,' Gregorovich explained. 'They could be naturally occurring and linked to the volcano or they could be man-made, indicating underground activity. The other images are unequivocal. They're men on snowmobiles. Whoever they were, they disappeared into holes in the ground moments after these shots were taken.'

Kurt studied the location of the snowmobile photos. 'Just inland from Winston Lagoon,' he said. 'A good place to shelter. But I don't see any ships there.'

'So they were dropped off,' Gregorovich said. 'This is Thero's way. His lab in Yagishiri was underground. His experiments involve delving deep into the Earth. Those hatches lead to Thero's compound. I'm sure of it.'

Kurt didn't doubt it. But nor did he doubt that Thero would be prepared for an assault. 'Do you think they heard your drones?'

'The men we spotted showed no sense of alarm,' Gregorovich said. 'Our drones are nearly silent, and almost invisible to the naked eye.'

Kurt nodded. The *Rama* was still over the horizon and making only enough steam to hold station in the current. 'Did you scan for radar sources?'

Gregorovich nodded. 'No emissions. It seems they're relying on stealth alone to protect them. They don't know we're coming.'

'There are other, more passive ways to detect an enemy's approach,' Kurt said. 'Infrared, like your drone used. Visual. He could have motion-detecting cameras or even track you by sound. You head right for him and he'll take your helicopters out before you hit the beach.

And since he's underground, lobbing a few missiles in his direction won't do much to him either.'

'We have no reason to believe Thero possesses anti-aircraft weapons,' Kirov sneered.

'He doesn't need them,' Kurt said. 'He has his death ray. If he spots this ship, he'll send a massive distortion out to crush it just like he did the *Orion*. And if he spots your birds in the air, he'll hit you with another weapon he's developed. Something they call a flash-draw. He used it on the ASIO. It will shut down every system on your aircraft including the pilot's nervous system. You'll all be dead on impact before anyone wakes up.'

Kurt was talking fast, urgently trying to seize the initiative before they decided they no longer needed him. The Russians stared at him as if he were making it up.

'You're just trying to save your neck,' Kirov guessed.

'Well, I'm rather fond of my neck,' he said. 'I've become attached to it after all these years.'

Kirov didn't seem to appreciate the humor.

Gregorovich glanced down at the map. 'We could hold our current position,' he began. 'Take the helicopters out to the north, well beyond visual range, and then swing around behind the island. By coming in from the north side of the island, we'll be using the central massif to conceal our approach. In that way, we should arrive undetected.'

'This is ridiculous,' Kirov said. 'Now we're taking orders and tactical advice from our prisoner?'

Gregorovich ignored him and pointed to a spot on

the map near the shoulder of Big Ben. 'If we come in over saddle point and set down here on the far side of Big Ben, they shouldn't be alerted to our presence. From there, it's no more than seven or eight miles to the Winston Lagoon. Most of it downhill.'

It was a good plan. And they certainly didn't need Kurt to pull it off. 'Well, there you go,' he said, his hand edging closer to the Makarov in case he'd just outlived his usefulness.

'Not just us,' Gregorovich replied.

Kurt narrowed his gaze.

'We're taking you and your crew with us.'

'Gonna be a little tight on those helicopters with so many people and the extra fuel you'll need for the long circular journey.'

'As it turns out, a few seats have become available,' Gregorovich said. 'Twelve of the commandos have been taken ill with a horrendous stomach virus.'

'So give them some fluids and tell them to quit gold-bricking,' Kurt said, hoping no one would actually listen to his advice.

Gregorovich shook his head. 'We're not going to hike a glacier with men puking their guts out every five minutes. They're too dehydrated and weak to be of any use. You and your people will take their place.'

'Not all of our people are healthy either,' Kurt said. 'Four of them are in your sick bay.'

'Only three,' Kirov corrected. 'It seems one of them died during the night. From lingering effects of shock.'

'All they needed were basic treatments,' Kurt said angrily. 'What kind of people are you?'

'The kind who will draw blood if we need to,' Gregorovich said, taking the conversation back from Kirov and unmistakably referencing their chess game and the altercation that nearly ended in both of their deaths. 'The others will get the attention they deserve as long as you cooperate.'

Kurt stared. 'Who do you want to bring?'

'You, your friend Zavala, and Ms Anderson.'

'There's no reason to bring her at this point,' Kurt said.

'I don't need a reason,' Gregorovich said.

Kurt wondered if the Russian knew this was exactly what he'd hoped for. 'Fine,' he said. 'But not until I'm sure the others have been treated.'

A smirk appeared on the Russian's rugged face. 'Still protecting your pawns?' he asked. 'So be it. They will receive what they need. But for you and I, the time has come. We'll finish our game tonight right here where you said we'd be: at the very ends of the Earth.'

32

NUMA vessel Gemini

Gamay Trout sat in the darkened room of the *Gemini*'s ROV control center. She stared at the flickering black-and-white monitor in front of her. Twelve thousand feet below them, one of the ship's deep-diving ROVs had come across a debris field.

Broken and mangled wreckage littered the seafloor in a familiar pattern. She had seen dozens like it before as NUMA explored and cataloged various wrecks. Only, this wreck was one of their own.

'Magnetometer reading peaking,' Paul said from beside her. 'She's got to be close.'

Paul and Gamay and the *Gemini*'s captain were crowded into the room along with three other techs. The quarters were tight, and no one wanted to see what they were about to find. Gamay slowed the ROV and tilted the camera upward. A moment later, the red hull plating of the *Orion*'s keel came into view along with her bent rudder and six-bladed propeller. The ship was lying on her side.

'That's her,' the captain said grimly. 'Bring the ROV up a hundred feet. Let's see the big picture.'

Gamay did as ordered, operating calmly, despite the sick feeling in her stomach.

The ROV rose above the wreckage to reveal the true extent of the damage. The ship's keel had been split wide open, like someone cracking a giant egg. Somehow, the two halves remained attached as she sank, but there was so much damage it was hard to make sense of it.

'No wonder they went down so fast,' Paul said.

As the ROV drifted on the current, they could see that the breach ran the width of the hull.

'Never seen a ship holed like that,' the captain said.

The ship began to drift out of view.

'Gamay?' Paul said, concerned at seeing her white face.

She stood up. 'Someone else take over, please.'

As one of the other techs took her seat, she stepped through the crowd and made her way to the aft deck. She pushed the hatch open and welcomed the icy chill of the outside air.

A deep breath helped ease the feeling that had come over her, but as her gaze fell upon a tarp lashed to the deck, the uncomfortable feeling returned. Under the tarp were three bodies they'd found and pulled from the sea. Crewmen from the *Orion* who'd drowned or died of hypothermia awaiting rescue. They now lay in bags on the deck. The ship had no cold storage, but the freezing air of the Antarctic waters was the next-best thing.

She turned away as Paul came out behind her.

'Are you okay?'

'No, I'm not okay. I can't treat this like some regular investigation. That's one of *our* ships down there. These people are our friends.'

'And we need to know why it went down,' Paul reminded her. 'We need to see if there are explosive burns or melted plates. We need to know if they were buckled from a mine or a torpedo or a missile impact, or if the plates were bent outward from some kind of an internal explosion. If the damage came from the outside, then we can rule out Ms Anderson's sensor device and activate our own.'

'I know all that,' she said.

'But?'

She sighed. 'What if we find Kurt or Joe in there? What if we put the ROV inside the hull and come face-to-face with one of them? Every time we plucked someone out of the sea, I was afraid it would be someone we knew.'

Paul took her hand. 'I understand,' he said. 'I'll have one of the other techs guide the ROV.'

She knew he was going to say that. She didn't want that result. She just needed a moment. 'Do you suppose there's any chance they're alive?'

Paul hesitated for a moment, then he shook his head. 'I don't see how they could be.'

She appreciated his honesty. Somehow, admitting it was a probability took the edge off the fear. 'All right,' she said, stepping back toward the door. 'I guess if I was gone, I'd want them to figure out what happened.'

'I would too,' Paul said. He opened the door and held it for her. She stepped inside, steeling herself for whatever they might find.

Kurt, Joe, and Hayley were given a modicum of winter clothing for the assault: a skintight base layer of wicking material, followed by a heavier thermal layer, and then outer shells of waterproof material. The pants, jackets and hoods were camouflaged in a pattern of white and light gray. They were given white boots, and white wraps to cover their rifles.

'How do I look?' Joe asked, fully garbed.

'Like the abominable snowman's little brother,' Kurt said.

'Apparently, they don't come in my size,' Hayley said, the sleeves of her jacket flopping around well past her hands.

'Best they could do,' Kurt said, standing and ready to go. He found the uniform stifling in the heat of the ship's cabin. He hoped it would do the trick out on the ice of the glacier.

Sliding the Makarov pistol into the holster strapped to his thigh, he stepped toward the hatch, pushed it open, and walked out on to the deck. There, beyond the stacked containers, were two of the ugliest gray helicopters he had ever seen.

'We're flying in those contraptions?' Hayley said, looking shocked.

Sleek was not a word used to describe the Russian-built Kamov Ka-32s, code-named Helix by NATO. They resembled old buses, with rounded corners and three tiny wheels underneath. A double tail looked as if it had been stuck on the back as an afterthought, as if the designers had forgotten to include it in the first place.

Making them appear even less airworthy was the Russian double-rotor system. Instead of a tail rotor for stability, the Russians had a penchant for using two rotors above the helicopter. They turned opposite each other, stabilizing the gyroscopic forces. The Russians had been using the system for decades, but on the ground, with the rotors drooping under their own weight, the Helix looked like a science project gone awry.

'I've always wondered how those rotors avoid getting tangled up,' Joe said. 'This thing's like a giant eggbeater. The blades really should chop each other off.'

Kurt shot Joe a look, but it was too late. Hayley was hanging on every word.

'Come on,' Kurt said, noticing that the wind had picked up and that snow flurries had begun to fall. 'We have less than eighteen hours.'

Gregorovich directed Zavala into one helicopter with Kirov and ordered Kurt and Hayley into the other. He climbed inside with them.

'How many men do we have?' Kurt asked as the door was buttoned tight and the engines began to wind up.

'Ten, not counting the pilots,' he said. 'You three, myself, Kirov, and five commandos.'

Kurt noticed three snowmobiles and piles of rope and climbing equipment in the rear section of the cavernous helicopter. 'Are we riding or walking?'

'Both,' Gregorovich said. 'We'll take the snowmobiles for most of the journey, but near the edge of the glacier the sound of the engines will carry through the cavern. At that point, we'll go on foot.'

As if on cue, the whine of the turbines reached a fever pitch, and the howl of the rotors' downwash began to shake the heavily laden copter. It rocked back and forth for a few seconds and then slowly began to rise. Kurt stared out the window as a crosswind caught them.

Still rising, they were blown sideways. The pilot corrected just in time to avoid clipping one of the shipping containers. After climbing another thirty feet higher, they peeled away to the port side, accelerating as they passed the bow of the *Rama*.

Since they were without headsets, the thundering sound of the rotors made it necessary to shout just to be heard. 'Think she'll be here when we get back?' Kurt yelled, taking one last look at the *Rama*.

Gregorovich shrugged. 'I really don't care one way or another.'

At least three commandos remained behind, not counting those who were sick with food poisoning. Kurt hoped they would honor the uneasy peace, and he figured Captain Winslow and his XO would put up a stiff fight if they didn't, but there was nothing more Kurt could do to protect them. All that mattered now was completing the mission ahead.

'So how do you plan to stop him?' Kurt asked.

'Take his compound by force,' Gregorovich said, and then pointed to a hard-shell suitcase strapped to the back of one snowmobile and marked with the international symbol for radiation. 'And then detonate it.'

'Is that what I think it is?' Hayley asked.

'Afraid so,' Kurt said.

She looked greener with each passing second. Kurt figured that sharing a cabin with a nuclear weapon was not going to help her fear of flying. On the other hand, like the Russian assassin he'd now partnered with, Kurt was glad to have a weapon aboard that would leave no doubt.

News reaching Washington in the dead of night was seldom good. Dirk Pitt was alone in his office as the clock neared midnight when the latest blow hit.

'*. . . so far, we've located eight bodies in the wreckage,*' Paul Trout's voice said from the speakerphone. The signal was scratchy and distorted from the continuing solar activity. '*Almost all of them trapped at or near their posts. Con-*

sidering the size of the hull breach, it seems like those belowdecks didn't have a chance.'

Pitt rubbed his temples. 'Can you tell what caused the breach?'

'The plating is twisted and badly deformed,' Paul said, *'but we've found no burn marks or signs of explosive impact. It does seem like the hull was bent outward in places. But I can't give you a definitive answer.'*

Pitt was back to square one. He'd hoped to find evidence of a missile or torpedo attack, even an internal explosion if they could prove the presence of explosives. Something that would have told him Ms Anderson's sensor array was not at fault. Without it, he couldn't order the *Gemini* to power up their system and risk the same fate.

'We've taken a vote,' Paul volunteered. *'Everyone on board is willing to risk using the sensor array if it means we might find the people who did this.'*

A thin smile creased Pitt's face. He was proud of the bravery displayed by the *Gemini*'s crew. 'Too bad NUMA's not a democracy,' he said. 'Keep that thing off until I tell you otherwise.'

'Will do.'

'Report in immediately if you learn anything new,' Pitt said.

'It's the middle of the night back there.'

'We have seventeen hours until the clock hits zero,' Pitt said. 'No one here is going home before then.'

'Understood,' Paul replied.

Pitt waited for him to sign off, but he didn't. 'Anything else, Paul?'

Static buzzed for a moment. *'You didn't ask. But I thought I should tell you we haven't found Kurt or Joe.'*

'Keep looking,' Pitt said.

'We will. Gemini *out.'*

The line went quiet, and Pitt leaned back in his chair. He glanced through the window at the lights twinkling in the dark on the other side of the Potomac. He could not in good conscience order the *Gemini* to risk the same fate as the *Orion*, but how else could they hope to find Thero and stop him?

He jabbed at the intercom switch, pressing in the number for Hiram Yaeger's floor.

'Yaeger here,' a tired voice said.

'Tell me you have something new, Hiram.'

'I have something,' Yaeger said sheepishly. 'But I don't think it's going to help.'

'I'll take anything at this point,' Pitt said.

'I have the computer on an autosearch mode,' Yaeger said. 'It's looking for anything of significance. The same way it found connections between the obituary notices of Cortland and Watterson.'

'And what has it found this time?'

'It's discovered another odd coincidence,' Yaeger said, 'regarding the handwritten notes sent to the ASIO.'

'Go on.'

'By comparing the samples, the computer determined with a ninety per cent probability that both the handwritten threat sent to Australia and the documents sent to the ASIO by the informant were penned by the same person.'

Pitt sat back. 'I thought the ASIO had ruled that out. One written by a lefty and the other by someone who was right-handed.'

'The handwriting is disguised to make it seem different,' Yaeger said, 'but the word choices, pressure points and stroke lengths are similar.'

Pitt's mind raced to the conclusion. 'But the threat letter has already been matched to Thero's handwriting sample.'

'I realize that,' Yaeger said. 'So either the computer is wrong or this man Thero is acting as both the perpetrator of the crime *and* the informant.'

Pitt had no idea what this latest bombshell might mean, but he guessed there was some sinister reason behind it. Certainly he knew better than to second-guess Yaeger's computer.

He glanced at the clock on the wall as the minute hand ticked over to the wrong side of midnight. Whatever the significance of this latest twist, it would have to wait till later.

'I don't care how you do it, Hiram, but you have two hours to figure out another way for us to find Thero. After that, I have to order *Gemini* to power up their sensor array.'

Yaeger grumbled something that Pitt couldn't make out and then said, 'I'm on it.'

Pitt cut the line and turned back toward the window. It was the dead of night in Washington, DC, but broad daylight over Australia. If they didn't find Thero and stop him, it might be the last peaceful day that nation experienced for a very long time.

33

The Russian helicopters had launched from the pitching deck of the MV *Rama* in the middle of a snow flurry. Loaded down with maximum fuel, they lumbered westward into an oncoming weather front. Turbulence shook them almost constantly. The visibility dropped to less than a mile. And, soon enough, the temperature had fallen so far that ice was forming on the *inside* of the unheated cabin.

Hayley scratched some of it off and it fluttered down like snow. 'Reminds me of my freezer back home.'

'Condensation,' Kurt said. 'From our breath.'

'Never thought I'd know what a box of frozen peas felt like,' she replied.

A new wave of turbulence buffeted them, and Hayley gripped the arm of the seat.

'You're holding up pretty well,' Kurt said.

'I'm kind of numb to it all now.'

'Look on the bright side,' Kurt said. 'If we survive, your fear of flying might be cured.'

He smiled, but she just stared blankly. He knew the look of someone falling into despondency. She was going forward now without much hope, emotions drained, doing what she was supposed to do.

Kurt let his smile fade. 'Once we get on the ground, who knows what's going to happen. I need to know if I can trust you.'

'You can,' she insisted.

'Then tell me what you're hiding,' he said. 'You've kept some secret locked away since the very start. Time to come clean.'

She stared up at him, her brown eyes quivering. 'I think I know who the informant is,' she said. 'It's Thero's son, George.'

'Thero's son?'

She nodded.

'What makes you think that?'

'The handwriting looked like his,' she said. 'And in the first letter the informant wrote that he was acting out of his *better conscience*. Most people say they're acting in *good conscience*, but George always used that other term instead. There were times he even insisted he was his father's conscience. Times he persuaded Thero not to take some risk or fly off the handle at some random event.'

'I thought he was dead.'

'So did I,' she said. 'But, then again, we all thought Thero was dead too, didn't we?'

Kurt nodded.

'There wasn't much left after the explosion,' she said. 'There were funerals but with empty caskets, you know?'

'So if Thero survived, it's possible his children did as well,' Kurt said. 'So why keep this to yourself?'

'I wasn't sure at first,' she said. 'By the time I convinced myself that it could be George, we'd already seen the first two couriers intercepted and killed. At that point, it became pretty clear there was a leak inside the ASIO. I figured any information I passed to Bradshaw might have wound up making its way back to Thero as well, so I kept it to myself. Assuming I was right and George did survive the Yagishiri explosion, I didn't want to get him killed for trying to stop us.'

'I think you probably made a wise choice,' Kurt said. 'Do you really think it could be him?'

'He was a good person,' she insisted. 'He didn't want to go to Japan. He didn't want to continue the experiments. But he figured if he didn't go, there would be no one to rein his father in.'

'That's why you're plowing forward? You think you owe him?'

'Don't I?'

'I'm not the one to answer that,' Kurt said.

'If we can get inside and find him,' she said, 'he may be able to help us.'

Kurt nodded. 'Maybe,' he said guardedly.

A new series of downdrafts hit the copter, and Hayley grabbed Kurt's arm. He patted her hand, and then took the opportunity to get up and make his way toward the cockpit. Poking his head in, he found Gregorovich and the pilot staring through helmet-mounted goggles. He sensed the craft slowing.

'Are we there yet?'

'Almost,' Gregorovich said.

Kurt glanced through the windshield. He saw nothing but white clouds and the snow streaking past them. He guessed the view through the goggles was better, probably enhanced by the laser range-finding and infrared pods he'd seen attached to the helicopter's nose.

'I hope you have our de-icing equipment on,' he added.

The helicopter was being buffeted sideways and descending. A radio altimeter was calling out distances to the ground in Russian. Kurt spotted the other helicopter up ahead for a second before it disappeared into the swirling clouds and snow once again.

More turbulence hit, threatening to spill the copter over sideways.

'Downdrafts coming off Big Ben,' the pilot said as he fought against it.

They finally dropped below the clouds, and Kurt could see they were only forty feet above the terrain. The other helicopter was ahead and to the right, cruising across the snowy ground. Without goggles, it was hard to tell where the sky ended and the ground began. Everything was white. But both helicopters slowed further and finally began maneuvering to land.

A man-made blizzard kicked up around them from the downwash of the rotors, and they were pushed sideways once again before the wheels finally touched the ground and sank into the snow.

Rarely had Kurt been so glad to be on the ground.

Five minutes later, after a quick recon of the area to make sure they hadn't been spotted, the helicopters were empty. Six snowmobiles, the climbing equipment and the suitcase bomb were unloaded and ready to roll.

They assembled in the shelter of the huge mountain, but the wind still whipped down off it, blowing the snow sideways. Kurt wondered how bad the weather would get. Most of Big Ben was already hidden in the clouds.

As Gregorovich whistled for the pilots to assemble, Kurt found Joe attaching a rope to his pack and what looked like a spearhead of some kind. He trudged toward him through the buffeting wind. 'You get your frequent-flier miles on this trip?'

'Yeah,' Joe said. 'What about yours?'

'I didn't sign up,' Kurt said. 'I'm hoping never to fly this airline again, so I figured there was no point.' He gestured to the spear. 'What's that?'

'RPH,' Joe said. 'Rocket-propelled harpoon. You can fire it into the face of the ice and avoid having to make a free climb.'

'Why'd they give it to you?'

'No one wants to carry it,' Joe said. 'The head is made of tungsten and lead. It weighs a ton.'

'At least that'll save us some time if we have to go up.'

'What'd you get to carry?' Joe asked.

'C-4 charges and some detonators,' Kurt said. 'In case we have to blast our way in.'

'Try not to blow yourself up,' Joe said. 'Like that

Fourth of July when you bought all those Roman candles from the discount store and –'

The sound of a Kalashnikov firing cut Joe off.

Kurt dove into the snow and pulled out the Makarov pistol. He whipped around, brandishing the weapon, as Joe dove down beside him, using the snowmobile as a shield.

Scanning the landing zone, Kurt saw no attackers, only the other Russians aiming their weapons and likewise looking for a target.

Finally, Gregorovich marched forward. A thin trail of smoke drifted from the rifle in his hands. 'The pilots are dead,' he announced.

'What?!' Kirov yelled. 'Are you insane?'

'Just cautious,' Gregorovich replied. 'I overheard them talking. They were planning to leave without us. To leave us behind and get back to the freighter before the weather made it impossible. That won't be happening now.'

The soldiers stirred nervously. Gregorovich stared at Kirov.

'Perhaps you were going to leave with them,' he said to his rival. 'To put a bullet in my back and then run home like a coward.'

'No,' Kirov insisted.

'But you do know how to fly?' Gregorovich clarified. 'It's on your dossier.'

'Yes, but –'

Gregorovich blasted him down before he could finish his sentence. Kirov fell backward, red blood staining the white snow beneath him.

'Wrong answer,' Kurt muttered to Joe.

'I know what to say if he asks me,' Joe replied.

The Russian commandos looked on in shock. 'How are we supposed to get out of here when the job is done?' one of them asked.

'I will fly you out myself,' Gregorovich said. 'I spent three years piloting attack craft in Afghanistan. Mi-17s and Mi-24s. These are not so different.'

'And somehow we're all going to fit on just one?' another soldier asked.

Gregorovich nodded. 'Without the equipment, there will be plenty of room. But no one is going anywhere until we find Thero's lair and set the bomb.'

The tension between the Russians felt like a pile of gunpowder just waiting to be lit. But Gregorovich had so completely seized the upper hand that the men could do nothing. Not if they ever wanted to see home again. In fact, they might need to guard Gregorovich with their lives.

They began to stow their weapons.

'Lucky for us,' Joe muttered. 'Caught in the middle of a Bolshevik revolution.'

'More like Cortés burning his ships in the harbor at Veracruz,' Kurt replied, 'to prevent his men from leaving Mexico.'

'This guy doesn't miss a trick,' Joe said.

'At some point, he will,' Kurt said. 'Whatever you do, don't tell him you're a pilot.'

Joe nodded, and Kurt began to hike back through the swirling snow to where Hayley stood.

'It's okay,' he said.

'No,' she replied harshly. 'It's not okay. I'm pretty sure nothing will ever be okay again.'

He climbed on the snowmobile and felt Hayley climb on behind him. As she wrapped her arms around his waist, he could feel her shaking. It wasn't from the cold.

There was nothing he could say to erase what she'd just seen. What's more, he was pretty certain it wouldn't be the last bloodshed they'd witness in the hours ahead.

Gregorovich waved his arm, and the lead commando gunned his throttle and moved off. Kurt strapped on a pair of orange-tinted goggles as Joe followed the lead sled.

A moment later, it was Kurt's turn. With a twist of the throttle, he accelerated and tucked in behind the Russians, gliding in their tracks. Gregorovich brought up the rear, unwilling to let anyone out of his sight.

The terrain map showed a seven-mile ride in the shadow of Big Ben, then a two-hundred-foot climb down a ridge. From there, it was a two-mile hike over the crevasse-infested field. Once across the far side, they'd reach the edge of the Winston Glacier, look for the hatches, and blast their way into Thero's stronghold.

It was a simple plan, Kurt thought; only about a million things could go wrong. But with a little luck, they'd be inside the lion's den by dusk with at least ten hours to spare.

34

NUMA Headquarters

Half the world away, Dirk Pitt had been forced to make a painful decision. With no answers from Hiram Yaeger, he had to risk the *Gemini.*

'You have the ship battened down?' he asked over the speakerphone.

'All watertight doors are sealed,' Paul Trout replied. *'The crew have donned survival suits and moved to the upper decks. The boats are ready. If this thing blows a hole in the bottom, or if Thero locks on to us and sends some kind of discharge our way that batters the ship, we'll be off the* Gemini *in sixty seconds.'*

Full precautions, Pitt thought. There was nothing more he could do. 'Let's hope we're just overreacting.'

'How's the telemetry link?' Paul asked.

Pitt glanced at the computer screen. 'We're receiving your data without any hiccups,' he said. 'The solar activity has faded a bit.'

'Good,' a female voice said. *'If we blow ourselves up, you'll be the first to know.'*

'I thought you were ordered topside,' Pitt said to Gamay.

'She was,' Paul replied. *'But she suddenly came down with a case of hearing impairment and missed that order.'*

'I understand,' Pitt said. 'Whenever you're ready.'

A few seconds of silence came next, and then Paul's voice. *'Initiating power-up sequence in five . . . four . . .'*

'Wait!' a voice shouted from Pitt's outer office. 'Wait!'

Hiram Yaeger rushed in with a set of papers in his hands. 'I've found something.'

'Stand by,' Pitt said into the phone. 'What do you have, Hiram? Tell me it's Thero.'

'Not exactly.' He handed over a printed page with a blue background and a jagged line crisscrossing it. It looked like a game of connect the dots.

'What is this?' Pitt asked.

'It's a ship's course over the last forty-eight hours,' Yaeger said.

'What ship?'

Hiram was panting. He'd run all the way up from the tenth floor when the elevator didn't respond fast enough. 'I don't know what ship exactly,' he said. 'But it's important – I'm sure of it.'

Pitt didn't doubt his friend but he needed clarity. 'What exactly are you talking about?'

'There's a storm brewing down there,' he said. 'Any ships in the area should be getting out of the way, or at least transiting with all due haste, but this one is changing course at odd hours and intervals and all but driving in circles. It's taken her two full days to arrive where she is now. Had she traveled straight, she could have done the trip in ten hours. In and of itself, that means nothing. But it is suspicious.'

Pitt didn't disagree. But there were reasons some ships took odd courses. One in particular came to mind.

'There's a lot of illegal fishing down there,' he said. 'The Aussies are always chasing ships off. Every year, they even capture a few. Those ships trawl for the biggest catch. But they stay out of the shipping lanes, and they don't stay in one place very long because they don't want to get caught.'

'My first thought,' Yaeger said, 'but this isn't a fishing trawler, it's a containership of some kind. And those turns are not as random as they seem. There's a pattern to them.'

Pitt looked at the jagged line. 'I don't see a pattern.'

Yaeger had a second item in his hand. It was a transparent overlay. He'd printed something on it.

'The angles are slightly off,' he said, 'and the legs aren't exactly the right lengths, but it's pretty close.'

He placed the overlay down and lined up the edges of the page. The left side of the pattern on the transparent sheet matched closely with the legs and courses the wandering mystery ship had taken.

Pitt recognized the full pattern instantly. 'The constellation of Orion.'

Yaeger nodded. 'For reasons I can't begin to guess at,

this lost containership has been tracing out half of the constellation. It's a mighty accurate effort at that.'

'Could it *possibly* be a coincidence?' Pitt wondered aloud.

Yaeger shook his head. 'Ten million to one for a ship to randomly make these turns and steam legs of the proper length. Add in the fact that our *Orion* just went down hours before this pattern started in the very same area, and the odds might hit a billion to one.'

Pitt nodded. Someone on that ship, someone in control of that ship, was trying to tell the world something. He couldn't fathom what circumstances might be creating this oddity, but he had a good idea who might be sly enough and intelligent enough to pull it off.

'Kurt,' he said almost unconsciously.

Yaeger nodded. 'He's the biggest astronomy buff in the department. He's always up on that roof with his telescope.'

'Where's the ship now?'

'Here,' Yaeger said, pointing to a position on the map. 'Three hundred miles east-southeast of Heard Island. It was holding station for a while, but now it's heading northeast at what must be flank speed.'

Pitt turned toward the speakerphone. 'Paul, have you been listening to this conversation?'

'Both of us have,' Paul said. *'In fact, Gamay's hearing seems to have made a rapid improvement. Not to mention both of our spirits.'*

'Mine as well,' Pitt said. 'But let's not get carried away. Get everybody back to their stations. Keep that device switched off, and tell the captain to head due west at flank speed. Don't spare the horses.'

'Should we try to contact them by radio?' Paul asked.

Pitt thought for a second. 'No,' he said. 'I don't know what's going on, but if we do have someone aboard that ship and he had access to a radio, he'd have called by now. Remain on radio silence until we know more. I'll have more orders for you in a while, but it wouldn't be a bad idea to start planning a boarding party.'

'Yes, sir,' Paul said. 'Gemini *out.'*

For the first time in days, Pitt felt a surge of positive energy. He looked back at the course line to make sure he hadn't imagined it.

'Find out what you can about that ship,' he said to Yaeger. 'I want to know who owns it, where it's been, and what it might be doing on the bottom of the world.'

Yaeger nodded. 'Should we give this info to the NSA?'

Pitt hesitated and then shook his head. 'Let's make sure we're not fooling ourselves first.'

35

Heard Island

Janko strode through a dimly lit tunnel several hundred feet below the surface of Heard Island. He traveled alongside a small conveyor belt that ran the length of the tunnel. The belt rumbled along continuously, carrying rock and other material in the opposite direction. At the far end, he came to a large, irregular-shaped room carved out of the rock.

The space was over a hundred feet in diameter and dropped down in sections like terraces. The air was thick with dust and the sound of hammering as two dozen workers toiled in the space under flood lamps. They dug with jackhammers and picks and carried the results of their labor to the conveyor belt in wheelbarrows.

Janko made his way to a burly foreman, who watched over the workers like a prison guard on a chain gang.

'Surprised to see you down here,' the foreman growled over the clamor.

'The yield has dropped,' Janko said angrily. 'You're sending up nothing but rock.'

The foreman shifted his weight, turning his stubble-covered face toward Janko with a sneer.

'I told you this would happen months ago,' he said. 'The diamonds in this mountain came up in kimberlite pipes. Brought to the surface by volcanic activity over the eons. The vein doesn't run horizontal, it runs vertical. We were lucky to find the top portion so rich. But the old man took the lion's share of that, didn't he?'

Janko didn't react.

'Well, anyway,' the foreman continued, 'the yield is gonna keep going down until you get me some heavy equipment, preferably the kind that can be used underwater.'

'We tried that,' Janko said. 'The ASIO intercepted the shipment.'

'Then you'd better get us more *employees*,' the foreman said without emotion.

Janko glanced around. Once, they'd had over a hundred workers, men and women captured or lured in by offers of big contracts. But the work was harsh, and accidents were common. Over the last year, half the crew had been killed, most in accidents, a few in escape attempts, a few others tortured and killed as examples to show the rest that working was better than rebelling.

An intercom box buzzed on the wall. Janko picked up the heavy receiver and was surprised to hear Thero's voice.

'We have a problem,' Thero said.

'What kind of problem?'

'We're no longer alone on our deserted island.'

Janko's body tensed. 'Is it someone we can allow to leave undisturbed, like those seal poachers who came ashore last year?'

'No,' Thero said. *'They're inland on snowmobiles. They must have been airlifted on to the glacier. That means they're military.'*

'What do you want me to do?'

'Get the hovercraft ready, and go deal with them.'

'On my way,' Janko said.

He hung up and exchanged glances with the foreman.

'The jig is up, isn't it?'

'Not necessarily,' Janko said. 'But we knew this wouldn't last forever. Maybe you'd better get the last shipment ready. If everything goes south, we're going to need some portable wealth fast.'

36

Stephenson Glacier, Heard Island

The group of snowmobiles crossed the winter landscape with deliberate caution. The heavy clouds, falling snow and gusting winds were creating a whiteout effect. It made the terrain hard to navigate.

Twice, the lead snowmobile got caught in deeper, softer snow and had to be pulled out. At one point, the grade became too steep for the machines to safely climb, and they were forced to back out and find another way.

Paused in a sheltered area while Gregorovich studied a map, Kurt flipped up his goggles and turned to Hayley. 'Are you okay?'

'Freezing,' she said. 'Can't feel my toes.'

She flipped up her own goggles. Her cheeks were windburned, her lips were blue, and strands of blond hair that had slipped out from under her cap were coated with ice.

He climbed off the seat. 'We should walk around while we're stopped. Get our blood pumping.'

Hayley agreed, and Kurt helped her off the machine.

'Where are you going?' one of the Russians asked.

'Out for a walk,' Kurt said. 'It's such a beautiful day.'

'Don't get lost.'

Kurt considered the statement. The blizzard would have been good cover if he'd wanted to make a break for it, but there was no point in that. There was nowhere to go.

He took a few steps and pointed up the slope. 'Tell the commissar I'm climbing that ridge to get a better look at what's ahead. Won't be gone long.'

With that, Kurt took Hayley's hand and began to hike upward. The exertion of trudging up a hill through knee-deep snow at a thirty-five-hundred-foot altitude was enough to get his heart pumping, all right. By the time they were halfway to the top, Kurt felt he'd lit an inner furnace; even his face was flushing.

'Feeling any better?' Kurt asked.

'I'm warming up, yes,' Hayley said. 'Any chance there's a ski lodge at the top?'

'Doubtful,' Kurt said. 'But just in case . . .'

He never finished the sentence, as his ears picked up an odd sound above the wind. It was a high-pitched whine, almost like a small jet engine. It faded and then returned.

Looking around, Kurt realized the confining ridge was shaped in a rough semicircle, a half bowl almost perfect for catching distant acoustics.

When the sound returned, he looked across the ice field. The falling snow made it hard to see anything. He flipped the orange-tinted goggles down to get a better contrast. In a second, he caught sight of movement. A group of small vehicles coming their way.

There was something odd about the way they moved, gliding over the snow with almost effortless ease.

'Houston, we have a problem.'

'What is it?'

'Trouble.'

He grabbed Hayley's hand and they began to climb down, hopping and jumping and sliding down the steep sections to cover as much ground as possible. They reached the bottom, just about tumbling into the group. 'Someone's coming,' he said sharply.

'From where?' Gregorovich asked.

'From the other side of the ridge.'

'On foot?'

'No,' Kurt said. 'I think they're using hovercraft.'

Seconds later, the high-pitched whine became audible on the ground.

'Move!' Gregorovich ordered.

In seconds, the snowmobiles were firing up, but they were almost too late. The group of hovercraft came charging up the slope, appearing out of the snowy haze like avenging ghosts.

Kurt and Hayley jumped on their machine. 'Hang on!' Kurt shouted as he pressed the starter and twisted the throttle.

She clung to him as the snowmobile leapt forward. The rest of the group scattered in different directions like a herd of gazelles set upon by lions. It was an unplanned tactic, but it was effective. There were six snowmobiles but only four hovercraft. Not all of them could be followed.

Racing down the slope and cutting around a snowdrift, Kurt glanced over his shoulder, looking past Hayley. Unfortunately, one of the sleek predatory craft was hot on their tail.

'Hang on tight!' he shouted. 'This is going to get rough.'

He turned his eyes forward, pinned the throttle full open, and began weaving back and forth across the snowfield. If there had been a forest on the island, he would have driven straight for it, but Heard Island was treeless, a fact that didn't bode well in terms of finding a spot to hide.

He cut to the right and caught sight of a small explosion from the corner of his eye. He avoided it and cut back to the left, only to see another one.

There was no sound to accompany the phenomenon, no concussion wave or smoke. In fact, the display looked more like the blurred pattern one sees out behind a running jet engine.

'Is that what I think it is?'

'Flash-draw,' Hayley yelled. 'Stay out of it.'

'Sound advice,' he said.

They continued on at breakneck speed, and Kurt strained to see details of the near-featureless terrain streaking past him. Even with the goggles, the light was so flat it was almost impossible to spot dips and rises.

Twice, uneven sections of the ground almost tipped them over, and then suddenly they were airborne, flying off the crest of a small ledge.

The snowmobile caught air at forty miles per hour, dropped about five feet, and landed solidly on the downslope like a contestant in the X Games.

Kurt's chin hit the windshield, gashing it and jarring him, while Hayley's boa-constrictor-like grip around his waist kept her on board.

The hovercraft launched itself over the same ridge without any hesitation. It dropped and landed smoothly on its cushion of air without any hint of the jarring impact Kurt and Hayley had felt. With his chin bleeding and his mind racing, Kurt realized what Joe had discovered in the outback: a hovercraft was the ultimate all-terrain vehicle.

He raced on, desperately trying to think of a way to escape its grasp.

As Kurt and Hayley raced off, Joe Zavala found himself pointed in the wrong direction, with the nose of his machine aimed toward the ridge that Kurt and Hayley had climbed. He got on the throttle fast and twisted the handgrips. The engine revved and the tracks spun, and Joe manhandled the nose of the snowmobile around to a new heading.

He shot forward, racing up a small hill and down the other side, almost T-boning one of the Russians.

Right behind the Russian sled, one of the gray hovercraft flew down the hill. The wide, flat vehicle reminded Joe of a stingray. The central portion of the machine was raised to hold a crew cabin and a turbine engine, while the thinner surrounding section and the rubber skirt that drooped from it were there primarily to create the cushion of air that it rode on.

As the gray machine followed the Russian commandos, Joe cut in behind it. He had the impression its driver hadn't seen him, since his attention remained locked on the original target. As they raced across the ice, Joe tried to get at the rifle strapped across his back, nearly wrecking in the process.

Eventually, he managed to slide the rifle around until it rested at his side. It was balanced by the strap that remained across his shoulder. Situated like this, he closed in on the target like a fighter pilot trying to save the life of his wingman. With the hovercraft crossing in front of him, Joe tried to flick off the safety, but the bulky gloves he wore made it impossible. He was still fumbling with it as the Russian snowmobile turned hard to the right.

The hovercraft followed, and Joe leaned into the turn, swinging wide, until he was back on target. He put the glove to his mouth, bit down on the fabric of the fingertips, and ripped the glove off. The frigid air chilled his fingers instantly, but with his bare hand he was able to grab the rifle grip, flip the safety off, and fire.

A spread of bullets lanced forth from the barrel to no effect.

The hovercraft turned left, and Joe fired again. This time, he hit the target – something confirmed by bits of fiberglass flying into the air – but still the hovercraft raced forward unaffected.

Ahead of them, the two Russian commandos had come to a narrow gap between a rocky ridge and a high drift of soft snow. They shot toward the gap, a fatal mistake.

The hovercraft's driver lined them up easily and triggered his own weapon. A direct hit from the flash-draw stunned the men into unconsciousness and stalled the snowmobile's engine. The fleeing sled turned sideways. Its right-hand ski caught a rut, and the machine tumbled out of control, ejecting the limp commandos in different directions.

Rather than repeat the snowmobile's mistake, the hovercraft turned right. It raced up the hill, skidded sideways, and pointed its nose back around and down toward Joe.

Joe flipped the selector to full auto and fired at will, tearing up the front end of the hovercraft and shattering its windshield. Despite the damage, the charging machine didn't stop.

Joe tried to dodge the oncoming craft, but he skidded on the ice. He was either about to get zapped or be decapitated. He dove off the snowmobile, throwing himself to the ground.

The hovercraft raced over the top of him, roaring like a tornado and hammering the snowmobile like a battering ram. The tremendous downward air pressure underneath the hovercraft's skirt blasted Joe out to the side as if he were a newspaper caught in the swirling air behind a truck on the highway.

As soon as he tumbled to a stop, Joe was up and running. Across from him, the hovercraft began to turn back. It swung around and charged back toward him. Joe could just imagine the thugs inside, drooling as they growled: 'Run him down!'

It wouldn't take long.

As Joe lumbered through the snow, the hovercraft bore down on him at ten times his speed.

The whine of the approaching vehicle rose in Joe's ears. He threw himself to the ground as the din of automatic gunfire rang out. He looked up just in time to see the hovercraft going off course and trailing smoke. It carried on for a hundred feet before losing power and crashing nose-first into the snow. It burrowed for ten feet before grinding to a halt.

Another snowmobile raced toward Joe and skidded to a stop.

'Get on!' Gregorovich yelled.

Joe normally preferred to drive, but he wasn't about to argue. He clambered on to the seat, barely grabbing the handholds before Gregorovich gunned the throttle and took off.

A half mile away, Kurt was doing a yeoman's job avoiding the stun blast of the flash-draw, but he could neither shake nor outrun their pursuer. He noticed only one advantage.

'We have better traction,' he yelled to Hayley.

'What?'

'That thing turns more like a boat or a plane, it skids and slides. But when we're not on ice, we're able to turn inside his radius every time.'

'How does that help us?'

'Watch,' he said, cutting hard to the right, racing back in the direction they'd just come.

The hovercraft dutifully followed, swinging wide, turning back on course, and then closing the gap again.

Kurt kept the throttle at full, almost losing control as they skipped across bumpier terrain.

Another miragelike apparition ripped past them to the right.

'That was awfully close,' Hayley said.

They'd come to a narrow section now, almost like a catwalk on a ski slope. The glacier dropped down to the right as a rocky ridge climbed up to the left and around the edge of Big Ben like a mountain road.

Kurt chose the ridge, hugging the wall, as the terrain beside them fell away precipitously. He backed off the throttle just a bit.

'They're closing in!' Hayley shouted.

As the ridge narrowed, Kurt hit the brake, turned the handlebars, and threw all his weight to the left side of the snowmobile. He leaned hard, like a motorcycle rider in a hairpin turn.

The snowmobile's skis dug in hard. And Kurt caught sight of the hovercraft, whipping into the turn behind them. Then he saw a flash of light in his mind and felt a falling sensation. It seemed as if everything went dark.

His limp body flew off the snowmobile and slid fifty feet into a thick bank of snow. He came to rest, all but buried and completely unconscious. Hayley tumbled off the snowmobile as well, but a handlebar caught her parka, tearing it open and yanking her to a halt like an arresting wire on an aircraft carrier. She ended up only a few yards from the damaged sled.

Kurt never saw her, nor did he see how effective his plan had truly been.

Just as he'd hoped, the snowmobile's sharp turn was beyond the hovercraft's ability to match. It skidded out over the sheer face of the ridge, carried sideways by its speed and momentum. A small cliff would have been no problem, but the eighty-foot drop was too much.

The hovercraft had to stay in close contact with the ground to generate lift, and with that ground suddenly gone, the craft dropped and rolled to the side as it fell.

It hit hard, landing on its side and tumbling in somersaults down the slope. Pieces of fiberglass sailed in all directions. It came to a stop in a heap, and no one climbed out of it.

Farther down the slope, Joe and Gregorovich were in trouble. Another of Thero's hovercraft had found them. It was driving them toward the towering wall of the glacier.

'He's going to trap us against the ice,' Joe shouted.

'I can't get around him,' Gregorovich said.

Joe looked over his shoulder. The hovercraft was hanging back, swerving from side to side. Any move Gregorovich made was easily countered. Joe knew he had to do something. He tried to pull the clip from his rifle, but by now his ungloved hand was completely numb. He pulled the other glove off, yanked the empty clip out, and jammed a new one in.

'This is my stop,' he shouted.

He pushed off Gregorovich and extended his legs, launching himself off the snowmobile, landing and tumbling through the snow for a second time.

Joe bounced and rolled and then slid face-first, cringing as the snow was shoveled through the gap in his collar. In seconds, he was up, shaking the snow from his face and getting his bearings.

Gregorovich was still heading toward the glacier. The hovercraft had ignored Joe and followed.

Joe raised the rifle and locked on to the hovercraft, calculating how much to lead it by. He was about to fire when a second high-pitched whine caught his attention.

He pulled the trigger, but the blur of Thero's stun gun had already hit him. The flare of blinding light seen only in Joe's mind encompassed him as it had in the outback and he collapsed in the snow, never knowing if he'd hit anything.

37

Thirty minutes later, with the white sky beginning to darken, the two remaining hovercraft made a cautious approach to the ridge where Kurt and Hayley had crashed. Using an infrared scope, Janko spied the wrecked vehicle at the bottom of the drop. Seconds later, he spotted the snowmobile.

He keyed the transmit switch on his radio. 'Unit two, make your way back down the slope and check for survivors. We're going up top.'

'Roger that,' the other driver replied.

As the two craft broke formation, Janko scanned the surrounding incline for heat sources. Only two signatures registered; the red-hot engine from the snowmobile and a figure lying ten feet away from it.

He pulled off his goggles and brought the hovercraft to a stop. As it settled, he threw open the hatch.

'Stay here,' he said to his gunner. 'Keep your eyes peeled.'

With a short-barreled submachine gun at his side, Janko climbed from the hovercraft and edged his way toward the wrecked sled. He found it to be inoperable, engine off, battery drained.

'At least they hit something,' he said to himself.

He moved to the body in the snow and rolled it over. To his surprise, a mop of blond hair spilled out from under the white hood of the parka.

Janko pulled the goggles from the woman's face. He recognized her. She was the woman he'd left tied up beside the explosives in the lab at the flooded mine.

'So you survived,' he muttered.

The radio crackled. *'Janko, this is unit two.'*

Janko lifted the portable radio to his mouth. 'Go ahead.'

'We've made it to the bottom of the ridge. Unit three is demolished. The driver and the gunner are both dead. No way to get it back up. Want us to burn it?'

'No,' Janko said. 'We don't need to draw any more attention to ourselves. The blizzard will dump a foot of snow in the next twelve hours. That will keep it out of sight.'

'And the men?'

'Get them out,' he said. 'I want all the bodies off this glacier. Ours and theirs.'

A double click told Janko his subordinate understood and would comply. Janko then switched channels and began a new transmission.

'Thero, this is Janko,' he said. 'Do you read?'

'Go ahead,' Thero's raspy voice replied.

'We're done out here.'

'Did you get them all?'

'All the snowmobiles have been accounted for,' Janko said. 'We lost two hovercraft in the process.'

'Who are they?' Thero asked tersely.

'Australians, I think,' Janko said. 'I recognize one of the survivors. A blond woman who was at the station in the outback when the ASIO tried to raid it.'

Silence for a moment, and then: *'Is she alive?'*

'Affirmative. We have two male captives as well. The rest are dead.'

'Bring them in,' Thero said. *'I want to interrogate them. We need to know if they're alone or not.'*

'My thoughts exactly,' Janko said.

He clipped the radio back on to his belt, scooped the woman up, and threw her over his shoulder.

Seconds later, he'd dumped her in the cargo bay of the hovercraft and was back in the cockpit, powering up the engines once again. As the sleek machine rose up off the ground, Janko eased it forward and then turned around only twenty yards from where Kurt lay.

The deep snow he'd become buried in masked Kurt's infrared signature, while his white camouflage, the failing light, and the continuing blizzard made him all but invisible to the naked eye. As a result, neither Janko nor his gunner saw Kurt as they trundled off into the graying horizon.

38

After a twelve-hour shift of breaking rocks and loading the rubble on to the endlessly moving conveyor belt, Patrick Devlin felt as if he'd been beaten with a club, run over by a truck, and forced to breathe in smoke all day.

He was surprised by the grace of a hot shower, even if it was a communal one. The water at his feet was dark sludge from the dust covering his body. A hearty dinner of seal meat and some kind of wild bird surprised him further, but then those things were in abundance on the island, and starving workers slowed down the production line.

After dinner, he was led to a room carved out of the rock. Bunks four high were spaced along two of the walls. Most of them were empty.

As the door was locked behind him, he spotted Masinga and the South American, playing cards.

'Which bunk?' he asked.

'Pick any of them,' Masinga said. 'There's plenty of space.'

He threw his stuff on one of the bunks and then sat down by the other men. 'Why is it so hot down here?'

Masinga played a card. 'Because we're in a volcano,'

he said. 'Where do you think the hot water comes from?'

'Geothermal?'

They nodded in unison.

Devlin looked around. There was no shaft leading to the surface here, only a thin grate above the door for ventilation.

'How far down are we?'

Neither man answered. The South American played a card. Masinga looked at it briefly and then reached for it. Devlin slammed his hand down on Masinga's. 'I said how far down are we?'

Masinga threw the table over and grabbed Devlin by the shirt, hauling him up and slamming him into a locker.

'You think you're the first one here with plans to get out?' Masinga shouted. 'The men who run this place aren't fools. They know that a death sentence awaits them for the things they've done. To think of escape is a crime, to talk of escape will land you in the torture chamber. And to actually try . . . The rule here is simple: one man fights back, three men die.'

Devlin shook loose of Masinga's grasp. 'So you just put up with it until they work you to death?'

Masinga glared at him. 'My father spent twelve years in a South African jail for his political activities. He survived by *putting up with it* until salvation came from the outside. That's the only way any of us are going to see home again, and I'll be damned if I'm going to let you get us killed with your rabid tongue before that happens.'

Devlin stared at his two roommates. 'Maybe that's how you're going to play it, but I'm going to get out of here or die trying.'

The South American spoke next. 'There are informers everywhere,' he warned, 'even among the men. Maybe even Masinga or me. So if I was you, I'd watch what I say. And who I say it to.'

Devlin took a deep breath and came to a decision. 'They brought me here on a ship. I'm going to find my way back to it at some point. If either of you are going to rat on me, then do it quick and put me out of my misery.'

They stared at him with sullen eyes. Finally, Masinga reached over and righted the table. 'And what do you know about sailing a ship, my friend?'

Devlin sat down and grinned at his fellow prisoners. 'Just about everything,' he said.

39

Kurt woke up from the flash-draw as disoriented as Joe had been in the desert. He thought he'd fallen asleep on his couch at home after a long day. But he couldn't ever remember it being so cold in his town house, even in the dead of winter.

As he moved about, the icy sensation on his face cleared the cobwebs a bit. He opened his eyes and saw nothing but white. Realizing it was snow, he brushed it away and dug himself out.

Once he'd burrowed clear of the snowbank, Kurt got to his feet and looked out over the escarpment. The flat light of the snowfield and the gray sky was broken only by a few jagged sections of black rock.

He quickly remembered where he was, how he'd gotten there, and who was with him.

He looked around, saw no trouble or any sign of movement. 'Hayley!' he shouted. 'Hayley!'

He heard nothing but the wind.

Forcing himself to stand and ignoring the aches and pains in his body, Kurt began to trudge forward to where the snowmobile lay on its side. Even if she was unconscious, Hayley should have been nearby, but she was nowhere to be seen.

He considered the wreck and where he'd ended up. He searched the snowbank and the surrounding ledge. Not finding any hump in the snow that might have been her, he returned to the snowmobile. He found a fragment of her coat caught on the handlebar and a trail of depressions almost covered in the falling snow that led back toward the glacier. It was hard to tell, as they had almost been filled in, but the depressions looked like they had once been footprints stamped deep into the soft snow.

He began to think Hayley had been captured. It made him wonder about the others, particularly his best friend. If either Joe or the Russians were around, they were keeping out of sight.

He climbed to a high point and scanned the distance. In the fading light, he saw no sign of the other snowmobiles. Considering how they'd scattered, that didn't surprise him, but it left him with a tough choice. He certainly couldn't wander around the glacier-covered island on foot, looking for help. Time was too precious now. Besides, he'd begun to think his own escape from capture was a fluke of some kind. Considering the effect of the flash-draw and how determined Thero's men seemed, he doubted they'd have just disappeared if they didn't think they'd rounded up the infiltrators.

He had to assume the worst: that Joe, Hayley and the others had been captured.

Stepping back to the snowmobile, Kurt grabbed the handlebars and forced the machine back up on to its tracks. The damage seemed mostly cosmetic, but a flick of the starter did nothing. Not even the lights would come on.

'This flash-draw is really starting to annoy me,' he muttered.

He flipped open a small cargo box on the back of the snowmobile and searched for anything useful. He found a flashlight, but it too was drained.

'Great,' he muttered.

He glanced up at the sky. The falling snow made it seem lighter than it really was, but the night was coming on fast. He had every intention of continuing on to Thero's lair, but it would be almost impossible in the utter darkness that was about to envelop the island.

He knew basically where he was. All he had to do was make his way down the cliff and across the snowfield and he'd run smack into the Winston Glacier. From there, he'd turn left and follow it toward the lagoon. Somewhere farther down, he'd encounter the hot spots photographed by the Russian drones.

He began to pick his way down the steep face of the bluff, studying the route carefully and noticing the wreckage of the hovercraft not far from the foot of the cliff.

When he reached the mangled shell of the vehicle, he found it half buried in the falling snow. Only the engine cowling, which was still venting heat, remained visible.

Kurt brushed the snow away and found the hatch ajar. He forced it open and climbed inside.

He was looking for anything useful: food, maps, radios, anything he could get his hands on. He found a flashlight and turned it on. Thankfully, it worked. He located the radio. The panel lit up as he flipped a toggle switch, but even with the headset on, Kurt heard no static. He figured something had blown. It didn't matter. It was a short-range unit anyway. He wasn't going to be able to reach help with it.

A few more minutes of rummaging provided him with some extra supplies, including a Zippo lighter, a few greasy rags that might burn if he needed a marker, and, most important, a set of night vision goggles.

Without them, the approaching darkness would have been Kurt's worst enemy. With the moon and stars blocked by thick clouds, and no source of artificial light on the island, the darkness would be like that of a cave, complete and all-encompassing.

To navigate through it without any type of aide would be impossible. To walk with the flashlight switched on or to carry a makeshift torch of flame was just asking to be seen and shot. But with the night vision goggles, Kurt could hike through the darkness like a bat using sonar.

He checked his watch. It was just past 8 p.m. local time. They had nine hours before Thero's promised attack. He figured a three-hour hike awaited him.

'No time like the present.'

He pulled his coat tight once again, forced the hatch open, and climbed out into the blowing snow. He left behind the only shelter for miles and trekked to the west, heading toward a confrontation he stood little chance of winning.

While Kurt was hoping to find a way into Thero's compound, Joe was wondering if he'd ever see the outside world again.

In the confines of the underground cavern, things were warmer but less hospitable. Joe was chained to a wall of black volcanic rock like a prisoner in a medieval dungeon. His hands were up high, stretched out to either side, and his feet were shackled and hooked to the floor. From the dried blood on the floor and the worn condition of the shackles, it was clear this wasn't the first torture session this room had seen.

Hayley and Gregorovich were chained up in similar fashion on either side of Joe. As an additional form of intimidation, the battered and broken bodies of the dead Russian commandos were paraded in and thrown in a heap on the floor one by one.

From the looks of it, three had been shot, while the other two seemed to have died from impact injuries.

'Tell us what we want to know or you'll end up like them.'

The question came from a bearded man who stood ramrod straight. His eyes were hard and his face a mask of determination. Joe had no way of knowing, but this was Janko, captain of Thero's guard.

Joe studied the bodies, taking in their faces. Instead

of fear, the sight gave Joe some hope. Kurt was not among them.

'Not willing to speak?' Janko asked. He nodded to a pair of muscle-bound henchmen and pointed to Gregorovich. 'Start with him.'

The two bruisers moved in on Gregorovich and began to soften him up with body blows. Kidney punches and uppercuts to the gut landed one after another. Gregorovich grunted and winced, but he never said a word, nor did he look away. At each pause in the beating, he straightened and eyed his torturers.

'How did you get to this island?' Janko demanded.

Gregorovich glared back.

'Wipe that look off his face,' Janko said calmly.

The thugs cracked their knuckles and moved the target zone from the Russian's torso to his head. They lined him up and connected with a series of haymakers that left his nose broken, his lips and mouth bleeding, and his right eye all but swollen shut.

They stepped back, surveying the damage. The Russian sagged in his chains, head down, blood dripping from his face. For several seconds, it seemed they might have killed him or knocked him out cold, but slowly and painfully Gregorovich straightened once again.

Joe had no love for the Russian, who'd basically kidnapped them, but he had to admit he was impressed.

Janko, on the other hand, was incensed. 'Break his legs!' he shouted.

The stockier of the henchmen rushed Gregorovich

and slammed a knee into his thigh with a sickening thud.

'Again!' Janko yelled.

Another hammer shot landed, and then a third.

'Hey!' Joe yelled. 'Save some of that for me!'

The group turned to him.

'You'll get your share,' Janko said.

Gregorovich was struggling to get back up, his legs all but useless even if they weren't broken. He pulled himself up on the chains, trying to straighten using only his arms.

'Come on,' Joe said. 'What, are you tired or something?'

Joe wasn't sure why he was trying to draw them off Gregorovich. Perhaps keeping the Russian from being beaten to death was a strategic move, perhaps it was pure emotion. All his life, Joe had been the guy to stand up for the underdog, though he'd never expected a Russian assassin to fall into that category.

Janko seemed nonplussed. With his arms folded across his chest, he motioned nonchalantly toward Joe. 'Give it to him.'

The first punch landed seconds later, and for the next few minutes Janko's strongmen kicked or punched Joe repeatedly, allowing just enough time between shots to get in a question or two.

Joe never answered, and the beating continued.

Unlike Gregorovich, who'd been intent on taking each hit as if he were unbreakable, Joe used his boxing skills both to harden himself against the rain of impacts and to reduce the damage by twisting and bending, turning the punches into glancing blows. Even then, after the fifteenth or sixteenth punch, he felt certain a rib or two had been cracked.

Finally, Janko raised a hand like a Roman emperor calling a halt to the gladiator games. 'All this is so unnecessary,' he said. 'Just tell us who you are. How you got here. And if there are any more of your people out there.'

Joe kept silent and was rewarded with a punch to the face. He turned away as best he could, but it caught him in the jaw, splitting his lip.

Joe looked up. 'I was just about to tell you,' he said, 'but you've given me amnesia.'

Janko gave up on him and pointed to Hayley. She cowered against the wall, trying desperately to pull her hands free from the shackles. Seeing the two men beaten to a pulp first had probably filled her with fear by now. That would only make it easier.

'Giving up so quickly?' Joe shouted, trying to draw their attention back to him.

The muscle-bound torturer looked over.

'And I thought we were just starting to bond,' Joe shouted. 'Really beginning to make a connection. I should have known you were too weak to finish the job.'

The guy fumed for a second, obviously aware it was a trick. He looked back toward Hayley, intent on intimidating her, only to have Joe spit a mix of blood and saliva at his face.

Furious, the thug stepped back over to Joe and slammed another fist into his stomach. Joe doubled over, only held up by the chains.

'How do you like that for a connection?' Janko asked sarcastically.

'Barely felt it,' Joe grunted, righting himself.

Janko nodded a green light to the thug, who stepped up and slammed Joe against the wall with his left hand, before connecting with a right cross and snapping Joe's head to the side. A huge welt, split down the middle, formed instantly and began bleeding. Joe's head hung for a moment.

Joe lifted his head. He made sure to look weary and woozy. 'Is that . . . all you've got?'

This time, the thug reared back and fired an overhand right at Joe's eye. Joe snapped his head to the side with surprising quickness. The torturer's fist slammed into the wall of rock behind Joe, and a sickening crack rang out.

The big thug shrieked in pain and dropped to his knees, cradling his wrist.

Joe managed a smile. Gregorovich laughed out loud.

'Enough of this!' Janko shouted. He stepped toward Hayley and grabbed her by the hair. 'Talk or I'll take it out on her!'

Before he could do anything more, the steel door opened. Three men stood there in the shadows. Joe's vision was a little fuzzy at this point, but he was fairly certain the man in the center was wearing some kind of mask.

They stepped into the room.

Janko snapped to attention.

'So these are our enemies,' the masked man said. His eyes lingered on Hayley until she returned his gaze. Next, he glanced at Joe, and finally Gregorovich.

'When they get done with you,' he said, 'you'll need a mask like mine.'

Gregorovich only stared.

'What did they bring?'

Janko pointed to the hard-shell-suitcase bomb.

'Has it been deactivated?'

'There was a timing device,' Janko said, 'but we have disabled it.'

The masked man looked to his guards. 'Bring it,' he said, and they quickly lifted it and took it out into the hall.

As the guards vanished into the hallway, the masked leader turned his attention back to Hayley. 'Get her cleaned up and bring her up to me,' he said. 'I have something to show her.'

'She's part of this,' Janko replied. 'She's been with the ASIO from the beginning. She knows what's at stake here.'

'Yes,' the man replied in a sinister, raspy voice. 'She knows more than you think.'

He turned around and left. Janko stood still, looking stunned.

Slowly, he began to act, doing as ordered, moving to unlock Hayley's cuffs and disconnect her shackles from the wall. He left with her in tow. The two interrogators followed him out. One of them, no doubt, headed for the sick bay.

As the steel door slammed and locked tight, Joe and Gregorovich were left in the room with the dead commandos.

Joe glanced over at Gregorovich. 'You're welcome,' he said.

Gregorovich turned back to Joe, his face mostly bruises and blood. 'I didn't need your help.'

'Really?'

'But thank you anyway.'

Joe figured that was the best he would get out of Gregorovich. 'You take a punch pretty well for a Russian.'

'Sure,' Gregorovich said. 'And you handled your pain fairly well for a decadent American. You didn't even need any whisky to make you strong.'

Joe accepted the backhanded compliment. 'I'd take some,' he admitted, 'if you happened to have a bottle on you.'

The two men stared at each other for a moment, and finally Gregorovich began to laugh. Joe joined him. It hurt like crazy, but it was worth it.

'What happened to you out there?' Gregorovich asked. 'I thought you were going to get the shot off.'

'Didn't count on their wingman coming up behind me,' Joe replied. 'What about you?'

'They sideswiped me and knocked me off the sled.'

'How'd they get so close?'

Gregorovich hesitated. 'I may have doubled back to look for you. An obvious tactical mistake.'

So Gregorovich hadn't been hit by the stun gun, but he'd been felled anyway, trying to help Joe.

'We all make them,' Joe said, looking at the bodies thrown in a heap on the floor. 'You notice something about these men?'

Gregorovich nodded. 'They're one short,' he said. 'The board hasn't been totally cleared just yet.'

'Kurt won't give up,' Joe insisted. 'If he's alive, he won't leave us here to die. If there's any way to get help or get us out, he'll find it.'

Gregorovich shook his head, but it was disbelief in the situation, not disagreement. 'One piece left,' he muttered dejectedly. 'One knight trying to save all the pawns. Hard for me to fathom that I'm one of them now.'

Joe smiled through his busted lip. 'Welcome to our side.'

40

Hayley shuffled along through the half-lit tunnels of Thero's underground nest. The man named Janko had given her a chance to clean up, and given her a change of clothes, before bringing her deeper into the lair.

She moved slowly, filled with trepidation and half wishing she was back with Joe and Gregorovich in the dungeonlike interrogation room. Something about being all alone made this fate seem worse.

'Be strong,' she whispered to herself. 'Whatever comes, face it bravely.'

Janko arrived at an open room filled with an eight-pack of electrical generators. The squat, cylindrical-shaped devices were the size of industrial washing machines. They were arranged in two rows, and Hayley was marched between them to a door on the far side.

Janko pressed an intercom button beside the door. 'I have the woman,' he said into the microphone.

'Bring her in,' a harsh voice replied.

Janko typed a code into the lock, and an electronic click was heard. He opened the door and ushered Hayley inside. She steeled herself for whatever lay ahead and stepped over the threshold.

This room looked different to the rest of the cave.

The walls were finished in a high-gloss white plastic. Computers, control panels and monitors were placed in various locations. Recessed lighting gave it a warmer look.

'Welcome to Master Control,' the man in the mask said to her.

The voice was distorted by the man's damaged vocal cords, but she was fairly certain who was speaking.

'Max?' she asked. 'Is that really you?'

The man stared at her for a moment and then looked at Janko. 'Leave us.'

'She could be dangerous,' Janko replied.

'Not to me,' Thero replied.

Janko exhaled sharply and then stepped out of the room.

As the door closed, Thero stepped closer to her. He held out a hand. She saw that it was burned and scarred.

'It's been so long,' Thero said. 'We've been so lonely.'

Despite the fear she felt, Hayley's mind was racing. 'We?' she said. 'Is George alive? Is he here with you?'

Thero nodded.

'Is he okay?' she asked, hopeful that George could help her put a stop to this madness and yet fearful that he might be horribly burned and scarred like Thero.

'He'll be along shortly,' Thero said. 'He knows you're here. In fact, it was he who suggested we talk to you alone. That perhaps you might understand.'

She smiled genuinely. George was the only hope. 'I'm thankful to hear that. What about Tessa?'

'No,' Thero said. 'They murdered her.'

Hayley cast her gaze down. George and Tessa had been like siblings. She'd hoped somehow both were alive, though she'd doubted it was possible. At least George had survived. Maybe there was a chance, she thought. Maybe reason could triumph at this last moment.

'My heart breaks for Tessa,' she said, 'though I'm thankful that you and George are still alive. How did you survive the explosion?'

'I'd begun working on a new theory,' Thero said. 'By using a spherical projector instead of a dome-shaped one, I thought the wave might be more stable. We'd only just begun the excavation when the shooting began. George and I escaped and sealed ourselves in while they shot the others.'

She stared.

'There was nothing we could do,' Thero insisted.

'I know,' she said softly. 'I understand.'

He glared at her for a moment before continuing. 'After the shooting ended and we heard nothing but silence, we unsealed the door. Seconds later, the explosions flashed. I was burned badly, though George was mostly spared. He cared for me until we made it to a hospital. We paid enough to keep it quiet. I didn't want them finding us after escaping with our lives. But we couldn't stay long. We had to find a place where we'd be safe.'

'And you came here?'

'Not at first,' he said, 'but eventually. We needed a place where no one would ever find us. A place with advantages. Here, we have geothermal power. We have food from the seals and the birds and the fishing grounds. And my study of geography proved most valuable when we discovered diamonds. A series of kimberlite pipes rich enough to fund our operations after the money Tokada had given us ran out.'

'Why not just take the money and run?' she asked. 'Live your life. You've given so much already.'

'What life?!' he shouted. 'We're hunted wherever we go. Banished here as much by their jealousy and hatred as by our own need to work without interference. You see, the world was not willing to let my light shine upon them. So now I will blind them and burn them instead.'

She considered her precarious position and Thero's obvious madness. She decided she'd better pander to his ego.

'The world is full of jealous fools,' she said. 'But wouldn't it be glorious to prove them wrong and become rich rather than begin a war that will only bring more death?'

'What good is wealth to a man who can't show his face or breathe the air?' he said. 'My lungs will burn without the proper humidity. My skin crawls if it meets the sunlight. I am no longer part of the world. I am doomed to live here on Tartarus, to live forever in darkness. So what good does the light afford me? Revenge is all I have left.'

'Revenge against Australia?'

'Against all of them,' Thero bellowed. 'Against an entire world set against us. Against any who challenge me!'

Hayley shrank back. It only seemed to anger Thero more.

'You have no reason to fear me,' he insisted.

'I have plenty of reason,' she replied. 'You've become a murderer. The man I knew was never like that. You wanted peace.'

'And this is what it got me!' He pulled off his mask to reveal a face horribly scarred by melted and burned skin. His nose had been burned off, the skin over his right eye scarred and twisted until that eye bulged grotesquely.

Thero stepped toward her angrily. She tried to back away but tripped and fell. Thero's gaze flicked off to the right and then settled back on her.

'Why shouldn't I?' he said aloud. 'She's a traitor. She betrayed us like all the rest.'

Hayley stared up at him, one hand raised to defend herself. She looked around but saw no one else in the room.

Still poised to assault her, Thero glanced over his shoulder. Finally, slowly, he lowered his hand and centered his gaze upon her once again. 'They're using you,' he told her.

'Who?'

'All of them,' he replied. 'The ASIO, the Americans, the Russians. All of them are out to destroy us together.'

Thero's paranoid delusions had always run to the grandiose. Strangely, his radical actions had now united much of the world against him.

'They forced me to come along,' she said, thinking quickly and playing to his thoughts. 'They were going to put me in prison if I didn't help. They claimed I was collaborating with you.'

Thero stared down at her. His scarred face showed no trace of emotion. She felt sorry for him in a way. Sorry and afraid and confused.

Thero glanced off to the side once again, staring into the distance. She found it frightening.

He shook his head as if responding to a question. 'No,' he muttered. 'No, I don't agree. We must be cautious. What makes you think she can be trusted?'

Once again, Hayley looked in the direction of Thero's gaze. There was no one there, not even in the distant shadows. Her mind whirled. She took a chance.

'George?' she whispered. 'George, I promise I've come to help you.'

Thero turned her way again.

'I looked for you both,' she insisted, gazing up into his eyes, her face quivering. 'I went to Japan after the explosions. I flew there to find you even though I was afraid to get on the plane. You know how I hate to travel. I was there at the memorial services for you and your father and Tessa. You have to know this. Now I've come all the way here to find you.'

Thero straightened a bit, and eased back. 'I told him you were always loyal,' he said in an odd tone.

He held out his hand, his left hand this time. The skin was smooth, unscarred. George had been left-handed, Thero used his right. She reached over and grasped the smooth palm.

'Come with me,' Thero said. 'I'll show you what Father and I have built.'

Father and I.

She now understood. Part of her recoiled at the thought, but she could not reject it any further. George was dead. She was certain of it. He'd died along with Tessa in Japan. Thero alone had survived. The pain and guilt of it had broken his already fragile mind and split his personality in two. Both the threat of destruction and the slim chance at salvation had come from the same body. In life, George Thero had been called his father's conscience. Now, after death, he'd become just that.

Hayley felt an all-encompassing sadness at this realization, but some part of her mind realized she needed to act. If she could use this break from reality to save her country, she must try, however distasteful it might be.

She reached out a hand and touched Thero's scarred face, looking into his eyes as if she were gazing at her old friend.

'It's good to see you, George,' she said. 'It's so good to see you again.'

The tears in her eyes were genuine. They seemed to touch this aspect of Thero's personality. 'It's good to see you too,' he replied softly. 'Father and I have missed you for so long.'

41

Hours of hiking through the blizzard and the frigid darkness brought Kurt to what geologists call a lateral moraine, a ridge of material deposited along the side of a glacier. Just beyond it, he could see the imposing wall of ice that made up the Winston Glacier.

Having made his first landmark, he turned south and began hiking down the slope toward the lagoon and the series of hot spots photographed by the Russian drones.

As he traveled, he received a low-battery warning on the night vision goggles.

He'd known the cold would drain the batteries and had been using them sparingly, turning them on, studying the terrain, and then switching them off as he hiked. Now as he forced his way down the rugged slope, he needed them almost constantly. When they finally shut down, Kurt was left in utter darkness.

Removing the goggles, Kurt trudged onward, holding the hood of his parka across everything but his eyes. He stumbled on a pile of unseen rocks, cursing under his breath as he smashed his shin. He fought his way over uneven terrain, and then he took a bad step in the dark.

He dropped and slid down a steep incline, causing a minor avalanche that took him for a ride and spat him out on flattish ground moments later.

Kurt allowed himself to rest for just a moment, but he knew better than to linger. The cold and fatigue would try to drag him into a sleep from which he would never awake. He found a spot to push off and forced himself to stand.

Breathing deeply, he noticed something. Not a sight or sound, but an odd scent. He couldn't quite place it, but it smelled like food cooking. Bad, greasy food, mixed with smoke. He couldn't exactly call it a pleasant smell, but it wasn't his imagination.

His fatigue was instantly forgotten as he thought about the reconnaissance photos and the hot spots near the front edge of the glacier.

'Even people who live underground need to eat,' he whispered.

Kurt sniffed the air in an attempt to locate the source of the smell, but he was no bloodhound. The best he could do was get a general sense that it was traveling upslope toward him. He eased forward until he found a treelike column of snow and ice.

He pulled the flashlight from a pocket, covered it, and then switched it on, allowing a tiny portion of light to escape from beneath his glove.

The column rose about ten feet. A few yards away, a second column stood only four feet high. And thirty or forty feet from that, he saw a third and a fourth and a fifth.

Kurt shut off the light and made his way to the shorter column. He found it was open at the top and roughly circular. As the wind gusted, it made a hollow sound, like someone blowing across the top of an open wine bottle.

He leaned over and peered down into the mouth of the icy tube. It was about the size of a manhole on a city street. Looking down into it, he saw nothing but darkness, nor did he detect a strong scent of food or grease. Still, he could feel warmth rising up and bathing his face. It felt almost surreal after so many hours in the cold. It also felt humid.

Kurt put a hand on the edge of the column and broke a piece off. It was just ice, and not very thick at that. It was also blackened with soot. He began to understand what he was looking at.

He'd been in Iceland a few years before and found similar structures near the geothermal vents up on the slopes of the active volcanic mountains. As the heated air from inside made its way to the surface, it brought humidity with it, some of which cooled and froze almost instantly as it mixed with the frigid outside air. Slowly, like coral building up a reef or the black smokers in the depths of the ocean, the freezing water vapor created chimneylike tubes. Since they were merely thin sheets of ice, they tended to topple in high winds. But as long as the vent was active, they would regrow.

Kurt risked another quick flash from his flashlight, aiming it down into the opening.

He could see nothing. He felt heat but didn't smell sulfur, like he'd have expected if they were volcanic.

He pulled out his Zippo lighter and one of the oily rags. He held the lighter against it and lit it, sheltering the rag from the wind until a third of it was burning. Next, he dropped it into the tube.

It fell through the darkness like a small meteorite, illuminating the smooth sides of the tunnel as it went, until suddenly it hit something and stopped.

As the rag burned, Kurt saw the outline of a grate. The chimney was not volcanic, it was man-made, designed to evacuate heat or smoke or something else undesirable from down below. It had to lead to Thero's lair. *It had to.*

Quickly, Kurt set up his rope. He found a section of the ice and rubble in the lateral moraine and hammered in three anchors to secure the rope. He didn't have a harness, or time to improvise one, but it didn't matter, he would rappel down, using his hands to control the descent.

He dropped the rope in and eased over the edge. The fit was tight. He could barely see past his boots. Twenty feet down, the tunnel was free of ice and consequently slightly wider. Kurt continued to descend. By the time his feet hit the grate, he figured he'd dropped about a hundred feet.

Pressing himself against one edge of the chimney, he studied the metal grate. He could see a dusty floor ten feet below it. He heard no sound of movement.

Bouncing up and down a bit, he tested the strength of the grate. On his third little hop, he felt it give.

'Time to drop in,' he muttered to himself.

He looped the rope through one of the bars and tied it. Then he jumped hard, and the grate broke free.

The sound of rock splinters hitting the floor was no louder than a whisper, and both Kurt and the heavy grate remained suspended by the rope.

Kurt lowered them both down gently and touched down without a sound.

He was in.

Exactly what he'd made his way into was another question entirely.

42

Paul Trout stood on the bridge of the *Gemini* as the ship surged through the waves toward the MV *Rama*. The merchant vessel had been traveling northeast since finishing its Orion-like pattern, and the *Gemini* had been racing to intercept it for the last eight hours. They were finally closing to within shouting distance.

'Think we're going to be able to do this alone?' Gamay asked from a spot beside him.

'We've got a fighting chance,' Paul said. He would have preferred some backup, but they were so far off the beaten track, there wasn't a military or coast guard vessel for a thousand miles.

'If it wasn't for the weather, we could at least get some air support,' she said. 'A few threatening passes by a formation of military jets or an Australian anti-submarine aircraft circling the ship relentlessly might have helped.'

Paul agreed completely, but the leading edge of a gale had reached the area. It was whipping up the seas and slinging freezing rain across the *Gemini*'s deck. Not the kind of conditions aircraft made low, showy passes in. Especially fifteen hundred miles from the nearest land.

All of which meant the unarmed *Gemini* was the only hope of stopping the MV *Rama* and finding out if any of the *Orion*'s crew were aboard.

'What's the range?' Paul asked.

They had the *Rama* painted on the radarscope, but with visibility at a quarter mile, they hadn't seen her in the dark yet.

'A thousand yards,' the radar officer said.

'That's it?' Paul replied. 'She must be running without lights.'

'In this soup, we might collide with her before we spot her,' the captain added.

'No, we won't,' Gamay said, looking through a pair of binoculars. 'I've got her. Just off the port bow.'

Paul followed her directions, spotting the shadow of a vessel plowing through the dark.

'Light her up,' the captain ordered.

The executive officer flicked a series of switches, and a trio of powerful spotlights came on, piercing the dark and the rain and converging on the lumbering vessel. At three times the *Gemini*'s size, the *Rama* pitched and rolled less noticeably in the swells, but there was a wallowing quality to her progress.

'Time to put on the show,' Paul said, handing his binoculars to the captain.

'I'll bring us up alongside her,' the captain said. 'You get ready to play commando.'

'I don't have to tell you to be careful,' Gamay said.

'No,' Paul replied grinning. 'No, you don't.'

With that, Paul left the bridge and raced down the stairwell. Minutes later, he was standing just inside the forward hatch with a dozen other volunteers. They all wore black, with hastily made arm patches that displayed an approximation of the Australian flag's blue field, with its stars of the Southern Cross and the Union Jack in the corner.

'Weapons, everyone,' Paul said. The *Gemini*'s weapons locker held six rifles and two pistols. The rest received wooden approximations of the M16 rifle that had been painted black. The volunteers from the crew laughed and pointed the guns at one another.

'What do we do if they don't surrender?' one man asked.

'Either dive overboard or swing these things like Reggie Jackson,' another one replied.

Paul hoped neither act would be necessary.

He cracked the hatch a few inches and peered through the rain and fog. The MV *Rama* was just across from them, bathed in the spotlights, as the *whoop-whoop* of *Gemini*'s alarm blared like a coast guard siren.

They chased and harried the *Rama* like this for several minutes to no effect. Finally, the intercom buzzed.

'They're not responding to our radio calls,' Gamay's voice announced.

'Understood,' Paul said. 'I'll man the rocket launchers. Tell the captain to get us in close. Real close. And be ready to give them your spiel over the loudspeaker.'

'Will do,' Gamay said. *'Good luck.'*

Paul looked at the chief. 'I'm heading forward. Get ready to take your positions on the deck.'

'We'll be ready,' the chief said.

Paul made his way to another door and pushed out through the hatch and on to the pitching deck. He crossed the foredeck to a squared-off structure that looked convincingly like a warship's turret, with multiple rocket-launching tubes on either side.

A hydraulic crane used to lift ROVs in and out of the water had occupied the spot hours before. The boom had been dismantled and the sheet metal façade of a turret welded on to the crane's turntable-like base. Metal air-duct tubing had been removed from parts of the ship, cut to the right length, and affixed to the sides. Painted battleship gray, with a fake antenna dish mounted on the top, the 'turret' gave off a reasonable impression of a lethal-weapons system.

Paul slipped inside, ducking through a gap in the metal. He found the *Gemini*'s crane operator at the controls.

Paul spoke into his radio. 'Light up the foredeck,' he said. 'Let them see what they're up against.'

Seconds later, additional lighting shone down on the turret as Gamay's voice sounded over the loudspeaker, roaring at the highest volume.

'This is Commander Matilda Wallaby of the Royal Australian Navy,' she called out. She was using a fake accent that was pretty close to the real thing. *'Your vessel has been spotted poaching fish in Australian territorial waters. You will*

reduce speed and prepare to be boarded or we will disable your ship.'

Paul stared through an aiming slit in the sheet metal. He detected no response from the *Rama*, but he saw lighting changes in the bridge area.

'Hopefully, they're looking this way,' he said.

By now, the *Gemini* had pulled directly alongside the blocky superstructure near the aft end of the containership. The captain had eased the ship in closer. No more than fifty feet separated the sides of the two ships. As one swell rolled through, the *Gemini* rode up and almost sideswiped the larger vessel.

'Anything?' Paul asked into the radio.

'Not yet,' Gamay replied.

'Give them another warning, and have the chief fire off a clip of tracer shells.'

Gamay's voice echoed over the loudspeaker again. *'Merchant vessel* Rama, *this is your last warning. Reduce speed and prepare to be boarded or we will open fire.'*

'Let's show them what we've got,' Paul said.

The crane operator powered up the base unit and pressed a small joystick to the side. The turret and its attached missile tubes began to pivot on the crane's turntable. It turned counterclockwise until the missile tubes were pointed at the *Rama*'s bridge.

Using a secondary actuator, Paul pitched the missile tubes up and down in an exaggerated motion designed to be obvious to the *Rama*'s crew. When he'd done as much as he thought he could get away with, he locked them in place again, pointed roughly at the *Rama*'s bridge.

'They have to see us,' he said.

The crane operator just shrugged.

Meanwhile, the chief and his commandos were deploying on to the deck with their rifles raised.

'*What do you think, Paul?*' the radio squawked.

'Go ahead and shoot, chief.'

The racket of gunfire rang out, sounding like a series of sharp pops over the wind. Paul watched as a series of glowing tracer shells raced past the bridge of the *Rama* and out into the night. Through his binoculars, Paul could see figures on the *Rama*'s bridge, staring out the windows. He hoped they were getting nervous.

'Our turn,' Paul said, lowering the binoculars.

Two makeshift rockets had been prepared using gunpowder, propellant from a box of flares, and the artistic skills of the men in the machine shop. They wouldn't cause any damage, but they might make an impression.

Paul loaded one of the rockets into the launch tube and shut the breach.

'Turn us five degrees to the right,' he said. It would do no good to have the rocket hit and prove itself to be a dud. The missile had to cross in front of the *Rama*, close enough to scare the crew, far enough away to be convincing.

The turret turned and stopped.

'Wait,' Paul said as the *Gemini* rode down a swell and

began to come back up. 'Wait . . .' He was gazing through the aiming slit like a World War One gunnery officer, guessing at the rate each ship would rise and fall on the waves.

'Wait . . .' he said again.

The *Gemini* reached the top of the swell and paused. 'Now!'

The crane operator pressed a switch, and the makeshift rocket ignited. It burst from the tube, showering the interior of the turret with sparks and smoke. It crossed the gap, spewing a tail of fire, and passing no more than twenty feet in front of the *Rama*'s bridge.

'Great shot!' Paul shouted, coughing because of the smoke. 'That was perfect.'

Seconds later, Gamay's voice sounded over the loudspeaker once again. *'The next missile will hit your bridge,'* she insisted. *'Reduce your speed or we will stop you by force.'*

Aboard the MV *Rama*, the ranking Russian commando had been arguing with the Vietnamese captain since the appearance of the *Gemini*. He'd ordered them to leave station off Heard Island to avoid any trouble or repercussions should Gregorovich succeed in detonating his bomb. Running into an Australian frigate was not the outcome he'd hoped for.

'I will not surrender!' he said.

'You can't fight them,' the captain said.

The tracer rounds flashed by in the dark. That concerned him but did not change his mind. Then the 'missile' was launched.

'Incoming!'

The commandos and the bridge crew hit the deck just as the missile lit up the world in front of them, rocketing past the main windows.

'That was too close,' the captain said.

'They wouldn't fire a missile at poachers,' another commando insisted. 'They must know we're here and what we've done. If we don't stop, we'll all be killed.'

'We cannot fight them,' the Vietnamese captain repeated. 'But you can negotiate once they're aboard. Diplomatic immunity. That's what you'll claim. But only if you're alive.'

The commando doubted the captain's take on International Maritime Law, but he believed he would be better served, and more likely to live, if he surrendered rather than fighting.

'Do as they say,' he agreed reluctantly.

On the *Gemini*'s bridge, Gamay waited tensely. If their bluff didn't work, they would have to try to risk a dangerous boarding maneuver in the storm.

She was about to make one more threat over the loudspeaker when the marine radio squawked.

'This is the MV Rama,*'* a voice said in accented English. *'We will reduce speed to seven knots and allow your men to come aboard.'*

A cheer went up on the bridge, and Gamay relayed the message to the others.

'Great work, Commander Wallaby,' the captain said.

She smiled. Now the boarding would only be risky, not foolhardy beyond belief.

43

'This is a mine,' Kurt whispered to himself.

He'd found quarried-out sections, discovered a conveyor belt loaded with gravel and a series of pipes along the wall that probably ran electrical wire. He'd found picks and a jackhammer and wheelbarrows.

What a mine was doing hidden on Heard Island, Kurt didn't know. Nor did it matter at the moment. His only concerns were finding Joe and Hayley, if they were alive, and stopping Thero no matter what.

He slipped off the heavy parka, stashed it, and pulled his backpack on once again. He began moving down the dark tunnel, his hand on the conveyor belt, his head ducked to avoid any dangerous outcroppings of rock he probably wouldn't see until it was too late.

After passing several other areas that had been quarried extensively, he came to a larger room. This one was dimly lit by a pair of exposed bulbs.

The conveyor belt ended there, beside a group of large machines designed to crush and sort the gravel. He'd seen this kind of setup before. It was an underground diamond mine. Suddenly, he had a better idea how Thero was financing the operation.

He saw a door on the far side and crossed the room

toward it. Just as he reached for the handle, the door moved, inching open. Kurt stepped back and raised the pistol as a trio of men came through.

'Don't move!' Kurt growled.

The men froze in place, and a tense standoff ensued. Kurt might have drilled all three of them, but without a silencer the gunshots would have echoed through the cave and brought the rest of Thero's men running.

As they stared at the gun, Kurt studied them. They carried sharpened staves made of crude metal instead of guns. Two of them appeared almost petrified, the third just as shocked but calmer.

'Put your weapons down,' he said, then added: 'Quietly.'

They did as ordered.

Kurt nodded toward one of the rock-crushing machines. 'Over there.'

The three men shuffled toward the machine. Kurt kept his distance in case they tried something rash.

'Two of you are going to end up tied to this machine,' he told them. 'Whoever doesn't want to spend the night like that can take me to Thero.'

'Take you to Thero?' one of them asked. He spoke with a South African accent.

'Who's Thero?' another said with an Irish lilt.

'The man who brought you here,' the South African said.

'Quiet,' Kurt said. 'Which one of you wants to show me the way?'

The three men looked at one another as if they were baffled by the question.

'Why would we take you?' the third man said.

'Because I have an appointment,' Kurt said, 'and I don't want to miss it.'

The confused look returned. Apparently, biting humor wasn't their strong suit.

'You mean, which one of us wants to go with you and die first,' the South African said.

Kurt stared at him. The statement made no sense. 'What are you talking about?'

'What are *you* talking about?' the South African repeated.

Kurt felt like he was in the Twilight Zone. He took another look at the men. They were filthy, wearing rags. Their weapons were crude. Suddenly, it made sense.

'You three are miners here,' he said. 'You're trying to escape. Whose idea was it?'

Two of them pointed at the Irishman.

'Rats,' the Irishman replied. 'The lot of you.'

A broad smile creased Kurt's face. 'More like three blind mice,' he said. 'The question is, exactly where were you running to?'

For the next few minutes, Kurt pried information out of the miners, learning their names and a little bit about the operation. Masinga, the South African, had been there right from the start.

'Eight months ago, I stole a key from one of the guards,' he explained. 'But he never reported it lost because Thero would kill him for losing it.'

'Took a lot of patience not to use it right away,' Kurt noted.

Devlin, the Irishman, spoke up. 'Apparently, patience runs in his family.'

Masinga smiled. 'I hoped a day would come when escape would mean more than just dying in the cold. Devlin here says he came on a ship. He says he knows how to get back to it.'

'I hate to tell you,' Kurt said, 'but you're going the wrong way. Nothing but excavation tunnels back this way.'

The other two prisoners looked menacingly toward Devlin.

'That's what you get for listening to me,' Devlin said. 'I've been here only two days.'

'So what's the deal with this mine anyway? I don't recall Thero having any mining expertise.'

'He has others,' Masinga explained. 'It's an uneasy relationship between him and the overseers. He keeps them on a short leash, yanking their chains from time to time, but for the most part he leaves them alone. They work us and sell the diamonds. Thero lets them keep a cut, or so I've heard.'

'Slave labor,' Kurt noted. 'That's one way to bump up the profit margin.'

'As we die off, they bring in more,' Masinga added. 'Kidnapping and luring in people who have little else in the way of opportunity.'

Kurt understood. It was a whole new reason to put

Thero out of business, but it ran a distant second to saving Australia. 'Any new arrivals in the last few hours?'

'Are you looking for someone specific?' Devlin replied.

'I started out with some friends,' Kurt said. 'Thero's men attacked us. We got separated. I think they were probably captured.'

'That's no good,' Masinga said. 'Thero will torture them, until they give in or die.'

Kurt studied Masinga's face. His nose had obviously been broken at some point, and a jagged scar next to his ear looked like the result of some violent blunt-force trauma. 'I'm guessing you know where that would take place.'

'I do,' Masinga said.

'I need you to show me.'

'That's back into the middle of this maze,' the third member of the trio said. 'You'll never get past Thero's men.'

'Maybe I won't,' Kurt corrected. 'But *we* are going to try. You're all coming with me.'

'Fine by me,' Devlin said. 'I've got a bone to pick with one of them.'

'I do also,' Masinga said.

'Just tie me to the machine,' the third man said. 'I'll wait for you to come back.'

Kurt glared at him.

'What's the difference? Three against thirty or four against thirty? Same odds, really. You don't need me.'

In a roundabout way, the man was right. Kurt had another idea. 'How many other prisoners down here?'

'Sixty or seventy,' Masinga replied.

'And how many of them might like a shot at revenge?'

'At least sixty or seventy,' the South African repeated, smiling.

'That makes the living quarters our first stop.'

Joe and Gregorovich remained in the interrogation room, sweating in what had to be hundred-degree heat. As the perspiration trickled down his face and dripped off his nose, Joe could barely believe the irony. 'An hour ago, I thought I'd freeze to death.'

'Now they're broiling us,' Gregorovich replied.

The small room had begun to feel stifling. Joe figured it was time to take drastic measures. He writhed around until he could rub the side of his wet face against the back of his hand. When the perspiration from his face and hair had coated his hand, he changed positions.

Squeezing his fingers together as tightly as he could, Joe eased his hand into the cuff. He felt like a contortionist, pulling and twisting.

'You'll never get free like that,' Gregorovich said.

'I have large wrists and average hands,' Joe said. 'And these old shackles have a lot of play in them.'

With the sweat acting as a lubricant, Joe finessed his hand deeper into the cuff. Finally, it came free.

Joe smiled, victorious. 'Blood, sweat and tears,' he said. 'That's all it takes.'

Gregorovich looked down. 'What about your feet? I don't suppose you have big ankles and narrow toes.'

Joe hadn't thought that far ahead.

'One step at a time,' he said. 'One step at a time.'

44

In the island's control room, Hayley was doing her best to act normal. She continued to speak to Thero as if addressing George, infusing her words with affection while trying not to look obvious.

As she fawned over him, Thero showed her the control panels for the great machine and led her to the viewing portal, through which she could see the great orb resting in the darkened cave.

He pressed a series of switches. Lights came on in a cave outside the window. A huge spherical construction appeared. She recognized it from a conceptual drawing Thero had shown her years ago.

'It's incredible,' she said.

'My father was right,' he said. 'This is proof. From here, we can direct vast amounts of energy through the Earth to any point on the globe. Energy we draw from the zero-point field.'

'You don't need the generators?' she asked.

'Only to start the wave,' he replied.

That gave her an idea. If they could possibly destroy the generators she'd seen outside, perhaps they could prevent the machine from engaging.

'This is amazing,' she said, gazing through the observation window at the latticework. 'How did you solve the dynamic feedback problem?'

'We've only partially solved it,' he admitted.

'Do you still end up with uncontrollable vibrations?'

'We use the water as a dampening field,' Thero said. 'It absorbs much of the energy. Also, by creating a spherical emitter instead of an open-ended conductor, we get a much more stable wave.'

'You were always a step ahead of us, George,' she said, smiling. 'That's really quite brilliant.'

'My father did most of the theoretical work,' he replied. 'But I crunched the numbers.'

As they spoke, she tried to gauge how strong a grip the George persona was exerting. Working on her own phobias, she'd learned a great deal about mental health. She'd heard of cases where subjects with multiple personality disorder had absolutely no idea what the other personalities in their minds were up to. To the point where they passed lie detector tests after committing crimes or even carried on affairs or entirely different lives when the dominant personality went dormant.

If that was the case here, perhaps she could coax George into letting them go, or surrendering, or at least giving them more time to come up with some plan to stop the lethal strike he was counting down to launch.

'It was you who sent the letters?' she asked hopefully.

A blank stare issued forth from Thero.

'To warn me,' she said, risking everything.

'Yes,' he replied finally. 'I was hoping we might still bring peaceful energy to the world.'

'Your father doesn't know,' she said. 'We have to keep it that way. We can still help him, but he won't understand.'

'I agree,' Thero said. 'He might hate me for it, but it's for our own good.'

'You helped the others to escape,' she prodded.

Thero nodded. 'I gave them a chance and the information. They never knew it was me. I passed notes. Made things possible.'

Inwardly, she cringed, imagining the turmoil. As George, he'd become the informant, he helped the couriers to make it to freedom. But then, as Thero, he hunted them down and had them killed. No wonder every meeting had been blown. There was no leak in the ASIO, the leak was at the source. It meant some information was passing from George's personality to Thero's. It made her more nervous than ever, but she had to press on.

'I thought reason might prevail,' George volunteered.

'It still can,' she said eagerly.

'No,' he replied sadly. 'They've come to kill us again. Only a show of unstoppable force will keep them away now.'

She had to think fast. 'I can negotiate with them for you,' she pleaded, squeezing his smooth hand. 'The

Americans have already promised amnesty,' she lied. 'All you have to do is return to the States with them.'

'Amnesty?'

'Yes,' she said. 'For you and your father,' she added, doing all she could to keep George's personality engaged and on the surface.

'Why would they offer that?'

'They're afraid of the Russians getting their hands on it.'

'They're working with the Russians,' George said forcefully.

'No,' she said. 'The Russians kidnapped us. They want to kill you. But if you get me to a radio, I can bring help.'

George hesitated. 'Are you sure?'

'I promise,' she said. 'I just need a chance to prove it.'

He stared at her for a long moment, as if pondering what she'd said.

'This is why you reached out to me,' she said, 'isn't it?'

Finally, he nodded. 'Come with me.'

He led her down the bank of control panels, stopping in his tracks as he passed the final console.

Hayley saw why. Lying on the floor were several men and a few women. They wore bloodstained lab coats. They'd been shot.

'Father, what have you done?'

Hayley tried to breathe. 'We have to hurry, George.'

Thero hesitated. He cocked his head to the side. 'What do you mean, they were traitors?' he asked the air.

She could see what was happening. 'No, George,' she urged. 'Don't talk to him.'

'They worked for you,' he said sharply, as if arguing with his father. 'They built this for you.'

A strange trancelike silence gripped Thero, and Hayley sensed him wavering.

'Stay with me!'

Thero hesitated. He stood with clumsy effort and let go of her hand.

'George?' she asked.

'No,' he said softly.

'George?'

'No!'

This time, the words were bellowed at her. The harshness returned to Thero's eyes with a rush, and he grabbed her by the throat with his right hand and slammed her into the wall. The impact stunned her, and Thero's hand crushing her windpipe seemed to cut off the blood from her brain.

'Please . . .' she gasped, crying out to the other side of Thero's mind. 'Please!'

Thero released her, and she dropped to the floor beside the heap of bodies.

'How dare you turn my son against me!'

'I didn't,' she managed. 'We were only . . . trying to help.'

'I don't need your help!' he shouted. 'Or my son's,

for that matter. I will bring the world to its knees. Once they see what I do to Australia, there will be no need for negotiations. They will beg me for mercy.'

He stepped back over to the control panel and shoved the master switch into the ON position. She heard the heavy circuit closing and the big generators in the other room switching on. The lights around them dimmed appreciably and then began to brighten.

Soon, the generators were humming, spinning up to a feverous pitch.

'No,' she begged. 'Please, don't do this.'

'I'm so glad you could be here,' Thero shouted. 'I will not even wait for zero hour. I will punish them immediately. And you will watch from my side as I wreak destruction on those who persecuted me.'

Out in the spherical cavern, the gears began to churn, and the giant collection of pipes and electrical conduits began to tilt. The weapon turned slowly, clinking like a roller coaster being dragged up the steep track to its release point.

Hayley found herself dizzy as the weapon slowly ratcheted itself toward a new position, an alignment that would aim the wave of distortion through the Earth's crust at the dormant rift in the Australian outback.

45

Kurt and his three newfound cohorts crept through several lengths of tunnel connecting various areas that the miners had quarried until eventually they arrived in a hub containing living quarters for the prisoners.

Every twenty feet or so, there was an alcove with a steel door. At the far end of the hall, a single guard sat at a desk, ostensibly watching the hub.

'How'd you get past him the first time?' Kurt asked.

'We waited for him to take a bathroom break,' Masinga replied.

'Unless he's been drinking coffee all night, I don't think we have time for that plan to work again. Get ready to use that skeleton key.'

He took a breath and let the tension fall away from his body. Then, calmly, he stepped out into the hall, leveled the Makarov, and advanced at a brisk pace.

When the guard looked up, Kurt had no choice. With two quick pulls, Kurt triggered the gun. The booming report surged through the narrow tunnel like thunder. The two shots hit the guard in the chest, knocking him off his chair and on to the floor.

He didn't move, but, to Kurt's surprise, a second guard appeared at the side of the first.

Kurt fired again. The guard crumpled to the ground, but his hand slammed down on an emergency alarm button as he fell.

The shriek of an electronic alarm rang out, and a thick steel-plated door began to close between Kurt and the guard post and whatever was beyond it. Kurt ran forward, but it shut just before he arrived.

Behind him, Masinga was already rushing to the dorm-like cells, letting the other prisoners free. They were shouting and thanking him in several different languages. Soon, they were filling the hall and surging toward Kurt, for whatever good it would do them.

Devlin arrived at Kurt's side before the rest of the mob. 'Now what?'

Kurt slid the backpack off his shoulders and dropped it to the floor. Opening it revealed the explosives he carried. 'Get everyone back into their cells.'

'You're gonna blow this thing?'

'No other choice,' Kurt said. 'Let's just hope I don't bring the roof down in the process.'

Kurt's instincts tended toward overkill. If a small hammer would do the job, a sledgehammer would leave no room for doubt. In this case, he tempered his basic inclinations, placing two bricks of the C-4 beside the door and jabbing a pair of blasting caps into each of them.

'Are you sure that's enough?' Devlin asked.

Kurt didn't reply.

'Could it be too much?' Devlin asked.

The wailing alarm was bad enough, Devlin's questions only made it worse. 'I guess we're going to find out one way or another,' Kurt said. 'Now, get these people back.'

As Kurt attached a wire to each of the caps, Devlin backed down the tunnel, ushering the others to keep away.

Kurt was soon backing away with them, spooling out the wire as he went. He reached the first of the alcoves and ducked into it. The newly freed prisoners crowded around him as he attached the wires from the detonator to a small handheld device that resembled one of those grip strengtheners tennis players are always squeezing.

'What's that?' Devlin asked.

'Some people call it a clacker,' Kurt said. 'It sets off the explosives.'

Around them, the prisoners ducked and covered their ears. Fortunately for Kurt, the clacker was a tiny generator, not a battery-powered object or it would have been drained by the flash-draw that took out the snowmobile.

'Ready?'

Devlin and Masinga nodded in unison. With a quick compression, Kurt squeezed the clacker. The action sent a tiny electrical pulse racing down the wire. The pulse set off the blasting caps, which in turn detonated the C-4.

A thunderous explosion racked the subterranean halls, and a concussion wave surged down the tunnel and into the alcove. Kurt felt the air knocked out of him and was thrown to the ground along with everyone else in the cavern.

Getting up quickly, he fought his way through clouds of dust and down the tunnel. As he neared the far end, the dust began to clear. He saw light and an open room ahead. The door lay on its side.

Stepping into the hall, Kurt found no resistance. 'It's clear,' he shouted. 'Let's go.'

Devlin and Masinga came running up first. Kurt handed them weapons taken from the dead guards, and the three of them moved out with the crowd of prisoners close behind.

The shrill call of the alarm caught Thero's attention as he began to run through the start-up checklist. He paused, wondering what could be happening.

As he waited, Hayley called out, 'George, it doesn't have to be like this. Tell your father there's another way.'

Thero looked to his left. His son was there, staring at Hayley like a lovesick schoolboy.

'Don't listen to her,' Thero shouted. 'She never cared for us. She would have come to Japan if she had. She betrayed us and brought these men to our door.'

'I only want to help,' Hayley said.

Thero was trying to concentrate on the start-up procedure. He had no time for his son's weakness.

'I can get you out of here,' Hayley said. 'Both of you. You can fulfill all your dreams peacefully. You know that's what you really want. You know that's the right thing to do.'

Thero began to feel confused. His son urged him to reconsider. 'Father, I think –'

A reverberating explosion shook the room. It came from somewhere deep in the cavern. Thero's mind cleared. The alarm, the explosion. They were under attack.

When Thero looked up, George was gone. He must have run off somewhere. 'Coward!'

'Please!' Hayley cried.

'Silence!' Thero shouted. He didn't have time to worry about his son anymore, he had to strike before he was trapped and buried like the last time in Yagishiri. Even if they stopped him, he would lash out and wound the world for what they'd done.

'If you do this,' Hayley said, 'they'll know where you are. They'll come here and destroy this place and you along with it.'

Thero looked down at her and stepped closer. 'Of course they will,' he said. 'But I'll be gone. And I'll take what they threatened me with to use against them.'

He pointed to an object resting by the wall. The Russian suitcase bomb. He could either use it to obliterate some enemy or sell it for millions.

Thero saw the fear in her eyes as she stared. He relished it and went back to his console, reaching over to the intercom and switching it on.

'Janko!' he shouted. 'What's happening?'

'We're under attack,' Janko said. *'Must have been . . .'*

The staccato sound of gunfire blocked out the rest of Janko's statement.

'Janko?'

'They've released the workers,' Janko shouted. *'There's a riot down here. We're being overwhelmed.'*

'Bring your men up here,' Thero ordered. 'We can hold them off from the control room.'

'I'll send them now,' Janko said, his words punctuated by another blast of gunfire.

Thero turned his attention back to the power grid. The levels were coming up. As soon as they reached the green margin, he began the initiation sequence, and the first ghosts of effervescent light began flittering through the cave on the other side of the window.

The sight mesmerized him, as it had always done before. So much so, he never saw Hayley Anderson sneak up on him.

She tackled him and threw a punch into his face, but Thero had few nerve endings left there. He felt the impact and little more. Enraged further, he flung her off and slammed her head against the console, knocking her out cold.

He felt a short spasm of remorse, but it passed. She deserved it. Another traitor.

He stood and went to the window. The orb had locked itself into place. Target: Australia. The system was beginning to draw energy from the zero-point field.

It wouldn't be long now.

46

With the gale rising in strength, Paul and the other NUMA commandos had a difficult time boarding the MV *Rama*, but once they were aboard, things calmed down. They marched to the bridge and took over command of the ship.

The Vietnamese captain then led them to the sick bay, where Captain Winslow and four members of the *Orion*'s crew were being held. They also found several of the Russian commandos laid up and dehydrated.

'Grab their weapons,' Paul said to the *Gemini*'s chief. As his men traded in their wooden rifles for real ones, Paul felt a sense of control building.

He made his way to Captain Winslow, who eyed him strangely.

'Paul?' the captain said, glancing at the Australian flag armband. 'You make a career change recently?'

'Sort of,' Paul said. '*Gemini* is standing by to help. What's the story here?'

Winslow explained about the sinking of the *Orion* and the rescue/abduction of the survivors at the hands of the Russians.

'How'd you get control of the ship?' Paul asked.

'Obviously, we didn't.'

'But this ship's been tracing out the path of the constellation of Orion for the past thirty hours,' Paul said. 'That can't be a coincidence.'

Winslow smiled. 'Kurt,' he explained. 'He had those Russians chasing their tails. Zigzagging all over the place. He said it was to keep the final destination secret. Who'd have thought he was sending up a message at the same time.'

'Where is he?' Paul said. 'We haven't found him.'

'The Russians took him, Joe and the Australian woman with them. They're staging some kind of raid on Heard Island. That's where Thero's base is. That's where he's hiding.'

Paul turned to the Vietnamese captain. 'Where's your communications center?'

The news that Kurt, Joe, and at least some of the *Orion*'s crew had survived was met with joy in Washington DC. It was tempered by the hands of the clock. Zero hour was a hundred and twenty minutes away.

Pitt looked at Heard Island on the map. Printouts of the Russian spy photos indicating Thero's assumed location were coming through on the fax machine. The more Pitt studied them, the more precarious the situation appeared.

'Everything this guy has done is underground,' Pitt said. 'Looks like he followed the pattern here. I have to give this info to the NSA.'

Yaeger looked grim. 'They're going to put a spread of missiles on that target.'

'I know,' Pitt said unemotionally.

Yaeger leaned in close. 'Kurt and Joe are probably there right now.'

'I'm well aware of that,' Pitt said.

'So they've been brought back from the dead just to be obliterated by Tomahawk missiles from our own submarines?'

Pitt glanced up at his old friend without a hint of malice. He understood exactly what Yaeger was saying. 'I don't do this lightly, Hiram. But we have no other choice.'

He pressed the intercom button. 'Get me Jim Culver at the NSA.'

47

Joe Zavala felt the rumble of the explosion as it surged through the cave. He and Gregorovich pricked up their ears and soon heard gunfire. It sounded as if a chaotic battle were raging in the cavern.

'It's coming this way,' Joe said.

Gregorovich nodded his agreement.

Joe went back to working on his freedom, straining and pulling and trying to rip his left hand free. It was no use, this cuff was a tighter fit.

Gregorovich pointed with his chin. 'Over there,' he said. 'Pliers. Maybe you can reach them.'

Joe looked at a cluttered desk across from them. Pliers, brass knuckles and a few other tools of the intimidation trade rested on it. He stretched toward them, but they were at least six inches out of reach.

'Come on,' Gregorovich urged.

'What am I, made of rubber?'

Gunfire and shouting echoed right outside the door.

Joe stretched again but flailed inches from the table.

The door swung open. One of Thero's men backed into the room, his eyes and his rifle aimed out through the door and down the hall.

As he fired off a burst at some unseen enemy, Joe

lunged for him, wrapping his free arm around the man's neck and yanking him backward.

The man dropped his rifle and grabbed at Joe's forearm, trying to pull it away from his windpipe. Joe held on, every muscle in his body straining, his powerful arm locked in a sleeper hold.

The man flailed and kicked, but Joe had all the leverage. Strangely, being anchored to the wall only helped. Soon, the man went limp in Joe's arm.

Joe held him like that for another full minute and then let him go. The man splayed out on the floor, and Joe stretched down and retrieved the rifle.

Twisting his body, he tried to aim the weapon at the chain cuffing his left hand to the wall, but the barrel was too long. He turned toward Gregorovich. 'Looks like you're first.'

Gregorovich stood and leaned away from the wall. 'Better make it quick. Before someone else shows up.'

Awkwardly, Joe tried to aim the rifle at Gregorovich's chains with only one hand on the grip.

'Watch it,' Gregorovich said as the rifle swayed toward his body.

Before Joe could steady his aim, the door flew open again. Joe swung the rifle toward it.

'Hold on, buddy!' a familiar voice called.

'Kurt!' Joe blared. He lowered the gun. 'It's about time you showed up. I almost had to rescue myself.'

'I don't know, you look like you have things well under control,' Kurt said. 'Can I offer some assistance?'

'Maybe you'd better do this,' Joe said, handing the rifle over.

Joe tensed as Kurt took careful aim and blasted the chain off his arm and then did the same for his feet. He stepped forward, glad to be free. Kurt freed Gregorovich the same way seconds later.

Kurt explained about the prisoners and the melee going on outside. He handed Gregorovich two pistols he'd confiscated from Thero's prison guards.

'I think we're gaining the upper hand, but we're running out of time,' he said. 'Any idea where Hayley is?'

'Thero took her,' Joe said. 'He had something he wanted to show her. I'm guessing we both know what that is.'

'Which way?'

'Not exactly sure,' Joe replied. 'But I believe he used the words *bring her up*. It's just a guess, but if I was a villain with an underground lair, I'd probably put my own quarters somewhere near the top.'

Seconds later, Devlin and Masinga came rushing in. Their status report seemed to mesh with Joe's guess.

'Thero's men are retreating up to the higher levels,' Devlin explained. 'We tried to follow, but they sealed off the corridor. We did find something of interest, though.'

'What's that?'

'The radio room.'

Kurt grinned. 'Now we're making progress. Time to call in the cavalry.'

48

Dirk Pitt's message to Jim Culver stirred up a hornet's nest of activity. Within ten minutes, a briefing was under way in the White House Situation Room. Culver was there, along with the President, Vice President Sandecker, and several ranking members of the Joint Chiefs of Staff. A cadre of advisers and aides backed them up, while Pitt and Yaeger watched the proceedings on a flat screen, patched in via a secure video link.

A brief set of remarks gave way to the prime question: With time almost up, could anything be done to stop Thero?

To that end, the only voice of importance was a rear admiral whose operational title was COMSUBLANT, an acronym that meant he was the Commander of US Submarine Forces in the Atlantic.

Even though Heard Island was a long way from the Atlantic, the admiral was also in charge of the submarines currently assigned to the Persian Gulf and the Indian Ocean. These were the closest vessels to what was now considered the target zone: Heard Island.

'. . . the Tomahawk missiles these ships carry have an extended range capability,' he said in answer to a question from the President, 'putting both the *Albany* and the *New Mexico* within range of Heard Island, but just barely.'

'So what's the problem?' Culver asked.

'The time frame. The Tomahawk is a subsonic weapon.'

'Meaning?'

The admiral sighed. 'Time from launch until impact is over three hours. According to the timetable you've given us, we have less than ninety minutes until this man acts.'

The room went silent. All of them knew what that meant.

'How could this happen?' Culver asked aggressively. 'We ordered vessels to begin moving into position two days ago.'

'The navy reacted as soon as we were directed to,' the admiral said. 'But Heard Island is one of the most remote spots on the face of the Earth, and we don't spend a great deal of time patrolling the bottom of the world. The USS *Albany* was the closest operational vessel at the time and it was over four thousand miles away.'

An aide rushed into the room and handed Culver a note.

'I guess it doesn't matter,' Culver said. 'Our early warning network has picked up a neutrino wave in the southern hemisphere. We don't have a location, but I'm pretty sure we can guess where it's coming from.'

'So Thero isn't going to give us ninety minutes,' the President said. 'Talk about jumping the gun.'

VP Sandecker spoke next. 'We'd better inform the Australian prime minister. Tell him doomsday is coming early.'

Pitt watched the proceedings stoically until the buzz of his intercom interrupted. It was Ms Conry from communications.

'I have an incoming radio call for you, Dirk.'

Pitt pressed the talk button. 'Now is not a good time.'

'It's Kurt Austin,' she replied. *'He's calling on a shortwave band. The signal is very weak.'*

'Put him through,' Pitt said without hesitation.

A distorted squeal of static and shortwave frequency interference came through the line seconds later.

'Kurt?' Pitt asked. 'Can you hear me?'

More static, and then finally Kurt's voice.

'Barely,' he said. *'We're on Heard Island. We found Thero's base of operations. It's underground. Near the front of the Winston Glacier.'*

'We know,' Pitt said. 'Hiram managed to figure out your signal and Paul and Gamay bluffed the MV *Rama* into surrendering. What's your situation?'

The sound wavered again, punctuated by bursts of interference. *'We've managed to start a small uprising and we've taken over half the station, but Thero and his men have walled themselves off on a higher level. We can't get to them.'*

'The NSA sensor grid is picking up neutrino emissions,' Pitt said. 'We believe Thero is charging his weapon now. Can you confirm that?'

'Not exactly, but it would explain the lighting issues we've been having,' Kurt said. *'You're going to have to hit this place hard to knock it out. We're at least a hundred feet below the surface.'*

'We can't get any ordinance on-site in time,' Pitt said. 'You're going to have to stop it from there.'

The silence and distortion returned.

'Kurt? Do you read me?'

'Loud and clear,' Kurt said. *'I'll see what we can do.'*

The static ended abruptly as Kurt cut the line.

Silence pervaded the radio room on Heard Island.

'No help coming,' Kurt said. 'It's up to us.'

'So what's the plan?' Joe asked.

Kurt looked at Gregorovich. 'Any idea what happened to that box of fireworks you brought from Moscow?'

'Thero's people took it with Hayley.'

'Then we'd better get to that control room,' Kurt said.

The lights dimmed, and a slight shudder went through the room as the first energy wave from Thero's weapon surged through the cavern. Kurt glanced up as dust drifted down on them from above.

'Is that what I think it is?' Joe said.

Kurt nodded. 'According to Dirk, the show's starting early.' He turned to the prisoners. 'Is there any other way up to the top level?'

Masinga spoke first. 'When we began to dig the mine, there was a vertical shaft. It was sealed off as soon as we began tunneling sideways into the kimberlite. You might be able to circumvent Thero's defenses if you use it.'

'Can you find it?'

Masinga nodded. 'I think so.'

'Let's go.'

Two minutes later, they were down the tunnel, prying a metal plate from a section of the wall. Once they'd pulled it aside, Kurt stuck his head in.

He looked up. A sixty-foot climb to the top. 'Could use that rocket-propelled harpoon of yours right now, Joe.'

'Better go search the lost and found, then,' Joe said.

'No time. We'll have to do this the old-fashioned way.'

Kurt glanced down. The shaft dropped another hundred feet or so. Kurt could swear he smelled the ocean. He turned to Devlin. 'I think I know where you'll find that ship of yours.'

Devlin nodded. 'I was thinking the same thing.'

'Gather up the prisoners. Get them down there.'

Devlin nodded. Masinga did the same. 'Once we've taken it over, we'll wait for you.'

'Don't bother,' Kurt insisted. 'Just head for the sea.'

Devlin stared at Kurt for a moment, offered him a salute, and then he and Masinga went back to round up the other prisoners.

'You should really go with them,' Kurt said to Joe.

'Sorry,' Joe said. 'Our last cruise made me seasick. Bad navigation. Poor accommodations. And don't get me started on the food. It was just awful. They should really put a health inspector aboard that vessel.'

Kurt laughed. He should have known better than to try benching his friend at this point in the proceedings. He turned to Gregorovich. 'Ready for one last gambit?'

'Ready to end this game,' Gregorovich said. 'Once and for all.'

49

Kurt, Joe and Gregorovich climbed up the abandoned shaft, while Devlin, Masinga and the South American led the surviving prisoners down toward the water level.

As they neared the top, another powerful vibration shook the cavern. In the hollow shaft, it made a sound like a rushing train.

Kurt gripped the scaffolding as the vibration came up. He noticed a strange luminescence to the metal work, something he hadn't seen before.

'We might want to hurry,' he suggested.

The other two fell behind, the beatings they'd taken slowing them down.

Kurt reached the top and braced himself, waiting as both Joe and Gregorovich caught up.

Another barrier of corrugated tin blocked whatever lay beyond. Kurt put his ear to it. A loud droning could be heard.

'What is it?' Joe asked.

'Generators.'

Kurt pulled his backpack off and wedged it into the scaffolding, taking out the last brick of C-4.

'What are you going to do?' Joe asked.

'Looks like it's only attached at four points,' Kurt said. 'One in each corner. If I wedge some explosives into the gap between the tin sheet and the wall and trigger them all at the same time, that should blast the corrugated sheet out into the room.'

'How much are you going to use?'

Kurt almost laughed. 'You and Devlin must have gone to the same school of asking too many questions.'

Unlike his effort with the heavy door he'd blown earlier, Kurt wanted to use as little explosive as possible in this case. Just enough to separate the sheet of tin from the opening it covered.

He tore off small sections of the plastic explosives and wedged them into the corners the way one might caulk a drafty window. Setting the detonators, he rigged his clacker once again.

'Hold on tight,' he said.

Both Joe and Gregorovich wrapped their arms and legs around the scaffolding, and Kurt did the same.

As the next wave of energy began to vibrate the cavern, Kurt figured he had the perfect opportunity. He squeezed the clacker tight. The four little charges blew simultaneously. The tin sheet flew out into the room, trailing smoke and clattering to the floor. The drone of humming generators doubled in volume.

Kurt looked inside.

A head poked out from behind one of the generators and seconds later gunfire burst forth from behind two others.

Kurt ducked back behind the edge of the rock as bullets tore up the inside of the mineshaft.

'So much for our surprise entrance,' Joe said.

A hundred and sixty feet below, Devlin and Masinga had reached the bottom level of the shaft. A short tunnel led to the cave where the black hulk of the *Voyager* remained docked.

From a side tunnel, Devlin noticed a man carrying a large crate toward it.

He put a finger to his lips and then jumped out, slamming the butt of the rifle down on the man's head. The man stumbled, dropped what he was carrying, and sprawled on the floor.

Devlin recognized him and stuck the business end of the rifle in his face. 'Running away again, Janko?'

Janko froze as he realized who was speaking.

'Look at this,' Masinga said, opening the crate. 'Diamonds.'

Devlin drew back and slugged Janko with the butt of the rifle once again, knocking him out.

A few minutes later, wearing Janko's clothes, he boarded the *Voyager* and took over the bridge. With the command crew under the gun, he waved Masinga and the other prisoners forward.

'Come on,' he shouted as the cave began to shake yet again. This series of tremors lasted longer and ran deeper than any of the others. Small rockslides could be seen throughout the cave.

As the last of the former prisoners climbed on board, Devlin turned to the helmsman. 'Fire this tub up.'

At the top of the shaft, just outside the generator room, Kurt, Joe and Gregorovich had run into better-prepared defenses than they'd expected. Eight of Thero's men were inside, hiding behind the generators.

'Getting through that cross fire is going to be suicide,' Joe pointed out.

'I have an idea,' Kurt said. He rigged up what remained of the C-4 and looked at Joe. 'Get ready,' he shouted.

Joe nodded, switching the selector on his rifle to full auto.

Kurt flung the pack around the corner and into the room, squeezing the clacker one last time. A booming explosion shook the generator room, hopefully knocking the defenders off their feet.

'Go!' Kurt shouted.

Joe went to rush in, but Gregorovich pulled him aside and climbed over him. He charged into the room, wielding his two pistols and blazing away. From the middle of the room, he fired in all directions, twirling and shooting, even as Thero's men fired back and hit him several times.

With Gregorovich drawing their fire, Joe and Kurt

rushed in behind him. They each took a side and gunned down the last of Thero's men in rapid sequence.

When the shooting stopped, only Kurt and Joe were standing. They rushed to Gregorovich, who was on the floor badly wounded.

50

Maxmillian Thero stood in the control room, bathed in the light of his great creation and oblivious to the gunfire outside. He gazed through the portal, mesmerized by the swirling galaxy-like pattern of the zero-point energy. It raced around the inside of the globelike structure, faster and faster, until finally disappearing in a blinding flash and heading toward Australia.

The first pulses probably hadn't been felt except by a few kangaroos in the outback. This surge would rattle windows and shake doors. It would cause tremors up and down the rift and set the stage for what was to come, as each reverberation built upon the previous one.

He checked the monitor. The next oscillation was beginning to build.

Suddenly, the door burst open behind him. He turned in time to hear the crack of the gunshot from Kurt Austin's weapon and see the flash of fire from the barrel. He fell backward, slammed into the viewing portal, collapsed, and slid down it, leaving a trail of blood on the thick Plexiglas.

As he slumped to the ground, he rolled toward Hayley. She was lying on the ground a few feet away.

'Thank . . . you,' he managed.

'George,' she whispered.

He nodded, and then his eyes closed.

Kurt rushed into the room and over to Hayley. 'Are you all right?'

'I think so,' she said, beginning to move.

As he helped her up, the room began shaking violently.

'What's happening?' she asked.

'Thero has engaged his weapon. You have to help me shut it off.'

Joe appeared in the door, supporting Gregorovich and lowering him to a seat, as Kurt led Hayley to the console. Kurt watched as she scanned everything, eyes going from one computer monitor to the next. A look of trepidation crept over her. 'I can't stop it,' she said.

'What?' Kurt asked. 'Why?'

'Thero's done something here. He's distorted the pattern, stretching it like a rubber band. The next wave will take longer to arrive, but it will be monstrous when it hits.'

'Not if we shut this thing off,' Kurt said, getting ready to fire a spread of shells into the computer.

'You don't understand,' she said. 'It's already off. What you're seeing is a free-form chain reaction. The energy is coming from the imbalance in the zero-point field itself.'

Kurt glanced out into the generator room. She was right. The last charge of C-4 had knocked the generators off-line; they were winding down on their own.

'How do we stop it, then?'

'We can't. It's like a car skidding out of control, overcorrecting back and forth. It will stop only when it finally crashes. When a large enough surge of energy overwhelms the wave and collapses it.'

'The rift giving way,' Kurt said.

She nodded.

He couldn't believe what he was hearing. There had to be a way. He looked around. His gaze fell on the Russian nuclear bomb. 'What if it found some other source of energy? A closer source.'

She turned toward the bomb. 'That might do it,' she said. 'From this range, that might just be enough to collapse the wave.'

Kurt moved to the bomb and opened the case. 'Gregorovich. How do I set this?'

'It's a simple timer,' the Russian managed. 'Set the time, press INITIATE, and it will blow at zero.'

Kurt looked for the timer. The control panel had been smashed. He flipped the timer switch to the ON position. Nothing happened. He toggled it several times. 'The timer is shot,' he said.

'Then you have to set it off manually,' Gregorovich said.

Kurt looked to Joe and Hayley. 'You two, get out of here,' he said. 'Take the vertical shaft. Get to the ship, if you can.'

'No,' Hayley said. 'You can't stay.'

'Not alone anyway,' Joe said.

The click of a pistol being cocked sounded.

All three of them looked up to see Gregorovich aiming his gun their way. 'All of you will leave,' he said. 'I will detonate the device.'

Kurt stared at him.

'Look at me,' he said. 'I'm not going home.'

'All right,' Kurt said, well aware that Gregorovich was dying. He slid the bomb over to where the Russian sat against the wall.

'Remove the timer,' Gregorovich said.

Kurt pulled the timer off. A simple detonation switch rested underneath.

'Arm it.'

Kurt turned the switch to the armed position. 'Are you sure you can do this?'

'It's a simple process,' Gregorovich said. 'All I have to do is press the button.'

'You know what I mean.'

'I finish what I start,' Gregorovich said.

'Eight minutes,' Hayley said, looking at the computer screen. 'At that moment the wave will be about to crest. It will be at its most unstable. Blow it then. No later or Australia will be in ruins.'

Gregorovich nodded as a new tremor shook the room.

Kurt noticed that this one felt different. Stronger.

It was time to go.

He offered a hand, and Gregorovich shook it. By the

time he let go, Joe and Hayley were already climbing down the scaffolding. He went to follow them.

'You were right,' Gregorovich called after him. 'Even pawns come in useful every once in a while.'

Kurt nodded and ducked out. He raced to the shaft and began climbing down. Halfway to the bottom, the cave shook again as if something solid had hit it. Cracks began snaking their way up and down the walls, and frigid, icy water began pouring in from above.

The tremors had caused a series of fissures to open at the base of the volcano. As magma and scalding heat flowed upward, the underside of the glacier began to melt. It shifted and slid forward. By the time Kurt reached the bottom of the shaft, an icy waterfall was pouring down on him.

He ran out from under it, catching up to Joe and Hayley as they reached the harborlike cave.

A strange black ship sat at the end of a narrow dock.

'Come on,' an Irish voice shouted from the deck. 'I'm not bloody well leaving anyone behind this time.'

Kurt was tremendously happy to see that Devlin had ignored his suggestion. He ran with Joe and Hayley. They climbed on board as the ship began to move. Inside, they found a few of Thero's men at the controls, guarded by Masinga and the other prisoners.

'Take us out,' Devlin ordered. 'And open the gates.'

As the cave shook, a stream of rubble fell from the roof. Fist-sized rocks pelted the *Voyager*, clanging off her decks, and a huge boulder crashed into the water only yards away. Seconds later, the *Voyager* was under way, submerging and heading for the slowly widening gap between the two doors.

'Increase the power,' Devlin ordered. 'Let's go!'

The helmsman did as he was told, and the *Voyager* began to push forward.

'Isn't this how Captain Nemo met his end?' Joe mentioned.

'Allegedly,' Kurt said. 'Allegedly met his end.'

Hayley gripped Kurt's hand, and everyone on the bridge held their breath as they stared at the slowly parting doors. The *Voyager* stabilized its depth and continued to pick up momentum. It passed through the gap in the doors, scraping badly against the right-hand plate.

'I'd give it full power, if I was you,' Kurt said.

'You heard the man,' Devlin ordered. 'Flank speed ahead.'

The helmsman didn't need to be told twice. He jammed the throttle lever to full. The big ship shuddered as the propellers increased their revolutions.

'We're much faster on the surface,' the helmsman suggested.

'Take us up,' ordered Devlin.

The crewman reached over and blew the tanks, and the *Voyager* began to rise. It breached the surface with a minute to go.

*

Back in the control room, half the ceiling had collapsed. A gap opened up between the control room and the level above, allowing the slush and water from the melting glacier to come pouring in.

This frozen mixture swept Gregorovich across to the far side of the control room, slamming him into the wall before its force lessened and sloughed away.

Gregorovich looked at his watch. He didn't know anything about waves or orders of magnitude in the zero-point field, all he knew was the promise he'd made. Eight minutes. He was supposed to detonate the bomb in eight minutes no matter what happened.

He tried to pull himself up. He had thirty seconds. He found he couldn't stand; the freezing water and slush was slopping around him, slowly filling the room.

He crawled through it, pushing floating debris out of the way. His eyesight was fading. His mind blurring. He thought back to the pain and the cold of the bog his father had once tortured him in and rose up, unwilling to give in.

He pushed forward through the flooding and made his way to the bomb. The secondhand on his watch hit zero, and he slammed his fist down on the detonator.

Kurt stared through the *Voyager*'s windows as the sea began flashing its brilliant white. He knew what was coming.

He looked back toward the island as a shock wave of energy erupted from the lagoon behind them. He saw a ball of white-orange flame. It raced outward as if it would engulf them and then just as suddenly collapsed back in on itself, like a bubble imploding at a great depth. A booming echo reverberated past them, and moments later a thin sheet of debris and water droplets pelted the *Voyager* like hail. But there was no fire, no heat. No angry flashing sea to be feared. Everything had gone dark and quiet.

At first, it seemed too good to be true. For a moment, no one spoke a word. Finally, Kurt asked the question on everyone's mind: 'Is it over?'

Hayley looked up at him and then back outside. The ship was rising and falling on the swells. The sea looked normal. The shuddering vibration was gone.

'I think so,' she said. 'I think he did it.'

Kurt continued to stare. Gregorovich had done exactly what he said he'd do. He'd finished the job.

'Somebody point me to a radio,' Kurt said. 'We need to find out if Australia is still in one piece.'

51

Eight hours after the explosion, the *Voyager* rendezvoused with the *Gemini* and the MV *Rama*. Kurt, Joe, Hayley and the other survivors were taken aboard the *Gemini* to a warm welcome led by Gamay Trout, who'd never met a celebration she didn't like. Amid the laughter, the iron words of Commander Matilda Wallaby were told and retold until Gamay was thoroughly embarrassed by it all. The story of Paul's home-built turret and his bluffing of the MV *Rama* received similar treatment, and both were sure to go down in NUMA lore.

'Remind me not to invite you guys to poker night,' Joe kidded.

For his part, Kurt remained quiet. Too many lives had been lost on his journey to feel anything but relief that it was over. And late one night he made his way to the radio suite and used the *Gemini*'s equipment to make a long-distance phone call.

'Hey, Dad,' Kurt said as his father picked up the phone. 'Hope it's not a bad time.'

It had been half a year since Kurt had seen his father and months since they'd had anything more than a cursory conversation. Life might have been busy, but that was far too long.

While the rest of the ship slept, Kurt and his dad spoke of old adventures and made firm plans for new ones in the near future.

A few days later, they finally docked in Perth. Debriefing and interrogations for the Russian commandos and the MV *Rama*'s crew followed. Eventually, the Australians released the impounded ship and allowed the Russian commandos to leave by air. They were flown to Tokyo and from there to Vladivostok, where they were repatriated and no doubt interrogated further by their own superiors.

Attempts to recover anything useful from Heard Island proved futile. On a teleconference with Dirk Pitt, Kurt explained.

'They've used ground-penetrating sonar to study the area where the tunnels and Thero's lab were located. There's no sign of any open spaces remaining. We're pretty sure the nuclear explosion vaporized Thero's lab and everything in it. It seems as though the concussion wave blew apart the structure of the natural cave, causing whatever remained to compress down upon itself. The rock below is now radioactive and will be for some years to come. Making any attempt at study even more problematic, the tremors and the explosion caused the underside of the Winston Glacier to liquefy. It surged forward. Whatever might be left down there has not only been vaporized but is now buried under several million tons of rock and ice.'

On-screen, Pitt nodded thoughtfully. 'Not altogether a bad thing.'

'My thoughts exactly,' Kurt said.

Pitt turned to Hayley. 'A UN treaty is being drawn up, banning the study of this type of energy. The sensors you developed are going to be a big part of enforcing that ban.'

'Good to know I've done something positive for a change,' she said.

'You may have prevented millions of deaths,' Pitt replied. 'It doesn't get more positive than that.'

She smiled.

'It was close,' she said. 'Apparently, they had a string of earthquakes out in the never-never. We're still feeling aftershocks, but there are less of them each day. And the rift appears to be stabilizing.'

'Good to hear,' Pitt said. 'Now, about these missing crates of diamonds. I've been asked by Cecil Bradshaw of the ASIO to inquire as to their possible whereabouts. As they came from Heard Island, they are, in fact, Australian property.'

Kurt, Joe and Hayley nodded.

'Any idea what happened to them?'

'I heard a rumor,' Kurt said. 'That Devlin –'

'Captain Devlin,' Joe corrected.

'That's right,' Kurt said. 'Captain Devlin and his intrepid first mate, Masinga, arranged for those diamonds to be divided up among the surviving miners and the families of those who were lost. But it's just a rumor. And as Captain Devlin is no longer on Australian soil, I'm not sure it'll ever be more than that.'

'Suits me fine,' Pitt said. He turned to Joe. 'In other business, I have a new job for you, Mr Zavala.'

Joe's eyebrows went up. 'I'm on vacation,' he said.

'By my calendar, your vacation just ended,' Pitt said. 'And your first mission back on the clock is to fly out to Cairns and explain to poor Ms Harrington of the Dooley Elementary School District why you disappointed her class and didn't show up for their scheduled field trip out on the reef.'

'Was she angry?' Joe asked.

Pitt nodded. 'Apparently. But she's willing to forgive you if you'll accompany her on an unsupervised field trip of her choosing. I believe you'll be needing a dinner jacket.'

Joe sighed and then perked up. 'The things I do for this agency,' he announced. 'I really should be getting a PR check in addition to my regular pay.'

Kurt laughed. 'Imagine that. All this talk about aliens, and a fifth-grade teacher is the one abducting you.'

'As long as it's in the name of science,' Joe said.

Pitt laughed. 'I'm proud of you all,' he said. 'I'll check in with you tomorrow.'

As Pitt signed off, Joe turned to Kurt and Hayley. 'I guess I'm out of here,' he said.

Hayley stretched up and hugged him. 'Travel safely,' she said with a laugh.

'Shall do.'

Kurt embraced his friend. 'If you're still in Australia when I get back to that side of the country, I'll look you up.'

'When do you think you'll get there?'

Kurt glanced at Hayley. 'Depends how long it takes to walk across the continent.'

Joe laughed. 'I won't wait up,' he said, and then ducked out the door.

Left alone with Hayley for the first time since they'd met, Kurt took her by the hand and kissed her.

'Come with me,' he said, leading her out into the hall.

'Where are we going?' she asked suspiciously.

'On a little trip,' he said.

She stiffened. 'I think I've done quite enough traveling for a while.'

He continued leading her down the hall. 'Your friend Bradshaw sent me some tickets to the rugby match at the Perth Oval tonight.'

She dutifully followed him but seemed confused. 'Tonight, under the lights?'

He nodded.

It was just past noon. 'Aren't we leaving a little early for that?'

'Not really,' he said, 'considering the form of transportation I've chosen.'

He opened the door for her and stepped outside. There, waiting by the curb, was a Victorian-style carriage with a docile chestnut-colored horse standing patiently in front of it.

'This is Inchworm,' Kurt said, patting the glossy brown animal on the shoulder. 'I'm promised he's the slowest, most sure-footed horse in all of the western territories.'

Hayley grinned broadly and scratched the horse behind the ears. He whinnied and seemed to like it.

'Nothing wrong with being slow and sure-footed,' she said to the animal. 'Or thoughtful,' she added, turning to Kurt.

He held her hand as she climbed in. 'Watch your step,' he said. 'Inchworm has never lost a passenger, and we don't want to start with you.'

She settled in, smiling so brightly her cheeks hurt. Kurt climbed in beside her and took the reins as she investigated the picnic basket he'd packed.

'How long do you think it will take to reach the stadium?' she asked.

'How long do you have?'

'All day,' she said. 'And all night.'

Kurt nodded. 'In that case, we'd better take a shortcut.'

He pulled on the horse's reins, and Inchworm began to move, plodding slowly and living up to his name. Hayley slid over to Kurt, wrapped an arm around his waist, and laid her head against his shoulder.

'This is my kind of speed,' she said.

Kurt put an arm around her and pulled her close. It suited him just fine as well.